Other Books by Jim Farrell

Novels

Brooklyn Boy (2013)

The Extraordinary Banana Tree (2015)

Mikey's Quest for Father God (2016)

Short Story Collections

Kiss Me, Kate, and Other Stories (2014)

The Committee and Other Stories (2016-2017)

The Barge of Curiosity

By

Jim Farrell

MRK Publishing

PO Box 353431

Palm Coast, FL 32135

This book is a work of fiction. Any resemblance to actual
people or circumstances is completely unintended.

Dedications

Sharon Corriveau, a good friend and East Providence, RI, firefighter, who is the model for Sandy Roberts on the cover. The cover photo was taken in Bunratty Village, County Clare, Ireland.

Photographer Larry Mingledorff who prepared Sharon's photograph to meet publication specifications.

Patty Gallagher, my cousin, good friend, and editor, who spends hours reviewing my manuscripts. Her corrections and suggestions are invaluable.

Marianne Collinson, my wife and best friend, without whose encouragement none of my writing would be possible.

Jim Villarreal, the friend of my youth, who offers advice, encouragement, and love.

Doctor Madeline Nixon, my sister, Professor at Rhode Island College, who has greatly supported and encouraged me in all my writing, especially with *Brooklyn Boy*.

Frank McGoff, a friend, who introduced me to James Joyce's *Ulysses*. Chapter Sixteen, *Stately Plump Buck Mulligan*, is dedicated to Frank. "Why are The Great Books called The Great Books? Because they are great books."

Contents

Introduction

Sandy Roberts and Mark Tuttle made their initial appearance in my collection of short stories, *Kiss Me, Kate, and Other Stories,* as the main characters in eight of the stories. A few readers suggested that I put the "Sandy and Mark" stories in a separate publication and add more stories about the young couple to the new collection.

I thought it was a great idea, but decided to do it differently.

I revised and coordinated the existing stories and made them chapters in a novel about Sandy and Mark, a novel that covers them from first grade through their adult years. If you have read the original eight short stories, you will find them changed for incorporation into the novel.

I added a new and exciting character to their lives, Peggy Mayhew, who is in love with both Mark and Sandy, especially with Sandy. I think you will find her engaging.

The cover photograph of Sandy is in Bunratty Village, County Clare, Ireland. The model is Sharon Corriveau, a friend from Rhode Island. When I saw that photo, I immediately envisioned Sharon as Sandy and asked for, and received, Sharon's permission to use the photograph on the front cover.

I hope you enjoy this expanded visit with Sandy Roberts and Mark Tuttle. I enjoyed writing about them and the amazing Peggy Mayhew, the "goddess".

Jim Farrell
Palm Coast, Florida
May 16, 2016

Chapter One
Seventh Grade Epiphany

During morning recess Rosalie Torino challenged my best girlfriend, Peggy Mayhew, to a fight after school behind the barn. Peggy, being Peggy, readily accepted the challenge. The barn is an abandoned farm building in a large vacant lot a quarter mile from our school, St. Michael's Parochial School in Coventry, Rhode Island. Peggy immediately came looking for me, Sandy Roberts. We were in seventh grade at the time.

What caused the challenge? Peggy was kissing Donna Martino in the girls' room when Rosalie and three friends entered that sanctuary. Rosalie had a crush on Donna. More than a crush; she considers Donna her girlfriend. Peggy, on the other hand, was just embarking on a curiosity binge, what Peggy calls "a ride on the Barge of Curiosity."

If there were a Miss St. Michael's Beauty Pageant with the winner to be selected by popular vote, I would vote for Peggy, and she would vote for me, for we honestly believe each other to be the prettiest girl in the school. But the remainder of the student body, with the exception of my Mark, Mark Tuttle, would vote for Donna Martino. She is the classic Italian beauty, the Sophia Loren of St. Michael's.

Peggy was merely inquisitive as to the feel, smell, and especially the taste inside the mouth of that young Italian beauty. She told me later that she just wanted to "get her tongue inside that *bella bocca italiana* to do a little tongue wrestling and to explore the mouthscape."

Rosalie was quite upset when she came upon Peggy and Donna *in flagrante delicto*. Peggy, as I said, was just curious; Donna was just being agreeable; but, to Rosalie, if was an act of infidelity.

"You fuckin' lez," she yelled at Peggy, not realizing the irony of that. She pushed Peggy away from Donna, and said to her, to Donna, "Are you all right, honey?" She assumed it was kiss-rape; Donna would never willingly kiss Peggy, or anyone else except Rosalie.

"Yes," gushed Donna, having been rescued by Rosalie, saved from a voluntary kiss.

Rosalie then turned on Peggy and yelled, "I'm gonna beat the shit outta you." They would have fought then and there, but Rosalie's friends restrained her.

"You'll get expelled, Roz," they said. The good Sisters of Notre Dame frown upon fighting or smoking in the restrooms.

"You wanna fight me after school behind the barn, bitch?" she asked Peggy.

"Sure," answered Peggy, never one to back away from a fight. "See you there."

Peggy then left the restroom and, as I told you, came searching for me.

"Sandy," she cried out, seeing me in front of my locker. "Come outside a minute." There were three minutes remaining before the resumption of classes.

When we got outside, she told me what had happened. After we stopped laughing, she asked me, "Will you come with me? Have my back? I'm sure I can take Rosalie, but she might come with friends."

"Of course," I said. "I'll ask Mark at lunch to come with us too."

"Great."

"How did that *bocca Italiana* taste?" I asked. *"Deliziosa?"*

"Buona, buona," she said. "I didn't get enough time in there. But it was good. I'll give you the details later after the fight." St. Michael's requires a foreign language starting in fifth grade. Peggy, Mark, and I had selected Italian as our foreign language. The choices were Spanish, French, or Italian. We chose the language of love, of Dante.

On the first day of fifth grade, when the three of us walked into Sister Angelica's Italian language class, we found *"**Nel mezzo del cammin di nostra vita**"* written on the board. Sister asked if anyone knew what that meant or where it was from.

I had no idea, but Mark Tuttle raised his hand and, when Sister called on him, said, "It means 'In the middle of the journey of our life,' and it's the first line of Dante's *Inferno*, the first book of his *Divine Comedy*."

"Very good, Mark," said Sister Angelica. "If you all study hard, some day you will be able to read that great poem in Italian."

After class I asked Mark how he knew that. He just shrugged. "I don't know. I read a lot," he said. I love him, but sometimes I hate him too. You know what I mean.

At lunch I asked Mark Tuttle to sit with me at one of the small tables in the rear of the lunchroom. He always complies with my requests. We were too young to be steady-dating, but we were best friends, had been since first grade. That's why I clarified above that Peggy was my best *girl*friend. Mark was/is/always will be my best friend.

"Rosalie Torino challenged Peggy to a fight after school, behind the barn," I said.

"What happened?"

"Peggy was kissing Donna Martino in the girls' room, and Rosalie caught them. She called Peggy a 'lez,' and they're going to fight after school. Rosalie wanted to fight in the girls' room, but her friends stopped her."

"Peggy's not a lez," Mark said.

"I know. How do **you** know?" I asked.

"Because she's attracted to me," he said. "Physically."

"**What?**" I cried out. But I already knew that. All the girls are attracted to Mark.

"Don't worry," he said. "She hasn't done or said anything, but I can tell."

"I'll kill her," I said.

"No need. She hasn't made any moves or said anything. I think she might be afraid of you."

"Not likely. She's not afraid of anyone."

"Then maybe she respects you or your friendship. She really likes you, you know."

"Yeah, I know. I like her too."

"I think she also knows that I've been in love with you since first grade, so I'm not available. Don't say anything to Peggy. I might be wrong, but I don't think so."

"You know, it's crazy. You and I love each other – everyone knows that -- but our parents say we're too young to date."

"We're always together, but we don't call it dating. I'm okay with that."

"Me too, I guess. So even though we're not dating, you're my boyfriend, right?"

"Yes, your not-so-secret secret boyfriend." He gave me a little kiss, a chaste kiss since we were in the lunch room.

"Anyway, will you go with us to the barn?" I asked. "Peggy and I would feel better if you were with us, for support."

"Yes, the three of us can walk over there together."

It was humorous after school. Peggy, Mark, Rosalie, Donna, and I are in the same class. We separated into two groups, and headed to the barn, walking on opposite sides of the street. We were three. They were four: Rosalie, Donna, and two tough Italian girls not in our class who accompanied them. Rosalie keep staring across at us, but she didn't say anything. I don't think she was happy to see Mark with us. When we arrived behind the barn, we discovered about thirty kids already there. Word of the fight had spread. Margie Baylor, who is in sixth grade, came over to join me, Peggy, and Mark. Margie loves me like an older sister.

Peggy took off her jacket and handed it to Margie, not to me. Peggy wanted me to have my hands free. Rosalie handed her jacket to one of the tough-looking girls. I handed my jacket and books to Mark. "Hold these for me, Mark. Just in case," I said.

"You ready to settle this, bitch?" Rosalie cried out.

"Any time you want," said Peggy.

Rosalie charged and threw a wild punch, which Peggy dodged. Peggy then grabbed Rosalie's shirt and twirled her to the ground. They rolled around a bit. Peggy ended up on top. Rosalie was screaming, "Get off me, bitch."

Why would any streetfighter let an opponent up when the opponent still wanted to fight? Give up a well-earned advantage? Peggy was in a position to pound Rosalie at this point, launch punch after punch into Rosalie's unprotected face, but Peggy didn't do that. She didn't want to hurt Rosalie. She had nothing against her. Peggy was not fighting to win Donna's hand (or mouth). She knelt on Rosalie's arms keeping her squirming body pinned to the grass.

"Had enough?" Peggy said.

"Get her off me," Rosalie yelled to her friends.

One of the tough-looking Italian girls came over and started to pull Peggy off. I ran over and pushed the second girl away from Peggy. I know Mark wanted to intervene, but he couldn't. It was a girls' fight.

The girl glared at me. I knew her from school; she's in eighth grade, Alex Something.

"Fuck off," she said.

"Make me," I said. "This is a one-on-one fight. So **you** fuck off." I don't usually use words like that, but under the circumstances.....I realized I wanted to fight her. I was excited.

Peggy allowed Rosalie to get up. Rosalie had had enough. Peggy had told her that she, Peggy, had no interest in Donna, so the reason for the conflict had evaporated.

Alex continued to stare at me.

"Do you still wanna fight me?" I asked. "Come on. I wanna fight you."

We stood face to face for an eternity. Then she said, "Fuck you, Roberts," and walked away. Without looking back, she gave me the finger. "Classy," I yelled.

I was relieved, so I guess I didn't really want to fight her.

Mark put his arm around my shoulder and said, "Do you know how hard it was for me to watch that and do nothing?"

"I know," I said. "I know. You wouldn't let me get hurt, would you?"

7

"Never."

"Let's go to McDonald's," said Peggy. Margie Baylor joined us.

"What started that?" she asked Peggy.

"Long story. I was kissing Donna Martino in the girls' room-"

"You were kissing Donna Martino?" said Margie. "I don't understand."

"You will when you get older," said Peggy. She winked at me.

When we got to McDonald's, I asked Peggy the question that I was dying to ask: "How was it kissing Donna?" Mark's ears perked up. Margie's eyes opened wide.

"*Buona*," she said again. "But, to be honest, I would rather kiss you."

"That's not going to happen, Mayhew," I said. "I only kiss him," pointing to Mark.

"We'll see," said Peggy.

"Do you really want to kiss Sandy?" Margie asked Peggy.

"Doesn't everyone? Don't you?" she answered. Margie turned as red as a tomato.

"Well, to answer your question about the kiss, it was nice. Her mouth is very wet with a very Italian flavor. It was like going to a Mediterranean feast in a damp, pleasant-smelling cave."

"What the hell does that mean?" I asked.

"A mixture of cheese, garlic, onions, prosciutto, pepperoni-----maybe a little goat, all within the slimy, slide-around texture of olive oil."

"But you kissed her before lunch," I objected.

"But after breakfast," Peggy said. "Maybe they eat grinders for breakfast in her house."

"Would you rather kiss boys or girls?" Mark asked Peggy. Boys love topics like this.

"Boys," she said. "It is fun to kiss a girl once in a while, but I prefer boys." She turned to me, "Sandy, don't worry about me and Mark. As attractive as he is, I will never come on to him. I know he's yours. Couldn't get anywhere if I did try. But I won't. You're my best friend, and I want it to stay that way. You can trust me."

"Thanks," I said. "I do trust you." *I guess I do, somewhat.*

"How about a kiss, Roberts? Just to compare with *bocca Italiana*," said Peggy.

I just smiled. "What did I tell you, Mayhew?"

"Sandy, be honest with me. Don't you ever feel tempted to kiss girls?" Peggy asked. "To kiss me? To swap saliva?"

"You're gross, Mayhew. I've never even **thought** about it," I said.

But that immediately was no longer true. Ever since that conversation, I have thought about kissing one girl, not Donna, the girl with the Italian sandwich mouth, but, you guessed it, Peggy.

I know it won't happen -- maybe *know* is too strong a word -- but I do think about it in bed at night.

I bet it would be nice.

Chapter Two
The Bully
Or
The Deflowering of Sandy Roberts

Mr. Wilson's Version: My name is Herb Wilson and I teach at Coventry High School. Coventry is a good school in a countrified small town, and we don't usually have the troubles that plague the inner-city schools, but we do have the occasional "occurrence", shall I say? I was leaving school last Friday – it was a beautiful fall day in mid-November -- when I noticed a large group of students over by the Athletic Center. They seemed to be watching something, and then they began to cheer. It wasn't a cheer you would hear if they were watching a fight or a disturbance of some kind, but the kind of clapping you would hear at the end of a concert, a cheer of appreciation. Then they started to break up.

I spotted a sophomore whom I have in my Honors Geometry class, a very nice young lady by the name of Margie Baylor. I stopped her and asked:

"Margie, what was all the commotion about?"

"Nothing happened, Mr. Wilson, except a bully got his comeuppance and walked away with his tail between his legs." She said it with delight.

"Tell me, Margie," I said. "What exactly happened?"

Margie Baylor's Version: I was walking over to the Athletic Center after school with Sandy Roberts, Peggy Mayhew, and a few of their friends. I wasn't really with them, just near them. They're all juniors, and I'm only a sophomore. Sandy is my heroine; she is the captain of the basketball team and the softball team, and she has a 4.0 average in the Honors Program. And she really is very nice. She never belittles you just because you're only a sophomore or a freshman. If Sandy and Peggy had been alone, I would have joined them.

Mr. Wilson Interruption: Sandy's mother, Madeline, teaches at Coventry High School, and is one of my dear friends. She doesn't teach in the Honors Program so she does not have her daughter, Peggy, or Margie, in any of her classes.

Margie Baylor's Version (continued): As Sandy was walking along, minding her own business, Mac came up and bumped into her, hard!

Mr. Wilson Interruption: Mac is Steve MacBride, the school bully. He is not a nice boy, and will probably end up in the ACI, the Adult Correctional Institute, someday.

Margie Baylor's Version (continued): I guess Mac is the only one in the school who doesn't know that Sandy is going steady with Mark Tuttle. But, unfortunately, Mark was not around. Mark is captain of the boys' basketball team and starting third baseman on the baseball team. He's dreamy, about six feet, four inches tall, and all muscle. All the girls love him. Anyway, as I said, he wasn't around. Sandy said something to Mac, and then he pushed her hard.

11

She went flying backwards. She didn't fall down, but she did drop all her books. Then he started going after her. She was trapped and she looked scared. Who wouldn't? Mac is mean. Believe me, Mr. Wilson, if he had hit her, I would have jumped on his back. I wouldn't let him beat up on Sandy. I'm sure Peggy would have gotten involved too. Peggy is tough, and she loves Sandy.

Peggy Mayhew's Comment: I got so mad when Mac pushed Sandy. She's my best friend. This would not have been a fight between Mac and Sandy, if Mac wanted to fight. It would have been between Mac on one side, and me and Sandy on the other. I always have her back; she always has mine. I think Margie Baylor would have gotten involved too. But then Mark Tuttle appeared.

Margie Baylor's Version (continued): All of a sudden, Mac stopped, and his glance was directed at something or someone behind Sandy. His demeanor changed from predator to prey. Now he was the one looking scared. I glanced at Peggy Mayhew, and I could see her relax. I looked behind Sandy and saw Mark Tuttle there with his left hand on her right shoulder. She looked at him and let out an audible sigh and gave him that smile of hers that will melt a glacier. He gave her a look of love that, if any man ever gives to me, will let me die a happy woman, and said something to her. I couldn't catch it. Then he gave her a kiss and walked over to Mac.

Mr. Wilson Interruption: "Mac just stood there?"

Margie Baylor's Version (continued): Yes, like a deer caught in a headlight. Mark picked him up with his left hand (I told you Mark is all muscle) and held him up against the Athletic Center wall. I didn't hear everything, but he essentially gave Mac a choice: leave Sandy alone or get beaten up. Mac chose the former and walked away with his tail between his legs. Mark then picked up Sandy's

12

books, and they started to walk toward the parking lot. They drive together to and from school every day. I began to clap, and then everyone picked it up. It was good to see Mac limp away like a beaten dog. Maybe he learned a lesson. You then stopped me. So nothing really happened, as I said, except a bully got put in his place.

Mr. Wilson's Version: I thanked Margie and then went to the faculty lounge where I found Madeline Roberts and a few other teachers.

Madeline asked me: "Well, what was that all about?"

I told her that her daughter got into a confrontation with Mac, but Mark Tuttle put an end to it. There was no fight. All the kids were clapping because a bully was put in his place.

Madeline said, "I put him on detention today for cutting up repeatedly in class. I bet he was just taking his anger out on Sandy. I will speak to him tomorrow."

I told her that it would probably be better not to do that. Mac was already chastised by Mark. "The situation is over, so why acerbate it?" She agreed.

Sandy Roberts's Full Version: I was heading over to the Athletic Center after school today with Peggy Mayhew, Marcia Snow, and Maria Coppocino. I told Mark I would meet him there after school; we drive to and from school together every day. I was talking to Peggy when, all of a sudden, Mac came barreling into me.

"Watch where you're going, bitch," he said.

I told him he had walked into me, not me into him.

"Are you calling me a liar?" he asked.

"No, I just said you walked into me; I didn't walk into you."

He then pushed me hard. I went flying backwards, but was able to maintain my balance with Peggy's assistance. My books did go flying, however.

I stood about eight feet from him, and he started to approach me slowly with a look of hate on his face. *What did I do to him to cause this? Did he have a problem with Mom today?* I saw Peggy tense up. I knew she had my back, but could the two of us handle Mac? He's a wild man.

 I had two thoughts:

Are Peggy and I going to have to fight this guy? and

Where are you, Mark?

Just then Mac stopped dead in his tracks. And he was looking over my right shoulder at something behind me. You won't believe this, but I could actually sense, physically, a change come over him. I could actually smell fear emanating off him. *Thank God, Mark is here,* I thought. And just then I felt a hand squeeze my right shoulder. I turned and looked into Mark's face and gave a sigh of relief, an audible sigh of relief. He gave me that look that he reserves for me (*God, I love that look*!), and then I smiled that smile that he loves. He has told me that I am a 10 under normal circumstances, but a 12 (on a scale of 10) when I smile. I'm not, but I'm glad he thinks so.

"Relax, Sandy, I'll take care of this," he said, and walked over to Mac.

He lifted Mac up with his left arm, twisting his hand around Mac's shirt up near his neck immobilizing him. I don't know how he accomplished that feat with his left hand; Mark is right handed. His arms, I have noticed, are like cables. Mac had no idea what to do. I don't know if he could even talk the way Mark was holding him.

Mark said to Mac, "Mac, I have never had a problem with you, and you have never had a problem with me, but Sandy is my girlfriend. So if you mess around with Sandy, then I **do** have a problem with you, and you **do** have a problem with me."

He stared at Mac and then continued, "Mac, I don't like to fight, although I am very, very good at it. I will usually walk away from a fight, because most fights are pointless. But if Sandy is involved, I won't walk away. And you **don't** want to fight me. Believe me, if I am defending Sandy, you **don't** want to fight me."

He then gave Mac a choice, "Now you can agree never to bother me, Peggy, or Sandy again, and I will put you down, shake hands with you, and we can live in peaceful coexistence. Or we can settle this right now. It's your choice. I don't care which way you want to go. In fact, I prefer that we settle it here and now, but you make the decision. What'll it be?"

Mac stammered, "I didn't know she was your girlfriend."

"That shouldn't make any difference. You should not be picking on girls. And you still didn't let me know your decision. Do you want to live in peaceful coexistence or do you want me to beat the shit out of you right now?"

"Peace," he managed to get out.

Mark let him down and shook his hand. As a parting warning, he said, "Remember, Mac, if you ever bother her again, I will hunt you down and pound you into the ground. Do you understand?"

"Yes," he said, as he turned and walked away.

Mark then came over and picked up my books. Peggy helped him. He put his right arm around my shoulder and said, "Let's get out of here."

I turned to Peggy and asked, "Do you need a ride?" Peggy lives with her mother, and we usually pick her up in the morning and take her home after school. Mark, Peggy, and I have been friends since first grade.

"No," she answered. "You two need to be alone today."

"Thanks for having my back today. I knew you were with me."

"You're welcome, Sandy. I always have your back."

I kissed her on the cheek, "I always have yours too." Then Mark and I headed to the parking lot. Mark looked back at Peggy and said, "Thanks."

As we were walking away, someone, I think it was Margie Baylor, started to clap, and then everyone picked it up. Margie's a good kid. On the way to Mark's car I was thinking, *I really want to spend the rest of my life with this young man…Grow old together.* Not a usual thought for a high school junior. *He's athletic, smart, a good man, responsible, and he loves me…He's been in love with me since first grade…Me too—in love with him…When we were six!..I would be foolish to look elsewhere for a life partner…I am going to make this work…He wants that too…I can tell.*

I looked at him and said, "You know, I didn't need your help back there. I could have taken Mac."

He gave me a look, an 'in your dreams' look. I laughed and said, "Thank you for being there for me, as always."

"No need to thank me," he said. "If any guy is fighting with you, he is going to have to fight me. Always."

Always! I liked the sound of that. "Always?" I said.

"Yes, always," he replied. "I told you I want to make this relationship work permanently."

Alleluia, I thought. *There is a God!* "Me too," I said.

I then told him I was lucky he came along when he did.

He gave me a very philosophical answer: "If I came along 30 seconds sooner, nothing would have happened. Mac would not have started a fight with you if I were there, I'm sure of that. But by coming when I did, he learned a lesson. Maybe he'll be less of a bully now, out of caution if for no other reason. And if I had come 30 seconds later, and found him fighting with you and Peggy or beating you up, I would have gone crazy. I might be in jail now for killing him."

"As I said," I replied, "I was very lucky you came along just when you did. I would have stopped you from killing him, by the way."

I gave him a kiss, a very passionate kiss, and then suggested we get inside the car and out of public view. After we were in the car, I snuggled up to him, and we continued to kiss passionately. I never felt so close to Mark, not since third grade anyway, the first time he saved my life. I then leaned back and asked him a question that surprised, and pleased, him greatly, "Do you have any condoms?"

The question actually surprised me as well. We're both virgins. At least Mark told me he is, and I believe him. We do kiss passionately whenever we're alone. We discovered we love to kiss each other in fourth grade at a birthday party when we became -- thank you, God -- spin the bottle partners. We went into a closet and, after a period of hesitation, we actually touched tongues. And we hugged. It was like an electric current ran through our bodies. And the taste of his mouth! I have always loved it, right from that first time. He told me I tasted like Breyer's vanilla bean ice cream. From Mark that is the ultimate compliment. We lost track of time in that closet and kissed until some jerk knocked on the door telling us to stop.

And we talk a lot about sex. There is no topic we won't discuss. You wouldn't believe the conversations Mark and I have. If Peggy is with us, which is often, she joins in. Mark has never badgered me about sex or suggested, in any way, that having sex was a *sine qua non* (remember, I'm an honors student) of our relationship.

But, for some reason, that day it was different. We were committed to each other and to our relationship. I didn't want to have sex with him; I wanted to make love with him. I was not trying to offer sex as a way of holding on to him. I didn't have to do that; I knew Mark was with me for the long haul. And I wasn't offering myself to Mark as a way of saying, "Thank you" for what he had done for me that afternoon. I knew that wasn't necessary. I just had an irresistible urge to share myself with him in the most intimate way. I think it was a combination of love, desire, and availability. Mom had a dinner meeting after school, and Dad was meeting my older brother at Fenway to see the Red Sox. My brother, Bobby, goes to Holy Cross College in Worcester and boards there. Our house would be empty until eight that evening.

Mark looked at me, smiled, and said, "Yes, back at my house."

"Why do you have condoms?" I asked, pretending to be angry.

"Just in case you would ask that question and only for that reason," he replied smiling.

"Good answer," I said. "In fact, the only acceptable answer."

"I'm no dummy," he said. "I'm in the Honors Program too, you know. Are you sure you want to do this?" he asked.

"Yes, aren't you?" I replied.

"Yes I am. There is nothing I want to do more than make love to you. In fact, I would like to do it every day for the rest of my life. Where?" he then asked. "Not here in the car. I would not want to make love with you in the back seat of a car."

"No, at my house. There will be no one home until after eight. Let's stop at your house first for the condoms, and then we'll go and use one, or maybe two," I said.

"Why not three?" he asked.

"Do you think you're man enough?"

"I guess we will find out," he said.

After we made love, we took a shower together. Mark was so gentle that first time. He just held me tight after the initial pain. Then I experienced pleasure. Oh, yes. We had spread an old beach towel on the bed. The shower was another pleasurable first for us. We discovered that we are as uninhibited in the bedroom and the bathroom as we are in conversation. I can't tell you how much I enjoyed standing naked in the shower hugging, kissing, soaping, and rinsing Mark. All over. And being soaped and rinsed and hugged and kissed by him. All over.

We then went out to a Chinese restaurant on Post Road. I called Peggy before we left the house. As I told you, she lives with her mother. Her mother doesn't get home from work until eight or later. When we were in grade school, Peggy ate at my house, or we both ate at Mark's house, almost every evening. The three of us still have dinner together most of the time.

"Hello," she said.

"Did you eat yet?" I asked.

"No, I was waiting for your call," Peggy answered.

"Presumptuous," I said.

"Well…..you called, didn't you?" She had me there.

"We're going to Chow Fun. Want to join us?"

"Of course," she said.

"We'll pick you up in fifteen minutes."

After we were seated, Peggy looked closely at me, then at Mark, then back at me. "About time!" she said.

"What?" I asked.

"What my ass," she said. "You two finally did it. I can tell. How was it?"

"Indescribable, so I won't try," I said laughing.

Dinner as always at Chow Fun was delicious. We always order a large bowl of soup, an appetizer selection, and two main courses, and share. White rice, of course. We take turns ordering. The owner, an older Chinese lady, knows us – we are frequent Chow Fun diners – and always greets us with a big *"Ni hao!"* To which we reply, *"Ni hao!"* Not the most intellectual conversation, but a full Chinese conversation nonetheless. She always gives me and Peggy pineapple cubes with our fortune cookies. Mark just gets the fortune cookie. She must be a feminist. When we leave we always tell her, *"Hen hao chi."* (It was very tasty.)

"You guys do your homework yet?" Peggy asked.

"No, we were a little busy," I said.

"Good. Can we go back to your place after dinner and look at the math? Couple of the problems were beyond my comprehension."

"Well, we do have the math guru with us. I'm sure he can figure them out and then explain them to us," I said. I punched Mark on the shoulder.

When Mom got home, the three of us were sitting innocently in the dining room doing our math homework.

We did **not** have sex on a regular basis after that. As much as we loved the experience and each other, there just were not many opportunities during our junior year. Oh there were opportunities to have sex, but, honestly, neither of us was interested in "having sex." We had too much respect for each other for that. I can't even imagine Mark asking me to have sex with him in the back of his car. Can't imagine it!   We both knew, now from experience, the delights that awaited us. We knew that we had a lifetime of lovemaking (note that I did not say "lifetime of sex") ahead of us. We could wait. Oh, don't misunderstand me. We did make love periodically during that year. And took those delightful showers together. But Mark insisted that we make love only at a time and in a place when and where there was no chance of discovery. He would never put me in a possibly embarrassing position.

Our situation changed overnight at the beginning of our senior year, as you will learn. As a consequence of that change, we enjoyed almost daily lovemaking during our final year at CHS.

Mark **and I** drove Peggy home that night. Just a precaution. I trust them, but do you think I was going to leave Mark alone with the gorgeous, sexy Peggy Mayhew? Just kidding. Even if I didn't trust Peggy, which I do, I trust Mark. I just wanted to be with him. With them.

I asked Mark to stop at Dunkin' Donuts on the return trip to my house. We like to talk at Dunkin' Donuts. After we obtained our coffees and were seated at a remote table, I said, "You know, now that you deflowered me, you have to marry me. That's the rules."

He just smiled at me.

"Say something," I said.

"I've wanted to marry you since I was six years old."

I leaned over and kissed him. I was crying.

By the way, we used all three condoms that afternoon, one before, and two after, the first shower, which, thankfully, led to a repeat shower. It was just as pleasurable as the first one. I am so glad we have no inhibitions! Believe me, Mark and I went to Heaven together that day.

Chapter Three
Peggy Mayhew

I know this book is about Sandy Roberts and Mark Tuttle, but you can't tell the story of Sandy and Mark without including me, Peggy Mayhew. We've been inseparable since we were six years old. I had the misfortune of falling in love with both Sandy and Mark when I was six. To add to my misfortune, they fell in love with each other at that same time. They do both love me, especially Sandy, but not in the way I love them. Well, that's not quite true. Sandy's love for me is different in degree, not in kind, from my love for her and her love for Mark. Her love for Mark is greater, not different, just greater. As I said, that is my misfortune.

I asked the editor if I could have a chapter or two early in this book to shed some light on my story. I can be found throughout the book, especially in the later chapters, but that is Peggy Mayhew as seen through Sandy Roberts's eyes and expressed in her words. Believe me, they are generous eyes and kind words; Sandy Roberts would never portray me in any other way. But I begged, and received, permission to contribute this little piece to depict how I see myself and our relationship.

Let me start with a little about my background and my introduction to Sandy and Mark in first grade. That day changed my life. For the better; definitely for the better.

I never knew my father. He and my mother, Nancy Mayhew, were not married. He wanted her to have an abortion when I was conceived. I thank my mother every day that she did not give in to his entreaties. He moved somewhere out west, I think California, before I was born, and we have never heard from him since. "Good riddance!" as Mom says. Friends (not Sandy or Mark – they know better) have asked me if I ever wanted to look up my father. I answer, "Hell, no" to that. Fucker didn't even want me to be born.

I am an only child so I grew up without any sibling interaction. Sandy and Mark became my missing siblings. Our interaction was critical to my development.

Physically I take after Mom, a second thing for which I am grateful to her. Mom is an attractive woman. She is tall, pretty, with sky blue eyes, brown hair, and a great figure. When I was six, when I met Sandy and Mark, I had Mom's pretty face, her sky blue eyes, and her brown hair. I was tall, strong, and athletic. My great figure came later. Yes, it did come.

Mom is a little rough around the edges, but she is a good mother. No, she is a great mother. She works hard to provide a good home for me. She is a sales manager at Kohl's Department Store in Warwick, and works the noon to eight P.M. shift. With that schedule she is there for me every morning to make sure I have a good breakfast and to prepare my lunch. She hated the fact that I was going to be a turnkey child, all alone from after school until she got home at eight-thirty. She also hated that my dinner menu would only have three choices: frozen TV dinners, dinners she had prepared and frozen for me, or cold cereal if I felt lazy. Too lazy to thaw out a frozen dinner? Don't forget:

thawing takes time. As you will see, I found a way to avoid both consequences of her work schedule.

Mom does date, and I have met a few boyfriends, but she does not let men sleep over in our apartment, and she is home every night. Beyond that I don't ask any questions. Her parents are deceased. I never met them. I never met my paternal grandparents either; I don't even think they know I exist. Mom was also an only child. So Mom has me, and I have her. That's it.

Mom, of necessity, is self-reliant, and has instilled that quality in me. On the first day of school, at St. Michael's Catholic School, before we left our apartment, she said to me, "Honey, don't take any shit from any of the girls or boys in your class. If any of the girls are bullies, pick out the toughest one and fight her. Then they will leave you alone. And don't ever give the sisters any trouble. I am working hard to earn the money to get you a good education." It didn't dawn on Mom that picking a fight with "the toughest" girl in class might not sit well with the good sisters. I did not have to do that. Why not?

Because the toughest girl in our class was either Sandy Roberts or me. And we liked each other from that first day of school. The second day of school, at recess, I watched her beat up one of the boys in our class. He didn't even fight back. I found out later, from Sandy, that she had wrongly accused him of ruining her Marble Composition book. She apologized after school, and they walked to the local candy store for a Coke, her treat. He held her hand after they left the candy store, and kissed her when they arrived at her house. Yep, Mark Tuttle. The beginning, on the second day of school, of a lifelong love affair. Maybe I should have beaten him up on the **first** day of school. To be honest, that would not have made any difference. Mark Tuttle has been in love with Sandy Roberts, and only Sandy

Roberts, since that first day of school. Can you blame him? I have been in love with her too. She is a special person.

You'll find out from Sandy's account that, throughout grade school, and especially during my sophomore year at CHS, I had an on-again, off-again crush on Mark Tuttle. How could I not? We were always in close proximity – the three of us were always together – and he is handsome, nice, strong, athletic, and smart. He smells good too. But the attraction was not reciprocal. He liked me; but he was drawn to Sandy like metal filings to a magnet.

My attraction for Sandy was also physical – she is beautiful, nice, strong, athletic, smart, and, believe me, she smells good too -- but it was more than physical, on my part anyway. Metaphysical? I knew she liked me, and I definitely did feel physical reciprocity, but the Sandy/Peggy relationship was not as strong as the Sandy/Mark relationship. Sandy/Mark would always come first for Sandy and for Mark. I did not, and still do not, have a problem with that. As long as Peggy/Sandy persists, I am happy. And Sandy/Peggy does persist.

The desire on my part to maintain that Sandy/Peggy relationship was the primary reason why I never made any moves toward Mark. Mark would not have accepted any advances from me anyway, and those advances would have caused a rift between Sandy and me. That I would not allow. To this day, and I am now an adult, Sandy Roberts, now Sandy Tuttle, is my best friend. And I still want to kiss her every time I see her. Occasionally I do. That physical attraction has never waned. She feels it too. We have a special bond.

When I started at St. Michael's, I definitely was, like Mom, a little rough around the edges. Sandy and Mark, and Sandy's Mom, became my personal pumice stones. When Mrs. Roberts found out that this little six-year-old girl went home to an empty house to have a solitary frozen TV dinner, she invited me to have dinner with them most school nights. Very often we were a family of six for dinner: Sandy's Mom, Sandy's Dad, her brother, Bobby, Sandy, Mark Tuttle, and me. Mrs. Roberts taught at the high school, and proper English, proper manners, and common courtesy were expected around the dinner table. I learned quickly. Occasionally Sandy and I would have dinner with Mark and the Tuttles. Mr. Tuttle called us "the three musketeers."

At the end of the evening, either Mr. Roberts or Mr. Tuttle would insist on driving me home, and neither would let me out of the car unless Mom was already home. Mom made me send "Thank You" notes to the Roberts and the Tuttles. Sandy, Mark, and I sat around the dining room table and did our homework after dinner. I realized right from the start that the two of them were in a class by themselves when it came to brains. Don't underestimate me; I am smart and was in the Honors Program at CHS and always on the honor roll at St. Michael's, but they were at that next higher level. They never made me feel inferior, however. In fact, their objective was always to lift me up to their level, and they succeeded most of the time. I can't tell you enough how much I loved sitting with the two of them doing intellectual work, being treated as an equal, being led upwards on the road to knowledge. The "road to knowledge"—that was Mark's expression.

We did school projects together. If the project was a two-person project, however, Sandy and Mark always teamed up. That was a given. But they insisted that my team, whoever my partner might be, worked with them. We became a two-team super team. My partner never objected; we always got A+ on the projects.

I had been a desultory reader growing up. Mom bought me books, but did not have the time to read to me. Both the Roberts and the Tuttles had libraries, a room set aside for books. I had never even thought of that before, home libraries. All four adults urged me to borrow any book I wanted from their home libraries. Mrs. Roberts even made up a reading list, "voluntary reading list" she called it, and encouraged the three of us to read books from the list. She updated it every six months all the way through senior year at CHS. I devour books today, thanks to Mrs. Roberts. I saved those lists and used them with Heather, Larry, and Candi, my children. I know Sandy and Mark used the lists with Maddie, Bobby, Jimmy, and Annie. Our kids are as close today as Mark, Sandy, and I were growing up. Sandy and I love that. Maddie is one year older than her brother, Bobby, and my Heather. All six of the younger children, even the boys, look up to Maddie as their leader. You could not find a better role model than Maddie Tuttle. I went up to Boston's Brigham and Women's Hospital the day she was born. I'll never forget the way Mark and Sandy looked at her. You knew she was going to have a wonderful life. How could she miss? Loving parents. Great genes.

I usually walked home together with Sandy and Mark, but I was not there the day in third grade when the pervert tried to kidnap Sandy -- Sandy will tell you about that. I had a doctor's appointment that day, and Mom took off from work early to take me to the doctor's office in Providence. We went to Chelo's for dinner. Mom had their famous Reuben; I had a hamburger. I did not know until the next morning what had happened. All the kids were talking about it. No one could believe that Mark had beaten up a thirty-five-year-old pervert.

I just smiled when I heard that. Mark would beat up ten 35-year-old perverts if they were trying to hurt Sandy Roberts or die trying. If you knew Mark, you knew that. When Sandy and Mark arrived at school – they arrived together – Sandy ran up to me and told me all about the attempted abduction.

I can still picture, even though I wasn't there, Mark standing over the fallen potential molester, holding his bat, focused, staring at his opponent, all muscles taut, ready to continue to do battle to protect his fair damsel. Only when Mr. Ross told him it was over, did he relax. And what was his first question? "Is Sandy all right?" What else would Mark Tuttle ask? Sandy told me she ran over to Mark and hugged him. To be honest, she has never let go.

After Sandy and I hugged, she told me, "Peggy, I am going to marry Mark. Do you believe that?"

"Yes," I said, "I have no doubt." And I didn't.

Mom and I are Catholics, but we didn't attend Mass or receive the sacraments before I started school. I was baptized, but that was the extent of my Catholic indoctrination. You might wonder why Mom sent me to a Catholic grade school. She wanted me to get the best possible education, and she was convinced that the Sisters of Notre Dame would provide that for me. She also liked the discipline the sisters enforced in their schools. Rotten apples didn't spoil the bushel; they were removed from the bushel before they could have any impact on the other apples. The public schools have to keep the rotten apples in the bushel.

Things changed for me after I started school. All the students attended Mass every Wednesday morning, we said prayers in school daily, we studied the Baltimore Catechism, and all students were expected, required I should say, to attend the nine o'clock children's Mass on Sundays.

I was at Sandy's house on the first Saturday of first grade. Mark was there too. We were playing basketball in Sandy's driveway where her father had erected a portable basket and backboard. Little Margie Baylor was playing with us. She had not started school yet, but lived near

Sandy. She idolized Sandy. Who didn't? We went into the house for lunch. Mrs. Roberts had set out a platter of sandwiches and a pitcher of Lipton's iced tea.

While we were eating, Mrs. Roberts asked me, "Peggy, how are you getting to church tomorrow morning?" I guess Sandy had told her mother that my mother did not go to church.

"I guess I'll walk," I said.

"No, you won't," Mrs. Roberts said. "We'll pick you up at eight forty-five."

That became our routine: Mr. and Mrs. Roberts in the front seat; Sandy, Bobby, and me in the back. Bobby sat with his class, the fifth grade, in church. Mark waited for me and Sandy at the door of the church, and the three of us sat together in the first grade section.

I was thinking church would be tedious, boring, unbearable, but, to my surprise, I liked it. I can still picture the three of us together during those grade school years, actually praying, singing the hymns, smiling at each other, exchanging the Kiss of Peace. Ah, the Kiss of Peace. I loved the Kiss of Peace. I looked forward to the Kiss of Peace. It was the only chance I had to kiss Sandy, to taste and touch her delightful skin with my lips. Even at that young age, I loved kissing her. Most of the time I kissed her cheek, and she kissed mine. But occasionally, if I was feeling adventurous, I would kiss her on the lips. It was an innocent, children's, inside-the-house-of-God kiss, but oh so wonderful. She always returned the kiss, never pulled away. Those lip-to-lip kisses stopped when Sister Mary Thomas, our fourth grade teacher, pulled us aside one Sunday after Mass and told us that kissing on the lips was inappropriate in church, "unless you are a married couple." I had to limit myself to kisses on Sandy's cheek after that, but I lengthened my lips' time on her face, inhaling her heavenly smell as I did so. It was still exciting -- it was all I had. *Peace be with you, my beloved Sandy.*

One Sunday during that first year at St. Michael's, after the final hymn, Sandy smiled at me, squeezed my hand and held it. Then Mark saw what she was doing, and he squeezed my other hand. I was between them that Sunday. Sandy said, "Friends forever." Mark and I repeated it. I don't think I had ever, in my young life, felt closer to two people than I did to Sandy and Mark that Sunday. I actually cried. Me, tough, hard Peggy Mayhew cried. I think that was when I fell in love with Sandy Roberts. I am still in love with her. Probably always will be.

Studying the Baltimore Catechism in the Roberts' dining room was another life-changing experience for me. In third grade, Sister Mary Angela had us review the first two questions in the catechism. "The answers to the first two questions," she told us, "are the most important things you will ever learn." At first I thought learning the answers would simply be an exercise in rote memorization. I should have known better. I was studying under the guidance of Mark Tuttle. He was drilling me and Sandy. This, remember, took place when we were in third grade. We were eight years old, not adults!

Mark asked, "Who made you?"

Sandy and I answered, "God made me."

Mark then asked, "Why did He make you?"

We answered, "To know Him, to love Him, and to serve Him in this world, and to be happy with Him forever in the next."

I thought we were finished, but, as I said, Mark Tuttle was leading the discussion. "Peggy," he asked, "do you believe that God made you?" He had put his catechism on the table and was looking at me.

I was silent. Then I said, "Yes, I guess so."

"Sandy?" he asked,

"Yes. He made everything," she answered.

"My father and I were discussing this the other night," Mark said. "He told me this is the most basic question of all. The way you live your whole life depends on the answer you give to this question. He made me take down the family Bible and read the first line from Genesis. He said that was the most critical verse in the Bible. Do you know what it says?"

Neither Sandy nor I did.

" '*In the beginning, when God created the heavens and the earth*.' It tells us God created everything, including us. And my father told me about the Jewish philosopher Maimonides. His great question: 'Why's there something and not nothing?' "

"The only answer to that question is 'God made it,' " I said. *How did I know that?*

Mark is like Socrates, pulling answers out from inside us…I loved studying with Mark.

Mrs. Roberts came in then with a platter of just-baked chocolate chip cookies. "What are you kids talking about? You look excited."

"God," we all said.

She looked startled. "God? You three amaze me. Have some cookies."

The only reason I mentioned the above episode in our young lives is to let you know what it was like on the "road to knowledge" with Mark Tuttle. For twelve years, the three of us studied together. We dissected every subject. If any one of us didn't fully grasp any point, we didn't move on until we all understood it. I might have slowed them down a bit at times, but Mark and Sandy never left me behind. "The ship doesn't sail until the full crew is aboard," Mark often said. "Get to the bottom of everything. Ask why," he urged. The first time he said that, I said, "Our ship is the Barge of Curiosity, and Mark's our tugboat."

"The Barge of Curiosity!" said Sandy. "I love that." It became a favorite expression of ours.

Mark Tuttle is the most amazing young man. You might think he was a bit of a nerd from the above. That would be furthest from the truth. He was probably the best high school athlete in the history of Rhode Island and, believe me, you would not want to fight Mark Tuttle, especially if he were defending Sandy Roberts (or me), as that 35-year-old pervert discovered. He is also an engaging conversationalist (there was nothing the three of us did not talk about), an avid reader and discusser of books, a lover of movies, especially Woody Allen movies, and the world's greatest **male** admirer of Sandy Roberts.

My Mom was ecstatic when I brought home my first report card from St. Michael's, all A's or A+'s in my academic subjects, and all E's (for excellent) on the conduct, behavior, and attitude side. I think the latter stunned her more than the former. My report cards stayed at that level of quality all the way through high school graduation. I loved sailing on the Barge of Curiosity with Mark and Sandy.

One of my personal best moments at St. Michael's came on a Sunday during my fourth grade year. As I was leaving church with Sandy and Mark, I noticed my mother kneeling in the rear of the church. I went over and hugged her.

"What are you doing here, Mom?" I asked. Dumb question.

"I've come home," she said. I knew what she meant.

I drove to Mass with Mom after that, but still sat with Mark and Sandy in our class's section in church. Mom often joined us at the Roberts's for Sunday breakfast after the service. Mrs. Roberts is as generous as her daughter. Or should I say: Sandy is as generous as her mother?

I have no proof of this, but I consider Mark responsible for my mother's return to the Catholic Church. I often discussed with Mom the theological topics that Mark, Sandy, and I discussed on the Barge of Curiosity. She told me one day that our (mine and her) talks had driven her to seek out Father Richard at St. Michael's.

The years at St. Michael's were enriching. To paraphrase Luke the Evangelist: The three children grew and became strong, filled with wisdom, and the favor of God was upon them.

There was a chance I would end up in a compromising position with Mark at Molly Davidson's ninth birthday party. Sandy, Mark, and I had been invited to Molly's after-school party. Molly was in our class, fourth grade at St. Michael's, but not very popular. We decided to accept the invitation because all three of us were invited. We felt we were doing her a favor.

After every one had arrived, Molly announced that we were going to play spin the bottle. She then announced the rules. Her party; her rules. There were six boys and six girls at the party. Each girl, except Molly, would pick a number, from two to six, out of a hat. Molly, since it was her birthday, was number one. Molly, as number one, would sit with all six boys in a circle and spin the bottle. She would then accompany the boy the bottle selected into the hall closet off the living room. They would stay in there for two minutes. Then girl number two would sit with the remaining five boys, and so on. Molly would control the in-closet time, even when she was in the closet.

Molly explained that the couples would go into the hall closet for privacy. She added that if any boy or girl did not want to kiss the bottle-selected partner, he or she didn't have to publicly embarrass his or her partner. Molly did not want anyone embarrassed at her party.

I picked number two; Sandy got four.

"I hope Mark's still left when I go," she whispered to me. "Four! That's so high."

Of the six boys at the party, Mark would have been my choice too, but I said, "Yeah, I hope so."

"Who do you want to kiss?" asked Sandy.

You…Definitely you. "Anyone but Mark," I said.

"You wouldn't want to kiss Mark?" Sandy asked, surprised.

"I would love to kiss Mark, but I don't want to kiss him because he's your boyfriend, and you're my best friend."

Sandy kissed me on the cheek. "You're a good friend, Peggy Mayhew." *Yes, I am.*

When Molly spun, the bottle pointed to Wally O'Malley. Sandy and I looked at each other and smiled. "Mark is still left," she whispered to me. "I hope you don't get him."

"Me too." *That would be awkward.*

It was now my turn to spin. I wanted to say, *Sandy, why don't you sit in the circle?* Imagine what a scandal that would have caused. I spun. I thought it was going to stop at Mark – *keep turning, keep turning* -- but it just passed him and pointed to Billy Walsh.

Billy's cute. We are friends in a broad sense. *I could have done worse.* Except for Mark during the Kiss of Peace, I had never kissed a boy before. What opportunity did I have? I did kiss Mark on the lips, just a little peck, especially when I was in the thrall of one of my on-again Mark crushes. But it was never the same as it was with Sandy.

When we were standing in the closet, I gave Billy a peck on the cheek. Then I started to return to the party.

"Don't leave yet, Peggy. That was not even a real kiss," he said.

"Sure it was," I said.

"A real kiss is on the lips," Billy protested, "unless you're kissing your sister."

"Okay," I agreed. I kissed him on the lips. "Satisfied?"

"Can we touch tongues?"

"No, we cannot."

"I'll give you a quarter if you let me touch your tongue," he said.

"Fifty cents," I said. I thought that would discourage him.

He surprised me. He handed me two quarters. I pocketed them and, putting my face up against his, I opened my mouth. I had never done this before; I wasn't sure how to proceed. He stuck his tongue into my opened mouth and touched my tongue. We held them together for about ten seconds. No movement; just touching tips. It wasn't bad. Actually it was fun. His breath was nice too. It smelled like cereal, like Kellogg's Sugar Smacks. I love them!

He had a big smile on his face when we finished. I reached into my pocket, took out the two quarters, and gave them back to him. "I don't want you to pay me, Billy. That kiss was very nice. We still have some time. Do you want to kiss me again?"

"Yes," he said. "You're very exciting, Peggy."

"Thank you. And let's move our tongues around."

I gave him the best kiss of his young life. We let our tongues explore each other and play. When we finished, I exhaled into his face. Why? I don't know. It sure pleased Billy.

"God, you smell great, Peggy," he said. "Thank you."

"You're welcome."

"Is Mark Tuttle your boyfriend?"

"No, just a very, very good friend. He will never let anyone mess with me."

"But he's not your boyfriend?"

"No, he's Sandy's boyfriend."

There was a knock on the door. Molly said, "Time's up."

I went back and sat with Sandy. "How was it?" she asked.

"Good. Actually very good. I think I made a friend for life." Sandy laughed.

Billy Walsh had a crush on me for years after that closet kiss. He followed me around like a dog follows a bitch in heat. But I was not ready to let anyone else join us on the Barge of Curiosity at that time. I did let him on the barge for a while in high school, but that's for later.

Marcia Snow was next. Sandy closed her eyes and crossed fingers on both hands while Marcia's bottle was turning. The bottle ended up pointing to Dave Abrams. Sandy squeezed my arm.

As if the gods had pre-ordained it, Sandy's bottle chose Mark. "Yes!" he said, and pumped his fist in the air. Sandy loved that. Molly had to knock three times to get them out of the closet. They came out holding hands. A few of the boys, Dave and Wally, began to tease Mark. He blushed, but I noticed he did not let go of Sandy's hand.

I asked Sandy how it was. "Better than I could have imagined," she said. "He told me my mouth tastes and smells like Breyer's vanilla bean ice cream. That's his favorite flavor."

"Mine too," I said.

She just looked at me. Then she blew air in my face. "It does smell like Breyer's vanilla," I said. *I bet it tastes like Breyer's vanilla too...God, I want to kiss her.*

That night, when I got home, I removed the half gallon of Breyer's vanilla bean ice cream from the freezer and was sitting at the kitchen table enjoying it. Mom came in and remarked that I was eating it very slowly.

"Just savoring the taste, Mom," I said.

In bed that night I kissed my pillow. I created a wet spot about the size of a quarter on the pillow case. But it wasn't Sandy. And my pillow did not have a tongue. Then I had a brainstorm. I went out to the kitchen, filled a little dish with Breyer's vanilla bean ice cream, and brought it back to my bedroom. I took a spoonful, spread it around my mouth, licked it until my tongue was coated, and then kissed the pillow. Not quite the real thing, but satisfying. You probably think that was weird. I don't care. I enjoyed it immensely.

We played a lot of basketball in the Roberts's driveway, the three of us and Margie Baylor. Mark was unbelievable, and Sandy, Margie, and I improved every single day playing with him. It was always Mark and Margie against me and Sandy. We won most of the time. How did we beat a team with Mark Tuttle on it? Easy. We learned to let Sandy shoot. Mark never blocked Sandy's shots. He blocked mine. Oh, yes, he blocked mine. Delighted in it. In a loving way. But never Sandy's. Even as adults, when we played with our kids in the Tuttle driveway, the Mark and Sandy Tuttle driveway, Sandy's team usually won. Why? Same reason. Mark never blocks Sandy's shots.

What developed out of that driveway basketball were two state championships for the CHS girls' basketball team. I learned in the Roberts's driveway to rebound and get the ball to Sandy as fast as I could. By the time we were juniors at CHS, it had become routine. I cleared the defensive boards, immediately threw an outlet pass to Sandy racing toward the other end of the court, and she either beat the field and laid it in or stopped and hit a fifteen foot jump shot. We were quite the pair, Roberts and Mayhew.

The only way to beat us at CHS was to get us out of the game. South Kingstown almost succeeded. Their coach, an evil bitch, sent in two subs to start a fight with us. After I objected to a hard foul, the South Kingstown player called me a "fucking cunt." I lost it and went after her. The other South Kingstown sub jumped on me which, of course, got Sandy involved in the fight. Sandy always had my back. All four of us were ejected. We were up by thirty-two when we left the game. CHS barely hung on to the lead and won by four.

Coach Thompson was furious. At us, yes, but even more at the South Kingstown coach. Coach Thompson told us if we ever got ejected for fighting again, she would personally whip our asses. Tough lady. We never got ejected again.

During the hot days of summer, short as summer is in New England, we lived in the Tuttle backyard. They had a pool. The Roberts and the Tuttles were so good to us kids. On Sundays, when my Mom was not working, she often came over to the Tuttle pool with me. She and Mrs. Tuttle had become friends. The Roberts were often there too. Mrs. Roberts sat with Mom and Mrs. Tuttle by the pool. The men snuck off to the den to watch the Red Sox. Mom was in her thirties, but did she ever look good in a two-piece bathing suit.

"I hope I look that good when I'm that old," I said to Sandy.

"You will. You have her genes."

We, Sandy and I, also wore two piece bathing suits. One day during the summer between seventh and eighth grade, Mark said to us, "Why do you two wear tops? You don't have anything up there to hide." We chased him around the yard and threw him in the pool when we caught him. That **was** true about Sandy at that time. She developed great breasts in high school, but was flat chested while at St. Michael's. I, however, started to develop breasts in seventh grade. Mom's great genes kicking in. I will let Sandy tell you what happened next. It was their first pre-sexual encounter.

Sandy's Input:

I jumped into the pool after we threw Mark in and said, "You just wanna see us topless, don't you? Especially Peggy." We were standing face to face, inches apart. I pretended I was angry. *How could I be angry at Mark?..He can see me topless if he wants, anytime he wants, although there is not much to see....But if he wants, it's okay...I hope he doesn't want to see Peggy topless...No he wants to see me...He knows I'm not angry...Of course, he knows.*

"I'd rather see you topless than Peggy," he said.

"Really," I said. *I knew it!..It's so exciting standing here like this...Where is this going?*

I kissed him. He had put his hands on my shoulders. *That feels so good.* Our bodies were actually touching, under the water.

"You don't want to see Peggy topless?" I asked.

"I didn't say that. I said I would rather see you topless than see Peggy topless."

"So you **would** like to see her topless."

"So would you, I bet," he said.

I laughed. "Yeah, I guess I would." *Yeah, I would like to see her topless...See those breasts that are developing so nicely...When will mine grow like that?..Maybe never...No, they will.*

"Sandy, let me tell you something that I swear is true. If I die without ever seeing Peggy Mayhew topless, I will feel aesthetically deprived, but otherwise I will be fine. If I die without ever seeing you topless, I will not die happy."

"Aesthetically deprived? Sometimes I don't believe you're only thirteen."

"Looking at Peggy naked would be like looking at a work of art, a statue of Venus."

I punched him in the shoulder. *I do that a lot...Mark knows it means I love him...Funny way for me to show it?..But he knows...I think he likes it...I do...It means he's my boyfriend.*

Mark suddenly grabbed me under the arms and tossed me toward the deeper part of the pool. I shrieked and, when I hit the water, started to go under. Then I shot out of the water sitting on Mark's shoulders. How he got under me and in position to raise me up so fast, I couldn't imagine. He was standing in four feet of water looking up at me, holding my ankles so I wouldn't fall off, water dripping off his face. *You say I have a beautiful face, Mark Tuttle, but you do too...I could kiss it all day, and when we're older, all night.*

He was smiling. I broke out in a smile too. "You know, you were right, about me anyway," I said. "I don't have any breasts, just little bumps."

"Can I see them and kiss them?" he asked. *Of course you can.*

"My bumps?"

"Yes, your bumps," he said.

"You want to look at and kiss my bumps?"

"Yes," Mark said. "I would love to look at your bumps, and kiss them."

"Am I getting you excited, Mark Tuttle?" *You're getting me excited.*

"Yes you are, Sandy Roberts. You always do."

I leaned over and kissed him. Then straightening up, and biting my lower lip, I smiled at him. He smiled back. *God, I love kissing that handsome, beautiful face.* I leaned toward him and blew a stream of breath at this nose. He inhaled deeply. *You belong to me, Mark Tuttle... Forever...God has put you on Earth to take care of me and to love me...And he's put me here to take care of you and to love you...And I will...And I know you will too...know it!*

"You get me excited too. Of course you can see and kiss my bumps, later in the pool shed. We can ride the Barge of Curiosity. You look funny with your face upside-down."

"So do you, but I still want to kiss you, my upside-down cake."

"Upside-down cake?" I leaned down and kissed Mark.

"Later, I'll kiss your bumps too, on the barge," he said. *Yes, you will.*

Back to me, Peggy:

Even with my "spectacular" seventh grade breasts, I was no competition for Sandy with Mark. She told me later that she let Mark take off her top in the pool shed. She knew it would be more exciting for him if he took it off. She filled me in on the details.

Sandy's Input (continued):

Twenty minutes later, Mark and I were sharing a pool chair at the side of the pool. He said, "Sandy, can you help me with something in the pool shed?"

I went with him to the shed. When we were inside, with the inner door locked, he asked, "Can I see them now? Twenty minutes was too long to wait."

"You really want to see my little bumps?"

"Yes, I really want to see your little bumps."

I turned my back to him and said, "Unhook the top." *He'll like doing that.*

After he had removed my top and placed it on the doorknob, I turned back around and said, "See. There's nothing to kiss or feel." *I hope he likes them...they are so small...he can feel them and kiss them if he wants...He can't take his eyes off them, my little bumps...That's good.*

"Oh yes there is," he said. "What do you think is getting me so excited?" he asked.

"My awesome bumps?" I was laughing. *I am getting excited too, Mark Tuttle…I'm standing topless in front of Mark Tuttle…He's loving it…I'm loving it too…No shyness, not with Mark…Never with Mark…He's my boyfriend…I wonder what Peggy's thinking…She knows why we came in here…I bet she'd like to be in here with us…With me, anyway…Maybe someday…I would like to see her breasts…So would Mark…We can ride the Barge of Curiosity.*

"Yes," he said. "Your fantastic little bumps. I love your bumps. And I love you standing here displaying them to me and to no one else. Now I can die happy. I have seen Sandy Roberts topless, and the sight has soothed my savage soul."

"You're not going to die any time soon, Mark Tuttle," I said. "I need you with me. We're going to grow old together. I will always soothe your savage soul – that's my job."

"No, I'm not going to die. There is too much of Sandy Roberts I still have to see, and too many things I want to do with Sandy Roberts before I die."

"What things?"

"Make love with you, of course, when we're older, but so much more: travel the world, hike in the Grand Canyon, walk on the Great Wall, look at the ceiling of the Sistine Chapel, admire Michelangelo's David in Florence, stand in St. Peter's Square, own our own house with a pool, share everything we have with each other, have children, maybe four, two boys and two girls, take them to Disney, go to Fenway, vacation on the Florida Atlantic coast, eat Chinese food whenever we want, go to sleep every night with you in my arms, wake up every morning looking at your glorious, beautiful, smiling face, kiss that face, fondle your breasts and your ass, bring you a cup of coffee in bed," Mark said.

I started crying. "I love you, Mark Tuttle. And I promise you we will do all those things." I pulled him to me. I wrapped him in my arms. *I love feeling your bare flesh against mine.* "And the two shall be as one flesh," I said. Our eyes and mouths were two inches apart. "You can fondle my ass now. You don't have to wait to do that."

Mark slid his right hand inside my bikini bottom and gently massaged. "I like that," I said. *Caress me, Mark, squeeze me...You get me so excited, Mark Tuttle...I guess I get you excited too...That's good...That's very good.* "We have so much to look forward to, don't we?" I said.

He kissed the top of my head and sniffed my hair. We were still hugging each other, feeling each other's bare skin. "Yes we do," he said. "I love the smell of your hair. I love all your smells, even those I haven't smelled yet."

"You will." *God, I want to kiss you, feel your tongue, taste your mouth.* "Kiss me, honey." *This is so nice...He's sucking on my tongue...He never did that before...Let me suck on his...Ooh, that is pleasurable...He's licking my nose!..That tickles.* "Stop that." "No." "Don't you dare say 'No' to me, Mark Tuttle." *He's hugging me tighter...We're both laughing...Let me lick his nose, see how he likes it...He loves it... I did too...Sandy and Mark, nose-lickers.* "I love it that you're my boyfriend, even though I can't say that." *I get you excited, don't I, Mark Tuttle?*

"I'm your boyfriend as long as you want me. Everyone knows that."

"That's forever," I said.

"Not forever," he said.

"What do you mean?" *What do you mean "not forever" Mark Tuttle?*

"Someday I'll be your husband, not your boyfriend. I'll still be your best friend though." *You had me scared there for a moment, Mark Tuttle...My **husband**...Yes, I want that!*

"We **are** going to get married someday, aren't we?"

"Yes, and have four kids. I love talking about our future," said Mark.

"Me too, and it **is** our future, not just a daydream. We better get back to the pool," I said. "Our moms might wonder what we're doing in here. We have the rest of our lives to enjoy moments like this. The rest of our lives!" *God, that's true…The rest of our lives…This was almost like sex today, but later we'll have real sex…For now, this will be wonderful…kissing…rubbing my little bumps against his bare chest…Licking noses…Mark kissing my bumps…Mark fondling my ass…Maybe I'll fondle his…very wonderful, Sandy, this will be very wonderful….Just sitting together by the pool in one of the long chairs…snuggling…maybe napping in his arms…smelling each other…someday we will sleep together every night…so loved, so safe in his arms…I can't imagine a safer place in the whole world…Mark will never let anything bad happen to me…I know that…I love that!*

"Do you know how great your breath smells?" Mark asked. "I know we have to get back to the pool, but I could stay like this forever, feeling your skin against mine, your bumps against my chest, smelling your breath, gently squeezing your soft ass. Just holding you. I love you, Sandy."

"Love you too. Don't worry. We'll spend a lot of time in the shed this summer. My bumps need cherishing and my ass needs massaging. By you. My personal *masseur*. Maybe I'll give your ass a little massage too. Like that?"

"Oh, yes," he said. We kissed again, and then headed back to the pool. I gave his ass a little squeeze before we left the inner room. "You can do that anytime," he said, smiling.

Back to me, Peggy:

Sandy told me all about the little adventure in the pool shed. I got excited just listening to her telling me about it. I wished I were Mark. I knew they had been up to something in the shed. They looked like two cats that had eaten the pet canary as they returned to poolside. I was waiting for little yellow feathers to pop out of their mouths, like in a cartoon.

You might be wondering why they would take a chance with their topless hugging in the pool shed so close to their mothers. Mark would never put Sandy in a position where she might be embarrassed. They knew what they were doing.

The pool shed had a large central area where the pump was located. During the winter months, all the pool furniture was stored in that section. Poles, nets, vacuum, and other maintenance equipment were also stored there. Off to the right side of the entrance was an inner room where the chemicals were stored. For some reason, the door to that storage room could be locked from the inside. There was no toilet in the shed. Bathers had to go up to the house if they needed to pee.

Mark had always helped his father maintain the pool. Beginning that summer, after seventh grade, Mr. Tuttle turned over pool maintenance control to Mark. Actually to Mark and Sandy. The first thing Sandy did each day was take the long pole and net and remove all leaves and other debris from the pool. Then she emptied the skimmer basket. Mark tested the pool, added chemicals, and vacuumed the pool as needed. The pool water was always clean and sparkling. If Mr. Tuttle graded them, he would have given them an A+.

Mr. Tuttle loved Sandy. He loved me too, and Margie Baylor, but he had a special place in his heart for Sandy. He knew she was going to be his daughter-in-law someday, and the mother of his grandchildren. Both of those thoughts made him very happy.

As the pool custodians, Mark and Sandy were the only ones who ordinarily used the shed. I helped them on occasion, but they were usually finished their chores before I arrived. As a further precaution, they performed their "admire and kiss the bumps" ritual (I'm not being catty; that's what Sandy called it) in the inner chemical storage area with the door locked. There was no reason whatsoever for any of the mothers to ever go into the shed. I don't think I ever saw one there.

I asked Sandy once if they ever played doctor in the shed. She just smiled at me, but did not answer. It was the only time Sandy ever clammed up on me. I concluded that they did. I would have if I had such a great opportunity, an opportunity to play doctor with Sandy, that is. I guess I would have played doctor with Mark too. Or, better yet, with both of them.

That night Sandy wrote out verbatim (as verbatim as she could remember) Mark's little speech about what they would be doing together. She hid it away in her desk drawer, but took it out from time to time to ponder it. Knowing Mark Tuttle, and no one knows Mark Tuttle better than Sandy Roberts, she knew they would be doing all those things one day.

One afternoon that summer, Billy Walsh was at the pool. I told you he followed me around like I was in heat. He was in our class, and Mark invited him over. We ended up having a chicken fight in the pool, me on Billy, and Sandy on Mark. Even though Sandy and I are best friends, we are both competitive. We wrestled for ten minutes, both determined not to be the first thrown in the pool. Mark was stronger than Billy, and a lot more athletic, giving Sandy the advantage. When I ended up falling off Billy, I said, "You only won because you were on Mark."

She jumped off Mark and said, "I'm not on Mark now," and lunged at me. We wrestled in the pool trying to put each other under. It was serious. Sandy and I were having a fight. Sandy Roberts and Peggy Mayhew having a fight. The unimaginable. We were both lucky Mark was there. He got between us.

"Stop it, you two," he said.

None of the adults had noticed what was happening in the pool.

We stared at each other.

"We were only playing," Sandy said.

But we weren't.

"We were not fighting, Mark," I said.

But we were.

"Of course not," said Sandy. Then she hugged me and kissed me. A warm kiss, a make-up kiss. "What the hell happened, Peggy? I'm sorry," she said.

"It's nothing," I said. "In fact, I liked wrestling with you."

"I did too." She kissed me again.

That night, lying in bed, I had my first experience with masturbation. I kept thinking about wrestling with Sandy, and kissing Sandy, and I started playing with myself and kissing the pillow. I went to the kitchen and came back with a little dish of Breyer's vanilla bean ice cream. *I love you, Sandy Roberts.* I woke up hugging my pillow. I couldn't wait to get back to the pool the next day. *How can that girl with her little bumps get me so excited?..I hope she's not mad at me.*

When I got to the Tuttle house, without Mom – it was not a Sunday; I went over on my bike – Sandy was already there. When I, nervous, arrived at the pool area, Sandy jumped up and ran to me.

"I thought you might be mad at me," she said, hugging me. "That would devastate me. Come with me to the pool shed. I want to talk privately."

We walked together to the shed. I was wearing my bathing suit under my white shirt and tan shorts. I removed the outer wear and sat facing her. We sat on two overturned chlorine buckets. She took my hands. God, she is beautiful. Even her little bumps are beautiful.

"I am too competitive sometimes, Peggy. When you said that I won only because I was on Mark, I got mad. I am so sorry."

"I should not have said that. I was just mad that you won. I'm sorry too."

"Let's make a pact," she said. "We will never fight with each other. Never. But we will fight like tigresses for each other."

"Agreed. Give me your pinky."

We locked pinkies, and each said, "I promise." And we have kept that promise, both parts of it.

"Let's kiss to seal the pinky promise," she said.

We kissed. We touched tongues. First time I did that with Sandy. "I love you, Peggy Mayhew," she said. First time for that too. "I don't ever want to lose you as a friend."

"I love you too, Sandy Roberts. And you **do** taste like Breyer's vanilla bean ice cream."

She blew a stream of air in my face. "Enjoy it," she said.

That might have been my best day at the Tuttle pool ever. That get-together in the pool shed was our first, private, two-person voyage on the Barge of Curiosity.

For the rest of the summer, Mark and Sandy always found some excuse to spend time alone in the pool shed. "I don't know why he loves to kiss my breasts so much,"

Sandy told me. "They're almost non-existent. But he does love to kiss and lick my little bumps. I like it too."

I knew Sandy loved Mark Tuttle, and he loved her. But she also loved me. She told me so. What more could I want?

Sandy and Mark hated it when September arrived -- the Tuttles closed up the pool. Even if they wanted to use the pool shed, they couldn't. It was full of pool furniture and equipment.

In December Mark told the two of us that he had convinced his father to open up the pool early.

"How early?" Sandy asked.

"January," he said.

She punched him on the shoulder – she liked to do that – and told him he could abstain. "It's good for the savage soul."

"But I need you to soothe my savage soul."

"I'll find some way, honey," Sandy said. "Don't worry. Your savage soul will be soothed."

I assume she did, but I don't know how.

Chapter Four
Peggy Mayhew II

At the end of eighth grade, I had a real scare. Sandy and Mark were both offered scholarships for high school, Sandy by Bayview Academy, and Mark by LaSalle Academy, two Catholic high schools noted for their academics and athletics.

"You're not going to accept them, are you?" I asked Sandy. I was almost in tears.

"No," she said.

Thank you, God.

"The commute for each of us would be forty-five minutes each way, and we would not be going together. Mom, obviously, thinks Coventry is as good a school as Bayview. And I want to go to high school with Mark and you, and the only way I can do that is if the three of us go to CHS."

"Mark and his parents agree?" I asked.

"When I told Mark I was going to CHS, he said he was going to CHS. My mother told the Tuttles that the Honors Program at CHS is as academically challenging as anything LaSalle can offer. After the Tuttles listened to Mom, they told Mark the choice was his. There is no way Mark is not going to high school with me. Especially now that I'm developing breasts. Know what he said to me?"

"No," I said, laughing at the breast comment. They **were** developing nicely.

"He said, 'The three of us will stay on the Barge of Curiosity for four more years.' I told him that sounded like an election slogan, 'four more years.' "

I liked the sound of "the three of us." *Oh, how I liked the sound of "the three of us."*

Before I get into my high school and later years, I want to tell you one more thing about the day Sandy first displayed her little bumps to Mark. She told me about it the following day. When everyone was finished using the pool, Sandy and Mark went to work. The second phase of their pool maintenance job was to clean up the pool area at the end of the day: straighten out the chairs, put things away, police the area around the pool, and wash down the tables. They were the only persons left at the pool that afternoon.

When they finished the cleanup, Mark stretched out on one of the long pool chairs. Sandy said, "Scootch over," and plopped into the chair and into his arms.

They lay on their sides, face to face, legs entwined, wrapped up in each other, stroking each other, smiling at each other, smelling each other, kissing with mouths open moistening each other's lips, occasionally sending a stream of breath in the other's direction, knowing their love was real....deep....abiding. They knew **that** since they were eight years old. Maybe earlier. What happened at eight might not have happened if they were not already in love.

"We really are going to spend the rest of our lives together, aren't we?" Sandy said.

"Yes," he said. "Don't ever doubt it."

"I don't. And, you know, we **are** going to stand together in the middle of St. Peter's Square. And walk on the Great Wall. We can and will do anything we want. Together. What is going to stop us?"

"Nothing. And make love, a lot."

Sandy told me she just hugged Mark tighter, her eyes filled with tears. "A lot," she said.

Two thirteen-year-old kids, but they knew each other and their future. They had no doubts.

Then they walked up to the Tuttle house holding hands. Sandy told me Mr. Tuttle was watching them, and he smiled. Sandy waved to him; he waved back. She thought, *You're going to be my father-in-law one day,* but that was not to be.

Near the end of freshman year at CHS, Mark and I were walking home from school together. Mark had just turned fifteen. Sandy and her mother had left school early; Sandy had an appointment with her dentist. We were still going to have dinner at the Roberts's house that evening. Mark and I decided to stop at McDonald's before heading over there -- just to share a large fries and to have Cokes, nothing to ruin our appetites, as if anything could ruin a teen-ager's appetite. If Sandy and Mrs. Roberts weren't home when we arrived, we planned to play basketball in their driveway.

On the way to McDonald's, Mark went into a convenience store to get something – I forget what – and I waited for him outside. I wasn't paying attention – I was reading a novel while I waited, *To Kill a Mockingbird* – and didn't notice the two hoody-looking guys approaching me. They starting giving me a hard time, something about reading a book, as if that were something to make fun of. I don't take bullying well. I said something like, "Fuck off, losers," which they took umbrage at. I don't know why. One of them pushed me. "Who you calling losers, cunt?" I pushed back and said, "You, fuckface." I hate the "cunt" word.

It didn't dawn on me that the odds were not in my favor. As I said, I don't take bullying well. And I don't back down from fights.

Mark came back out at that moment. "Hey, what's going on here?" he said.

"This bitch your girlfriend?"

"Yes," said Mark, and he winked at me.

"You gotta teach her some manners. She's got a shit mouth."

"I think she has a pretty mouth," said Mark. "Now why don't you two just take off?"

"Because we're gonna teach her a lesson. Teach her not to have such a shit mouth."

"No, you're not," said Mark. That's when the fight started. Mark was stronger than they, and more athletic, but they were street fighters, probably gangbangers. The fight wasn't two on one; I wasn't going to let Mark fight alone, especially since he was fighting for me. It was a short, but a vicious fight. Luckily for us, they did not have knives. The owner of the convenience store came out yelling, "I just called the cops. Stop this." When the gangbangers heard "cops," they ran.

Mark had a black eye and a cut on his cheek. I had a bruise on the side of my forehead and a cut under my left eye. I did get in three good punches, head shots. I took a few too, obviously. Mark did some damage too. We couldn't assess the extent of it because our foes had fled.

"Thank you," I said to Mark.

"I didn't call the cops," said the owner. "I just wanted to scare them off. Are you kids okay?"

"Yes," said Mark. And, "You're very welcome," to me.

"Do you still want to stop at McDonald's?" I asked.

"Yes. We can clean up there."

"Sandy's going to kill me when she sees you," I said.

"No, she won't. She would kill me if I didn't fight for you."

I knew that was true.

When we got to McDonald's, even before we ordered, we had to tell about eight people what happened. CHS students. Everyone wanted to know where Sandy was. Mark and Peggy without Sandy? Doesn't happen. We commandeered a table, and then I went to the ladies' room. When I got back, Mark went to clean up in the men's room. Then we ordered.

"I never lost a fight before," he said. We had dumped the French fries on the table between us and were sharing them, dipping them in the ketchup mountain we had created.

"You didn't lose today," I said.

"I sure as hell didn't win," he retorted.

That was true. "We did hold our own."

"I should have been able to protect you, Peggy, without you having to fight. I have to be able to protect Sandy and you. Margie Baylor too. But especially Sandy and you."

"I started it with my 'shit mouth,' " I said.

"You don't have a 'shit mouth.' You have a beautiful mouth."

"Do you want to kiss it? I shouldn't say that. Sandy would kill me. But I do want to kiss you today. A thank you kiss, for standing up for me." *I've always wanted to kiss Mark Tuttle….Just a thank you kiss…Not impinging on Sandy's turf…I wouldn't do that.*

"I'll always stand up for you," Mark said.

So we kissed. The only time other than the Kiss of Peace. We had earned that kiss; it was a vicious fight. We did not touch tongues. The only tongue Mark Tuttle will ever touch belongs to Sandy Roberts. The only breast he will ever fondle belongs to her too.

Sandy and Mrs. Roberts could not believe what they found in their driveway when they came home: two wounded combatants. Mrs. Roberts disinfected our cuts and put a steak on Mark's eye.

Sandy asked, "Are you two okay? What happened?" She kept looking from one face to the other.

"I got in a fight with a couple of hoods, and Mark protected me. I have to learn to curb my tongue."

"What did you say?"

"I called them losers and told the one who called me a 'cunt' that he was a 'fuckface.' "

"He called you a 'cunt'?"

"Yeah."

"I would have fought him too. Good thing Mark was there."

"You better believe it. Sandy, I gave him a kiss at McDonald's, but it was just a thank-you kiss."

"That's okay." And I knew it was.

After Mr. Roberts drove me home, Mark and Sandy sat on her porch. He gave her all the details. Sandy later gave me full details of **their** conversation.

"I am so glad you were there. Does it hurt when I hug you?"

"No. Not at all."

"Good. I want to hug and kiss you so bad."

They were locked in an embrace, kissing passionately, when Mr. Roberts came home. He cleared his throat loudly so they would know he was there.

Sandy just looked up and said, "Hi, Dad."

He just smiled. He has loved Mark Tuttle since Mark was eight years old. There is nothing he wants more than Mark Tuttle as his son-in-law. Sandy and Mark want that too.

Two days later, again at McDonald's, the three of us together this time, Mark said, "It's never going to happen again."

"What?" we asked.

"Getting beaten up trying to protect one or both of you," he said. "I want you two to feel safe when you're with me."

"We do," we both said.

"I asked around. There is an ex-Special Forces Sergeant, Ben Kravey, who has a studio in the Stop & Shop Plaza here in Coventry where he teaches street fighting and self-defense. Not Karate or Judo, street fighting. How to protect yourself on the street, how to fight more than one person, how to handle someone with a weapon. I had no problem convincing my father to pay for the lessons. He did not like that black eye the other night, Peggy. One hour each week for the first three months, then one hour each month for as long as I want. Private lessons. I asked if you two could watch, and he said, 'Yes, as long as they're quiet.' That might be impossible with you guys."

Sandy punched him on the shoulder. "We'll be quiet."

We went with Mark every week. Ben Kravey was scary good. At first Mark was severely overmatched. But rapidly, he and his teacher became equals.

Sandy and I picked up a lot just observing in the studio. To enhance our skills, the three of us laid out mats in the CHS gym and practiced tactics. Mark was our teacher. A crowd of students, mostly boys, gathered to watch. Can you blame them? Two pretty girls in gym shorts fighting. Sandy's breasts were no longer little bumps. Believe me, Sandy and I were very careful. We did not want a repeat of the pool fight. It didn't happen. We had made a promise to each other. And to quote Mark's favorite poet – yes, Mark Tuttle has a favorite poet, Robert Service, who is now my and Sandy's favorite poet too -- "A promise made is a debt unpaid." After a few months of these sessions with Mark, we were a fearsome duo.

Mr. Kravey told me and Sandy one day, when Mark was in the changing room, "I never had a pupil who learned so well and so fast."

"He was embarrassed that day," I said. "He didn't lose, but he didn't like it that he didn't win, and that he needed my help."

Mr. Kravey looked at us and said, "You know he's doing this for you two. He never wants either of you to be threatened when he's around. Peggy, he wasn't embarrassed because he didn't win. He was embarrassed because he let you get hurt. You got hurt on his watch, as we say in the military."

"I would have gotten hurt a lot worse if he wasn't there."

"He knows that, but he has a zero tolerance policy when it comes to you or Sandy getting hurt. Zero tolerance.

"And Sandy, you know he would die for you, don't you? Every other word out of his mouth is 'Sandy.'"

"Yes," she said. "I would die for him too."

Mr. Kravey had three rules posted on the rear wall:

1. Always avoid a fight if at all possible.

2. Only fight if you are boxed into a corner or if you are defending your woman.

3. If a fight starts, fight to win. That's the most important rule.

Sandy and I loved rule number two: ***Only fight ... if you are defending your woman***.

"He's a lucky guy," Ben said. "He has two women." Sandy and I knew that wasn't true.

I mentioned that Sandy and I led CHS to two state championships in basketball. That was not even our best sport. I have never seen anyone who could pitch a softball more accurately and faster than Sandy Roberts. We played seven inning games, and she averaged eighteen strikeouts per game, and only one walk. No-hitters were the norm; and she had seven perfect games in our senior year alone! And could she hit, not with the power I had, but for average. She sprayed singles and doubles all over the field. I, on the other hand, hit for power. I averaged two home runs per game during those two championship years usually with Sandy on base. She seemed to be always on base when I came up to bat. I played third and handled the defensive duties well. Mark called me "a female Brooks Robinson."

Coach Thompson, our basketball coach, also coached the softball team. Coach Wilson, the boys' basketball coach, was the athletic director at CHS, and he was at all our games. Bill Reynolds, the famous columnist for the *Providence Journal*, was at many of our games during our senior year. Sandy will tell you later in this narrative how that relationship developed. Bill was a fine athlete during his high school and Brown University days. He asked Coach Thompson before one game if he could take some swings against Sandy. Coach Thompson laughed, but said, "Go ahead." Nine pitches, nine swings, nine misses. When he rejoined Mark in the stands, Mark said, "Don't feel bad. Nobody can hit her." Bill asked Mark if he could. Mark laughed and said, "I never try. I just warm her up with a very padded glove."

Mark warmed Sandy up before all our games. Coach Thompson would come over to the fence, toss Mark a catcher's mitt, and ask him to warm up Sandy. Mark would swing himself over the five-foot high chain link fence with the ease of a gymnast. He and Sandy then walked down to the bullpen area in right field. Her pitches gradually increased in speed until she felt ready. They walked back to the dugout holding hands. Then they kissed – that was their pre-game, never-to-be-altered, ritual – and then Mark hopped back over the fence, again with ease. He sat with Sandy's parents who were at the games. During our junior year, Mr. Tuttle often came to the games as well. You could tell that he loved Sandy and cherished the thought of having her as his second daughter. Mr. Roberts always asked, "Mark, how's your left hand?" Mark just held up his very red left hand. Even with the padded catcher's mitt, that hand displayed the fury of Sandy's pitches. It would have taken more than a red hand to keep Mark from warming up Sandy.

Before we reached junior year, CHS had won only one state championship in any sport, girls' cross country twenty years in the past. We, the CHS girls, won four, two in basketball, and two in softball. The boys won two in basketball. That four to two advantage was a point of pride for me and Sandy. The boys' baseball team came close in Mark's senior year. They lost in the state final to LaSalle, eighteen to seventeen. The game was played in McCoy Stadium, the home of the Triple-A Pawtucket Red Sox, a stadium with major-league dimensions. Mark hit three home runs, one a grand slam, but CHS did not have any pitching. Mark, like I, played third.

During our sophomore year, Mark put his Ben Kravey training to amazingly good use. Mark did follow Ben's rule number one: *always avoid a fight if at all possible*. But you better believe he was always ready to follow rule number two, especially the second part of it: *protect your woman*, or, in his case, *women*. That was the reason he went to Ben Kravey in the first place, because I got hurt on his watch.

Sandy and I were sitting behind the gym at one of the outdoor picnic tables waiting for Mark, who was showering and changing after basketball practice. The girls' team practiced first, then the boys. The three of us walked to and from school together every day, so, after Sandy and I showered, we either watched the boys practice or, on nice fall days, sat behind the gym talking. Sandy and I loved to be together. I like to think we loved each other. I definitely loved her; I think it was reciprocal. Both the girls' and the boys' teams were very good that year, but not quite ready to challenge for the state title. That stage was coming.

During eighth grade and during our first two years at CHS, Sandy's parents did not think she should have a steady boyfriend. "You're too young," her mother said. I don't think Mr. Roberts agreed with that, but he did not oppose his wife. I think Mrs. Roberts feared the big "S" word: SEX. She, Mrs. Roberts, wanted and foresaw a Tuttle-Roberts wedding in the future, but she wanted to keep "the kids" out of trouble.

One evening in June, just before we graduated from St. Michael's, Mrs. Roberts asked Mark and Sandy to join her in the Roberts's den. Sandy, as always, gave me the details the next day.

"You know I think you two are made for each other. I really believe that. I have never seen two people, of any age, more attuned to each other---"

"I can hear a 'but' coming, Mom," said Sandy.

"Yes, you do, honey. I think if you two are together all the time, alone together, it can lead to problems. I don't think you should date each other on a steady basis. I don't think you should be boyfriend and girlfriend. You're too young."

"I'm not **not** going to be with Mark, Mom. He's my best friend. He's my protector. You should appreciate that."

"I do, honey. And I don't want you **not** to be with Mark. But not dating. I don't want you dating anyone else. I don't want you dating at all yet. Be with Mark but in groups. No one-on-one time."

"Peggy's always with us, Mom."

"Yes, that's good."

"We don't do anything bad, Mom," pleaded Sandy.

"What were you two doing in the pool shed last summer?"

Sandy was caught by surprise. "We take care of the pool, Mom!"

"I mean during the day. You two were always disappearing into the shed during the day."

Sandy blushed.

"Why are you blushing? What did you two do in there? That's what I am afraid of."

"We just kissed and talked, Mom," Sandy lied.

"Mark?"

"It's my fault, Mrs. Roberts. I asked Sandy to take off her bathing suit top, and she did. I just wanted to see what she looked like on top." He didn't tell Mrs. Roberts that he kissed the bumps and massaged Sandy's ass.

"You went in there almost every day. You just looked?"

Mark just hung his head. He was embarrassed. More for Sandy than for himself.

"I assume you two did not do anything rash. Can I assume that?"

"Yes," they both said.

"Good, but I think we need some rules for the time being," said Mrs. Roberts.

"What rules?" asked Sandy.

"You can continue taking care of the pool, but no time alone in the pool shed during the day, or at the end of the day for that matter...

"No one-on-one dating...

"You can kiss, even hug at times, but nothing more than that...

"Don't call yourselves boyfriend and girlfriend. You can still say, 'best friends'....

"You can be together as much as you like, but not alone. Agreed?"

"Yes," said Sandy.

"Mark?"

"Yes, Mrs. Roberts."

"Don't get me wrong. I love both of you. I want you two to get married someday. I think you will get married, and you'll be very happy together. You'll give me fine grandchildren. But take it slow. Don't miss out on your youth." She then hugged and kissed each of them.

As Mrs. Roberts had hoped, that did slow down Sandy and Mark's sexual progress. They missed the pool shed time that summer – they both had been looking forward to that – but, in retrospect, Mrs. Roberts's caution was probably for the best. Mark was shocked, but pleasantly so, three years later when he again feasted his eyes on those little bumps. They weren't so little, and they were no longer bumps. And they were still his, and always would be, to share with their children.

Mark took the rules more seriously than Sandy. He did not ask her out on any dates. He never called her his "girlfriend." Sometimes that bothered Sandy. But, in his defense, he was always with her. And he never stopped being her protector. And he dreamed at night about those awesome little bumps. But he wanted to remain in Mrs. Roberts's good graces.

That day behind the gym, after basketball practice, while we were waiting for Mark, engrossed in girl conversation, a senior football player came over and patted Sandy on the ass. I couldn't believe his audacity.

"Excuse me," Sandy said, "What are you doing?"

"I saw you two young ladies over here by yourselves and said to myself, 'They need a man to take care of them.'"

"I have a man," said Sandy.

"I don't see a man," he said.

"He's changing after basketball practice. He'll be here soon," Sandy said.

"You mean that sophomore, that little boy, who hangs out with you two? The kid who can't make up his mind which of you two he wants?"

"He wants **me**," said Sandy.

"I do too, and I know what to do with you."

Sandy slapped him. I stood up ready to fight. I saw Mark running over. He looked mad.

"What the fuck are you doing?" he said to the much bigger, older football player.

They were standing face to face, eye to eye, Mark not backing down.

"What the fuck you think I'm doing? Get lost before I beat the shit out of you."

Mark just stood there, not terminating eye contact. The senior cocked his right arm, preparing to punch Mark. I don't even think I saw what happened next. The senior surely did not. Mark hit him with two punches, a left and a right, and the football player was down holding his neck. He was not getting up any time soon.

Mark helped us gather up our books and other items. "Peggy, Sandy, let's get out of here," he said. The seniors who were watching parted like the Red Sea and let us pass unmolested like the Israelites fleeing Egypt. I don't think, from that time on, any student at CHS ever bothered Sandy, Mark, or me. Except for "stupid Mac," but as I just said, Mac was "stupid." Word got around the school fast: "Don't mess with Sandy Roberts or Peggy Mayhew."

After we left the school grounds, on the way to McDonald's – where else? – Sandy dropped her books and hugged Mark. They knew I was watching, but they kissed passionately. They might not be "boyfriend" and "girlfriend," but I wouldn't mess with Sandy if I were you. Ben Kravey's rule number two. And as that senior found out, Ben Kravey's rule number three as well: *if you're going to fight, fight to win.* If Mark is fighting for Sandy, he is going to fight to win.

Sandy and Mark entered one of those zones that afternoon, a zone of exclusion, where no one exists but the two of them. I had seen them lose themselves in such a zone before. It's a wonderful sight. When they stopped kissing, Sandy put her right arm around Mark, pressed her face into his shirt, and rubbed his chest with her left hand. He hugged her with both hands and smelled her hair. He loves to do that. She then looked up into his face and said, "Thank you."

"You're welcome, Sandy, but you don't have to thank me. I will never let anyone hurt you."

She just stared into his eyes, her eyes filling with tears, continuing to rub his chest, and said, "I know. I know that, Mark, and that's one of the reasons why I love you so much." *I loved that "I know."*

"I love you too," he said. "Always have; always will."

They hugged so tightly that I thought they had become one person.

Then Sandy exploded out of the zone, hugged me, and said, "Off to McDonald's."

We walked holding hands, Mark in the middle. Maybe you couldn't tell which one he wanted, but I knew. Sandy knew. Mark knew. He knew since he was six years old. Believe me , he knew.

I let Billy Walsh -- remember him? – get on the Barge of Curiosity during the latter half of my junior year. I was not an ingénue, but neither was I the sexual animal that some thought I was. I did talk a good game, but much of that was talk. The only person whom I always wanted to make love with, who always, **always** turned me on was, and is, Sandy Roberts. But Sandy was not available.

I did sleep with Billy a few times. He was good during the act itself, but sorely lacking in foreplay and postplay. His idea of foreplay was saying, "Wanna fuck?", and his idea of postplay was asking if I wanted a beer too. He was also sorely lacking in brains. Sandy convinced me to drop him. I started dating an honors student in our class, Fred Williams. Billy Walsh wanted to make trouble for Fred, but Mark let Billy know that any action on his part would be ill advised. Billy understood, and never bothered me or Fred after that. No one at CHS ever messed with Mark.

By the fall of our junior year, Sandy and Mark had stopped the charade of not dating – Sandy brought that situation to a head the night of the East Greenwich basketball game – and the four of us often double dated: movies and the country-western line dancing that Sandy loved. Sandy and Mark both liked Fred. He could put together a complete sentence, a task Billy never mastered, and Fred's sentences were interesting. Fred and I did make love a few times, not excessively, and he understood the concepts of foreplay and postplay. That was nice. We would often lay in bed and talk after sex. Billy would have called that "wasting beer time."

There was a lesbian couple in our class at CHS, Gina Victoriano and Betsy Roche. I made love with them -- both of them together! – a few times. It was exciting, playing with vaginas and boobs, things neither Billy nor Fred had. Gina and I had such fun together that Betsy got mad, and they broke up. During my senior year, Gina and I made love occasionally, but the only vagina, the only boobs, I hungered after belonged to Sandy Roberts.

Mark's sister gave Mark her old Ford Falcon when she bought a new car. Mark loved that Falcon. Sandy, Mark, and I now had transportation. Mark would not let anyone drive the Falcon, except Sandy Roberts of course. They referred to the Falcon as "our car." People who knew how possessive Mark was with the car were amazed when Sandy would say things like, "Mark, I have to go to Kohl's. Can I have the keys?", and he would just toss them to her. (She never said, "Can I borrow the car?" You don't borrow your own car!)

Mark had one rule for the car that I found endearing. If there were ever a conflict, when he and Sandy needed the car at the same time, Sandy always had priority. Always. Mark insisted on that, not Sandy.

I had a two o'clock dental appointment one afternoon. I had obtained an early release from school, and Mom was going to pick me up. The morning of the appointment, Mom told me she had an important meeting at work and couldn't take me.

"What will I do?" I asked.

"Borrow Mark's car. He'll let you," Mom said.

"Mom, he doesn't let anyone drive his car."

"He lets Sandy," she said.

"Mom, I'm not Sandy."

"Just ask him. All he can say is, 'No.' "

I was apprehensive when I got in the back seat that morning. I leaned forward and put my right hand on Mark's shoulder.

"Mark, can I ask a favor, a big favor?"

"Sure," he said.

"I have a dental appointment this afternoon at two. Mom was going to pick me up, but she can't. I have no way to get there."

"Take our car," Sandy said.

"I didn't think Mark would let me drive it."

Mark reached up and squeezed my right hand. "Of course you can drive it," said Sandy. "That doesn't apply to you. If you ever need anything from either of us, just ask. We won't say 'No' to you, Peggy."

That's true. I asked Sandy many years later for the favor of favors, and she came through. God did she ever come through. I am crying now just thinking about it. I was desperate and didn't know where to turn. Then I thought *Sandy*! As soon as I told her my problem, she solved it -- before I even had a chance to ask her for help. She always has my back. She did the greatest thing for me that one mother can do for another. Did I ever tell you that I love Sandy Roberts? As Mark would say, "Always have; always will."

When we got out of the car, Mark handed me the keys. "Meet us at the Roberts's for dinner."

We had lasagna. Delicious. But more delicious than the lasagna was the taste of the friendship I have with Sandy Roberts and Mark Tuttle. And unlike the taste of the lasagna, the taste of our friendship has endured a lifetime. The two of them drove me home that night after we did our school work. Then they went back to the Roberts's home for some allowable hugging and kissing.

Did you notice above that Sandy spoke for Mark when I asked to borrow the car? They were a couple already. "Take **our** car." I loved it.

When I got home, I told Mom, "Mark let me use his car."

She smiled. "There was never any doubt in my mind, Peg."

Our senior year at CHS was a whirlwind. Sandy has given her account of all these incidents in other parts of this narrative, but I will briefly touch on them.

In September, Mark's parents were killed in a freak automobile accident. That was the worst day of Sandy's and Mark's lives. I was there for them throughout that whole harrowing time. Mark's sister, Patty, had graduated from Rhode Island College and was teaching at that time in North Providence. She had an apartment in that suburban city. Patty and Mark agreed that he would live in the Tuttle house until he left for college. Then the siblings would sell the house. During the remainder of our senior year, Sandy spent as much time at that house as Mark did. Not quite! Sandy didn't sleep there, but she and Mark made love almost every day. They were engaged after all. The three of us, sometimes four if Fred Williams joined us, often ate dinner there. Sandy and I did the cooking, and Mark and Fred handled the cleanup. Chinese take-out was also a favorite.

"It's like you're married," I told Sandy one day.

"Not quite. I want to sleep with him. Literally sleep with him," she said.

"You will in eight months," I said. The wedding date was set for June.

They got engaged the afternoon of the Tuttles's wake. Mark gave Sandy his mother's diamond ring and his mother's pearl necklace, with Patty's blessing. At the wake and at the funeral, Sandy was the most attractive woman, young or old, I have ever seen. I do love her, but I think I was being objective. She wore a long black dress and had her hair twirled on top of her head. The white pearl necklace between her perfect breasts contrasted spectacularly with the black dress, adding the final mesmerizing touch.

Mark's father had two large insurance policies. The proceeds paid off the mortgage, all final expenses and debts of the Tuttles's, and left a little in excess of $650,000 to both Patty and Mark. Sandy and Mark would have no financial worries during their college years. As you will find out, that was a real understatement.

During our senior year, Sandy and I scratched the itch we had. I will let Sandy tell you about that event, but it created an even stronger bond between the two of us, a bond which has lasted a lifetime.

I was offered a few basketball scholarships to smaller, Division II, colleges, but chose to go the University of Rhode Island (URI) on a Centennial Scholarship: free tuition, room, and board for the top high school seniors in Rhode Island. An attempt to keep the talent at home. Riding the Barge of Curiosity with Mark and Sandy definitely made me one of the top high school seniors in the Ocean State.

Fred Williams was accepted in to RPI, his first choice. I knew that was the end of our relationship. Mark said "GUDs" did not work -- GUD, a Geographically Unacceptable Date. He was right. We ended as a couple the day Fred left for Troy, New York.

Mark and Sandy got married in June, a few weeks after graduation. I was the maid of honor. They went to Italy on their honeymoon. Sandy had written down the litany of things Mark proclaimed he wanted to do with her before he died. When they came home she said to me, "We can cross off three. We saw the ceiling of the Sistine Chapel, and the Last Judgment on the wall of the chapel; we saw Michelangelo's David in Florence; and we stood and walked for hours in St. Peter's Square. I didn't want to leave the *Piazza San Pietro*. We stood arm in arm near the obelisk in the center. I felt more love for Mark at that time than I can explain. I said, 'You told me we would be here, and we are.' He kissed me and asked, 'Did you doubt me?' I said, 'Never.' " She told me the eight years of Italian, four at St. Michael's, four at CHS, really paid off. They were conversationally fluent.

Sandy accepted a full scholarship to Harvard, and Mark accepted a full scholarship to MIT, both in Cambridge, Mass. They each received a housing and meals allowance which more than covered their rent, food, and entertainment (movies, Red Sox, Chinese restaurants) costs. They also had more than $650,000 in their

69

investment account. The Monday after the wedding, Mark changed that account to joint. The Falcon went with them to Cambridge, but they used it almost exclusively for trips to Rhode Island or New Hampshire. They used public transportation or walked within the Boston-Cambridge area. Sandy told me they rented a plot of dirt near their apartment to park the car. "Two hundred dollars a month!" she complained.

You might think that the distance between Kingston, Rhode Island, and Cambridge, Massachusetts, would have created problems for the Peggy/Sandy relationship. It did not. We would never let that happen. I was in Cambridge twice a month on average the five years they were there. Sandy referred to the guest room as "Peggy's room." Most other visitors, except couples, slept on the couch whether I was there or not. Sandy and Mark came to Rhode Island frequently. During freshmen year, they picked me up in Kingston on Friday after classes, and dropped me back off on Sunday before they headed back north. After that, I had my own transportation.

My sexual appetites matured at URI. I no longer sought out the occasional vagina. As I told you earlier, there was only one vagina that I ever hungered for, and that vagina was in Cambridge and married. I met a fellow Rhode Islander, Warren Jones, from East Greenwich during my sophomore year. He had played basketball for East Greenwich High School, and held Mark Tuttle in awe. He was guarding Mark the night Mark scored fifty-seven points! Warren was amazed to discover that Mark was one of my two closest friends. Warren had a car and we either went together to Cambridge or, if he was busy, I took the car north. We usually went together. Warren could not believe he was friends with Mark Tuttle – they were, and are, good friends – and looked forward to our week-ends together with the Tuttles.

Warren and I got married the month after Maddie, the Tuttles's first, was born. Sandy was my matron of honor, and Mark was our best man. Our first, a girl Heather, was born a year after our wedding. Bobby Tuttle was born at the same time. All three of my children had a Tuttle contemporary, Heather with Bobby as I said, Larry with Jimmy, and Candi with Annie. The six of them looked up to Maddie. Maddie was the leader of the Tuttle/Jones contingent. I mentioned earlier that my kids and Sandy's were best of friends. They grew up together, they played together, and as you'll learn, some of them married.

After Maddie's birth, and before my wedding, I received the best phone call of my life.

"Peggy, it's me." I knew Sandy Tuttle's voice. "We decided to move back to Coventry. I want our kids to grow up around their grandparents and their aunts and uncles. And I want them to grow up with your kids, when you have them. And I miss the daily contact with you."

"I do too, miss that daily contact." I was crying.

"My brother, Bobby, and Leslie are moving back to Coventry too."

"I bet your mom is happy."

"She's ecstatic."

"Get a house with a pool," I said laughing. "And a pool shed."

"Oh, we will. That's a requirement."

We did have daily contact after they moved back. Did I ever tell you that Sandy and I love each other? We do.

I was hired by CHS to teach Phys. Ed. and to coach basketball. I started as JV coach, but later took over the varsity when Coach Thompson retired. I brought two more championships to CHS. They say a good coach is a great coach if she has the players. I had Maddie Tuttle, Heather Jones, and Melanie Roberts. They made me a great coach.

71

Warren taught English at Bishop Hendricken High School in Warwick. We bought a ranch house in Coventry. It did not have a pool, but we didn't need one. Our other house, the Tuttle house, had one.

Mom passed away when I was forty-five. I could not have gotten through that ordeal without Sandy. She always has my back. Mom was a great mother. And a great grandmother. My three children, and the Tuttle children, adored her. She and Maddie frequently had long conversations by the pool or on the Tuttle porch in cooler weather. When I asked Mom what they talked about, she told me, "Philosophy." *Philosophy?* Love that Maddie.

I often think back to that first day of school. "If any of the girls are bullies, pick out the toughest one and fight her." Well, the toughest one was Sandy, and I did not have to fight her. Sandy Roberts was no bully!

I cry when I think of what Mom did for me.

Thank you, Mom, for not having that abortion.

Thank you, Mom, for sending me to St. Michael's...What would my life be like if I had never met Mark and Sandy?..If I had never ridden on the Barge of Curiosity with them?

I can't imagine a life without Sandy Roberts in it. Or Mark Tuttle.

One final point: I knew Sandy was not really looking for soap that momentous day in the CHS girls' locker room. She'll tell you about that.

Chapter Five
The Dance and the Trinity

Can you love all of your children equally, and yet love one more than the others? It sounds like a paradox, a contradiction, and Mark and I will go to our graves insisting, and believing, that we love all four of our children equally, and yet we know, deep in our hearts, that we love Maddie more than the others without loving the others any less. Maddie is our first born, our *primogenita*, the little girl who taught us to really understand the meaning of love, and who taught me, at least, how to comprehend that great mystery of Christianity, the Trinity.

While Mark was at MIT and I was at Harvard, Mark met and befriended a shy young man from Seattle, Bill Skwor, who had remarkable marketing skills, but lacked Mark's unbelievable computing skills. Mark is truly a genius. I know I'm prejudiced, but it's true. Mark and Bill combined their skills, developed a very popular software package while freshmen, and then marketed it quite successfully. They added a third partner, a venture capitalist, Philip Andrews, also from Seattle, greatly increased the production and distribution of the product, and their company, Alpha-Omega Data Systems, went public in a very lucrative IPO during Mark's junior year. Bill Skwor, the marketing guru, owned 40% of the company, Philip Andrews owned 30%, and Mark and I owned the remaining 30%, JTWROS (jointly with right of survivorship). Mark and I share everything; we have since we were six years old. We would never consider any other option.

Mark and I are anal, and we developed, while still dating, what we called The Rules to Make Our Relationship **Prosper** – emphasis is mine! There are six rules, and we have kept them religiously ever since we created them. *Rule Five* is *Share Everything*. *Rule Four*, closely related, is *Either One of Us Can Make Decisions for Both of Us*. (Within reason, of course. Mark would never commit us to a *ménage a trois,* for example, even with Peggy Mayhew, which might be pleasant for all three of us! Not only is that something I would never do, but I would probably kill him for suggesting it, especially if he suggested the gorgeous, sexy Peggy.)

Back to the IPO: overnight, my and Mark's net worth went from $800,000 (it had grown) to $450 million dollars. Very few people, other than Denny McIntyre, our financial advisor, Mom, Dad, Patty, and Peggy Mayhew – Peggy and I have no secrets -- know our net worth. In fact, today, eleven years later, our net worth is significantly higher. Mark and I do not spend money profligately. He drives a Honda Accord, and I drive a Volkswagen Passat. We donated $300,000 to our church, St. Michael's in Coventry, last year for a new roof, but that gift was anonymous, so don't tell anyone.

The night after the IPO, Bill, Philip, and the two of us were sitting around our apartment in Cambridge. We had just finished a baked macaroni and cheese casserole that I had prepared. That dish carried us through our years in Cambridge, and, if I say so myself, I do make a mean mac and cheese. Bill looked over at Mark and said, "I guess our lives are going to get a lot better now."

I loved Mark's answer: "Bill," he said, "I have to disagree. Sandy and I are married, we love each other, we're healthy and intelligent, we're lovers, we sleep in each other's arms every night, and we're best friends. How can life get better than that? I agree that our lives will be easier, and that we will never have any financial problems as long as we live, but better, no, our lives cannot get better. They're perfect now."

I gave him a kiss, a well-deserved kiss. *It's great to be married to your best friend.*

Bill Skwor left MIT after his junior year and returned to the west coast where he set up the headquarters of the new publicly owned company, Alpha-Omega Data Systems. Mark and I finished college, both graduating with high honors. A year later we returned to our home town, Coventry, bought a large house with a pool and a pool shed near my parents' house, and did what we always wanted to do, write. We still own approximately ten percent of AODS, and Mark is on the Board of Directors.

Mark has published four novels, three of them best sellers, and I have published numerous short stories and, after Maddie's birth, twenty seven children's books, a series about the exploits of *Alexandra the Mouse*, who is Maddie in prose. I like to point out to Mark that I have twenty-three more published books than he has, but he counters with the observation that my books are, on average, thirty pages of large print with a lot of pictures. We love our life. We love to travel. Mark occasionally journeys out to Seattle for board meetings or to do some consulting for Bill Skwor, who has remained a good friend. I accompany Mark on these trips – I can't sleep unless I'm wrapped up in his arms. Mom, Patty, or Peggy watch our children. Yes, children. We have four, Maddie, now 11, Bobby, 10, Jimmy, 8, and our baby, Annie, 7.

Our fifteen year marriage is stronger today than it was the day we committed to each other. *Rules One, Two,* and *Three* have contributed to that: *Rule One* is *Never Argue or Fight.* Sounds impossible, but we have not had a real fight or argument since we began dating. I did get mad at him, unjustifiably, for ten seconds at *Lago Maggiore* – I'll tell you about that later. *Rule Two: If We Break Rule One, Never Go to Sleep Angry*, was becoming obsolete through lack of use, so we added *And Always Sleep Together* as a *Rule Two Addendum*. That's why I go with him to Seattle; neither one of us can imagine getting into bed without the other at the end of the day. *Rule Three*, I believe, is the main ingredient in our happy relationship: *Never Lie to Each Other, and Never Keep Secrets from Each Other*. We never do either. You can avoid so many problems in life by following those three rules. And, as I said, we're anal, and we follow them. I agree with Mark's 'Night of the IPO' comment that our life together could not get better. We have remained best friends as well as spouses and lovers. But being extremely wealthy does make life easier and less stressful!

Bill Skwor often comes for a visit when he feels overwhelmed at work. He refers to our house as his private retreat house. He tells acquaintances out west that he visits the Coventry House of Christian Love when he needs to refresh his soul. The Coventry House of Christian Love is, of course, our home. He made the comment once that, in all the years he has known us, both in Cambridge and in Coventry, he has never sensed the slightest tension in our apartment or house. He says our home is the only place he knows where he is absolutely positive he will be at ease at all times. I thank God, and Mark, every day that that is true!

This story actually begins one August day during the summer that Maddie was eleven. Bill Skwor was visiting as well as two of Mark's cousins from Ohio, Annie and Luisa. I love Annie; I named my youngest after her. We invited Mark's sister, Patty, her husband, Bill, my brother, Bobby, his wife, Leslie, their two children, Melanie and Robby, my parents, my best girlfriend, Peggy Mayhew, now Peggy Jones, her husband, Warren, their three children, Heather, Larry, and Candi, and our parish priest over for a cookout and swim in our back yard. Whew! That was a mouthful. Father Hanson came at 5:15, after celebrating the 4 o'clock Mass at St. Michael's, and arrived just in time for the dance. Peggy and her children practically lived at our house – Peggy and I would have it no other way – and they would have been there anyway.

Maddie, Annie, Melanie, my niece, and Heather and Candi, Peggy's girls, looking like five sisters with their matching ponytails, khaki shorts, and white T-shirts, approached me and Peggy who were lounging by the pool. Maddie, always the spokesperson, said, "Mommy, Aunt Peggy, can we perform a dance for our guests?" I love to do modern dance with the girls, so, of course, I said, "Yes." Peggy often dances with us, but she said, "Today I'll just be part of the audience." Peggy Mayhew is still the most beautiful woman I have ever seen. In high school the boys called her "the goddess." Her Heather will be as beautiful as she is.

While I was setting up the music, Maddie ran over to Mark and said, "Daddy, come dance with us." Mark never refuses any reasonable request from Maddie, so we were seven lined up to dance when the music started. I have often said, "If you ever need something from Mark, have

Maddie ask him." I guess you could equally well use me or Annie as an agent – Mark has a weakness for the girls in his life. But Maddie is special, special from the day she was born, when they looked at each other in the hospital room and both smiled. Yes, Maddie smiled. They tell me that's not possible, but I saw her smile at her daddy.

From the audience's point of view, Melanie was on the far right, then Heather, then me, Maddie in the middle, then Mark, and finally little Annie and Candi on the far left. Annie and Candi remind me and Peggy of ourselves when we were their age. They're inseparable.

"It's like we're looking back in time," Peggy said to me one day.

"God, do they ever look like us," I said.

Mark, who overheard, said, "Lucky kids." I kissed him.

And Bobby and Heather are like me and Mark. My Jimmy told me one day last week that Bobby beat up a sixth grader – Bobby is in fifth grade – for giving Heather a hard time. He added that Heather gave Bobby a hug and a kiss. Yes they are definitely like me and Mark. Heather, like Candi, is as beautiful as her mother. Jimmy wasn't being a tattletale; he was proud of his brother.

We dance together a lot, but never plan the actual dance moves in advance. The girls and Mark just follow my lead and, occasionally, my whispered instructions. If you taped the dance and played it back in slow motion, you could discern that their movements follow mine by a split, a very split, second. But in real time, you would swear that all our movements were simultaneous. Even the little ones, Annie and Candi, keep up with the timing. I might whisper, "Left turn," and then we all slowly make a full turn to the left stomping a foot at each quarter turn in the circle. Then I will whisper, "Reverse," and we'll slowly go back the other way. Our hands are perfectly synchronized as well, perfectly timed hand claps or arm movements. Much of it is simply that we have danced together so often that the girls know my next step before I take it. I love dancing with my girls, and I include Melanie, Heather, and Candi in that description. Melanie, Heather, and Candi **are** my girls. Mark and I, as I have said many times, are simply two bodies with one mind, as our volleyball opponents have discovered.

If Mark is dancing with us, Maddie will whisper at some point, "Twirl pony tails," and the six of us girls will slowly spin our heads creating pony tail circles in the air. Or she'll whisper, "Side to side," or "Front to back," and the six of us will execute the ponytail maneuver in perfectly matching movements. Maddie loves this because Mark does not have a ponytail, and he has to follow our moves without the effect. Mark is a good sport and pretends he has a ponytail. There is nothing Mark will not do for Maddie.

On this day I happened to look at Mark, and he was looking at me with that look I love, the look that says, "I love having you as my wife. I love sharing my life with you." I smiled the smile that he says will melt a glacier, a smile I reserve for him and the children. Maddie whispered something to me at this point, and we had a little private mother-daughter exchange that I will tell you about later. We did not miss a beat in the dance during the exchange.

The dance ended after four minutes, and it was a good performance. A friend has told me that we should take this show on the road. The girls are so cute and the synchronization is amazing. In fact as Mark was heading over to the grill to finish the hamburgers, chicken, and hot dogs, Father Hanson came up to him and asked, "How long did you guys work on that dance routine?"

Mark laughed and said, "It's completely spontaneous, Father. The six of us just follow Sandy's lead. You can't go wrong following her lead."

Father shook his head and said, "That's amazing. How can the kids maintain such good timing? There aren't any mistakes."

Mark said, "You're forgetting something, Father. They're not just any kids, they're Sandy's kids; they're little Sandys. They think like her; they act like her; they even look like her! Melanie, our niece, shares a lot of DNA with Sandy. Sandy's parents are her grandparents after all. And Heather and Candi are her godchildren, and they spend more time at our house than I do. Notice that all the girls wear ponytails because Sandy wears a ponytail."

Father just said, "I still think it's amazing."

When the food was ready, Maddie, Melanie, Heather, Peggy, and I helped Mark carry all the food, the chicken, the hot dogs, the hamburgers, the cheeseburgers, the green salad, the potato salad, the macaroni salad, and the baked beans, to the smaller picnic table off to the side, and then I gathered everyone around the big picnic table in the center of the yard.

"Before I ask Father Hanson to say grace," I began, "I want to tell you about an incident that took place in my kitchen this morning. Maddie and I were baking a chocolate cake, actually I was helping Maddie bake a cake, when, out of the blue, she said, 'Mommy, I hope someday I find a man who'll love me as much as Daddy loves you.' "

"I said, 'Maddie, I hope so too.' And then I smiled and asked her, 'How do you know that Daddy loves me so much?'

"She laughed and said, 'Mommy, it's so obvious. That look he always gives you is a giveaway. Plus he always,

always treats you with respect. And we all know that he will never let anyone hurt you.'"

I then looked at Mark, sitting at the other end of the table, and said, "Even though I walk through the Valley of Death, I will fear no evil because you, Mark, are with me, and always will be."

He smiled at me and said, "Yes, I will be."

I answered, "I know." *I do know that, and I love it that I know that...Mark will never let anyone hurt me...Do you know how great that is?..I do...And I appreciate it...More than I can tell you...Look at him smiling at me...He loves me...Always has...Always will...Thank you, God...I love you too, Mark, always have, always will.*

I then continued my little story, "Maddie then said, 'Mommy, you know Daddy gives us that same look, and we all know he will never let anyone hurt us. I think he is the ideal husband and the ideal Daddy.' "

I agreed with her. I was temporarily speechless.

I looked down at Mark and he had a tear in his eye. He looked over at Maddie and said, "Do you really believe that, honey?"

"Yes, Daddy," she answered.

"Thank you," he stammered.

"It's true, Daddy." I was tearing up too. So were Mom and Dad. Imagine having a granddaughter like Maddie! Someday I would, but I didn't know that at the time.

I then finished my little story. I didn't want the food to get cold, or hot in the case of the salads. "I don't know if you all noticed during our dance that Maddie whispered something to me at one point. Mark was looking at me, and she said, nodding her head in his direction, '**That** look.' I whispered to her, 'I see what you mean,' and gave her my sweetest smile. She looked at me and said, 'Mommy, now you're giving me that look. You must love me.' 'Very, very much,' I said. She just said, 'Good,' and continued with the dance."

Father Hanson then said the grace, and I told everyone to help themselves. "Don't forget to take a piece of Maddie's cake," I encouraged them. "It's delicious."

I then motioned to Mark to come to me and led him out by the pool for a little private talk. Neither one of us would ever give priority to eating a hamburger while it's hot to having a conversation if the other wanted to talk. It would not even be a consideration. When we arrived by the pool, I gave Mark a big hug. He is still so handsome, so strong, and he smells so good. Now his own smell, that I love, was masked by a chicken-hamburger-hot dog smell. I would say he smelled good enough to eat, but that would be trite.

"God, I want to make love with you right now," I said, "but that's not why I dragged you out here. But maybe we **could** grab a *quickie* before dinner. No, that won't work because I want a *longie*, not a *quickie*, and our guests would wonder where we disappeared to. So you're going to have to wait until later."

"I can wait. Knowing what's coming, I can wait," he said. "What did you want to talk about?"

"Maddie's kitchen talk got me thinking. You know I love you, and I know you love me, but sometimes I don't tell you how much I love some of the things you **do**. I don't ever want you to think I take you for granted, not that that's such a bad thing. It just means that I am completely at ease with you, and I am."

"I never think you take me for granted," Mark said. "I know you are absolutely comfortable with me, and I love that. Totally uninhibited too. There's nothing we can't say to each other. That's the way it should be for two people who are in love. That's the way it is with you and Peggy too. I think that's wonderful. I understand how important her friendship is to you. You two have been friends since you were six. The three of us riding the Barge of Curiosity."

"Thank you, but let me tell you some things you do which I simply love, and never tell you I love, or don't tell you enough---

"I love the way I feel so safe because of you. I know that you will not let anything bad happen to me or the children. Ever. Taking that course from Ben Kravey so you could protect me and Peggy." I leaned over and kissed him. I was getting horny. He always makes me horny. I'm not complaining, just stating a fact. "Do you know that Bobby beat up a sixth grader who was hassling Heather? He takes after his father; no one messes with his woman. Jimmy told me. He was so proud of Bobby."

"When Bobby and Jimmy are a little older, I'll teach them some of the techniques that Ben taught me. Bobby and Heather, eh? She is pretty; she looks like her mother."

"She's smart and nice too."

"We better keep them out of the pool shed," Mark said.

"You don't want Bobby to play with Heather's bumps?" I said laughing.

"God, I loved playing with your bumps that summer, until your mother put a stop to it."

"Yes, that was nice. Bobby and Heather are a lot younger than we were then. We were thirteen, teen-agers."

"You and Peggy are not trying to arrange anything, are you?"

"No. That never works. They are great kids, and they will be great adults, and Peggy and I would love to see them get together, but, no, we are not trying to arrange anything."

(Another of our rules, *Rule Six*, is: *Defend Each Other with Our Lives*. I have not had to do any defending, but

Mark has observed this rule a few times, beginning with that aggressive senior football player when we were sophomores. Actually beginning with that pervert when we were eight years old.)

I stepped back and placed his head between my palms. "I love the way you look at me, that look that says, 'This is my woman and I love her and I always will.' The way you're looking at me now. The way you **always** look at me. Maddie and the younger ones see that---

"I love the way you respect me. Maddie was right; in all the years we have been together, you have always treated me with respect. You still even open the car door for me. You have never talked down to me or talked disparagingly of me to anyone---

"I love the way you still find me physically attractive and still love to fuck me because I still love to fuck you. I love to use that word, fuck, with you. It makes me horny. I really don't think you've ever thought about fucking anyone else, not even Peggy."

"I haven't," he said. "Why would I? I have you, and you take care of me. When I get horny, I think of you. And when I think of you, I get horny. Only you. I'm horny now."

"Thanks. Me too. I'm all yours tonight. Every night actually." I laughed and kissed him. "I love the way we end each day wrapped in each other's arms discussing the important and the mundane, laughing over the adventures of the day just ended and planning the adventures of the day to come. You've never said, 'I'm tired, honey. Let's just go to sleep.' And we share equally in the conversation; it's not just me talking and you listening while you hope I will soon shut up so you can go to sleep. And I love that we wrap up in each other's arms, and legs, to sleep. I can't tell you how loved and how safe that makes me feel. During our senior year, when we were making love almost every day, Peggy said to me, 'It's like you two are already married.' I said, 'Not quite. I want to sleep with him.' I love sleeping with you, breathing in your smell, feeling your whole body against mine, your chest against my bumps---"

"I love it too," Mark said. "I don't think you even know how great you smell, especially after we've made love."

"Thank you. You smell great too. And, to keep this short so the hamburgers don't get too cold, I love the way every day begins with you smiling at me and saying, 'Good morning, honey. I love you and always will. And I thank God every day that you're my wife.' I love your breath in the morning. So sweet. So arousing. So mine, if you know what I mean...

"In short, I love living with you and I want you to know that."

"I do know that," he said. "Never think I don't. And I love living with you. Now how are we going to get rid of everyone early tonight? Especially the people who are staying here?"

I laughed and gave him a kiss, with a little tongue as a tease. "We'll manage," I said. "God, I'm horny."

"Me too," he said.

"How many married couples with four kids are this horny all the time?" I asked.

Mark just laughed and squeezed my ass. He has class.

We then headed over to the picnic table and joined the others. The hamburgers were still warm. Annie came over and squeezed between the two of us. She greeted Mark with her deep-voiced imitation of Seinfeld's Newman salutation: "Hellooo, Daddy." To which he responded in the same manner, "Hellooo, Annie."

She then said, "You know, Maddie was right."

"Maddie's always right," said Mark.

"Yeah, yeah I know," she said dismissively.

"What was Maddie right about?" I asked.

"She's right about it being obvious that you two love each other, and do you know how great that is for us kids? We feel so safe and so happy living here."

Out of the mouth of a seven-year-old… I cried and gave her a big hug. So did Mark. We love our little Annie. Don't ever misunderstand – Mark and I love Annie as much as we love Maddie. Maddie is just our *primogenita*.

I had an experience with Annie last week that would not have ended so smoothly if the experience had been with Maddie. It was a Saturday, and we were all sleeping in. Mark and I made love when we woke up, and then I suggested that he take a shower and get dressed while I went to the kitchen to get some coffee and to see if any of the children were up. I was sitting at the breakfast bar on one of the tall stools when Annie came into the kitchen. She came over to me and buried her head into my lap as she gave me a big hug.

She pulled back and said, "You smell like Daddy."

"Well, we sleep together, Pumpkin," I said.

"No, I mean you **really** smell like Daddy, strong and good," she said.

I didn't know what to say, but suddenly inspiration hit me. "Annie, Daddy and I share everything, even our smells."

"Oh, that's nice," she said. "Do we have any orange juice?"

Whew, I thought, *that answer would never have worked with Maddie…She would have asked, not rhetorically, "How do you share smells?", and she would have waited for an answer, a good answer, an answer I would not have been able to give.*

But it was Annie, and not Maddie, and I got away with it.

Mark was still working on his hamburger when Bobby, Jimmy, Robby, our nephew, and Peggy's son, Larry, came over and asked him to play basketball with them when he finished.

"You too, Mom, and Aunt Peggy, and the girls," said Bobby. We don't play girls against the boys, as you might expect, but Mark and the girls against me, Peggy, and the boys. "In ten minutes," said Mark.

The game was fun and we won, as we usually do, not because the boys, Peggy, and I are better, but because Mark never shoots. He just feeds Melanie, Maddie, Heather, Candi, and Annie – it gets crowded on the court, but everyone plays -- and he plays very loose defense on me. Love that man. Never once in his life has he blocked one of my shots. Heather is going to be the awesome rebounder that her mother was. I noticed, and pointed out to Peggy and Mark, that Bobby never blocks Heather's shots.

Maddie is becoming quite good. In a few years, she'll be leading the Coventry girls' team to the state championship. Coach Jones, Peggy, is salivating over the prospect of having Maddie, Heather, and Melanie on her team. Melanie is not as good as Maddie or Heather, but she has an uncanny way of getting open for one of Maddie's passes and she never misses when she gets open. Maybe she is as good as her cousin and friend.

And Bobby and Jimmy are little Marks. They're equal in height now, but Bobby is two years older. Jimmy will reach 6'3" or 6'4", and will be formidable in high school. I see glory days returning to Coventry sports, both the boys' and the girls' teams!

There was one controversy in the game, and we handled it as we usually do, by negotiation. Maddie passed to her father who took the ball and handed it to Annie who was on his shoulder. Mark than ran to the basket, and Annie dunked the ball for two points. The boys screamed, "Traveling," but Mark argued that he could not have been traveling because he did not have the ball, and Annie could not have been traveling because her legs never moved. The compromise solution: we let them count that basket, but outlawed the move in the future.

As you can see, Maddie occupies a good part of my thoughts, and my story-telling, especially with *Alexandra the Mouse*, revolves around her. I believe the same is true for Mark. I want to return now to the question that I raised in the opening sentence of this chapter: Can you love all of your children equally, and yet love one more than the others? And I wanted to explain how Maddie could possibly tie in with the Trinity, in my thoughts, at least.

I have to take you back to the day Maddie was born. Mark was with me in the delivery room holding my hand while I was going through child-birth, an unbelievably painful experience as any mother can tell you, and which no man can ever comprehend, unless he has passed a kidney stone. But Mark was there with me through it all, which I did appreciate. The nurses took Maddie off to be cleaned up and returned me to my room to await her. Mark of course was with me the whole time. After the nurse left, Mark helped me shower. He stripped down to his boxers to shower me. As tired and spent as I was, I did feel a little tingle as he cleaned me. Mark is a very handsome, very athletic man. And he is mine!

"Are you enjoying this?" I asked.

"Most definitely, my love, especially washing your bumps."

"In a couple of days---"

"Don't think about that now," he said.

"I bet you will," I said.

"You **hope** I will," he said. Then he kissed me before drying me and covering me in the sexy hospital gown. "You are ravishing," he said, "even in this." He carried me back to the bed. "And did I ever tell you that you have the most beautiful face in the world? And how much I love to wake up looking at it?"

I laughed. As I have said before, it is great to be married to your best friend. *Wow!..We've been married five years already...And we have a baby girl...Little Mark Tuttle and little Sandy Roberts have a baby girl...Thank you, God.* "I love you, Mark Tuttle," I said.

He just smiled and kissed me.

When the duty nurse brought Maddie in and placed her in my arms, I forgot the pain. She was beautiful, and Mark and I had created her, rather our love had created her! I gave her to Mark to hold, and he gave her the look that I had never seen him give to anyone but me. And I realized something. Mark loved her as much as he loved me, but his love for me was in no way diminished. He had not taken a chunk of the love that he felt for me, and given that piece to Maddie. Our love had expanded to include Maddie; our love was infinite. I would experience this later with Bobby, Jimmy, and Annie, but it was Maddie's birth that taught this to me: God is Love, and Love therefore is infinite! And by creating Maddie, Mark and I were sharing in God's Love! I will never forget that moment and that insight as long as I live. Saint Augustine named his son *Adeodatus*, Gift from God. At that moment I thought of naming our child, *Adeodata*, the female equivalent. But the thought passed. I'm sure Maddie is glad now that it did.

When I handed Maddie to Mark, a mutual love affair commenced that lasted from that moment until the moment Mark died. It was only fitting that Maddie was with him at the end, and more fitting that they were at a basketball game, a Providence College game at The Dunk. They smiled at each other that day in Brigham and Women's Hospital. The nurse told me that newborns don't smile, but Maddie smiled at Mark. I saw it. And she squeezed his pinky. I saw that too. I don't think any father ever loved his daughter, or daughter loved her father, more than they loved each other. Right to the end.

Don't think that Mark didn't love Annie. He adored Annie as much as he adored Maddie. He had the same father-daughter relationship with Annie that he had with her sister. But there was always something intangible, something special, in his relationship with Maddie. Maddie taught him, as she taught me, that Love is infinite. Mark told me once that, if he had not believed in God before Maddie was born (he did), he would have become a believer the moment he held her in his hands. I cried when he said that, and loved him even more.

Also lying in bed watching Mark hold Maddie, I had my great insight on the Trinity. As Mark loves me, and our love created Maddie, so, in some similar way, the Father loves the Son, and the Son loves the Father, and from that love proceeds the Holy Spirit, a real being representing that love. Eternally existing, always loving, always loved. I know that my insight is just seeing *through a mirror darkly,* but, at least for me, the Trinity is less of a mystery. Three Persons in One God: the Lover, the Loved, and the Love Itself. Three persons in one loving relationship: Mark, me, and Maddie. Not the same, but maybe…

That's why, even though we love all our children equally, perhaps there is a little extra part of that infinity for Maddie. I'll never admit it; but I can't deny it either.

The visitors started pouring into our room that afternoon: Billy Smith and Maureen Sullivan, soon to be

Maureen Smith, Bill Reynolds of the *Providence Journal,* Patty and Bill, Mom and Dad, Bobby and a very pregnant Leslie, Margie Baylor, and, of course, my beloved Peggy Mayhew and her soon-to-be husband Warren Jones.

"You going to be up for the wedding?" Peggy asked. I was to be her matron of honor for the wedding the following month.

"I wouldn't miss Peggy Mayhew's wedding for the world," I said. She kissed me. I love Peggy Mayhew. And she loves me.

Patty said to Mark, "Too bad Mom and Dad aren't here for this."

Mark replied, "They are, Patty, they are."

He and Patty hugged each other and cried.

I asked Mark, *sotto voce,* if he was wearing wet boxers.

"No, there's nothing underneath," he answered, smiling. "Getting excited?"

"Everything you do is exciting to me, Mr. Tuttle," I said. I was joking, but not really. Everything he does **is** exciting to me.

It was wonderful in Brigham and Women's that day. My family and friends gathered to welcome little Maddie into the world. And the two people that I love, Mark and Peggy, at my side. We were about to embark on another voyage on the Barge of Curiosity!

Chapter Six
The First Date

My good friend Margie Baylor suggested that I tell the story of how Mark and I first started dating. Margie didn't know that I had already decided to write that chapter. In fact, I had already decided to tell our entire life story. Any reader with children is familiar with my other works, my series of picture books on *Alexandra the Mouse*, which are really stories about my beloved Maddie. Most little girls have *Alexandra the Mouse* dolls and lunch boxes.

When did Mark and I have our first date? A lot earlier than you think, Margie Baylor. On our second day of first grade, at St. Michael's Catholic School, Missy O'Donnell, whom I have never forgiven, lied to me and said that Mark Tuttle had scribbled on the cover of my new Marble Composition book. I was so mad and so hurt that I challenged Mark to a fight during morning recess. Imagine me challenging Mark Tuttle to a fight. Mark, of course, would not fight with me and allowed me to hit him again and again. He just covered his head with his arms. At lunch, he dragged the real culprits to me. I apologized and invited him to have a Coke on the way home. We did. I'll give you all the details in a later chapter.

That stop for the Cokes could have been considered our first date, but I regard the walk from the candy store to my house as our first date. Mark asked if he could walk me home. Halfway to my house, he took my left hand in his right one. When he saw that I was going to let him walk hand-in-hand with me, he smiled and said, "I like you a lot, Sandy Roberts." I just smiled back, but he knew I liked him too. I also knew, really knew, all those years ago that he would never let anyone hurt me. God's honest truth! I could tell by the way he squeezed my hand. He kissed me when we arrived at my house. But that is not the date I'm talking about in this chapter.

The day Margie is referring to is a day early in the basketball season during our junior year at Coventry High School. It was the day of our "coming out" as a couple. Mark had committed to be my "not-so-secret secret boyfriend" in seventh grade, and, even before that, we were always together. We loved being together, but neither my parents nor Mark's thought we were old enough for steady dating. So we were always together, but never dating, if that makes any sense. My best *girl*friend, Peggy Mayhew, had a crush on Mark on and off throughout grade school, and, I later found out, she had a serious crush on him during our sophomore year at CHS. But she never acted on that crush, for two reasons. She knew Mark belonged to me, but, more importantly, I was, am, and always will be her best friend. She values our friendship over everything, and would never do anything to cause a rift. She loves me. I love her too.

Mark and I were in the Honors Program and, being athletes as well, we spent a lot of time together, but always in a group and never as a dating couple. I sometimes wondered why Mark didn't ask me out – I didn't consider my mother's prohibition to be still valid now that we were juniors. And I sometimes **worried** that he didn't ask me out. Had he lost interest in me as a potential girlfriend? I didn't think so – hadn't he destroyed that senior who insulted me, and hadn't we kissed and hugged violently after that? -- but I worried. *Violently?..Funny word to describe a kiss...But it was violent, in a pleasantly violent way...Exciting too...He says he loves me, but he never refers to me his "girlfriend", and he never asks me out on a date...He is always with me...Isn't that enough?..No...I want to be alone with him...I want him to be alone with me...How can he love me and **not** be my boyfriend?..Does he love me like a sister?..No, you don't kiss your sister the way he kisses me...Stop worrying, Sandy...Mark is yours.*

I had no need to worry about Mark's intentions. What I discovered was that Mark still considered Mom's edict as binding. He didn't fear my mother, but he held her in great regard, and did not want to do anything to turn her against him. He still felt embarrassed over his confession to Mom—telling her he had asked me to show him my bumps in the pool shed. I also found out that I had grown so high in his estimation that he was afraid to ask me out. Afraid that I might say "No." Can you believe that: me saying "No" to Mark Tuttle? Mark Tuttle had me on a pedestal.

He drove me and Peggy to and from school every day. We had practice or after-school activities most days, but we always waited for each other and went home together. We usually stopped at McDonald's for Cokes and French fries, which the three of us shared. The three of us had great discussions, sometimes about sex, but usually not. Infrequently Mark and I ate lunch as a twosome, but mostly as a threesome with Peggy or in a larger group. Mark and I did our school projects together with Peggy and her project partner, whoever it might be. The three of us had dinner at my house most evenings, and the three of us did our homework together in the dining room after we did the dishes. We loved riding "the Barge of Curiosity" together.

I loved being with both Peggy and Mark, but sometimes I wanted to be with him alone. I just got that urge to kiss and hug him. To be honest, I sometimes got that urge with Peggy too, but not as strongly or as frequently. But Mark never asked me for a date. Never asked me to go to a movie or to a dance. I can say that he never showed any interest in any other girl, even Peggy. But I did wonder what was in his head. I probably should have asked.

I never considered dating anyone else. I always believed in my heart that Mark and I would start dating someday, but I was beginning to be a bit apprehensive. I even began to entertain self-doubts, to question whether he thought I was pretty enough or interesting enough for him. Maybe he wanted to play the field, but felt trapped by earlier commitments. There was no reason for any of these fears, but they began to fester.

I brought up the subject with Peggy one day. Peggy and I talk about everything, including sex!

"Do you think Mark still likes me?" I asked.

"**What?**" she exclaimed. "**Likes** you? He loves you, always has, always will."

"Then why doesn't he ask me for a date?"

"He probably thinks you two are already dating," she said. "Everyone else does."

I laughed. "Everyone does?"

"Of course. You know what I think?"

"What do you think, Peggy Mayhew?"

"I think you two need to start fucking," she said.

I punched her on the shoulder. "**Peggy**!"

"I'm serious, Sandy."

"I know you are. To be honest, I have thought about that." *I don't need to spread my legs to keep Mark from going elsewhere…No other girl can take him from me…If any girl tries, she is in for one hell of a fight, a fucking*

95

*fistfight…He only wants me, I believe that, I know that…He has never even hinted that we have to have sex…Or else…Can you imagine Mark Tuttle giving me an ultimatum?..I can't…He'd rather just be with me than fuck some other girl…Is that true?..Yes…He'd come to me if he needed sex…Wouldn't go elsewhere…A prostitute?..Never…I have to let him know that he can always come to me…He must know that…I want to have sex with him…Where can we do it?..Not in our car…No way…That would be so unromantic, so uncomfortable!..But it is a very pleasant thought, fucking Mark…Like those thoughts I have of kissing Peggy…That would be fun…Maybe we'll do that…She wants to…I bet her mouth is deliziosa…Now I'm getting horny for Peggy…Stop thinking of her…Mark and I do kiss, occasionally very passionately, should I say violently?..We nibble on each other's lips…I did make him bleed once…That made both of us so horny…Tasted good too…Remember the day last year when that senior was aggressive with me…Boy was Mark ever mad that day…'What the fuck are you doing?'..He **is** my boyfriend, my protector…But I want more…I want him to fuck me, to eat me…Eat me?..Where did that thought come from?..All boys like to do that…That's what Peggy tells me…She knows about those things…I wonder if he'll like the smell…Yes, he will…He likes all my smells: my hair, my breath, my body, even my feet…My farts?..Probably… Don't be silly…He'll like my pussy's smell…And taste…What does it taste like?..I bet he wants to taste me…Fuck me and eat me…Soon, Mark Tuttle, soon…I want it …I know you do…This is why Mom didn't want us dating…We were only thirteen then…We're almost seventeen now…Peggy's right…We have to do it…It is so exciting to think about this…How should I bring it up* *with Mark?..When?..God, you're making me horny, Mark Tuttle...We will fuck soon.*

"Do more than think about it," said Peggy, pulling me back down to earth.

"I will." *I will.*

"You look like you were someplace else," Peggy said. "What were you thinking about?"

"Mark," I said. *And you.* "And your suggestion."

I brought things to a head one night in early November after the girls' game against East Greenwich High. We won, by the way, 85 - 48. I had thirty-seven points, five assists and twelve rebounds. Twelve rebounds and I'm only five feet, six inches tall. But I can jump; can I jump! Peggy had a monster game, twenty-four points and seventeen rebounds. As a combo, we make the CHS girls' team unbeatable. Her seventeen rebounds were followed by seventeen sharp outlet passes to me, but they led to only sixteen baskets. I missed an open ten-foot jump shot. So unlike me.

As I headed toward the locker room at the conclusion of the game, Mark was standing at the end of the tunnel leading back to the dressing rooms. Peggy patted me on the ass, whispered, "Go get him, girl," and continued on into the locker room. She turned and winked before disappearing into the changing area.

Mark asked if I was going to Chelo's after the second game for something to eat. He said everyone was going, including both coaches.

"I really would like it if you came," he added.

Unfortunately I had left home without my wallet, so I had to tell him that I would not be able to join him.

"Why don't you come as my date?" he asked.

Be still my heart! But I wasn't sure he was really asking me for a date or just funding my attendance at Chelo's. I decided to bring our situation to a head.

"Mark," I said, "You know I've been in love with you since I was six years old, six! I have assumed since I was a little girl that we would always be a couple, always. And no matter what we do, even drive to and from school, we do it together. I think you love kissing me as much as I love kissing you. But you have never asked me out on a date, to the movies, to go line-dancing together, just the two of us. Are you asking me out on a real date now or are you just being nice and giving me a way to go out with the gang? If it's not a real date, I think I'll go home."

He looked stunned, but happily stunned. And then he broke out in a big smile and began to laugh. "Come over here," he said, pulling me to a private spot under the stairs leading to the balcony.

"What's so funny?" I asked. He hugged me and kissed the top of my head.

"I am so sorry," he said. "I thought we **were** dating in a secret sort of way. I have always been in love with you, ever since first grade. Ever since that day you beat me up at recess. I always will be. You should never doubt that. But, to be honest, as we got older, I was a little afraid to ask you out. For two reasons. First, your mother's prohibition. I felt so awful when I confessed to her that I had asked you to remove your top in the pool shed. I wanted to regain her trust—"

"You never lost my mother's trust. Believe me, she loves you. And my Dad thinks you walk on water, can turn water into wine, can raise the dead. You won his everlasting thanks in third grade. I overheard my Mom telling my Dad that you wanted to see my 'bumps.' They were both laughing about it. What's the other reason?"

Mark took a deep breath. "I was afraid you might say 'No.' I was just avoiding that risk. Didn't you notice how I always hang out next to you when we're all together? How mad I got when that senior bothered you? How I light up when I see your face in the morning? I think you have the most beautiful face in the world. How I love to kiss you? How I never look at any other girl?"

"Even Peggy?"

"Even Peggy," he said. "Peggy is beautiful, but I don't have feelings for Peggy. Oh, she is a friend, a good friend, but I only have feelings for you. Since the day you pounded the shit out of me in first grade."

I started laughing. "Then why in God's name did you ever think I would say 'No'? I would have said 'Yes' a long time ago! I will never say 'No' to you, Mark Tuttle."

"I've considered you an untouchable," he said.

"Now **that's** a compliment," I said.

He blushed. "Not in the dot-Indian sense," he said.

"In what sense?" I asked.

"You're the prettiest, nicest, most athletic, most physically attractive, smartest girl I know. You have a personality straight out of heaven, and a smile that will melt a glacier. I always love being with you, but I was just too afraid to ask you out, just me and you."

"Wow," I said.

"You're intimidating, like Psyche or the P-GOAT."

"So I'm intimidating and an untouchable, and who are Psyche and the P-GOAT?" I said befuddled.

"Psyche was a princess in Greek mythology so beautiful that no man had the courage to ask for her hand in marriage. The P-GOAT, an acronym for Prettiest Girl of All Time, is one of the main characters in David Foster Wallace's *Infinite Jest.* She was intimidatingly (if that's a word) pretty; so much so, that all the boys in her school were afraid to ask her out. I read a lot."

"I'm impressed with your literary knowledge, and I appreciate the compliment, but I think you've over-estimated my beauty, by a long shot."

"No I haven't. You're very special, Sandy," he answered.

"I'm not too special for you, believe me," I said. "I was starting to think you wanted to play the field, but didn't want to hurt me."

"Oh, God, no. There has never been any other girl for me, Sandy, not even in my dreams. I'm completely Sandified."

"Sandified?" I said. "I like that. What does that mean exactly?"

"Completely satisfied with Sandy. Saturated with thoughts of Sandy, so saturated that there is no room for thoughts about any other girl."

"You never think about other girls?"

"No."

"Really. No?"

"Really. No."

"What do you think about when you think about me and you?" I asked.

"Everything."

I smiled and punched him on the shoulder. "Me too," I said. "And only with you."

"Now that I realize what a fool I've been," Mark said, "Yes, I am asking you on real date, I hope the first of many, a lifetime of dates. I will give you one hundred percent of my attention, treat you with the respect you deserve, and deliver you safely to your door whenever you want to go home. In fact, I would like to apply right here and now for the job of being your official, out-in-the-open boyfriend.

Let me ask you formally. Do you want me to get on my knees for this?"

"Not here. Everyone's looking at us," I said. *A lifetime of dates!*

Remaining standing, but taking my hands in his, he said, "Sandy, do you want to go to Chelo's tonight as my date, as my real date, as my girlfriend? It would make me the happiest boy in Coventry, actually in all of Rhode Island!"

"Yes," I said. "Now that was easy, wasn't it?"

"Yes, it was," he answered.

We agreed to meet in the same spot after the second game.

"I better get into the locker room to change before Coach Wilson comes looking for me," he said, "and you have to take a shower."

"Why, do I stink?" I asked, teasing him.

"No. In fact you smell so good that I could lick every inch of your body from the top of your head to the bottom of your feet," he answered, smiling. "God, I have always loved the way you smell. Even that day you peed your pants."

I punched his shoulder again. *Maybe Peggy is right, and it's time to take this relationship to the next level... 'From the top of your head to the bottom of your feet.'...With a long stop in the middle?..We have so much to look forward to...Get ready, Mark Tuttle...I am going to take you to Heaven...And I'm going there with you...I bet you **would** like the smell of my farts...I'll have to test you...Just kidding...Love you, Mark Tuttle...My boyfriend...My official boyfriend.*

I gave him a little kiss, our first true boyfriend-girlfriend kiss (not our first kiss; we had a very wonderful kiss in fourth grade, and many deep kisses since), and wished him good luck in the boys' game. The boys had beaten East Greenwich 63 - 45 on the road two weeks ago. Mark had led the way with twenty-three points. As I ran into the girls' locker room, he called out my name. When I turned, he tossed me his wallet.

"There's cash in there. Get yourself something to eat or drink; it will be three hours before we get to Chelo's," he said.

"Thanks," I said. I didn't protest or say anything stupid like, "I can't take your money." It's our money now. I'm his girlfriend, after all. From now on, we share things. And we have.

I heard later from some of the guys on the team that Mark was ecstatic in the locker room. He wouldn't tell anyone why, but two of the players had seen him kiss me before rushing in to change. Word started spreading: "Mark and Sandy are a couple." That was big news at Coventry High School. Many, if not most, thought we already were a couple.

I locked Mark's wallet in my locker while I showered and didn't look inside until I was dressed again in street clothes. He had a very Spartan wallet: his driver's license, his Coventry High ID, his Ocean State library card, and a MasterCard in the left side wallet pockets. I didn't know he had a credit card. On the right side he had one picture: me! Cut out of last year's yearbook and laminated. I liked that. In the back, he had fifty-two dollars.

Peggy came up and put her arm around my shoulder. "Mark's wallet? Must have gone well. Or else my best friend has turned into a thief."

"Very well. You were right; he already thought we were dating. He actually said that he didn't ask me on dates because he thought I might say 'No.' "

"Why did he think **that**?"

"Because I am the most beautiful girl in the world and, possibly, too good for him."

"He said **that**?"

"Yes."

"I agree with him, on the first part. You are the most beautiful girl in the world."

I gave her a raised eyebrows look.

"You are." Peggy then kissed me on the top of my head, same place where Mark had just kissed it. "And I am going to get my real kiss, too. Just you wait."

"Maybe," I said.

"That's encouraging," she said. "Gives me something to dream about."

I then called home. Mom, of course, knew my feelings for Mark. How could she not? He was at our house every day.

"Mom, guess what I'm doing later tonight after the boys' game," I said when she answered the phone. (She and Dad usually come to my games, and to the boys' games as well, but tonight they were unable to make it.)

"I don't know. Tell me, honey," she said.

"Going on a date, a real date, with my boyfriend."

"Mark?" she asked. She knew only Mark would fit that description.

"Yes!" I almost shouted. "He asked me to go with him to Chelo's as his date after the boys' game. And he asked me to be his girlfriend. I said 'Yes' to both."

"I thought you two were already dating. And I thought he was already your boyfriend," Mom said, a little puzzled.

"He still thought your prohibition was in effect," I said.

"Oh, gosh. Tell him he has my blessing to date you," Mom said laughing. "And Dad's. Have a great time. What time will you get home?"

"Mark said he would get me home whenever I needed to be home. What time do you want me home?" I asked.

"Well, the second game will be over by eight thirty. Say eleven, how does that sound?" Mom asked.

"Great. I'll be home by eleven. Mom, I am so excited. I really believe this is the starting point of our life together. Our personal Alpha Point. I really believe that."

"Your Alpha Point occurred when you two were six. I have absolutely no doubt of that. What are you going to do now?"

"Get a cheeseburger and a Coke at the stand here and then watch Mark's game with Peggy."

"Do you have any money? You left your wallet on the kitchen table."

"Mark gave me some to get something to eat. In fact he tossed me his wallet before he went in to change."

"Enjoy the game and Chelo's, honey. Oh, I almost forgot. How did you girls do in the first game?"

"We won 85 - 48. I had thirty-seven points, five assists and twelve rebounds."

"Sorry we missed tonight. Twelve rebounds, Wow!" she said before she hung up.

After hanging up, Mom told Dad that Mark asked me out on a date and asked me to be his girlfriend. Mom told me about their conversation when I got home that night.

"I thought they were already dating. He lives here, for God's said. And he **is** her boyfriend, isn't he?" asked Dad.

"I thought so too, Bob. But I guess there are dating rules, and, until tonight, he was not officially her boyfriend. Now he is. He still thought my prohibition was in effect."

"Aah. If only our two were so obedient. But I'm glad. Always loved that boy, since he was eight anyway. I would love him as my son-in-law."

"Me too, Bob," said Mom. "Believe me there is nothing I want more than that. I'm pretty sure he will be."

Mom said Dad just smiled.

Mark led the boys' team out onto the court. He had a big smile on his face; I was pretty sure I knew why. Mark had been having a very good year. He was averaging a little over twenty-three points a game, and the team was 4 - 1, the only loss to powerful LaSalle Academy. In that game, at LaSalle, Mark had twenty-nine points, and we almost pulled it off. We lost by three in overtime. Mark couldn't wait to get revenge on our court in early December. We, the girls' team, beat Bayview, our main competition, on the road 55 - 51. We were still undefeated.

The CHS boys' team had beaten East Greenwich High on the road in the season opener by seven. But on that November night, Coach Johnson and his East Greenwich players were in for a surprise. Mark had changed. He was no longer the Mark they had faced in October; he had become the second coming of Jerry West! I think I can take credit for that.

He opened the game with four threes, four driving dunks, and three steals. He blocked two shots during that stretch and dominated the boards. Before the game was four minutes old, we led 22 - 0. The twenty-first and twenty-second points were scored on a layup off an assist from Mark. The East Greenwich coach called time out and looked over at Mark in amazement.

Mark had forty-one at half-time along with five assists and fourteen rebounds. Three or four blocks as well. Coventry led 55 - 17. Coach Johnson of East Greenwich wondered if this was the same team they had played a month earlier.

As a little aside, the poor East Greenwich junior who was tasked with guarding Mark Tuttle was a young man named Warren Jones. After Mark took him for forty-one points in the first half, and blocked his only two attempted shots, he held Mark in awe. Little did he realize at the time that the girl he would meet and fall in love with at URI, Peggy Mayhew, was one of Mark's two closest friends. Nor did he ever dream that night that Mark Tuttle would be the best man at his and Peggy's wedding, and a good friend for life. Things happen that you never expect, don't they?

In the locker room, Coach Wilson looked at Mark and said, "Tuttle, what are you high on tonight?"

"Nothing, Coach," said Mark.

"He's high on love," said Bobby Wilcox, one of his teammates, from the back of the room.

Mark blushed, but said nothing.

"He's just showing off for his girlfriend," said Craig White, another player. "He can show off all he wants if he plays like that," added Craig.

Bobby Wilcox chimed back in, "He's just trying to prove he's a better player than his girlfriend, but the jury's still out on that."

They all laughed.

Mark picked up right where he had left off in the first half. He poured in sixteen additional points in the first four minutes of the second half, giving him a total of fifty-seven for the game. Poor Warren Jones! Coach Wilson, to show mercy, took Mark out and kept him on the bench for the rest of the game. Mark turned, found me, and winked. Everyone saw Mark turn and wink, but most in the stands didn't know to whom he was winking. I knew. So did Peggy Mayhew, Marcia Snow, and Maria Coppocino, who were sitting with me. They knew that I had Mark's wallet in my pocket.

After the game, the East Greenwich coach asked Coach Wilson what happened to Mark. "He's not the same player I saw in October."

"I don't know," answered the Coventry coach. "He was amazing, wasn't he? At halftime a couple of the players were kidding him about being in love. Can love do that?"

"I know Faith can move mountains, but Love, I don't know," said Coach Johnson.

Coach Johnson was waiting for his players outside the locker room when Mark came out of the home locker room. The coach went over, introduced himself (Mark told him he knew who he was), and congratulated Mark on a great game. I was waiting there as well and, when Coach Johnson started walking away, I went over to Mark. As I approached, I tossed him his wallet.

Mark stopped Coach Johnson and introduced me to him. (I found out years later, from Coach Johnson's wife whom I ran into at Stop & Shop, that he told her that night that I was the most beautiful girl he had ever seen, "not in a model sense, but in an athlete sense," whatever that means. It was flattering, nonetheless.)

"Coach, this is my girlfriend, Sandy Roberts."

Coach Johnson gave me a big smile, shook my hand, and then asked if I played on the girls' team. When I said "Yes" he asked how we had done. "You won, didn't you?"

"Yes, 85 - 48," I answered.

"How did you do?" he asked.

"I had a good game, thirty-seven points, five assists, and twelve rebounds."

"Wow," he said. "You're not that tall. How did you get twelve rebounds?"

"I have great reflexes and instincts, and I can really jump well," I replied.

"Yes, she has great legs," said Mark.

As we were leaving the gym, I turned to Mark and said, "Something you said back there made me very proud and very happy."

"What, that you have great legs?" he asked.

"You jerk," I said, and punched him in the shoulder.

"You can't call me a jerk," he said, "I'm your boyfriend."

"*Al contrario*," I replied. "It is precisely because you are my boyfriend and I love you that I can call you that."

"I love you too," he replied. "Can I call you a jerk?"

"No, never."

"Why not?"

"Because boys stop growing emotionally in the fourth grade. They retain their jerkdom into adult life. Girls, on the other hand, outgrow jerkdom."

"What did I say that made you so happy then?" Mark asked.

"You introduced me as your girlfriend. You don't know how happy that makes me feel. I always thought I was your girlfriend, but now the whole world will know. It's about time we ended that damn charade."

"I think the whole world already knew," said Mark. He gave me another kiss, and then we headed out to the parking lot to get his (our) car to drive to Chelo's.

Coach Wilson later told me that Coach Johnson sought him out before leaving that night. "I found out your secret weapon, Coach."

"What?"

"Mark Tuttle introduced me to his girlfriend, Sandy Roberts. I believe she is his inspiration."

Coach Wilson laughed. "I should have guessed that. One of the other players said at half time that he was trying to prove he's better than his girlfriend. She would be my starting point guard if she were a boy, or if the team were co-ed."

"She's that good?" asked Coach Johnson.

"Yes. Sandy will definitely lead the girls to the state title. And probably in softball too. God, can she pitch. I thought, before tonight, that the boys' team also had a shot at the state championship. Now I think it's going to happen with Mark playing like that. They make a good pair. Both are honor students too, did you know?"

"No, I didn't," answered Coach Johnson.

We had a great time at Chelo's in our first appearance as a couple. I don't think anyone noticed anything different. Peggy was with us as always. Mark and I each ordered a corned beef Rueben with fried onion rings and Cokes. Peggy ordered a Reuben too with steak fries. We took some of her steak fries, and she took some of our onion rings. Things were the same.

Mark and I have a lot of likes in common, not only in our food tastes, but also in our love of books and movies and sports, both playing and watching. We already knew that. It might be hard to believe, since we really had been going together for eleven years, but that night was a turning point in my life – our personal Alpha Point. All the tension that had been building up unnecessarily inside my brain vanished. Poof! The misgivings, the lack of confidence, the fears that Mark might have lost interest in me, the thought that there might be some other girl, all of that flew out of my head and didn't come back. Still hasn't. I realized what I never should have doubted: Mark Tuttle is my man, and I am his woman. That has been the case since we were six years old! And Mark Tuttle is a one-woman man.

I was so at ease that night at Chelo's; so was Mark. There was no stress, no tension, no 'let's pretend' going on. To be honest with you, none of those things have ever made an appearance inside our relationship. I can't tell you how nice that is. I never have to worry about what I say or do in Mark's presence. Mark doesn't ever have to worry about what he says or does around me. Never. At ten fifteen I told him we had to hit the road.

After we dropped off Peggy, and before we got back in the car, he told me that he would do everything possible to make this relationship work. I not only liked that; I knew it was true. I told him I would do the same. He took my right hand in his left hand, and gave it a little squeeze, like he did on the walk home after school the second day at St. Michael's. Same hands, same squeeze, same meaning. I already liked having him as my boyfriend, and I knew this was the beginning of a long-term arrangement. Well, it actually began eleven years earlier, as Mom said, but this was the official beginning – our Alpha Point. We got in the car and headed home.

"Sandy," he said. "I am so sorry I created some tension. I never wanted that. I'm yours until you get rid of me. That has always been my intention."

I looked at him with tears in my eyes. "Pull over at some deserted spot, Mark."

He pulled into a closed service station. "I am never getting rid of you. Never." I slid over and kissed him. I let my tongue roam throughout his mouth. His tongue was just as active.

"God, you smell and taste so good," he said. "There's something there beyond the Reuben. Something delightful, a special Sandy taste that I love."

"You taste great too," I said.

"I could do this all night," he said.

"Me too, but we have to be home at eleven. We still have ten minutes."

We took full advantage of those ten minutes.

When we finished, I said, "I'm yours until you push me away too."

"Not gonna happen," he said. "Never gonna happen."

As we drove home, I thought, *Soon...Peggy's right...We have to start making love...I want him to eat me too...Not tonight...Soon, Mark, soon... But not in the back of our car...You wouldn't want that either.*

"Penny for your thoughts," he said.

"Just thinking how much I love you."

Mom invited us in and offered us both Cokes. We sat on the couch.

My father came into the living room. Mark stood up. "Well, Mr. Tuttle," Dad said, "I want to ask you one question. Whether or not we ever become friends may well depend on your answer." In reality, Mark was and always would always be Dad's friend.

"Dad!" I exclaimed.

"It's important, honey," he said.

Turning back to Mark, he asked, "Now that you're dating my daughter, even though I thought you already were, what do you consider you main responsibility to be regarding her?"

"Dad!" I said again.

"It's okay, Sandy," said Mark. "Sir, I think it's twofold, to treat her with respect at all times and to defend her with my life if need be."

Dad, impressed, said, "You mean both of those things?"

"Completely," answered Mark.

I think Dad was satisfied. "I like you already, Mr. Tuttle," he said, shaking Mark's hand.

After Mark finished his Coke, as I was walking him to the front door, I apologized for Dad.

"Don't worry about that," he said. "Fathers worry about their daughters. If we have daughters, I will act the same." *Oh, you will, Mark Tuttle. Believe me, you will.*

The next day was Saturday.

"Let me cook breakfast for you tomorrow morning. I'll call Peggy and let her know we will not be having breakfast with her tomorrow. She'll understand. Mom, Dad, and my aunt and uncle are going to Cracker Barrel for breakfast, so the kitchen will be all mine. Then we can go over to the gym and play some basketball."

"Sounds great," he said. "What time?"

"Around nine," I answered.

"I will see you at nine." He then gave me another kiss, a little more subdued than the kiss at the gas station.

Uncle Ron, Mom's brother, and Aunt Betsy came over at eight forty-five the next morning and found me busy in the kitchen preparing a bowl of scrambled eggs. Thick ham steaks were on the stove, and four pieces of multi-grain bread were sitting in the toaster awaiting toasting.

"What are you up to, Sandy?" asked Uncle Ron.

"Making breakfast for my boyfriend, Mark," I answered. "I want to show him that I'm more than just a pretty face."

"He knows that," said Mom. Then turning to her brother, she said, "Mark is in the Honors Program with Sandy. He knows she is more than just a pretty face."

"So you're dating a geek," said Uncle Ron.

"A geek who got fifty-seven against EG last night," I said.

"Fifty-seven points in a high school basketball game?" said Uncle Ron, disbelieving.

"And he only played twenty minutes. Coach Wilson took him out to show mercy to the other team."

"I can hardly wait to meet this young man," he said.

He didn't have to wait long. Mark arrived at nine on the dot; he is very punctual, as am I. We're also both very anal. We do have a lot in common.

Uncle Ron, who is six feet, two inches tall, had to look up to Mark. And Mark's catcher's mitt hand completely surrounded Uncle Ron's much smaller hand. Uncle Ron was impressed. I think Aunt Betsy was more impressed with the fact that he was in the Honors Program. She never much cared for sports and often thought I was wasting too much time with athletics. Luckily, Mom was of a different mindset.

After the introductions, Mark came into the kitchen, gave me a kiss, and asked if he could help with anything.

"You have the dish-washing duty," I said.

"One of my specialties," he answered. "Especially pots and pans."

"We make a good team," I said, continuing my preparations.

"In many ways," he said and gave me a big smile.

We had a great day. We picked up Peggy on the way to CHS. At the gym, we played two-on-two, Mark and me, Mark and Peggy, or me and Peggy, against all comers. No team could beat us no matter the combination we used; no team could come close to beating us. There were not two males, excluding Mark, at CHS who could beat Peggy and me!

Mark and Peggy came back for dinner at my house that night, and then we three went to Showcase to see a movie. I didn't find it strange bringing Peggy along on our movie date. We always rode the Barge of Curiosity together. Mark sat between us, lucky guy. I rested my head on his shoulder and kept kissing, and smelling, the side of his face. When he looked at me, I blew a stream of air into his face. The three of us shared a large popcorn, which Mark held on his lap. I don't even remember the name of the movie. I think it was an early Woody Allen movie. *Bananas? Take the Money and Run?*

When Peggy started going with Billy Walsh – God, I thought he was a jerk, and told Peggy so – and then with Fred Williams, we double dated, but prior to that, we always went out as a threesome. That never bothered me, or Mark. I never felt she was intruding. I just felt that I was going out with two people I love, my boyfriend, and my best girlfriend. Mark and I always found private time to kiss and hug.

Mark came over that Sunday morning at nine thirty and joined Mom, Dad, and me for the ten o'clock Mass at St. Michael's. Peggy drove to church with her mom and joined us in the pew. After Mass we all went to my house for breakfast. Mrs. Mayhew and Peggy stopped at the Coventry Bake Shoppe and arrived with an Ebinger's crumb cake and a dozen Jewish hard rolls. Mom and Mrs. Mayhew cooked; Peggy and I set the table. Don't think Mark didn't have an assignment; he and my father did the dishes. Mark, Peggy, and I each made a fried egg, ham, and ketchup sandwich on a Jewish hard roll. The runny yolk mixed with the ketchup and soaked into the roll. This was another treat that Mark introduced to his two best friends. I tried to eat it without getting yolk all over my right hand. I didn't succeed too well. The first time, I held my hand out to Mark and asked him if he wanted to lick it off. Mom gave a disapproving look, and I quickly retrieved my extended hand. "Sorry, Mom."

Mark's and my relationship kept getting better. I don't remember any fights or real disagreements. And as you know from *The Dance and the Trinity* chapter, we are still together, still very much in love, and the proud parents of four children, including the inimitable Maddie. He still makes me so horny, and I know I still make him horny. How great is that?

By the way, with the new, improved Mark Tuttle, Coventry defeated LaSalle by twenty in the rematch at Coventry in December, and by twenty-three on a neutral court for the state championship. Need I say that Mark was unstoppable? And not to be outdone, the girls' team beat Bayview Academy in the state final 67 - 60 capping off an undefeated season.

We did win the softball title as well. I pitched a no-hitter, and Peggy slammed four home runs in the title game against East Providence. We won 14 - 0.

Those were Coventry's first three state titles in twenty years. We added three more the following year.

The Wednesday after the "first date," the stars aligned. Mom had that dinner at school. Dad went to Fenway with Bobby to see the Sox. Mac tried to bully me. Mark defended me. We kissed passionately, "violently," in our car. And then I asked that magic question: "Do you have any condoms?"

The two of us picked up Peggy that evening, and we went to Chow Fun for dinner. Peggy knew immediately – Our smell? Our smiles? Our behavior? -- but I didn't give her the details at the Chinese restaurant. I gave those to her the next day when we were alone together. We have no secrets.

"So you followed my advice," she said.

"Yes. Good advice it was, too."

"I always give you good advice."

"That's why I love you, Peggy."

"I love you too, Sandy."

We hugged.

I bet it would be nice to kiss her.

115

Chapter Seven
The Unexpected Answer

Did you ever get an answer to a question that was so unexpected that you thought the responder was answering a different question than the one you had asked? Coach Wilson did when he asked me a question during the summer following our junior year at Coventry High.

It was a Friday, and I was sitting in the gym reading a novel while waiting for Mark who was in the shower room. Coach Wilson approached me and, to break the ice, asked what I was reading.

"*Time and Again* by Jack Finney," I answered.

"Isn't Mark reading the same book?" he asked.

"Yes, we always read the same novel so we can discuss it. We buy three copies of any book we are going to read, for me, Mark, and Peggy Mayhew," I answered.

"You three are unbelievable," he said. "I never heard of people doing that."

"Book clubs do it all the time," I said. "We're a little three-person book club."

"Whatever," he said. I hate it when kids say that. I guess I hate it as much when adults say it.

He then asked the question that he came over to ask: "Did you and Mark have a fight today?"

"How did you know that?" I asked. "Did Billy Smith tell you?"

"No, I haven't seen Billy today. I have my ways of finding out things," he answered. Then he gave a little conspiratorial laugh.

"Was it serious?" he then asked.

"It was me and Mark against two punks, big guys too. Actually Mark did all the fighting, but I was ready to join in if he needed me. He didn't. One of our little relationship rules is *Defend Each Other with Our Lives*. I will always fight like a tigress if Mark needs my help. In this case, he handled it very quickly and very efficiently, as you would expect with Mark. Was it serious? When we left, those two pieces of trash were hurting bad, but they won't get any pity from me. I wanted to kick the one who was fondling my backside in the face, but Mark stopped me."

"**What** are you talking about?" asked Coach Wilson who obviously was not expecting that answer. He also seemed a little shocked by my final comment.

"What are **you** talking about?" I asked in return.

"Someone told me that you two ate lunch at one of the picnic tables behind the gym in a very uncharacteristic fashion, uncharacteristic for you two at any rate. No interplay, no joking, no smiling. Serious and silent. Not at all like you two. She wondered if you two had had a fight," said the coach.

"She?" I asked.

"Well it was a girl, but I can't tell you who," he answered. "She did say that you two made up at the end of lunch. She said you went over and gave him a big hug."

"That's your evidence for a fight between me and Mark, that we had a serious and quiet lunch? That is so wrong. One of our rules is *Never Fight, Never Argue*, and in the seven months we have been going together, I should say in the eleven years we have been going together, believe it or not, we have not had a serious argument. In fact, Coach, the only fight we had was in first grade, and I beat him up."

"You beat Mark up in first grade?"

"Yes, he didn't even get off a punch."

Coach Wilson shook his head, in disbelief.

I think Coach Wilson was concerned when he heard that Mark and I had a fight because, ever since Mark and I have been officially dating, Mark has improved immensely on the basketball court. He scored fifty-seven points against EG (East Greenwich High) the first night we dated. But Coach Wilson had nothing to worry about.

"Do you want to know what happened today, Coach?" I asked.

"Yes I do," he answered.

"We were playing ball here in the gym this morning, as you know. At around eleven thirty, I said to Mark, 'I'm getting hungry. Want to get something to eat at Joey's?' (Joey's is a hamburger joint on Route 2 here in Coventry.) He said, 'That sounds great.' So, after a stop at Peggy's, we headed over there."

"Why did you stop at Peggy's?"

"She's sick today. Otherwise she would have been with us. We stopped in for a half-hour visit before going to Joey's," I said. If Peggy had been with us, this whole day would have been different, for us, and especially for Billy Smith, but I am getting ahead of myself. Billy Smith's whole life might have been different. There is no way Peggy would have done nothing when the shit hit the fan.

Coach Wilson asked, "Who pays when you two date? I'm just curious."

"From the first night we dated, when Mark tossed me his wallet to get something to eat between the two games, we have shared everything," I answered. "That's another one of our rules. Today Mark only had five dollars, and Joey's only takes cash, so he asked me how much I had. I had ten dollars, so together we had enough. The bill actually came to ten fifty and, after paying it, Mark took two dollars and a quarter and gave me two dollars and a quarter so we would each have money in our pockets. I didn't say, 'Hey, all the change is mine; you didn't even have enough to cover your lunch.' We don't work like that."

"That doesn't surprise me," he said.

"Anyway, we ordered two cheeseburgers, two large fries and two Cokes---"

"That's a healthy lunch," said Coach Wilson.

"Yeah, I know. That's a rare lunch for us; we usually go to my house for lunch. Mom gives us soup and a sandwich. But we played hard this morning and decided to splurge. I carried the bag with the food, and Mark carried the two Cokes. When we got to one of the picnic tables in front of Joey's, I looked in the bag and saw that we were missing ketchup and napkins. Mark said he would go back in to get them, and he put the two Cokes on the table next to the bag I had carried out. No sooner was he inside the restaurant then two big South County hicks came over to me. The bigger one put his arm around my shoulder and the other one came up and grabbed my behind---"

"He did what?" said Coach Wilson.

"He grabbed my behind. I couldn't believe it either. I tried to swat away his hand, but he just grabbed tighter and whispered to me, 'Behave, Missy.'"

"Behave, Missy! Do you believe that, Coach?"

"Were you scared?" asked the coach.

"Yes, also very mad. But I was smart enough not to try to fight them and did the best possible thing under those circumstances, the same thing I will do any time in my life when I am in trouble. I yelled out, 'Mark' as loud as I could."

"My God, Sandy," said Coach Wilson. "Did Mark get there quickly?"

"Yes, but I also saw Billy Smith heading over toward us carrying a two by four. He yelled out, 'Hey, leave her alone.' Just then Mark arrived, told Billy, 'I'll take care of this,' and then he, Mark, approached the two shits. Excuse my language, Coach."

"You're excused. What did Mark do?"

"Billy said to Mark, 'I've got your back.' Mark pointed a finger at him, nodded, and then turned back to me and the two punks. Mark and I both appreciated what Billy had done. Mark looked so mad; I have never seen him look so angry. I think seeing the guy grabbing my behind really got to Mark.

"He said, 'Get your hands off her or I will kill you.' The big one, the one with his arm on my shoulder, leaned over as if to kiss me and said to Mark, 'You gonna make us, college boy?' He obviously thought we were older than we are."

"Did he kiss you?" asked the coach.

"He never got the chance. God, Coach, his breath, even just in the approach, was foul. What occurred next happened too fast for me to see, but he, the big guy, ended up on the ground out cold with blood pouring out of his nose."

"Oh my God," said Coach Wilson again.

"The second guy let go of my backside and, not being too bright, went after Mark. Again too fast for me to see how it happened, the second guy ended up on the ground with one hand on his groin and the other on his neck, and he was retching. I was reminded of what Mark told Mac the

Bully a few months back: 'I don't like to fight, although I'm very good at it.' This was the only the second time I saw Mark fight. The first time was when that senior football player insulted me last year---"

"I didn't know about that," said Coach Wilson.

"The senior told me that he knew what to do with me – he meant it sexually – and I slapped him. It would have been ugly. Peggy was there, ready to fight with me, but Mark came out of the gym and pummeled him---"

" 'Pummeled.' Good word."

"You hang around with Mark, Coach, and your vocabulary grows. And he's right – he is an awesome fighter. A good guy to have on my side! And he **is** on my side. I told my father once that Mark is my Michael the Archangel, with an avenging sword."

"I never heard about Mark having fights, except that time with Mac," said Coach Wilson.

"No, Coach, he never fights unless he is defending me or Peggy or Margie Baylor. Then you don't want to fight him. There was no fight with Mac. Mac backed off.

"Back to the story, Mark then turned to me and said, 'Grab the bag, honey, and I'll get the Cokes, and let's get out of here.' It was the first time he had ever called me 'honey'. Before it was always 'Sandy.' I really wanted to kick the guy who had grabbed my butt, but Mark stopped me.

" 'I can't let him get away with what he did,' I said.

" 'I saw what he was doing, Sandy, and he didn't get away with anything. Look at him,' said Mark. The punk was still retching.

"I had to agree he had not gotten away with anything. I tapped Mark on the chest with the side of my fist and said, 'Let's go.'

"As I turned, I saw Billy Smith and, trailing him by quite a few yards, Bobby O'Connor. I went over to Billy and kissed him on the forehead. 'Thanks,' I said. 'That was brave.'

" 'You're welcome,' said Billy. Then he turned to Mark, 'The way you handled that was amazing. Before you came back out, I told Bobby that we can't let them molest Sandy. I was scared shitless, but I was coming over to do something, I don't know what. But I was not going to just watch them hurt Sandy.'

" 'Thanks,' said Mark. 'You better get out of here before they revive. Do you need a ride?'

" 'No,' said Billy. 'I have my bike.' "

Billy Smith's Insert:

It's funny how one act of bravery can change your life. It was as if I was being tested, by God maybe. I was just enjoying my cheeseburger when I saw the two tough-looking characters grab Sandy, one on the butt. I had seen Mark go back into Joey's, so I knew Sandy was alone.

I said to Bobby (Bobby O'Connor), "We've gotta do something."

"What?" he asked. "What can we possibly do against those two guys?"

"I don't know," I answered, "but we have to do something." I noticed an old two by four on the ground near our table. I picked it up and headed over to help Sandy. Bobby followed reluctantly and at a distance. Sure I was scared, very scared, but at times you have to overcome your fear and take action. I didn't know if I had that ability or not, but if this were my test, I passed. As I got close to them, I heard Sandy call out for Mark in a very loud voice. I held up the two by four and yelled, "Hey, leave her alone." I don't know what would have happened next, but just then Mark appeared on the scene. I was not going to let them hurt Sandy.

"I'll take care of this, Billy," he said.

"I've got your back," I said, bravely. I meant it too.

He pointed his finger at me, like it was a pistol, and then turned to Sandy and her two assailants.

He told them to get their "fucking" hands off her or he would kill them. And when they didn't, he did. Not actually kill them, but put them both in pain and out of commission very, very efficiently. I was amazed. I knew he was a great athlete, but I had never seen him fight before. Sandy wanted to kick the one who had grabbed her ass, but Mark stopped her.

As they were leaving, Sandy kissed me on the forehead and thanked me. I don't think I washed that part of my body for a month. Mark also thanked me and advised me to get out of there right away.

Going back to what I said at the start, that one moment of bravery changed my life. Bobby O'Connor's life did not change. I could have sat there and done nothing. Maybe Mark and Sandy would not have seen me, and my life would not have changed. But what would they have thought of me if they did notice me just sitting and watching? And what would I have thought of myself if I had done nothing?

As it turned out, my action, little as it was, changed me from just another non-descript sophomore, an acquaintance, a benchwarmer on the basketball team, to their friend. To this day, and I am now forty, we are friends. We spent less time together after they moved to Cambridge for college, but after they returned to Coventry, we became adult friends. I received my doctorate in Pharmacy at URI, and am now the chief pharmacist at the Coventry CVS. My kids go to school and play with their kids, and Maureen (that's my wife) and I spend a lot of time at their house. They have a huge piece of property with a large pool in the backyard. Mark told me we are always welcome at the pool, and he meant it. Sandy will often call Maureen and ask if we would like to catch a movie and dinner on a Friday evening. We usually go to the Cable Car Theatre in downtown Providence, and snuggle on the comfortable two-person couches they have. The movies are often off-the-wall with subtitles, but we enjoy them. Post-movie, we cross South Main to a great Thai restaurant. Peggy Mayhew, now Peggy Jones, and her husband, Warren, usually join us. Peggy and Sandy are still best friends.

The Monday after the incident at Joey's, I was sitting behind the gym at a picnic table eating a PBJ sandwich I made at home. I looked up to see Peggy Mayhew, "the goddess," approaching me. She sat next to me on the bench seat, put her arm around my shoulder, kissed me on the cheek, and said, "Thanks, Billy, for sticking up for Sandy Friday. That took courage." God did she ever smell good.

"I couldn't do nothing." I replied, sounding ungrammatical, but actually correct.

"You didn't do nothing, Billy. That's what matters." She kissed my cheek again, and headed back to the gym. She looked back and gave me a thumbs up sign and a big smile.

Wow, I thought. *Kissed by the two prettiest girls in school within four days.* I definitely consider Donna Martino a distant third to Sandy and Peggy.

During my junior year, Mark and Sandy's senior year, one of the starting guards, Ronnie Simpson, got sick, and the coach told me I was starting against Cranston East. I rarely got the chance to play important minutes with Mark. I usually just got in during garbage time, which there was plenty of that year as we rolled to another state championship. Before the game, Mark put his hand on my shoulder and said, "Be ready for a pass every time I have the ball. Don't assume I'm going to shoot and turn and face the basket. Every time!" I told him I would.

And I did, and Mark hit me with perfect passes all night. I made 17 baskets, on 17 assists from Mark, and ended up as high scorer with 34 points! Mark had 28. After the halftime pep talk from Coach Wilson ("This game is not over yet," although we had a thirty-point lead!), the coach passed me the ball and said, "Smith, lead us back on the court." Proudest moment of my basketball life, leading the best team in the state back onto the court before a sold-out crowd in the Coventry gym! After the game I sought Mark out in the locker room. He was sitting in the corner talking to Coach Wilson. I approached him.

"Great game, Billy," said Coach Wilson.

"Thanks, Coach," I answered. Then I turned to Mark, "Thanks, Mark. I will never forget this night."

He answered, "You don't have to thank me, Billy. That was for Joey's last summer." Then he high-fived me. That was the only time Mark or Sandy ever mentioned Joey's (with one big exception), but I knew it had earned me their everlasting respect and friendship. I went home that night on a cloud. Would I ever have had a 34-point night if I had just sat on my rump cowering that day at Joey's? No, I would not have. Would Mark Tuttle and Sandy Roberts be my friends? Would "the goddess" Peggy Mayhew be my friend. No, they would not.

I still have the clipping (laminated now and hanging on the wall in my den) from the following day's *Providence Journal.* The headline on the high school sports' page was: SMITH LEADS COVENTRY OVER CRANSTON EAST WITH 34 POINTS.

And I still treasure the invitation I received that summer after my junior year: *Mr. and Mrs. Robert Roberts cordially invite you to the wedding of their daughter, Sandy, to Mark Tuttle, Saturday, June 13, 19xx, at 2 PM in St. Michael's Church, Coventry. Reception at 4 PM at the Coventry Country Club.* I attended with Maureen Sullivan who later became Maureen Smith. The fact that I was a friend of the King and Queen of Coventry impressed her. But what happened at the reception **really** impressed her.

Mark and Sandy started the dancing with an exclusive performance. Then Sandy danced with her father and Mark, being an orphan, danced concurrently with his sister. Then the master of ceremonies announced it was time for the special "Bride's Choice" dance. Sandy took the mike and stepped out onto the center of the dance floor.

"When I told Mark whom I had selected for this dance, he immediately knew why and thought it was a great idea. I do too. Mark is the most courageous man I know. He told my father the night of our first date that he would protect me with his life if need be. And he has. And he will. But, with the exception of Mark, the young man I have chosen for this special dance is the most courageous man I know---

"What is courage?" she continued. "Courage is doing the right thing, coming to the aid of a friend in need, when you could easily do nothing and nobody would know. When you are really scared, when the situation is risky and dangerous, and yet you still do the right thing---"

At this point, I knew she was talking about me, and whispered that thought to Maureen. Maureen did not know about the day at Joey's, and wondered what Sandy could be talking about.

Sandy then headed over to our table and said, "Billy, Mark and I will be forever grateful for what you did for me last summer at Joey's. (Heads were turning to see just who this "Billy" was.)

"We will always consider you a friend, and if you ever need anything – and these are not empty words. I mean them – just come to me or to Mark, and we will be there for you---

"So, Billy Smith, on this the happiest day of my life, will you do me the honor of having this special dance with me?"

I stood up, admittedly with tears in my eyes, with Maureen looking at me adoringly, and said, "Sandy, I will be happy to have this dance with you. And the honor is all mine."

We danced and everyone watched us, wondering just what Billy Smith had done, knowing that is was something very courageous and very special. I didn't know which was the highlight of my life to that point, and still don't: that dance with Sandy or the 34-point night. But both occurred only because I answered the call on that day the previous summer.

At the conclusion of the dance, Sandy accompanied me back to the table. When I objected, she said, "I left the mike there," and I felt a little foolish. As she was leaving the table, she turned to Maureen and said, "He's a good man to have at your side." Maureen said, "I know." I think that's when Maureen decided that we might have a good future together.

Back to my story (Sandy):

"Mark led me over to our car, and as he always does, came around to the passenger side to open my door for me. He told my father the night of our first date that he would always treat me with respect, and he always has, and, I'm sure, always will.

"As we were driving away, he said, 'I've got the ketchup and napkins in my pocket.'

"I looked at him and said, 'You are amazing. That's why I love you so much.' (I actually said, "fucking amazing," but I didn't use the f-word with Coach Wilson.)

"He answered, 'Well you can't have French fries without ketchup, can you?' Then he turned to me and added, 'And I love you too, very, very much.'

"I began to cry. I took his right hand, squeezed it, and said, 'I know.' We rode in blissful silence back to the gym where we sat at one of the picnic tables out back to have our lunch. We did eat in silence, but we had just gone through an ordeal, and we were just enjoying the peace and quiet and each other's company. We were not having a fight, Coach."

"Yeah, I should have known that."

"Coach, I always tell Mark what's on my mind. In fact another of our little rules is: *Never Tell Each Other Lies and Don't Keep Secrets from Each Other.* After finishing my cheeseburger, I said, 'Mark, what I am going to tell you has nothing to do with what you did for me today. I know you will always defend me, in fact I expect it, and I love you because I know I can expect it. What I was just thinking is: I don't think it is possible, even remotely possible, for me to find someone to spend my life with better than you. We belong together.'

"Mark was silent, smiling but silent. I wondered if I had gone too far too soon. I had never been this direct before.

"Then he said, 'Sandy, I feel the same way. Why don't we do it?'

" 'Do what?' I asked to make sure we were on the same wavelength.

" 'Spend our lives together,' he answered.

"Now I was quiet. I don't think I was ever happier in my life, but I was speechless. Actually breathless.

"Now he misunderstood my silence and tried to sell himself, 'I promise I will do everything I can to make your life happy and good---

" 'And if you had to choose one word to describe me, 'faithful' would be a good word. I will never be unfaithful to you.'

"I said, 'Be quiet. You don't have to sell yourself to me.'

"Suddenly I got up, went around to Mark's side of the table, and, after motioning to him to get up, I buried my face in his chest. I began to cry.

" 'What's wrong?' he asked.

" 'Nothing. I'm happy,' I answered. 'I always cry when I'm happy.'

"Then I gave him a kiss, definitely not a brother-sister kiss, and said, 'I accept your offer.'

" 'Thank you,' he said. 'You will never regret it.'

" 'Neither will you,' I replied.

"And that was our rumored fight, Coach."

"I should have known better than to think you two were fighting. I am relieved nonetheless."

After we left the gym, we stopped again at Peggy's. Her mother was happy to see us. "She is bored stiff up there. The only thing she liked today was your visit. Go on up."

"Hey," I said, coming into her room. Her face lit up. She was reading *Time and Again.*

It was a little after four when we got there. We stayed until six. I told her the whole story of the rumble at Joey's.

"So little Billy Smith came over with a two by four. I'll have to give him a kiss when I'm better. I should be up and around on Sunday."

"I'll come over and make you breakfast tomorrow," I said. "Mark can clean up behind me. I'll let him eat with us too."

Peggy smiled, but she was crying. Big, tough Peggy Mayhew crying. I leaned over and kissed her on the lips. "I hope I don't catch something," I said.

"What I have is not catching, according to my doctor," she said. "So you can kiss me again."

I did, holding our lips together a little longer this time, a little bit longer than appropriate.

"I love you Peggy Mayhew," I said. "So do I," said Mark.

Peggy was still crying, happy crying. "I love you guys too."

Mark surprised me, no astonished me, on the ride to my house. Holding the steering wheel with his left hand, he reached over with his right hand and squeezed my thigh.

"I want to tell you something, honey," he said.

"What?"

"It doesn't bother me when you kiss Peggy. I know how much you love her, and you two kissing doesn't make me jealous. I think it's wonderful. I want you to enjoy that friendship."

"Remember the lecture with Mr. Corda last semester, the one on intelligence among the primates?" I asked.

"Yes."

"How he talked about difference in kind and difference in degree?"

"Yes."

"I have been thinking about that, without knowing the names, since seventh grade. I loved both you and Peggy, but I knew I loved you more. Still do. But the love I have for you and for her is not different in kind, just different in degree. Does that make sense?"

"Yes, it does," Mark said.

"So you don't mind if I kiss Peggy?"

"No. As long as you still kiss me."

"That I will never stop."

Mark joined me for dinner that night as usual. Mom's brother, Uncle Ron, and his wife, Aunt Betsy, were also there.

During soup I opened the conversation with, "We had an adventure today."

"Who?" asked Mom.

"Me and my hero here," I answered, punching Mark on the shoulder.

"What happened?" she asked.

I told the story again. When I got to Mark's first line to the punks, I said, "What did you say, Mark?" I love to put him on the spot, in a loving way of course.

Mom, Dad, Uncle Ron, and Aunt Betsy looked at Mark expectantly.

"I said, 'Get your fucking hands off her or I will kill you.' Excuse the language. I was very angry."

Aunt Betsy blushed, but Mom was not phased. Dad was ecstatic.

When I got to the line of mine about Mark not forgetting the ketchup, I continued my discretion. "You are *absolutely* amazing," I used in the second retelling, again leaving out the f-word.

Uncle Ron was amazed when he heard how Mark handled my two assailants. "I know you're a great athlete, strong and quick, but you couldn't do that without training."

"When I was fifteen, I got into a fight with two guys and lost. Or, at least, I didn't win. I was defending Peggy," he said to Mom and Dad. "I ended up with a black eye, and she had some bruises. I recognized that I had great natural ability, but I had no idea how to take care of myself if I ran into problems. I found a retired Special Forces sergeant who gave lessons, not in Karate or anything like that, but in street fighting: how to protect yourself on the street against someone with a weapon or against a couple of guys. I met with him once a week for three months. Now I see him once a month so I don't lose what he taught me.

"The first rule, and he stressed this over and over, is: avoid a fight at all costs. Only fight if you absolutely have to, if you're trapped or defending a loved one---"

"That's me," I said.

Mark looked at me and said, "There is no doubt about that."

"This is fascinating," said Uncle Ron. I think Aunt Betsy was in shock.

"Who's Peggy?" he asked.

"My best girlfriend," I said. "She, Mark, and I are best friends. She would probably be here tonight, but she's home sick. Mark and I visited her before dinner."

"You always try to give your opponent a way out," Mark continued. "a way to avoid an actual confrontation. That was the purpose of my opening statement to those two guys."

"I think," interjected Mom, "that if you're trying to pour water on a fire, it might be good to leave out the f-word."

"I don't know if I really wanted to give them a way out in this case."

"Good," said Dad.

Looking back at Uncle Ron, Mark said, "If it gets to a fight, Uncle Ron, you fight to win. That is the only purpose of a fight. And if you're up against two or more guys, you're always at a disadvantage no matter how good you are. Your first move has to be to eliminate one of them, preferably the bigger one. To make it a fair fight. That's why I broke the big guy's nose and knocked him out."

"How did you do that?" asked Uncle Ron. Aunt Betsy did not believe she was hearing this.

"Two very quick rights, one to the base of the nose, the other to his temple. He had no idea what hit him."

Uncle Ron was dumbfounded. "I better never mess with Sandy."

"You're family; I wouldn't hurt you---

"But I would never let you hurt Sandy either. I would never let anyone hurt Sandy."

There was silence at the table. Dad was looking at Mark adoringly, a look that said, *I know my daughter is safe with you.*

"Let's eat the soup before it gets cold," said Mom.

I kissed Mark on the cheek and then started in on my soup. "Corn chowder, Mom," I said, "my favorite."

We brought ham, eggs, and rye bread to the Mayhew house the next morning. I scrambled some eggs and fried the ham, four big slices. Peggy was feeling good enough to join us at the table. Mrs. Mayhew ate with us too.

When Peggy went to the bathroom, Mrs. Mayhew said, "I don't know how to thank you two, not for breakfast, but for your friendship with Peggy. From the day I enrolled her in St. Michael's, you two have been her best friends. I love the way she puts it. She says, 'Mom, we ride the Barge of Curiosity, Sandy and I, and Mark is our tugboat.' "

"I love your daughter, Mrs. Mayhew. So does Mark," I said.

"She sure loves you two," she said.

When Peggy got back to the table, she asked what we had been talking about.

133

"Riding the Barge of Curiosity with you," I said, "with Mark as our tugboat, and loving the ride."

Peggy came over to me, hugged me, and kissed me. "*Ti amo, amica mia.*"

"*Anche ti amo,*" I replied.

On the way back to her seat, she said to Mark, "I love you too, Mark. You're the only boy to ever fight for me, and you're not even my boyfriend."

Mark said, "It was my pleasure, Peggy, even if I did end up with a black eye."

"That was a vicious fight, Mom," she said. "My mouth almost got me killed. If Mark wasn't there, I would have been in trouble."

"I know, honey. I saw how you two looked that night when Mark brought you home."

"The Captain of the Barge has to defend his crew," Mark said.

"See you at church tomorrow?" I asked.

"We'll be there," said Mrs. Mayhew.

"Then back to my house for breakfast," I said.

"Of course," answered Peggy. "This is definitely my last day of house confinement."

Chapter Eight
Precursor Incidents

Remember at my wedding, when I was inviting Billy Smith to share my special dance, I announced that, with the exception of Mark, Billy was the bravest man I knew? I want to relate two childhood occurrences that not only show how brave Mark has always been, at least when it concerns protecting me, but also illustrate why I always believed Mark and I would get together some day -- despite that three plus years hiatus imposed by the mother. I needlessly worried during the first two years of high school, and part of my junior year, because of that prohibition.

The first incident occurred when we were in third grade at St. Michael's Catholic School in Coventry, Rhode Island. Mark and I had been good friends, very good friends, since we started at St. Michael's together in first grade. We were, by third grade, two eight-year-olds who loved to be together. The walkway winding down from the front door of the school to the street in front of the school was about fifty yards in length. On the day of our incident, Mark and I were alone at the street end of the walkway. Peggy Mayhew, who made up the third member of our triumvirate, had a doctor's appointment that day, and her mother had picked her up early from school. Otherwise she would have been with us.

Mr. Ross, the Physical Education teacher for the school, two male parents, and two nuns were standing fifty yards away at the door of the school with a group of students. I waved good-bye to Mark and started home. Mark headed off in the opposite direction for baseball practice. Thank God he had baseball practice that day because that meant he had his Louisville Slugger baseball bat with him.

After Mark and I separated, a car screeched to a stop at the curb, and the driver, a scruffy, mean-looking man, jumped out, grabbed me, and started to push me into the back seat of the car. I screamed loud enough for the adults at the school door to hear me, but they were fifty yards away. Mr. Ross, the two fathers, and a young nun started running toward us, but both they and I knew they would never get there in time. As I was beginning to despair, I heard Mark yell out, "Leave her alone!" The pervert screamed out in pain and released his hold on me.

"Run, Sandy, run," yelled Mark. Mark had hit the pervert across the lower back with his Louisville Slugger. Mr. Ross later described the swing as a "home run swing." Being freed from the man's grasp, I ran as fast as I could away from the car, glancing back to see what was going on. I saw the pervert turn on Mark who held his ground with the bat held high. I think the pervert expected Mark to swing at his upper body, but Mark later told me that, if he had swung high, the man might have been able to block the swing or even grab the bat and take it from him. So Mark, always a resourceful young man, swung low, hitting the pervert on the side of his left knee.

Mr. Ross, the two fathers, the nuns, the children, and I heard the crack. It sounded like a limb, heavy with snow, breaking off from a tree. Mark had broken the man's knee. As the pervert began to topple, Mark hit him again across the left side of his head, breaking his jaw and knocking him out. The man fell and lay face down on the sidewalk. Mr. Ross, still approaching, thought Mark might have killed him. The two male parents reached the scene at the same time as Mr. Ross. Mr. Ross went straight to Mark; the fathers hovered over the fallen attacker. The young nun ran straight to me.

"He's out cold, but alive," said one of the fathers. "It looks like he met his match." You could hear the sound of sirens coming from two directions. One of the nuns had called the police, and nothing brings them faster than an "abduction in progress" call from a grade school. Especially a call from a nun!

Mr. Ross was amazed by the scene. A thirty-five-year-old man, looking strong, obviously dangerous, defeated in battle by an eight-year-old boy defending a little eight-year-old girl.

Mr. Ross put his arm around Mark and told him, "You did good, Mark. You did good."

Mark relaxed a bit and said, "Is Sandy all right? Is she safe?"

When Mr. Ross said, "Yes, she's fine, thanks to you," Mark let out an audible sigh. "He was going to do bad things to Sandy, and I couldn't allow that. Sandy is my best friend, and I'll never let anyone hurt her."

The young nun, Sister Mary Angela, our third grade teacher, had taken me in her arms and was telling me that everything was all right. I broke free and ran back to Mark and gave him the biggest hug I had ever given anyone. Mr. Ross later said what happened between me and Mark at that point was beautiful. We existed in our own little private world, our cone of exclusion. We spoke as if Mr. Ross were not there. I could not stop thanking Mark.

"You don't have to thank me, Sandy. I will never let anyone hurt you."

"I know," I said. "I know." I was rubbing his chest with the palm of my right hand. I did know, even then as a little girl, I instinctively knew that Mark Tuttle would never let anyone hurt me.

I looked at his handsome face and said, "Mark, I'm very embarrassed. When the man grabbed me, I got scared and peed my pants. Do I stink?" I was still rubbing his chest.

"No," he said, "you smell wonderful. You always smell wonderful to me. (I smiled.) And there is no reason to be embarrassed. It's normal for that to happen when you're scared like that. I'm sure Nurse Smith can give you something dry to wear home. And, anyway, who's going to know? It's our secret."

I stood back, took both his hands in mine, and, looking directly into his eyes, said, "I am going to marry you someday, Mark Tuttle."

"Nothing will make me happier, Sandy Roberts," he said. "We will be married."

"Promise?"

"Promise."

"I'm going to hold you to that, Mark Tuttle." And I did!

"I hope you do, Sandy Roberts" he said and smiled. What a lovely smile!

I kissed him, on the mouth, an innocent little girl kiss, but from the bottom of my heart. And he knew it was from the bottom of my heart. And he kissed me back. And I knew it was from the bottom of his heart. We were both so happy despite what had almost happened. But it didn't happen, because Mark did not let it happen. Mark never lets anything bad happen to me.

Mother Mary Agnes, the principal, then arrived on the scene, out of breath, huffing and puffing, but also very relieved that we were safe.

"Oh, I am so glad you're both safe. And thank God, Mark, that you had your bat and the courage to use it. Don't feel bad about that man; he deserved what you gave him. Now let's go up to the school to see Nurse Smith. She is waiting to see both of you."

As we started walking back up to the school, I took Mark's left hand in my right hand and I would not let go. He squeezed my hand; that made me feel so safe. Except when we, separately, were with Nurse Smith, I did not let go of his hand for the rest of the day. If he didn't have to go home, I might be still holding it.

When we arrived at Mother Mary Agnes's office, she instructed Mark and me to sit in the outer office, and she went in and called Nurse Smith. Maybe it was nervousness, but I couldn't stop talking, and I did not let go of Mark's hand. What did I talk about? Everything and anything other than what had just happened. When Nurse Smith came to the outer office, she asked me to follow her to her office.

"Can Mark come with me?" I asked.

"No, honey," said Nurse Smith, "I want to talk to each of you privately."

I then turned to Mark and made him promise to wait for me. "Don't go home without me today, Mark Tuttle."

"I won't," he promised. I hated to let go of his hand, but, of course, I had to. Nurse Smith asked me if the man had touched me anywhere where he should not have touched me. "No," I replied. "There wasn't enough time. He had just grabbed me around the waist and was pushing me into the car when Mark hit him with his bat. Mark yelled for me to run, and I did, as fast as I could. I peed my pants when he grabbed me. Do you have anything dry I can wear home?" I asked.

Nurse Smith smiled and said she did. She reached into her bottom drawer and pulled out a pair of plastic, absorbent, paper-lined panties and told me to go in the lavatory in her office to clean up and put on these plastic things. *Ugh,* I thought. *Where did she get these?* But at least they were dry. She gave me a paper bag for my wet panties and then led me back to the principal's outer office. Mark, as I expected, was waiting for me. His welcoming smile gave me such a warm feeling throughout my body. *I am so glad you're my boyfriend, Mark Tuttle.* I did think "boyfriend". Before I had a chance to re-capture his hand, however, Nurse Smith led him away. He looked back at me as they headed to her office and said, "Now you wait for me." I just smiled. *I'm not going anywhere without you, Mark Tuttle…I love you.*

Nurse Smith noticed that he looked upset and told him that what he had done was a good thing and he should not let it bother him. He told her it didn't bother him, not at all, but he was afraid they might put him in jail for hitting someone with a bat.

"No, honey, no one's going to put you in jail. If anyone goes to jail, it will be that man. What you did was a good thing. You should not feel bad about it."

"I don't, not at all," he said. "I would do the same thing tomorrow if I had to. I will never let anyone hurt Sandy. Never."

Nurse Smith was surprised by the intensity of his remark.

When we were together again, I told him about the plastic panties. "I feel like a baby," I said, "in a diaper."

"At least you're dry, and I won't tell too many people," he said with a smile. I punched him on the shoulder and said, "You better not tell anyone, Mark Tuttle."

"Don't worry, I was just kidding," he said.

"I know," I said. "I just wanted to hit you."

Mother Mary Agnes then called my Mom. She started with a line that was sure to upset Mom although her intention was exactly the opposite. "Hi, Mrs. Roberts,

Mother Mary Agnes from St. Michael's. I want to tell you up front that Sandy is fine. She and Mark Tuttle are sitting in my outer office, holding hands and chatting away."

"What happened to her and Mark?" asked my Mom.

"Sandy was just starting to head home when a man jumped out of his car and grabbed her---"

"Oh my God!" said Mom. "How did she get away?"

"She was too far away for Mr. Ross or any of the men near the school to do anything and my heart sank, but then little Mark Tuttle hit the pervert as hard as he could across the lower back with his baseball bat, and Sandy was able to run away."

"Did he hurt Mark?"

"No, Mark hurt him. He hit him two more times, broke his knee and then his jaw and knocked him out. It was the most amazing thing, and the bravest, I have ever seen. When Mr. Ross got there, the first thing Mark said was, 'Is Sandy okay?' He said he would never let anyone hurt her because she's his best friend."

"I'll be right over," Mom said. *Thank you, Mark Tuttle,* she thought. "How is she holding up?"

"She seems fine. Nurse Smith examined her. The man didn't get a chance to touch her anywhere. She and Mark are chatting away in the outer office. I don't know what they're talking about, but they haven't stopped talking. And she won't let go of his right hand."

"I'll be right there," Mom repeated. Before she left Coventry High School, where she teaches, she called Dad and let him know what had happened. "I'd like to give that boy a hug," he said. "I'll be right home."

"I want to give him a hug too," said Mom, "and I will as soon as I see him."

Mother Mary Agnes also called the Tuttle's, but Mrs. Tuttle was not at home. She had gone grocery shopping.

When Mom arrived, she gave me and Mark big hugs. She was crying, but it was happy crying. I asked her if we could give Mark a ride home and maybe stop at McDonald's for Cokes and fries.

"You and Mark can have anything you want, anywhere you want," she said.

"Cokes and fries will be fine," I said.

When I sat down next to Mark at McDonald's, I crinkled. *Darn plastic panties*, I thought. He started to laugh but I gave him a stare and said, "Don't you dare laugh at me, Mark Tuttle." But then we both laughed because it was funny.

When we got to Mark's house, he turned to me and said, "Do you want me to walk with you to school tomorrow morning?"

"Yes," said Mom from the front seat.

"Yes," I said from the back seat. Before he got out, I gave him a little kiss. I think I was beginning to like giving him little kisses. And I think he liked them too.

"I'll come by at eight o'clock," he said. And as he was walking to his door, he turned around and said, "And I'll bring my bat."

That evening at dinner Dad was very restless. He kept looking at me and smiling and asking, "Are you sure you're all right, honey?" I assured him I was. Suddenly he stood up and said, "Madeline, I'm going over to see the Tuttles. I have to thank that boy."

"Can I go with you, Daddy?" I asked.

"Sure, honey. Let's go."

When we rang the bell, Mr. Tuttle came to the door. He seemed very surprised to see us. "Hi, Sandy. What's up?"

"Mr. Tuttle, this is my father, Bob Roberts. He wants to thank Mark."

Dad held out his hand to a surprised Mr. Tuttle who invited us into the house.

"Thank Mark for what?" he asked.

"Didn't he tell you?" asked Dad.

"No. Tell me what?"

"He single-handedly beat off a thirty-five-year-old pervert who was trying to abduct Sandy. All the adults were too far away to help, and, if it wasn't for Mark, I hate to imagine where Sandy might be now. He clobbered the man with his wooden baseball bat. Broke his knee and his jaw and gave him a concussion. And I bet his back isn't in too good shape either."

Mr. Tuttle was stunned. "Come into the dining room. We're just finishing up dessert. Have a cup of coffee and tell my wife what he did. My God, he said nothing."

When we reached the door of the dining room, Mrs. Tuttle and Patty, Mark's older sister who's in eighth grade at St. Michael's, looked at us, also surprised by our visit. Mark, who, of course, knew what this was all about, just smiled at me.

"Hi, Sandy," said Patty. "What's up?"

"Is anything wrong?" asked Mrs. Tuttle.

"No, everything is very right," said Mr. Tuttle. "Mark, why didn't you tell us what you did today?"

"It was no big thing, Dad," he said. "Somebody was trying to hurt Sandy and I stopped him. I'll never let anyone hurt Sandy."

"No big thing? No big thing?" said Mr. Tuttle, and then turning to his wife, he said, "Sandy was being kidnapped by a thirty-five-year-old pervert, and Mark, who was the only one near enough to help her, beat him senseless with his baseball bat. If he didn't react, Sandy wouldn't be with us tonight. Oh my God, Mark, I am so proud of you."

"Patty, pull up a chair for Mr. Roberts. Bob, join us for coffee and dessert," said Mrs. Tuttle.

"Thanks," said Dad, "but first I'm going to do what I came over here to do." Then, with tears in his eyes (I had

143

never seen Dad cry before) he went over to Mark and gave him a big hug saying the same thing I had said to Mark that afternoon: "Thank you, thank you, thank you---" Mark just blushed.

"Mark, get a chair for Sandy," said Mrs. Tuttle.

"That's okay, Mom, she can sit with me." And he moved over making room for me on the chair. I occupied that space very quickly. I loved sitting next to him, touching his leg with mine. Nothing sexual – we were only eight – but something very warm, very nice.

"You're not crinkling," he whispered to me.

I punched him on the shoulder.

"What was that about, Mark?" asked his mother.

"Just a little private joke, Mom," he answered.

"Sandy, would you like some ice cream?" asked Mr. Tuttle.

Mrs. Tuttle gave her husband a dirty look. "I just dished out the last of it," she said.

"That's okay, Mom," Mark said, "Sandy can share mine." He moved his dish of Breyer's vanilla bean ice cream between us and handed me a spoon.

"You never share ice cream with me," kidded Patty.

Again Mark just blushed.

Dad told Mom later that night that, for the one and only time in his life, he had a vision while sitting at the table.

He looked across the table and saw me, but I was a young lady and I was wearing a wedding gown. Mark, and he was sure it was Mark, was sitting next to me in a tuxedo with his arm around my shoulder. We were smiling and I was feeding him a piece of wedding cake. Dad said he blinked and when he looked again, he saw two little, smiling, happy children sharing a chair and a dish of Breyer's vanilla bean ice cream.

Dad told me about the vision on our wedding day itself, right after he saw me feed Mark a piece of our wedding cake. It happened exactly as he had seen it. Strange but true.

The second incident occurred three years later, when Mark and I were in sixth grade at St. Michael's. It happened after school one day when we were playing, just the two of us, one-on-one basketball on the outdoor court behind the school. Peggy Mayhew was usually with us when we played basketball, or did anything for that matter, but she was not there that day. I think she had to go to the dentist. I noticed that the school bully, I think he was in eighth grade, and two of his friends were watching us play, and they were making nasty comments.

"Just ignore them," said Mark. "They'll go away."

That was fine with me, so we just continued to play. They then came and stood on a little hill overlooking the court and started making some uncomplimentary comments about me, personal comments. The bully said something like, "That's two boys out there, right?" "Yeah," agreed his sidekicks.

"And the one in the blue shirt (I was wearing a blue T-shirt that day) sure is one ugly little boy," he added, and the three of them laughed. Mark could see that this was bothering me, so, contrary to his advice to ignore them, he put down the basketball and walked over and stood two feet in front of the bully himself.

"You can make fun of me all you want," he said, "but if you make fun of Sandy, we're gonna fight."

"You're gonna have to fight one against three," said the bully indicating his two smaller companions.

Mark stared at the two, at one and then at the other, and said, "If you two want to join in, yeah, then it will be one against three, but I'm not backing down. And if you two do join in, I will get you both alone and beat the crap outta you." Then to the bully, "It's you I want to fight, me against you, unless you're chicken. And I promise you this, no matter what happens to me, you're going home crying, hurting, and bleeding."

I had picked up a broom stick and had come up behind Mark. He didn't know it, but the flunkies did. I was not going to let him fight one against three. The two sidekicks then started moving to the side leaving their leader to handle Mark alone.

"Come on," said Mark. "I'm ready."

The bully looked at him, realized he was in for a real fight, and decided to back off. "Can't you take a joke? I was just kidding." He then motioned to his two followers, "Come on, let's get out of here." And they walked away while Mark watched them to make sure they were really leaving.

Mark then turned, saw me holding the broom stick, laughed, and said, "What are you doing with that?"

"I wasn't going to let you fight one against three," I answered.

"Thank you," he said.

"No, thank you," I replied.

He then put his arm around my shoulder, and I put my arm around his waist, and we walked back to the court.

"Were you scared?" I asked.

"Yes, but I had a big advantage," he answered.

"What?"

"I was willing to fight and he wasn't. Bullies never are if you call their bluff."

"What if he was willing?"

"Then I would have fought him, and, win or lose, he would have regretted it because I would have hurt him."

I gave his waist a squeeze and, when we reached the court, gave him a kiss reminiscent of the spin the bottle kiss from fourth grade.

Then standing back, and holding both of his hands in mine, I said, "Mark Tuttle, someday I'm going to marry you. That's a promise, and our life is going to be very good and very happy."

"Nothing would make me happier, Sandy Roberts," he replied.

We had that same conversation when we were eight.

Then we squeezed hands and stared at each other for an eternity, an eleven-year-old's eternity. I don't know how long an eternity is, and maybe that's not even a valid question, but I do know that time stood still for us on that basketball court. Finally Mark broke back into the present with the question, "Do you want to go get a Coke?"

"I only have fifteen cents," I said.

"I have three dollars," he said, "so we have enough."

"I like that," I said.

"What?" he asked.

"The 'we,' " I answered.

"We make a good 'we,' don't we?" he asked.

"We sure do," I answered.

Mark Tuttle, you and I make a great 'we'....We will always be a great 'we'...Because I promise you that no one will come between us...no thing will come between us...And if anyone tries, I will fight her – I assume it will be a her – with every ounce of strength in my body.

We walked off to McDonald's hand in hand. Two young lovers with our whole lives ahead of us, not realizing what our life together would produce, but confident that it would be wonderful.

I am going to marry you someday, Mark Tuttle...Nothing would make me happier, Sandy Roberts.

Chapter Nine
We Love You, Bill Reynolds

I have mentioned Margie Baylor a few times in this memoir. I consider Margie my little sister. The Baylor house was next door to the Roberts house, and she was always at my house when we were growing up. She is one year younger than I am, and, I think, she idolizes me. How could she not? Just kidding.

Margie suggested that I include a chapter about Mark's and my developing relationship with Bill Reynolds. Margie was instrumental in introducing us to the famous Bill Reynolds, sports columnist for the *Providence Journal*, and writer of the world's greatest column, his collection of off-the-wall observations published every Saturday. Everyone in Rhode Island and Southeastern Massachusetts reads that column which is accompanied by a little head shot of Mr. Reynolds.

During the summer after our junior year, Mark and I had signed up for a mixed doubles beach volleyball tournament at Narragansett Beach on the Rhode Island shore. The teams, mostly college kids, came from all over the northeast. Coach Thompson, my basketball coach at CHS, had given me a flyer which contained an application. Mark and I sent it in immediately with the twenty-five dollar entry fee.

I suggested to Peggy that she and Billy Walsh sign up. She asked Billy and he said, "Volleyball is a girl's sport."

"Mark and Sandy signed up. Is Mark a girl?"

"No, but he's pussy whipped," Billy said.

"Do you want me to tell him that?" Peggy asked.

"I don't care….Well, I guess not," he said.

Of course, Peggy told us. Mark just laughed. "What an idiot."

"You have to drop him, Peggy," I said. "He's such a nothing, and you're such a …..…a……..a something."

We were both laughing so hard, we peed our pants. Just a few drops. Peggy gave him his walking papers the next day.

Mark and I, as you know from previous chapters, are very athletic. But what makes us so good in two-person volleyball is the fact that we are like two bodies with one mind. I know what he's going to do, and he knows what I am going to do, before we do it. Amazing, but true. Another advantage we had that day in Narragansett was the presence of a cheering contingent, twenty or so of our classmates, all wearing Coventry High T-shirts, who were quite vocal when we were competing. Peggy Mayhew and Margie Baylor were the primary cheerleaders.

The tournament took place one week after the Rumble at Joey's – that's what I started calling that episode in our lives. Margie and Peggy rode down to Narragansett with us.

On the way down, I rested my hand on Mark's shoulder and turned to face Margie in the back. "Do you know what Mark told my Uncle Ron at dinner the night of the Rumble at Joey's?"

"No," Margie answered.

"He said that he only fights to protect me, Peggy, and you."

Margie was surprised. "Did you say that, Mark? You would fight for me?"

"Of course, Margie," he said. "I hope I never have to, but, yes, I would. We've been friends for eleven years."

Margie sat back and said, "Wow. Thank you."

Peggy put her arm around her and said, "Margie, we would all fight for you. You're part of us."

I was surprised to find so many CHS students at courtside. Margie told me she had spread the word.

Bill Reynolds had the day off and went to Narragansett to get away from the heat of the city. He had no idea there was a beach volleyball tournament scheduled for that day. He ran into an old Brown classmate who told him about the tournament: "Bill, you should take it in. The players are really athletic, and all the girls play in bikinis. Not a bad spectator sport. College kids from all over the east coast."

Bill decided to check it out. I am not insinuating that the bikini-clad female athletes were incentives, but he, being a newspaperman, followed up on the lead from a friend. He soon discovered that the best team there, a team that seemed to be unbeatable, was made up of two high school kids from Rhode Island, me and Mark. Bill called the *Journal* and had them send down a photographer. Bill doesn't usually cover high school sports so, even though he knew that Mark Tuttle and Sandy Roberts had led Coventry High to two state championships in basketball that year, he didn't have any idea who we were or what we looked like.

Bill approached a young girl watching the match and asked who we were. The young girl, Margie Baylor, said, "Mr. Reynolds, you should know who they are."

He looked puzzled. "You know me?" he asked.

"My father and I read your column every Saturday. And your picture is next to the column," answered Margie.

Bill was flattered. "Do you like the column?"

"We love it. Who doesn't?" asked Margie.

Bill liked hearing that. "And you are?"

"Margie Baylor, Mr. Reynolds."

"And, Margie Baylor, why should I know who they are?"

"Mr. Reynolds, look around. We're all wearing Coventry High School T-shirts. Two great athletes, one male, one female, from Coventry High School. Duh! Everyone in Rhode Island who follows sports knows them."

Bill still looked puzzled.

"Sandy Roberts and Mark Tuttle," she said.

"Oh, the basketball players," he observed, the light dawning.

"They're a lot more than basketball players," she said, and then, pointing to the court, she added, "That's not basketball, is it?"

"Point taken, Margie Baylor."

Margie then proceeded to give Bill Reynolds a lecture, as only Margie can do. "They are not only good athletes, Mr. Reynolds, but the smartest two people I know. They both have 4.0 averages in the Honors Program at school, and both scored 1600 on the SATs---"

"1600?" said Mr. Reynolds. "No one gets 1600." This was back when the SAT only had two sections, and 1600 was the maximum score possible.

"Well they both did," said Margie.

"Wow," said Mr. Reynolds, properly impressed.

"They're also the nicest two people I know, and they really love each other. In fact, if any man ever loves me as much as Mark loves Sandy, I will die a happy woman. And they're best friends to boot. How would you like to be in love with your best friend? I think it's great."

"It sounds like you're their PR person, Margie Baylor. Do they pay you?" asked Mr. Reynolds, smiling.

"No, just an admirer and a friend," said Margie. "Sandy also led us to the state championship in softball. This," she added, pointing to Peggy, "is Peggy Mayhew. She and Sandy were our one-two punch in basketball and softball."

Bill was impressed. Peggy Mayhew is impressive.

Bill stayed for the entire tournament. We not only won every match capturing the title; we won every game. We were awesome, if I say so myself. After the final match, Margie introduced us to Bill Reynolds. He and Margie, it seemed, had become friends. The *Journal* photographer had arrived, and he took some nice pictures of us playing and of us with Bill Reynolds after the final match.

During the interview, Bill asked Mark how we got to be so good.

Mark told him, "We're very athletic. I guess it just comes naturally to us."

I added, "Our friends say we are like two bodies with one mind."

Mark then made one of his famous observations, which became the following Saturday's *Quote of the Week* in Bill's column: "I just thank God one of the bodies is female!"

Well, that was our introduction to Bill Reynolds, but the relationship continued to mature after that.

Coach Wilson, the boys' basketball coach and Athletic Director at Coventry High, had been a classmate of Bill's at Brown. Bill called Coach that night to discuss the volleyball tournament. Coach Wilson didn't know anything about the tournament, but figured out immediately who the high school athletes were.

"How did you figure that out?" asked Bill Reynolds.

"Bill, I'm a Brown graduate, so I must be smart," said Coach Wilson. "Two great high school athletes, one male, one female, from Coventry High School – you wouldn't be calling me unless they were my kids – and you don't think I'd know who they had to be? They're great kids, by the way, and smart as Hell. They each scored a 1600 on the SATs, imagine that."

"Yeah, I heard that. From another of your kids, Margie Baylor. That is impressive."

"You met Margie? Another good kid. She idolizes Sandy."

"I gathered that. I asked her if she were their PR person."

"Mark and Sandy will both be getting a lot of basketball scholarship offers; I know UConn and Tennessee are after Sandy, and at least a half dozen big name schools, including Duke, are after Mark, but they're going to accept academic scholarships to Harvard and MIT. Many college coaches are going to cry over that, I can tell you."

"I think I'd like to get to know them better," said Bill Reynolds.

"That's not a bad idea, Bill," said Coach Wilson. "They're going to dominate Rhode Island high school sports next winter and spring. You know, don't you, that Sandy is a fantastic softball pitcher, the best I have ever seen. Coventry not only won the boys' and girls' basketball titles this past year, we also won the state championship in girls' softball this past spring. First state titles in twenty years."

"Yes, Margie Baylor told me that," answered Bill Reynolds. "And she introduced me to Peggy Mayhew, who was watching the match. Now there is one beautiful young woman."

"Best female rebounder I ever saw, and a home run risk every time she came to the plate. She and Sandy make a great combination. And they're best friends. Come over to the gym any day but Sunday – today was an exception – and watch them play two-on-two hoops against all comers. They never lose, no matter which two happen to be playing, Mark and Sandy, Mark and Peggy, or Peggy and Sandy. Peggy and Sandy can beat any two boys in the school, excluding Mark Tuttle of course."

"I'll take you up on that," he answered, and he did, quite often the rest of that summer.

The next day's *Journal* had three pictures of me and Mark on the top of the high school sports page; there's not much to report on that page during the summer months.

The picture on the left showed me from behind, in my black bikini, slamming home the tournament-winning point. Mark's in the picture, off to my left. I told him he was looking at my ass. He claims he was watching the ball. Look at the picture and decide for yourself. I think it's pretty obvious that he is looking at my ass! But can you blame him? It *is* quite attractive. (I rarely wear dresses. I am more the casual, sporty type: slacks in winter, shorts in summer. On one of those rare occasions when I was in a dress, however, a friend, Molly O'Rourke, suggested that I should wear high heels when I dress up. "It will give your backside more definition." I told her, "Molly, two things: one, I will never wear high heels. And two, Mark loves my backside's definition just the way it is.")

Mark has loved my ass since the day I let him squeeze it in the pool shed...before that actually, but that was when he first got to enjoy it...Now that we're intimate, he loves to play with it...Bury his head in it...I love it too when he plays with it, squeezes it ...Boy was he ever surprised when he saw my bumps again after three years...I know my ass and bumps are sufficient for his needs and desires now, but I can't believe he loved them when I was thirteen...But he did...No doubt about that...He masturbated thinking about them...Now he doesn't have too...Masturbate that is...He still thinks about them..Neither do I have to masturbate...We take care of each other...in every way.

The picture in the center was probably the sexiest picture ever published on the *Journal*'s high school sports page. I had jumped up into Mark's arms after the final point was scored, had my bare legs wrapped around his waist, and he had one hand on my bikini-clad backside and the other on my back as we exchanged a passionate, celebratory kiss. That picture definitely showed the whole world, all of Rhode Island and Southeastern Massachusetts at any rate, that we were much more than volleyball teammates.

The picture on the right showed the two of us, wearing Coventry High School T-shirts, with Bill Reynolds. I am on Bill's left holding the trophy aloft with my left hand, and my right hand is around Bill's waist; Mark is on Bill's right with his left arm around Bill's shoulder. All three of us have huge smiles on our faces. Bill still has that picture on his desk in his office at the *Journal*.

Bill followed our progress very closely during our senior year. Even though he was not officially covering the high school sports scene, he was at most of our games, both Mark's and mine, and interviewed us and Peggy after most games. We appeared fairly regularly in his famous Saturday column.

He was not at the boys' game against Cranston East and was surprised to read in the following day's *Journal* the headline, "SMITH LEADS COVENTRY OVER CRANSTON EAST WITH 34 POINTS."

He called his former classmate, Coach Wilson, the day after the game and asked, "Who is your new star, this Billy Smith?"

Coach Wilson told him of the post-game conversation in the locker room between Mark and Billy. "After the game, Bill, I was talking to Mark off in a corner of the locker room when Billy Smith came over. Billy rarely plays, but one of our starters was home sick, and Mark had asked me to give Billy the start. I agreed. It turned out quite well. Billy had thirty-four points, seventeen baskets on seventeen assists from Mark. It was an amazing display. After I told Billy that he had played a great game, he thanked me and then turned to Mark and said, 'Thanks, Mark, I will never forget this night.' Mark then high-fived him and said, 'You don't have to thank me, Billy. That was for Joey's last summer.' Joey's is a hamburger joint here in Coventry. Billy Smith had come to Sandy's defense at Joey's when a couple of hoods were giving her a hard time. Sandy had told me about the incident the day that it happened, but I had forgotten about it, forgotten Billy's involvement at any rate. Mark eventually took care of the situation, but Billy had stepped up to her defense before Mark got there. Standing up for Sandy – that's a sure way to turn Mark into a friend."

Bill Reynolds even came to most of my softball games that year. One day during pre-game warm-ups, he asked Coach Thompson if he could take a few swings against me. He couldn't get around on any of my pitches: nine pitches, nine swings, nine misses. At that point, he said, "I'm duly impressed," and returned to Mark in the stands. He had played baseball at Brown.

"Don't be embarrassed," said Mark. "Nobody can hit her."

"Can you?" asked Bill.

"I never try," laughed Mark. "I just catch her when she wants to practice, and I use a very padded glove."

I averaged eighteen strike outs a game that year. We play seven-inning games; that means that eighteen out of a total of twenty-one outs each game came via the strike out. With Peggy's slugging, and my pitching, we were repeating state softball champs our senior year.

We invited Bill Reynolds to our wedding after our senior year, and he came. That surprised a lot of people, having the famous Bill Reynolds show up at our wedding and reception, but it didn't surprise us. When we told him we were getting married and asked if he would like to attend, he had said that he would be honored. By that time, we were no longer just a couple of interesting subjects for his reporting; we had actually become friends. He was one of the few attendees at the wedding who wasn't surprised when I chose Billy Smith for the "Bride's Choice" dance. When I said, 'With the exception of Mark, the young man I have chosen is the most courageous man I know,' Bill knew immediately that I was referring to Billy. So did Coach Wilson who, of course, was also at the wedding.

Bill kept in touch with us during the Cambridge years. We were back in Rhode Island many week-ends and had dinner with him a few times. When he was up in Boston, to cover the Celtics, the Red Sox, or the Bruins, he often crashed at our pad for the night instead of driving back to Providence after late games. Our couch opened up into a bed. Billy Smith used to sleep on that couch a lot too. Our apartment did have a guest room, but I called that "Peggy's Sanctuary," and it was reserved for her use; later her and Warren's use. Peggy stayed with us a lot. Bobby and Leslie used the guest room when they stayed overnight, but single guests slept on the couch.

Bill Reynolds could enjoy a few cold beers with us without worrying about the drive back to Rhode Island. I remember that we laughed a lot during those visits. The *Journal* would have paid for a hotel room, but I think Bill enjoyed spending the time with us.

Bill knew Mark was involved in a start-up venture with an MIT classmate, but never gave it much thought. He was sitting at his desk one day when one of the *Journal's* business writers stuck his head into Bill's office. "Did you read my article today on the Alpha-Omega Data Systems IPO?"

"No," answered Bill. "Should I have?"

"Well, everyone upstairs is saying I scooped Reynolds."

That made Bill sit up straight in his chair!

"Let me read you the last paragraph," said the business writer.

"The Alpha-Omega Data Systems IPO, one of the most successful in history, made overnight mega-millionaires of the original owners: Bill Skwor, MIT Junior, of Seattle, Washington, 40%; Philip Andrews, Venture Capitalist, also from Seattle, 30%; and Mark Tuttle, MIT Junior, and his wife, Sandy Roberts Tuttle, Harvard Junior, of Coventry, Rhode Island, joint owners of the remaining 30%. Readers of this paper will be familiar with the Tuttles, but from a different section of the paper. Mark Tuttle and Sandy Roberts filled the sports pages of the *Journal* with their exploits at Coventry High School a few years ago before heading north to Cambridge."

Bill sat there with his mouth open.

Bill called and asked us to meet him for dinner. I was home when he called and agreed, for both of us, to have dinner with him the following Friday at the Seven Suns Chinese restaurant in North Kingstown, Rhode Island. We drove straight from Cambridge to North Kingstown after classes, and Mark dropped me off at the restaurant's door before he parked the car. As I approached Bill's table, he put down his drink, a gin and tonic, and stood up to greet me.

"Well, you look great, Sandy Roberts," he said. He liked to call me by my maiden name, the name he first knew me by. "You look like you could suit up and get 23 against Bayview tonight."

"Bill, I could get 30 against Bayview tonight," I said laughing. "As long as I had Peggy rebounding for me." He gave me a big hug and then asked, "Where's Mark?"

"Parking the car; he'll be right in."

Standing back, he smiled and said, "Well, Sandy Roberts, you have done quite well for yourself."

"Did you ever have any doubts?" I asked, taking him by surprise with my less-than-modest reply. That was not my usual manner of speaking.

He was at a loss for words, but I came to his rescue. "Bill, you misunderstand my meaning."

"Oh?" he asked.

"Yes, I'm married to the most amazing and smartest man I have ever met, and he loves me, and he always will. And I love him, and I always will. How could my life be anything but great?"

"Yeah, I see what you mean," he said. Mark joined us and we had a great meal. The sweet and sour fish was to die for. It was just three old friends reminiscing about the good old days, the glory days of three and four years ago. Mark and I did merit a mention in the following Saturday's column, something about local kids striking gold.

I told Bill a funny story about one of our closest friends in Cambridge, an MIT classmate of Mark's from Croatia, Kristijian (Christian) Kovasevic. Bill had met Kristijian at our apartment a few times when he, Bill, was staying overnight with us. Kristijian was another of the MIT/Harvard crowd that survived college on my homemade mac and cheese and Mark's lasagna.

We had a gang over for a little party, and Kristijian quieted the gathering and posed a question. I remember Peggy and Warren were there that night. Bill Reynolds remembered Peggy from our softball games. Very few people ever forgot Peggy Mayhew. Kristijian's question: "If you took a Playboy bunny, a beautiful Playboy bunny, blonde, nice teeth, without clothes, and placed her in front of Mark, what would he say?"

The question took us by surprise. "Nice teeth?" commented Peggy. We had all had a few Miller Lites by then.

"I don't know," said Bill Skwor, "Maybe 'Hello'?"

"No," said Kristijian. "He would not say, 'Hello.' "

"We give up," Peggy said. "What would he say to this beauty with nice teeth?"

Kristijian cleared his throat, sipped a little Miller Lite, and said, "He would say, 'Will you please move. I cannot see Sandy.' "

I loved it. And so did Bill Reynolds when I told him the story at the Seven Suns. It is very funny, but it is so true. That's why I love Mark so much. Mark would much rather look at me clothed than any other girl nude. Including Peggy! I am not being self-deceptive. He knows what's under the clothes, and he knows he is going to have full access to it later.

A year after our graduations, with honors of course, when we were still living in an apartment in Cambridge, Billy Smith called the *Journal's* Sports Department one Friday morning and asked for Bill Reynolds.

"I'll see if he's here," said Bill's secretary. "Can I ask who is calling?"

"Billy Smith. Tell him Mark Tuttle asked me to give him a message."

The secretary, Bertha, caught Bill as he was leaving the office. "Mr. Reynolds, a call from a Billy Smith. He says he has a message for you from Mark Tuttle."

"I'll take it, Bertha. Put it through to my office," Bill said as he hurried back to his desk.

"Hi, Billy. What's up?" Bill asked.

"Mark called me at four this morning to tell me Sandy gave birth to a very healthy little girl. Mark asked me to call you at a reasonable hour," said Billy.

"That's great news. Do they have a name for the baby?" asked Bill.

"Yes, Madeline, and they are going to call her Maddie."

"Are you going up to Cambridge today?" asked Bill.

"Yes. My girlfriend, Maureen, and I are going up early this afternoon."

"Do you mind if I join you?" asked Bill.

"Not at all," answered Billy. "Do you want us to pick you up?"

"Yes, that would be great. At the *Journal?*" asked Bill. "I will just leave my car in the lot."

"Be happy to," said Billy. "Around one thirty?"

"Fine, thanks."

"One other thing, Mr. Reynolds. Mark said the most amazing thing to me this morning."

"What? And call me Bill."

"He said, 'Billy, I was holding Maddie for the first time this morning, and all of a sudden I realized that I loved her as much as I love Sandy, and I did not think it was possible that I would ever love anyone that much.' It brought a tear to my eye."

After Bill hung up, he called to Bertha, "Is my Saturday column still here?"

"Yes, Sir," she replied. "I just finished proofing it."

"Please bring it in here. I want to make a change."

Bill usually did not write the headline for his column, but he wrote the one on that Saturday's piece. And he devoted the first bullet point to me and Mark.

A PRINCESS IS BORN

- Sandy Roberts Tuttle gave birth yesterday morning to a healthy baby girl in Boston's Brigham and Women's Hospital. The girl will be named Madeline, and they will call her Maddie. The proud father, Mark Tuttle, said that the first time he held little Maddie, he realized that he loved her as much as he loves Sandy, and he did not think it was possible for him to ever love anyone that much.

Congratulations to the young couple, two of the nicest people ever to come out of Rhode Island.

And best wishes to young Maddie. Can you just imagine what a jump shot that little girl will have!

Chapter Ten
The Tuttles' Wake

The third Monday in September of my senior year at Coventry High was the darkest day of my young life, and of Mark's. I helped Mark get through that week, but it was Peggy who helped both of us survive it. We grew from children to adults that week.

Mark, Peggy, and I were in Advanced Placement Calculus class (we call it AP Calc) taught by Mr. Roger Wilson, Coach Wilson's brother, when the vice principal, Mr. Orlowski, knocked on our classroom door and motioned for Mr. Wilson to join him in the hall. Mr. Wilson then returned to the classroom and called Mark out into the hall. That got my attention. After a few minutes, Mr. Wilson returned without Mark. I looked at Peggy, and we both shrugged our shoulders.

"Mark has been called away on a personal matter. Let's get back to our latest problem," he said to us.

How could I think of calculus if Mark has been "called away on a personal matter"? I looked out a window and saw Mark getting into a police car that was parked outside the main entrance. Mark got in the front with the officer, not in the back, so I knew he wasn't being arrested, but what had happened?

"He got in a police car," I whispered to Peggy. "In the front."

"What's going on?" she asked.

"I have no idea," I said.

Sitting there for fifty minutes (it was our final period of the day), I understood what St. John of the Cross went through when he endured his *Dark Night of the Soul.* But I didn't know if I would come through my dark night into Paradise or into Hell. I did not give much thought to calculus, and Mr. Wilson, sensing that my mind was far from the classroom, did not call on me that period.

Peggy and I ran directly to the teachers' lounge after class to find Mom. She teaches at Coventry High, and I hoped she would know what had happened. She did, and when she told me, I was devastated. Mark's parents, both of them, had been killed in an automobile accident that morning on Route 95, the north-south interstate highway running through Rhode Island. No other cars were involved. Mr. Tuttle lost control (it was not known how at that point), and the car rolled over into a ditch. When the rescue workers arrived, they found Mark's mother and father dead: major head trauma. I couldn't believe what I was hearing.

Mom asked how Peggy and I were getting home. I answered that Mark, as usual, would drive us home. I was in a daze. "Honey, Mark is not at school now. You know that."

"Oh, yeah," I answered. As I said, I was really in a daze. "I have a key for Mark's car. Peggy and I will take that. I'm sure Mark will expect that. When we got in the car, Peggy and I hugged. "Oh my God, Sandy," she kept repeating. "Whatever you need this week, count on me," she said.

"I will...we will," I said. "I know I can count on you."

We drove to my house in silence. At home I just walked up and down in the living room; I had no desire to eat or even to sit. Peggy sat on the couch. Occasionally I would go over and hug her and cry. There was no need for words. I had to see Mark. I kept saying to Mom: "Should I go over to Mark's house?" She suggested I wait a bit. "He's probably not home yet. I'm sure he will call you if he needs you over there." *If he needs me! Of course he needs me!* After repeating this exchange a few times, I said to Mom, "Peggy and I are going over there now. I have to be with Mark." Mom hugged me and sent us on our way.

"Honey, you and Peggy take care of Mark and each other. I'll see you when you get home. I'll wait up. Stay with Mark as late as necessary."

"Thanks, Mom," I said, giving her a big hug and a kiss. "We'll take care of each other. Mark is always so strong for me; this week I'll be strong for him." There was a little tear in Mom's eye as she watched us leave. Her little daughter had become a woman.

While we were driving over, I later found out, Mark was pacing up and down in his living room, also unable to eat, and wondering, as he later told me, if he should call me. I don't know why he even gave that any thought. Of course, he should call me. But he didn't really mean 'if' he should call me, but 'when' he should call me. His sister, Patricia, a teacher in North Providence, and his Aunt Marion, his mother's sister, who had driven up from New York as soon as she heard the bad news, were sitting at the kitchen table drinking tea. Finally Patricia called Mark into the kitchen. "Why don't you call Sandy?" she suggested.

"Great idea, Patty," he said. "I'll do it right now."

After he left the kitchen, Aunt Marion asked Patricia who Sandy was.

"His girlfriend," said Patricia.

165

"Oh," said Aunt Marion. "Isn't he a little young for a girlfriend?"

"He's seventeen, Aunt Marion, and Sandy is actually much more that a girlfriend. She's his best friend. She's going to be my sister-in-law; I have no doubt of that. Mom and Dad loved her."

"Oh," repeated Aunt Marion.

When Mark called my house, my father answered the phone.

"Hi, Mr. Roberts, is Sandy there?" Mark asked.

"No, she's on the way over to your house. She and Peggy. She has your car."

"Great," said Mark. "Great."

"I'm so sorry about your----" Mark had hung up.

After telling his sister and Aunt Marion that I was on the way, with Peggy, Mark went out to the front porch and sat on one of the rockers waiting for us.

Aunt Marion asked Patricia who Peggy was. "A good friend," said Patty.

That caused a raised eyebrow.

On the way to Mark's house, I told Peggy that I was not going to school that week. She said she would go to keep us abreast of the material covered. She said she would be with us every day after school. I thanked her. I love Peggy Mayhew.

When Mark saw the car drive up, he quickly rose from the rocker and started walking toward the street. I parked the car and started walking toward him. As we got closer, we both accelerated. I fell into his arms and we hugged each other, both crying profusely. I said, "I am so sorry, Mark," and he said, "I just called your house, and your father told me you were on the way over. That made me feel so good. I am so glad you're here, Sandy."

"So am I," I said. "So am I. I will be with you all week if you want." I took out a tissue and wiped my tears and his as well.

"Of course I want that," he said.

Peggy followed me, but she held back a bit to let us hug and commiserate.

Peggy then approached us. She wrapped her arms around both of us and told Mark how sorry she was. "Anything you two need, Mark, you can count on me."

"I know that, Peggy." And he did know that. I did too.

Our relationship ostensibly began the night of the East Greenwich basketball game during our junior year. I called that our personal Alpha Point. But I said at the time (you can look it up!) that I always knew, since we were little kids, we would get together someday.

I already had a crush on Mark when we were six and had just started first grade at St. Michael's Parochial School. I think that crush began the moment I laid eyes upon him. I remember one incident that occurred back then with crystal clarity. Mom had bought me a new Marble Composition book. I loved that book and wrote my name in big letters in the little white box on the cover. On the second day of school, I discovered that someone had scribbled all over the cover with a purple crayon. I stood there shocked. Then Missy O'Donnell told me that Mark Tuttle had done it. I didn't know what upset me more: that the book was ruined or that Mark Tuttle had done it. Probably the latter. I had a crush on Mark, on the first day of school!

At recess time I went out to the playground and found Mark. Holding up the book, I yelled, "Why did you do this?" I was crying.

"I didn't do it," he protested. "I wouldn't do anything like that especially to **your** book."

"I know you did!" I cried, having been misinformed by Missy O'Donnell.

I then punched Mark, and, still crying, shouted, "Come on, fight with me. I want to fight with you." I kept hitting him.

He just covered his head with his hands saying, "Sandy, I didn't do it."

Mark was saved by the bell ending recess, and I ran into the classroom. At lunchtime I was sitting outside with little Peggy Mayhew at one of the picnic tables when Mark came up with Larry Rossi, the toughest kid in class (actually Mark was the toughest, but he was nice so nobody knew that yet) and his sidekick, Eddie Reuther. Larry had a bloody nose.

"He wants to tell you something," said Mark pointing to Larry.

"I scribbled on your book," Larry said.

"Why?" I asked.

"I dunno. For laughs maybe," he said. "Eddie thought it would be fun."

"Mark told us to say we're sorry," said Eddie. "And he told us if we ever bother you again, he will beat us up again."

"And he told me to give you this," said Larry, handing me a quarter.

After they had left, I turned to Mark and said, "Why didn't you fight back when I was hitting you?"

"I don't want to fight you," he answered. "I want to be your friend."

"You can be my friend," I said. "No, you **are** my friend. Can you walk me home today after school? We can stop at the candy store and get two Cokes. My treat. And

I'll get a new Marble Composition book at Coventry Drug Store on the way."

"Sure," he said, smiling.

When I told him that it was Missy O'Donnell who said he did it, and that I was going to beat her up, he told me to just ignore her. "She's just jealous that I like you better than I like her."

"You do like me?" I asked.

"Yes," he said.

The three of us walked back to the classroom after lunch, three happy youngsters, not knowing it but beginning a lifetime friendship.

I always knew Mark and I would be together!

And then there was Molly Davidson's birthday party when we were in fourth grade, nine years old. Twelve of us, six boys and six girls, attended Molly's party, and she announced we would play Spin the Bottle. Molly gave herself number one, and the five remaining girls picked numbers from a hat. Peggy got two; I got four. That meant Molly sat in the circle with all six boys when she spun the bottle. Peggy, being number two, would spin with the five remaining boys. When it got to me, there would only be three boys left. I had two worries: would Mark still be left when it got to me? And, Heaven forbid, what if Peggy got Mark? Even in fourth grade, Peggy was beautiful. I found out years later that Peggy really wanted to kiss me, but that wasn't possible under Molly's rules.

The gods were with me. When it was my turn to spin, Mark was still in the pool of eligible boys. As I gave the Coke bottle a spin, I prayed (silently of course), "Please stop at Mark...Please stop at Mark." The bottle ended up pointing at Mark, directly at Mark, no question about it. Mark pumped his fist in the air and said, "Yes." That surprised and pleased me. We looked at each other and smiled, and then walked into the coat closet off the living room. Molly had suggested using the closet. That way, if any boy or girl did not want to kiss the other, the refusal could be kept private. We went into the closet and knelt down. I don't know why we knelt down, but we did. It was dark in the closet, but, after a few moments, we could see. With our hands at our sides, we kissed. He wrapped his lips around my top lip, and I wrapped my lips around his lower lip. I was thinking, *He tastes like chocolate candy, and his mouth smells so sweet.* We separated and, moistening our lips with our tongues, we stared at each other. *That was nice...I want to kiss him some more...I never felt like this...What is happening to me?..Does he want to kiss me?..I hope so...I bet he does.*

"Do you want to kiss me some more?" I asked.

He said, "Yes, very much," and we rejoined our lips. This time he put his right hand on my shoulder and we actually touched tongues. It was electric for me, and, I hoped, for him. I don't know how long we kissed, but we didn't stop until someone banged on the door yelling, "What are you two doing in there?" The tips of our tongues never separated.

Mark and I stopped, and he said to me, "Your mouth tastes like Breyer's vanilla bean ice cream."

"And yours tastes like chocolate," I replied. "Did you like kissing me?" I asked.

"Yes," he said.

"Come out, you two," a young female voice shouted. Molly? There was laughing in the living room.

"One more quick kiss?" he asked.

"Yes," I said. And we rejoined our tongues. And blew breath into each other's mouth. That was nice. He was rubbing my back.

Bang! Bang! Bang! On the door.

"I guess we better go back out," I said.

"We'll do this again," he said.

"Yes, we will."

Yes we will, Mark Tuttle...A lot...God I loved that...I think you did too...Are you my boyfriend?..I hope so...What was that feeling?..So warm...Whatever it is, I love it.

He squeezed me tight, and then we got up. *I'm feeling it again...How nice.*

We came out of the closet holding hands. All the boys were teasing him: "Wow, what a long kiss!" and "Look at the lovebirds." Stuff like that. Mark was blushing, but he did not let go of my hand. He..did..not..let..go..of..my..hand!

Two innocent children, experiencing something magical and mysterious, beyond their comprehension, but never to be forgotten.

I always knew Mark and I would be together!

It's funny how stream of consciousness works. (I took a one-semester course on James Joyce's *Ulysses* at Harvard.) Thinking of Molly's party brought my mind to a recent evening at Chelo's, the restaurant where we had our first real date. I was sitting at one end of the table, Mark at the other end, with our girls, Maddie and Annie, at Mark's end of the table, and our boys, Bobby and Jimmy, at mine, with Mom and Dad sitting in the middle between their grandchildren. Mark got up to talk to someone at the bar, I forget who, but when he came back, he came to my end of the table.

"Excuse me, ma'am, are these your children?" he asked.

"Yes," I said, playing along.

"They're well behaved," he said.

"They have a very strict father. He beats them if they misbehave."

"Does he beat you too?" he then asked.

"Only when I deserve it," I replied. *I can't even imagine Mark beating me or the kids!*

"He sounds like a very good man," said Mark.

"Oh, he is, he is," I answered.

He then leaned over and kissed me, and then pulled back smiling.

"What?" I asked.

"You taste like Breyer's vanilla bean ice cream," he said.

"And you taste like chocolate," I said. "So you remember that time in the closet at Molly's party?"

"I have never forgotten it," he said. "A highlight of my life."

"Now go back to your end of the table and spend time with the other women in your life, but remember, you're sleeping with me tonight."

"That's another thing I don't forget," he said laughing.

Stream of consciousness again: that same night after we had been served our soup and salad, I asked Maddie to say Grace. We always say Grace, even when out in public.

We all joined hands, and Maddie said, "God, thank You for our food, and thank You for bringing Mommy and Daddy together, for only good things have happened since then. Amen."

Silence. All four adults had tears in their eyes.

"Maddie, that was beautiful," I said. "And you are one of the good things that has happened. You and Bobby and Jimmy and Annie."

"I know, Mommy, I know."

God how I love that Maddie.

I noticed that Mark was giving her the look that, in the days before Maddie's arrival, he reserved only for me. Does Mark ever love Maddie! Always has, from the day she was born. No, from the day she was conceived. *I have loved you in your mother's womb.* And she loves her father. Does that make me jealous, that I have to share that look? God, no. To know that your man loves your children and will protect them at all times, what mother wouldn't love that? I know I do! I also know he will die for me. A very nice thing to know. Reassuring, to say the least.

I caught Mark's eye and mouthed to him, "I love you," and he mouthed back to me, "I love you too." Then I said, "Let's have our soup before it gets cold."

Getting back to that awful night in September of our senior year: When Mark, Peggy, and I went into the house, I hugged Patty and told her how sorry I was. Patty introduced me and Peggy to Aunt Marion, and I hugged her as well. Her hug was not as loving as Patty's hug, however. Oh well, she was just meeting me.

"Patty, whatever you need us to do, we will do. I am not going to school this week, so both Mark and I are available for whatever you need done," I said. "Peggy's going to school, but she'll be here every evening."

"What I would like," she answered, "is for you three to take care of the kitchen. People will be bringing over food, and we'll be buying rolls and cold cuts. I'll stay out of the kitchen, and you guys can take care of that. Also I would like you to be my gophers and chauffeurs: shopping for things we need and picking up people at the airport and shuttling them from the hotels to the funeral parlor or here."

"We can do all of that," I said. "Don't give it another thought."

"You can start by running to Dave's to get cold cuts and breads. Use your own judgment."

As we were heading out, she called me back. "Sandy, there's one very special thing you can do for me."

"Anything, Patty," I answered.

"Stay at Mark's side all this week. At the wake, at the funeral. He needs you, and that's where you belong."

"It will be my pleasure. And, I agree, that **is** where I belong."

After we left, Aunt Marion said to Patty, "Should she be at Mark's side at the wake and funeral. She's not family."

"Aunt Marion, Sandy means more to him than anyone, including me. She definitely belongs at his side at the wake and the funeral. She might not be family now, but she will be."

Aunt Marion never raised the objection again. She knew that Patty, who was only twenty-two, was running the show. Patty told me about it later that night.

We dropped off Peggy at ten forty-five, and Mark brought me home around eleven. We sat and rocked on my front porch for another half hour. We talked and we cried and we hugged. I think we both knew then that we would be together forever, and the thought brought us peace in that time of sorrow. Yes, this was a terrible time, a devastating time, but it was nice to know that we had each other, and always would. We would get through this. We were passing through our *Dark Night of the Soul*, but we would be coming out of it, and out of it into Paradise.

Mom came out at eleven thirty and suggested we get some sleep. "You both will have a busy day tomorrow," she said.

"Mom, I'm not going to school this week. I'm going to stay with Mark."

"We can make up any school work on our own," added Mark. "Peggy will see us every afternoon, and she'll make sure we get what we need."

"I'm not worried about you two making up school work. And I agree, Sandy, that you should stay with Mark and skip school this week. I just assumed you would do that. I'll tell Mr. Wells (the principal) tomorrow morning."

Sometimes Mom surprises. But I guess she knew there was no way I was going to school under these circumstances. Also, she really did agree with me on this one.

"You're right, Mrs. Roberts, we will have a busy day tomorrow," said Mark. And to me, "I'll pick you up at eight."

He then gave me a kiss and headed home. We survived the first day, Monday.

Mark picked me up at eight Tuesday morning. We are both very punctual, so I knew he would be on time, and I was ready when he arrived. He told me that he and I would be preparing breakfast for ourselves, Patty, and Aunt Marion at nine – part of our kitchen duties -- and suggested that we stop at Dunkin' Donuts for a coffee to go over what we had to do and when we had to do it. As you know, we are both anal, and I agreed it was a great idea. We love to sit, drink coffee, and talk in Dunkin' Donuts.

Mark told me that Patty had made the arrangements with the funeral parlor and St. Michael's Church Monday afternoon. "The wake will be from five to eight on Thursday, and the family, and that includes you, will gather at the funeral parlor at nine on Friday. The Mass will be at ten."

His mother's other sister, Aunt Margie, who lives in Ohio, would be arriving by car that afternoon, Tuesday, along with her husband, Uncle Bill, and their two oldest daughters, Annie and Luisa, sixteen and fifteen. They had been visiting Uncle Bill's sister near Philadelphia, and would leave eastern Pennsylvania early Tuesday morning.

His mother's brother, Uncle Andrew, would be flying in from California Wednesday evening at nine with his wife, Aunt Millie. We would be chauffeuring them from the airport to the house and later to their hotel. Mark's father's family, all from the New York City area, would be driving up on Thursday for the wake or early Friday morning for the funeral.

I asked him about Aunt Marion. "She seems a little cold to me. Do you know why?"

"She's my godmother, and she just wants to make sure you're worthy."

I gave him a funny look, "Really?"

"I don't know," he answered laughing, "but I wouldn't doubt it. She's very protective. I'm her godson. But don't worry. I think you're worthy."

I punched him in the shoulder and said, "You better believe I'm worthy."

He laughed and kissed me. "The only thing I ever questioned is: am I worthy for you?"

"You are. I do have a problem though, Mark," I said.

"What?" he asked.

"I don't have a black dress, black dress shoes, or black underwear."

"We'll go shopping after breakfast," he said, "and get what you need."

We had been sharing everything since I officially became his girlfriend, but I was afraid this would be too much and told him so.

"Sandy, this may be presumptuous, but in the not too distant future, everything I have will be yours, and everything you have will be mine. Also nothing would give

176

me more pleasure than buying you a nice dress for the wake and funeral."

I kissed him. "Okay, we'll go to Kohl's after breakfast. You know I love you, don't you?"

"Yes, I do," he said, "and I love you."

We made scrambled eggs and ham steaks with rye toast and coffee. Aunt Marion seemed much friendlier to me over breakfast. She even gave me a kiss when we first arrived at the house. After we did the dishes, we headed over to Kohl's. I picked out a beautiful mid-calf length black dress, elegant but simple. When I came out of the dressing room, Mark just smiled and said, "Wow, you are beautiful."

"Thanks," I said.

Mrs. Mayhew, Peggy's mom, who works at Kohl's, spotted us and came over. She hugged Mark and told him how sorry she was. "Peggy told me she's meeting up with you two after school," said Mrs. Mayhew.

"Yes," Mark said. "I'll make sure she gets home safely."

"I know you will, Mark. I was asleep when she got home last night. I came down this morning and found her crying at the kitchen table. She said she really loved your parents."

"They loved her too," Mark said. "She's a great person."

"Yeah, she is, isn't she?" said Mrs. Mayhew. "And I think a lot of that has to do with you two. I am so glad you three are friends." She kissed Mark and me and said, "I have to get back to work."

We then went over to the shoe department. "Do you want me to get high heels?" I asked.

"I've never seen you in high heels. I've read they're not good for your back," he said.

"I never wear them, but I've been told they make your behind look alluring."

"I love your ass just the way it is," he said. "It doesn't need any enhancement to allure me."

"Don't be crude," I said. "Don't say 'ass' at least not in public. You can say anything you want when we're alone."

"Anything?"

"Anything, honey," I said. I realized it was the first time I had called him "honey."

"I'll remember that, honey," he said. We stood there staring at each other, and then my eyes filled up with tears.

"What's wrong, Sandy?" he asked.

"Nothing. I'm happy. I always cry when I'm happy, and I am very happy right now."

I then buried my face in his chest and hugged him as tightly as I could. He hugged me and rocked me back and forth. It didn't bother either of us that we were standing in the middle of Kohl's Shoe Department. I don't think I had ever loved Mark more than I did at that moment, up until that time at least.

My mother says I have a way of bringing any situation back down to earth. I looked up at Mark at that point and said, "Let's get me some shoes." He laughed and said, "Yeah, let's."

I picked out a nice pair of black dress shoes *without high heels*, and a pair of colorless stockings. Then we headed over to the underwear department. I held up a pair of black panties and asked, "How will I look in these?" "Great," he said. I added a black bra, and my shopping was complete. I held up the bra and panties and said, teasingly, "Someday you'll see me wearing these."

"I already have," He replied.

"When?" I asked, puzzled.

"I've seen you in a black bikini," Mark answered. "Playing volleyball. At the beach. Lots of times."

"It's not the same. Not the same at all."

"How are they different?" he asked.

"A bikini is for everyone to see. Panties and a bra are just for my lover to see, just for you to see. For you to take off. Different," I answered. *Getting horny, Mark?..I am...Not the time for that...Not the place for that...Well, I guess anytime is okay to get horny with your man...Just can't act on it all the time.*

"Then it will give me something to look forward to," he said.

"Yes, it will." I smiled and gave him a little peck on the cheek.

I took all the clothes back to Mark's house and hung them up in his closet. I planned to shower and change there on Thursday before the wake. Mark has his own bathroom.

Aunt Margie, Uncle Bill, and Mark's two younger cousins arrived at the house in mid-afternoon. After I was introduced, Aunt Margie gave me a big hug and kiss: a much warmer welcome than I'd received from her older sister, Marion. I hit it off immediately with the girls, especially Annie. Peggy arrived at four straight from school. Annie and Luisa loved her too. Uncle Bill told Mark that he had two beautiful friends.

"Uncle Bill," I said, "I think Sandy is the most beautiful young woman I have ever seen, but do you know what the boys at school call Peggy?"

"What?" he asked.

"The goddess."

"I can see why," he said.

Peggy blushed.

Patty insisted we all eat together ("We have so much food. All the neighbors brought over casseroles," she said), and Mark, Peggy, and I recruited Annie and Luisa to work with us in the kitchen. After dinner, Aunt Margie and Uncle Bill went to their hotel (Aunt Marion was staying in Mark's house), but the girls begged to stay with us. Mark promised to bring them to the hotel safely by ten o'clock, and Uncle Bill agreed to let them stay. After we did the dishes, the five of us teen-agers sat in the den and got acquainted. Annie and Luisa were the first teen-age members of Mark's family that I had met. Despite the occasion, we did a lot of laughing that evening. At nine forty-five, Mark, Peggy, and I brought the girls to the Holiday Inn where they were staying and delivered them safely to their parents. We promised to pick them up at eight the next morning to take them to a teen-agers only breakfast. Aunt Margie thought that was a great idea. Peggy had a free first period, and told us she would join us for breakfast.

We dropped Peggy off and arrived at my house at ten fifteen, and sat, for an hour, on my porch. I wrapped myself up in Mark's arms, and we talked. We talked about our future and made promises and commitments, generally putting into words things we had both thought, but never said (we had come close to committing to marriage after the Rumble at Joey's). I could have stayed wrapped up in his arms all night, the rest of my life, but Mom interrupted with a bedtime call at eleven thirty. *I can't wait until we sleep together, Mark Tuttle...Not euphemistically, really sleep together...I want to wrap myself in your arms and sleep...How wonderful that will be...How safe and secure...Like two little kids cuddling, smelling each other...I love the way you smell...You love the way I smell too, don't you?..We have the rest of our lives to enjoy those smells...I want to wake you up blowing my breath into your face...Licking you too...That would surprise you...Maybe nibble on your nose...Silly thoughts...But nice thoughts…We're going to have a good life, Mark Tuttle…We'll take care of each other.*

"I don't want to let you go, but I have to," I said. "See you in the morning. I will think about you all night."

"Me too," he said, and gave me a final kiss. Mom smiled watching us.

After Mark left, Mom asked me what I was going to wear to the wake and funeral.

"Mark and I went shopping this morning, and I got a nice black dress and black shoes." I didn't mention the black panties and bra. Maybe too much information for Mom.

"How did you pay for them?" she asked.

"Mark paid," I said. Before she could say anything, I added, "He insisted, Mom. We have been sharing everything ever since we started dating. It made him happy to buy it."

"Where is the dress?" asked Mom. "I'd like to see it."

"Hanging in Mark's closet. You'll see it at the wake. I think you'll love it."

"Are you going to stay at the wake the whole time?" she asked.

"Yes, I am going to be at Mark's side in the receiving line."

"That will send a certain message. Are you both okay with that?"

"Yes, Mom, we are. Very much so."

"And is it okay with Patty since you're not family?"

"She insisted on it. You're beginning to sound like Mark's Aunt Marion."

"Was she against it?" asked Mom.

"Patty told me that Aunt Marion raised the 'not family' point with her, but Patty told her I belonged there at Mark's side, and that was that. Aunt Marion's okay with it now.

181

You know, I think Patty and I are going to become very good friends, the sisters we each did not have."

"Give me a hug, sweetie," said Mom. "I really think it's where you belong too. Now give me a kiss and get to bed."

So we survived the second day, Tuesday.

Mark picked me up at seven thirty on Wednesday, and then we picked up Peggy before heading over to the Holiday Inn to get Annie and Luisa. We were going to take them to IHOP, but decided to eat at a local breakfast and lunch place where the prices were more reasonable. I really bonded with Annie that morning. As you know, our youngest daughter is Annie. We named her after her Ohio cousin, actually her first cousin once removed. Mark is the only person I know (except for me and Peggy, of course, since he taught us) who understands the cousin relationships: something about rungs on a ladder, each rung representing a generation. Everyone in the restaurant, Louie's Diner, knew me, Peggy, and Mark, and all offered their condolences. I think they were a little surprised that Peggy and I were with Mark on a school day, but no one said anything.

During breakfast, Annie became the first member of Mark's family to know we planned to get married. Uncle Andrew became the second, later that same day. I asked Annie if she would be in our wedding party. "I want someone from Mark's family represented," I told her. "Peggy doesn't know it yet, but she will be the maid of honor."

"I better be," said Peggy, who gave me a kiss.

"I would be honored," Annie said. "Have you planned a date?"

"Not definitely," I said, "but we are looking at the second Saturday in June next summer as a real possibility. We are both planning to go to college up in Cambridge, and we want to go up there as a married couple." We had talked about this, but this was the first time it came out into the open. "Don't tell Patty or your parents yet. We haven't announced anything." Looking at Mark, I asked, "Does that date seem good to you?"

"Yes," he said. "Very good."

"I turn eighteen next May, Annie, so June seems right to us," I said. "Mark will already be eighteen by then."

The four of us dropped Peggy off at CHS, and then went over to Mark's house.

Later Mark said to me, privately, "You mean I have to wait until next June to see you in your black panties and bra." We were already lovers, so I knew he was kidding.

"We'll see about that," I answered, "but you can look at me in my bikini and make believe."

We went over to the airport at eight that evening to get Uncle Andrew and Aunt Millie, whom he always called "Mildred." Uncle Andrew was very proper in his manner and his speech. He sat in front with Mark, and Peggy and I rode in the back with Aunt Millie. (We called her "Aunt Millie," not "Aunt Mildred.") Uncle Andrew could sense the special relationship between me and Mark, and asked, out of the blue, "Mark, is this young lady going to join our family in the near future?" We both said, simultaneously and immediately, "Yes."

"Have you set a date?" he asked.

"We're thinking of next June," I said.

"You must invite us to the wedding. You know that Mark is my godson, don't you?"

"No, I didn't, but you both will definitely be invited." Aunt Millie gave me a big hug, warm and loving. "Peggy's going to be my maid of honor and Annie will be in the wedding party."

I realized at this point just how far things had come since Monday. I always knew that Mark and I would be together permanently. But in three days, without actually planning it, we had made the final commitment and even had a wedding date. How did that happen? Who cares; we both were very satisfied with the outcome!

Uncle Andrew said, at around ten-thirty, that he and Mildred were ready to go to the Holiday Inn. Aunt Margie and Uncle Bill, tired, had left earlier. Mark would take Uncle Andrew and Aunt Millie and, upon his return, he, Peggy, and I would take Annie and Luisa to the hotel. We teen-agers wanted to spend as much time together as possible. Then, after dropping off Peggy, Mark would take me home where we planned to break the big news to Mom and Dad.

Uncle Andrew caused a little excitement before leaving, however.

"Patty, I think you're going to love your new sister-in-law," he said.

"What?" said Patty and Aunt Marion, simultaneously.

"Sandy's joining our family. Isn't that wonderful?"

"How do you know that?" asked Patty.

"Uncle Andrew knows all. Actually, I asked and they told me," he said. "You have to be direct to get any information in this family," he answered.

Patty looked at us. "Is this true?" she asked. I thought she might be upset or hurt finding out from Uncle Andrew and not from her brother and me directly.

"Yes," we both said. "We just decided last night. Actually we decided a while ago, but made the commitment last night," I said.

Instead of being upset, Patty lunged at me, hugged me, and screamed, "Congratulations. I always wanted you as my sister, ever since I first met you. I am so happy." Even

Aunt Marion gave me a big hug. We women had a good cry.

"I knew you two would get married when you were eight, and Mark shared his Breyer's vanilla bean ice cream with you. You had to be special for him to do that. Have you set a date?" asked Patty.

"Next June," I said. "We're going to tell my mother tonight." *Tell Mom tonight,* I thought. *I hope that goes well... I think it will...Mom and Dad love Mark.*

It did. Mom broke into tears and hugged us both in one embrace. She then called to my father who also gave us his blessing. He always loved Mark.

"Eighteen is so young, but you two are ready for it. I have no fears for the success of your marriage. Just promise me one thing," said Mom.

"Anything," we said.

"Graduate from college, both of you. As much as I want grandchildren, wait until after you graduate."

"You have our word," I said.

"Mark?" she said turning to him.

"You have my word, Mrs. Roberts."

So we survived the third day. Wednesday actually ended on a very high note.

We picked up Annie and Luisa again on Thursday morning and took them to Dunkin' Donuts for a pre-breakfast coffee. Peggy had an early class and couldn't join us. Luisa, who didn't like coffee, had a hot chocolate. We then went back to Mark's house where the four of us, Mark, Annie, Luisa, and I, prepared breakfast for all our guests and ourselves. Aunt Margie and Uncle Bill had brought Uncle Andrew and Aunt Millie to the house while we were at Dunkin' Donuts.

"Where's Peggy?" asked Uncle Bill.

"At school. She'll be at the wake tonight."

"Good," he said.

At three, Mark brought the cousins to the Holiday Inn, and I went back to Mark's room to shower and change for the wake. I made sure he was back before I made my entrance into the living room. Actually, I called him into his room and asked him to zipper me up. I knew that was exciting for him; it was also exciting for me. I then entered the living room where Patty and Aunt Marion were waiting to see "how I cleaned up." With my hair twirled up on top of my head, instead of in my usual ponytail, and with the new black dress and new shoes, I have to admit I looked good, even without any high-heel posterior enhancement. Mark, who had just seen me in his room, still said, "Wow! You are beautiful." I said, "Thanks, honey."

Patty said, "I agree you are beautiful, but something is missing. I think I have the perfect accessory." She then left the room and came back with a pearl necklace, absolutely stunning, which she asked Mark to put around my neck. God, it looked fantastic contrasted with the black dress.

"Sandy, that necklace was my Mom's," said Patty. "I know she would want you to have it. She wanted, and I want, that necklace to stay in the family, but after that little disclosure last night, I know it will. But there are no strings attached. If you and Mark don't get married, that necklace is still yours."

I teared up and said, "It's staying in the family, Patty. In fact I will give that to my firstborn girl on her wedding day as a gift from her grandmother and her aunt." We both cried and hugged at that promise.

Mark then went in to shower and change. He came out in a black suit with a red and blue striped tie and white dress shirt. We made a handsome couple.

Then something completely unexpected happened, something absolutely surprising. My eyes are filling with tears as I write this. Suddenly Mark was on one knee in front of me.

"What we decided last night was like a decision by committee, a committee of two," he began. "Now I want to do this right--- Sandy Roberts, will you marry me, will you be my partner for life?"

"Yes, Mark Tuttle, of course I will," and I hugged him, still kneeling, and cried, of course. When I broke the hug, and stood back, he hit me with another surprise, something also completely unexpected. He reached into his suit jacket pocket and brought out the most gorgeous, largest diamond ring I had ever seen. He slid it on to the ring finger of my left hand. Amazingly, it fit.

"This was my mother's," Mark said. "Patty asked me to join her in the living room last night when I got home. I thought she was going to have a serious talk with me about marriage at our age. But that wasn't it at all. She handed me this ring and said, 'Mom wanted this to go to your wife when the time came. The time has come. Give it to Sandy tomorrow.' "

I didn't know what to say. I kissed Mark and hugged Patty. Aunt Marion also came over and gave me a hug and a kiss. I guess she found me worthy, after all.

"I know this is a wake, but we are only burying their bodies," said Patty. "I'm sure they're looking down from Heaven and smiling, especially Dad. He told Mark he would be crazy not to marry you. And I agree, Sister."

Mark and I then went over to the Holiday Inn to pick up Uncle Andrew and Aunt Millie to take them to the funeral parlor. We dropped them off at the door, and then I went with Mark to park the car. Before we got out, I turned to Mark and said, "I know this is going to be very hard for you, but remember that I love you and am at your side. I will always be at your side."

His eyes were filled with tears. He turned to me and replied, "I love you so much, Sandy. I could not have gotten through this week without you. And I am so glad we are going to be together for life. I am so glad----" We hugged and then walked, holding hands, into the funeral parlor.

Seeing the two coffins side by side was sobering. We knelt before them and I put my arm around his waist. We both cried and said a prayer and then took our place on the receiving line just behind Patty and in front of Aunt Marion, Uncle Bill, and Aunt Margie. His father's two surviving brothers, and their wives, stood on the line after Uncle Andrew and Aunt Millie. Mark introduced me to them as his "fiancé." That took me by surprise for a second, but then I realized that was what I now was. I liked it.

When Mom and Dad came into the viewing room, Dad took one look at me and said, "My God, she is beautiful."

"She's smart too," said Mom.

"Don't be sarcastic," he said, "and look at the jewelry she's wearing."

"Around her neck or on her left hand?" asked Mom, who never misses a thing.

"What?" said Dad.

"Look at the ring finger on her left hand," said Mom.

"Oh my God," he exclaimed.

"I bet it was Mark's mother's ring, and the pearl necklace too," said Mom.

A lot of people at the wake, teachers, students, Mark's New York family, were surprised to see me with him on the receiving line. The few who noticed the ring congratulated us; I didn't show it off at the wake. But Mark did introduce me all night as his fiancé.

Peggy came in with her mother. Peggy was wearing a long blue dress. It was only the second time I had seen Peggy in a dress; the first time was at our junior prom. Believe me, Peggy is the most beautiful woman I have ever seen. The CHS boys are right; she is a goddess. Even at a wake, all the men sneaked glances at her. When she got to us, she hugged Mark and cried. I joined the hug, and the three of us stayed like than for an eternity.

"I loved your parents, Mark. They were so good to us," she said. "I am so sorry."

When we finally broke apart, Mrs. Mayhew, a beautiful older version of her daughter, gave Mark another Mayhew hug.

"Peggy, why don't you go with us to Chelo's when we finish here?" said Mark. "Mrs. Mayhew, we will make sure she gets home safely."

"I know you will, Mark. I know how safe my baby is with you."

"Mom!" said Peggy

"You will always be my baby, honey."

For the rest of the evening, about an hour, Peggy stood behind us on the receiving line.

After the wake, the whole family went to Chelo's where I was able to get better acquainted with the Tuttle side of the family. None of them even knew Mark had a girlfriend, so I was a major surprise. As was to be expected, Mark, Peggy, and I had Reubens. What else would we have at Chelo's? And we shared our onion rings and steak fries.

So we survived the fourth day, Thursday, as well.

The day of the funeral was almost anticlimactic. Mark, with me on his arm, followed Patty and the two coffins up the aisle. I did one of the readings, Paul's poem to love from First Corinthians. Annie, at Mark's request, gave a short talk after Communion. She said that Mark's father was the only adult she had ever known who treated children as persons. A few of the New York Tuttles stood and told stories about Mark's parents from their younger days.

At the cemetery, we gathered around the plot waiting for the priest to say the final prayers from the Catholic burial rite. I stood at Mark's side. Suddenly a hand was placed on Mark's shoulder and on mine. Peggy had come up to stand with us. Mark looked at her, kissed her on the cheek, and said, "Thank you, Peggy, for everything."

Peggy's response was a line I have never forgotten. She said, "You're welcome, my Captain." *Mark Tuttle, Captain of the Barge of Curiosity.* Mark smiled for the first time that day. He then looked at Peggy and squeezed my hand. "I love you two," he said. A feeling of warmth filled my whole being.

"What did your father call us, Mark?" Peggy asked.

"The three musketeers," he said.

"One for all, and all for one," she said. The three of us were crying.

After the bodies were lowered into the ground, it was time for Patty and Mark to throw a handful of dirt onto the coffins. Patty went first.

Then Mark turned to me and said, "Come with me." I didn't object. I knew I belonged at his side. He then turned to Peggy, and said, "You too, Peggy. It's time for the three musketeers to make a final tribute to my mom and dad."

We stood side by side and each threw a handful of dirt on the Tuttles.

"I promise I will be the best daughter-in-law for you," I said. "And I will give you grandchildren to carry on your name."

We buried Mark's parents that day, but they still live on in our memories and in our children.

Mark told us later at the collation that his father would have been so proud of his son, paying his final tribute surrounded by two extremely beautiful women, both of whom Mr. Tuttle loved.

I walked back up that aisle in nine months, in white instead of black, and to Mark not with him. All the way up the aisle I looked at him, and he looked at me. It was the beginning of phase two of our life together, with Maddie, Bobby, Jimmy, and Annie as the results. As Maddie said, "Only good things have happened since they got together."

Despite the many differences between the two walks up the aisle, one thing was the same. I was wearing my pearl necklace both times. And someday, Maddie will wear it as she goes up the aisle to her man. And that man had better be special if Mark is going to give him his Maddie.

Chapter Eleven
Scratching an Itch

There are only two people I have ever loved, Mark Tuttle and Peggy Mayhew. The love I have for them is the same, but it is greater in Mark's case. Technically, the difference is in degree, not in kind. If I had to choose, and I guess I did, I would choose Mark. But that does not mean that I can't, or don't, love Peggy. I do. Every time I see her, I want to kiss her. I know she feels the same urge.

Of course I love my parents and my children. I would protect my children like a lioness protects her cubs. With Mark and Peggy, however, I am talking about a different **kind** of love, a visceral, passionate, sensual, sexual love. A very different kind of love than the maternal love I have for Maddie, Bobby, Jimmy, and Annie. Which love is stronger? It is easy to say maternal love is stronger, but I hope I never have to choose between Mark and any of my children. That would be an almost impossible choice. Maternal love would win, but I would be destroyed in the choosing. I love Mark that much. Can I say I love the children, even Maddie, more than I love Mark? No. So how could I choose without destroying myself? Knowing Mark, I will never have to make that choice.

I have loved Peggy since I was six years old. It started as friendship, but it has grown to much more than that.

There has always been a physical attraction drawing me and Peggy toward each other. When we talk or when we're just sitting or standing together, we constantly touch each other -- on the arm, on the shoulder, on the leg. We love being together. We have each other's back. If Peggy is in a fight, I'm in a fight. If I'm in a fight, Peggy is in a fight. She always says she wants to kiss me. I laugh about it; I kid about it; but I also think about it – a lot!

I have always had the same kind of attraction to Mark, a little stronger, maybe a lot stronger, but the same, also since I was six. I never looked at Mark and Peggy as competitors for my affections. I always knew, and I have told you this, that I would have a lifelong love affair with Mark Tuttle, would bear his children, would be his wife, his best friend, his lover, his partner, would never let anything, or anyone, including Peggy, come between us, but I also knew that I would have a lifelong relationship with Peggy, a warm, loving relationship. I did not see any incongruity in that. I still don't. Mark is my husband, my lover; Peggy is my friend. We are friends who love each other.

It amazed me that Mark and Peggy never had a mutual attraction to each other, the most attractive guy and girl in St. Michael's School and Coventry High School, and they were always together, but never alone. I was always with them. Peggy did tell me that she had on-again, off-again crushes on Mark culminating in a giant crush during our sophomore year. But she loved me so much that she never took any action on those impulses. She did not want to ruin what we had. They did kiss once, the day in sophomore year that Mark defended Peggy, the day that propelled him into Ben Kravey's studio. But that was a "thank you" kiss, not a passionate one.

Mark admitted to me that he thought Peggy was beautiful, but "not as beautiful as you." The only other person who thought I was prettier than Peggy was Peggy. I truly believe Mark never was tempted to get involved with Peggy. So since he didn't want involvement, and she abstained from it, the relationship between Mark and Peggy never developed.

A lot happened between the end of our junior year and graduation the following May. I have added a chapter later, Senior Moments, to describe some of those happenings. This chapter is about a series of events involving me and Peggy, events that brought our relationship to a new level.

The Rumble at Joey's brought Billy Smith into our circle of friends. He and his wife, Maureen, are still our good friends, and their children and ours, and Peggy's, are the best of friends. On the day of the Rumble, Mark and I visited Peggy who was home sick. Peggy and I had our longest kiss that day, not a passionate kiss, but a long, lingering, loving kiss. Back during the summer after seventh grade, on the day after my and Peggy's fight, when we made up in the pool shed, we had our most passionate kiss. We touched and held our tongues together. Make-up sex for two thirteen year olds. But the kiss in her bedroom that day was much more meaningful. It was a definite "I love you" kiss.

After the seventh grade pool fight, which Mark broke up, we promised never to fight **against** each other again – only to fight **for** each other. We have kept that promise. I don't know who would win if Peggy and I fought. It would be one hell of a fight; men would pay money to see that fight.

After leaving Peggy's house the day of my and Peggy's long, lingering, loving kiss, Mark told me that he had no problem with me and Peggy kissing. It did not make him jealous. He thought the love we (Peggy and I) had for each other was a thing to be cherished. Mark really surprises me at times. He never saw Peggy as a rival. She wasn't. With Mark's blessing, I began to entertain frequent thoughts about kissing Peggy, sensually kissing Peggy.

I always felt that Peggy was beautiful: tall, athletic, sexy, great breasts, great ass, great legs, and she emanated excitement. She felt the same about me.

One fall day during that senior year, Peggy, Marcia Snow, Maria Coppocino, Margie Baylor, and I were sitting at a picnic table behind the gym. I don't know how the conversation got around to pubic hair, but it did. Girls discuss sex as much as boys do, only we are more discrete. The question boiled down to: did you, or are you going to, shave off your pubic hair? The three "M" girls, Marcia, Maria, and Margie, all said they had already shaved off their bushes. They were as smooth as babies' bums down there. Peggy laughed and said, "I love my bush. So do the boys."

"Boys, plural?" I said.

"Yes, boys plural," she said. "Billy, Fred. Girls too."

The four of us looked at her with open mouths.

"Don't tell me you've never done it with a girl," she said. She addressed the question to all of us, but she was looking directly at me. "You don't have to be a lesbian to enjoy sex from a different angle once in a while."

"I've never even done it with a boy," said Margie, blushing.

Marcia and Maria remained silent on the issue. I believe the subject was getting a little too intrusive for them.

Peggy turned to me. "You never answered the question, Sandy. Do you still have your bush?" We change in private cubicles and shower in separate stalls in the girls' locker room, so Peggy had never seen me nude. I likewise had never seen her nude. I had never thought about that before. *I bet she would be awesome naked.* I actually blushed. The others thought I was blushing because of Peggy's question. I wasn't.

"Don't be shy, Sandy. Tell us," Peggy said.

"I still have my bush," I said. "I trim it, but I will never shave it off."

"Why not?" said Peggy.

"I like it," I said. "So does Mark."

"Mark has seen your bush?" Margie exclaimed. *The innocence of juniors.*

Just then, before the discussion could develop further, Mark arrived. He, Peggy, and I usually drive together to and from school every day. Today it was going to be just me and Mark. Peggy was meeting Fred Williams.

"What are you girls giggling about?" he asked.

"We were just talking about pubic hair," said Peggy. "Female pubic hair."

"Female pubic hair?" said Mark. "Interesting subject. Can I join in?"

"No," I said. "Let's go."

"Sandy said she'll never shave her bush because you like it," said Peggy. I shot her a dirty look.

"There's no part of Sandy I don't like," Mark said.

We then left. Mark asked me for details of our discussion. I think he was a little excited. Boys get excited so easily. I told him Peggy had brought it up. "She asked who shaved their hair and who didn't."

"And?"

"Margie, Marcia, and Maria are smooth as babies. Peggy and I still have our hair."

"I prefer hair," he said.

"I know," I said. "Mine is the only bush you've ever seen, right?"

"Yes."

"Good. If you had said 'No' we'd be fighting now."

He smiled. "Have you ever seen Peggy naked?" he asked.

"No," I said. "We have separate cubicles and shower stalls in the girls' locker room."

"God, I bet she would look great naked," Mark said. I punched him, but I agreed. "That's something you'll never see."

"Just an observation. I am very satisfied with what I have."

"You better be." I'm very satisfied with what I have too, but I was curious. Thinking about Peggy naked was making me horny, surprisingly horny for Mark, not for Peggy.

After the Tuttles died, we had an available location for sex, Mark's house. His sister had her own apartment in North Providence, near the school where she taught. Mark and Patty had agreed that Mark would stay in the house until he left for MIT; then they would sell it. His father had life insurance which paid off the mortgage on the house, all debts, all funeral costs, and left Mark and Patty with close to $650,000 each. Mark invested $600,000 with his father's investment advisor, Denny McIntyre, and kept $50,000 with Citizens Bank to cover living expenses until the stipends from MIT and Harvard kicked in for us. We got engaged the night of the Tuttles' wake and set a date in June, after our graduation, for the wedding. Now that we were engaged, and had a place that was like a home for us, we became regular sex partners. I still hated the fact that we did not sleep together. I looked forward to the day Mark did not have to take me home at night.

The talk about pubic hair with the girls, especially with Peggy, had made me horny. I really wanted to see Peggy nude. I didn't want to make love with her; I wanted to make love with Mark. I wanted Mark to play with my pubic hair and my pussy, eat me, fuck me. But I was curious. As soon as we entered the house, I was all over Mark. We were kissing tongue to tongue as we moved locked together into the bedroom. He pulled off my panties and caressed my bush and my wetness.

"I am so glad you don't shave," he said, twirling my little hairs in his fingers.

I came twice and then pulled him into me. We climaxed together and then embraced each other for twenty minutes while we came back to Earth. *God, that was good.* I did not think of Peggy while Mark and I were having sex, but I did think of her when we finished. *This is just an innocent fantasy,* I tried to convince myself. *I just want to see if I compare…I have no feelings for Peggy…I just think she's sexually exciting…Sexually exciting?..Whoa, girl, this is getting dangerous…And don't kid yourself – you definitely have feelings for Peggy.*

A few weeks later during basketball season, Peggy and I were the last two in locker room after practice. She was in one of the shower stalls. I could hear the water running. My desire to see her nude was becoming an obsession. *What the hell. It's just a look.* I knocked on her stall door. I was wrapped in a towel.

"Sandy?" she asked. I was the only other person in the locker room.

"Yes. Can I borrow some soap?" I asked.

"Sure. Come on in," she said, unlocking the door.

I entered, and there she was, completely naked. Venus at CHS. I was glad that I did not feel arousal. Just admiration and envy. My breasts are nice; Peggy's are sensational.

"I see why the boys call you 'the goddess,' " I said.

"There are two goddesses in this shower stall, Sandy, not one," she said.

"Here's some soap," she added, "but you have to pay for it."

"How?" I asked innocently.

"With a kiss. And hang your towel on the door so it doesn't get wet. I want to see you now that you're seeing me. That's only fair."

I should have left her stall at that point, but I didn't. I hung my towel on the door over her towel and moved under the shower. I knew we would be in a lot of trouble if someone came into the locker room. How could I explain Peggy and me in the same shower stall naked? "I was just borrowing some soap." *Yeah, sure.*

"I see why Mark likes your bush," she said. "I like it too. Creative. You've made an inverted triangle. How cute. Points to the house of treasures. Signpost for Mark. I let mine grow wild. I just snip off the outer edges so it doesn't escape my bikini bottoms."

"Can I have the soap?" I asked. "We should not be like this together."

"Here's the soap. Can I have my kiss?"

"We shouldn't, Peggy."

"Why not. No one will know." She put her face up against mine and kissed me on the lips. She slid her tongue into my mouth. That scared the shit out of me because I liked it. Her mouth tasted so good. We explored tongues; she massaged my ass while we kissed. I wanted to do the same to her, but I didn't. Our bumps, not bumps anymore, were touching. When I realized I was aroused, I grabbed my towel and left her stall. I left the soap. I never wanted that damn soap.

Later after we had dressed, she approached me and said, "Don't worry, Sandy. A kiss doesn't make you a lez."

"I know," I said.

"But it was nice, wasn't it?" she said. "Any time you want to kiss me, you can." She patted me on the ass, gave it a little squeeze, and, smiling, started out of the room. Then she turned back and said, "You're not mad at me, are you?"

"No," I said, "No, no, no, no, NO! How can I be mad at my best girlfriend? I love you, Peggy Mayhew, but I'm just a little scared because I don't understand what happened."

She came back, kissed me gently on top of my head and said, "I'll see you tomorrow. I'm meeting Fred. I love you too. More than you can know."

I do know, Peggy Mayhew...I definitely do know...I love you the same.

I sat and tried to calm myself before leaving the lockers. I was meeting Mark near the parking lot, and I was shaking. *I don't have feelings for girls...I don't have feelings for girls...I love sex with Mark...I don't want to have sex with Peggy...But that fucking kiss was nice...Shit! Shit! Shit!..Damn Peggy...God, she did look great naked...And what a wild bush...I didn't see her vagina...Don't go there...Stop!*

After five minutes of attempted self-calming, I went out to Mark. I gave him a big kiss. It was better than my kiss with Peggy. Much better. I was not just telling myself that. *I love Mark much more than I love Peggy...She is fucking exciting though.*

"Shall we go out for Chinese tonight?" he asked.

"Yes, but not until we make love. I am so horny right now."

The chicken *chow mein* tasted so satisfying after the sex.

I now had a new obsession: seeing Peggy's vagina. I had read that they differ from woman to woman. Some are pink, like mine, others darker. And each one has a distinctive smell. *What does Peggy's look like?..What does it smell like?..What does it taste like?..Am I really thinking about smelling and tasting Peggy's pussy?..No...Yes...Shit! Shit! Shit!*

I tried to avoid being alone with Peggy. I was feeling contrasting pulls, away from Peggy, toward her vagina. I succeeded for a few days, but then, again after practice, we were the last two in the locker room. I was sitting on one of the common benches putting on my sneakers when Peggy came up to me.

"Have you been avoiding me?"

"No. Well, maybe a little."

"Why? The kiss?"

"Yes. Ever since that day we were talking about pubic hair, I wanted to see you naked. Curiosity more than sex. I didn't need soap that day. That was a ruse."

"Ruse? Good word. I forget you're the smartest girl in school, as well as the most athletic. And the sexiest. And the prettiest. I figured you didn't need the soap."

"When I saw you naked, I was impressed. Peggy, you really are a goddess. But I was not aroused. I was in awe, but not aroused. But when our tongues touched, I liked it. I felt something sexual. I became aroused. That scared me. I love sex with Mark. I don't want to ever do anything that will screw that up. That's why I got out of that stall fast."

Peggy laughed. "Sandy, I am not a lesbian. I love sex with boys. But I appreciate the beauty of the female body. I think I wanted to see you naked as much as you wanted to see me naked. I should have left it at that, but, seeing you, I wanted more. I **was** aroused. Thus the kiss. It **was** nice, wasn't it?"

"Yes." *God, I want to see your vagina...Not just see it...Taste it...Smell it...Lick it...Play with it...Play with those wild pubic hairs.*

"That doesn't make us lesbians. Just friends who kissed. You know Gina and Betsy are lesbians---"

"Yes, I figured that," I said.

"When I want to ride that pony, I get together with one or both of them."

"Both?"

"Yeah, it's pretty exciting. Am I getting you hot?"

"A little," I said.

"Want to meet me somewhere? My house? My Mom's not home." Peggy and her Mom live alone.

"No," I said. *Yes,* I thought. *What the fuck!* I appended.

"Okay, sorry. Go fuck Mark, and thank me if it's great."

Unbelievably I kissed her before leaving the locker room. No tongues. Okay, we did touch tips, but not for long. And, God, did I ever fuck Mark that afternoon. Mark should thank Peggy.

Now, not only did I have a mental picture of a naked Peggy running through my thoughts with her wild, brown bush, but I also had naked Gina and Betsy in there with her. I had to imagine what they looked like nude. *What did they do, three of them together?* I gave Gina a wild, black bush. She's Italian after all. I shaved Betsy.

Mark had to stay late one Monday for a Student Council meeting. Neither the boys' nor the girls' basketball teams practiced on Mondays. I told him I would pick him up after the meeting. I asked Peggy if she wanted to have a coffee after school. We drove over to Dunkin' Donuts in Mark's car. I felt like a traitor. We took a table in the back corner; the nearby tables were not in use.

"You want to take me up on my offer?" she asked.

"No, not yet," I said.

"Not **yet**. That sounds encouraging," Peggy said.

"Let's talk about it," I said.

"Gladly," said Peggy.

"It's my curiosity again. I was obsessed to see you naked. I did. That should have been enough for me---"

"But it wasn't?"

"No. Now I want to see your vagina, maybe more than just see it. I keep picturing you together with Gina and Betsy. I love sex with Mark. I love Mark, period. I am absolutely satisfied with Mark. I know he's satisfied with me. Gina and Betsy can't fuck you unless they use some device. Why bother with a device when you have Fred?"

"You're missing something, girl," she said.

"What?"

"Actually two things. Girls are softer than boys, more tender, have more feelings. It's great cuddling and playing with Fred, but he becomes impatient. He's a lot better than Billy was, but still---

"And he doesn't have breasts. Do you know how nice it is, and arousing, to suck on and play with a girl's breasts?

"Girls smell different too. There's a wild, jungle smell that boys don't have. It turns me on, Sandy. Does Mark ever tell you he loves the way you smell?"

"All the time," I said.

"It's that woman smell. Drives men, and me, crazy. Gina and Betsy smell different, but both are exciting. Wouldn't you like to smell me, especially if I'm aroused? I'm actually a little aroused now. I'm getting wet. I would love to smell you. Want to go into the ladies room?"

I just stared at her. *Is she serious? At Dunkin' Donuts?*

"Just kidding." *It's hard to believe, but I was tempted to say, "Yes"...I'm wet too.*

203

This was the discussion I wanted, but I was getting nervous. I took a large sip from my cup and then asked, "And what's the other reason?"

"Does Mark eat you?"

Where is this going? "Yes," I said.

"I know you like it, but does he like it?"

"Yes, a lot."

"You'll never get a chance to do that."

"Do what?"

"Duh. Eat pussy. Fred is okay, but I would bet a million dollars that Mark is a better, more sensitive lover. Sex with Mark is probably ecstatic – like that word, huh? And I know you two love each other. He makes you come with his tongue, doesn't he? Am I right?"

"Yes, on all counts. Mark is a great lover. I come, multiple times, every time we make love. Sometimes we cuddle and kiss for a half hour before we actually begin the sex. And we curl up together, arms and legs entwined, kissing and smelling each other for a long time after sex. And, yes, he does love the way I smell. He says I smell different before and after sex, and he loves both smells. He says my smell before says, 'Fuck me,' and after says, 'Protect me.'

"I would love to smell you sometime," Peggy said. "Wouldn't you like to smell me?"

"We'll see," I said, laughing. "And even if Mark and I didn't have sex, we are still best friends. I would never want to jeopardize that.He has been my protector ever since I was eight years old. When he was eight, eight!, he beat the shit out of a thirty-five year old pervert to save me."

"Back at St. Michael's, right? I remember that."

"Yes. So, Peggy, as tempting as your offer is, I don't want to screw up what I have with Mark. I think you'll have to remain a pleasant daydream with a mystery vagina. And my best girlfriend. I don't want that to change."

" '*A pleasant daydream with a mystery vagina.*' Wow! If I had a car, I'd get that as a bumper sticker. Don't worry. We'll always be friends. I love you. But remember, Sandy, the offer is still on the table. If you want to taste and smell pussy, I'm available. No strings. I don't want a lesbian relationship. I'm not gay. Bi? Maybe. I know it's you and Mark. I envy you that relationship, as I think you know. This would just be a little diversion. I think it's going to be hanging out there until we satisfy our curiosities. A ride on the Barge of Curiosity – that's all it will be. Then we can put it to bed."

I laughed at her phrasing. *Put it to bed.*

"Thanks, Peggy. Can I drop you off at your house before I go back to school to get Mark?"

"Yes, thanks. What time do you have to pick up Mark?"

"Six," I answered.

"It's only four-thirty now," Peggy said. "A little sexual exploration on the barge would be a nice way to pass the time." She had her left hand on my thigh as I drove her home. It felt nice.

When I dropped her off, she stuck her head through the window and continued the sales pitch, "This might be your only chance to explore unimaginable wonders. No strings."

"No, thanks, Peggy. Still friends?"

"Friends," she said. "Always." She leaned in and we kissed.

I returned to Dunkin' Donuts and ordered a coffee. *She's right...This will be hanging out there until we take care of it...What the fuck, it will only be one time.* I left my coffee untouched and drove back to Peggy's house.

"I thought you'd be back," she said, opening the door.

"You're right. This will be hanging over us, creating tension, 'until we put it to bed,' to quote Peggy Mayhew."

"I agree. Sit down," she said motioning to the couch. "Want a Coke?"

"Yes, I'd love one." God, I was nervous.

She brought out two cans and sat next to me.

"How do we get started?" I asked.

"We're not lovers, not going to be lovers---"

"In a sense," I interrupted, "we are lovers. We do love each other, don't we?"

"Yes. But, even if I would like it, we are not ever going to be lovers like you and Mark, are we?"

"No, but there is a physical attraction, isn't there?" I asked. "I have dreamed about kissing you, passionately, at night in bed."

"Just kissing me?" she asked.

I blushed, but said nothing.

"How do we start now? Do we just kiss?" I asked.

"I have an idea," Peggy said. "After that day in the pool, the day of the infamous fight, I dreamed about wrestling with you. It turns me on, just thinking about it---"

"So you want to wrestle?" I asked. The thought of wrestling with Peggy was turning me on too. *Will we wrestle nude?..Mark would love to see that...God, I am getting horny...I am glad I came back here...It will just be this one time...I am finally going to see your vagina, Peggy Mayhew...This won't hurt our friendship...I won't let it.*

"Let's move the coffee table and those two chairs," said Peggy. "We can wrestle right here in the living room. Carpet is thick and soft."

We moved the table and chairs to the side of the room.

"Should we take off our shoes?" I asked.

"Take off everything but your panties," she said. We both did. God, did she have a nice body. *She is probably thinking the same of me...I hope so...We're both wearing white panties... There is not a man alive who wouldn't pay big bucks to see this...I would pay to see it!..Your panties are coming off, Miss Mayhew.*

"Start on our knees," Peggy instructed.

We began to fight. As I expected, we were an equal match. She is a little taller and, possibly, a little stronger, but I'm quicker, and Mark has shown me many moves over the years, some that he hadn't shown Peggy. Peggy and I are both competitive. That almost resulted in a real fight. Almost, not quite. We did not break our promise. *A promise made is a debt unpaid.* No punches, no hair pulling, but we were really fighting. She got on top of me, but I was able to roll her off. We were stretched out on our sides facing each other, our arms and legs twisted together, our faces nose to nose. I opened my mouth to get some air. Peggy inserted her tongue into my open mouth. I willingly received it. That stopped the fight. Our tongues began playing with each other, as our hands began exploring each other's bodies. We were both getting hot. I expelled my breath into her mouth. She did the same to me. Her mouth tasted good. Earthy. Different than Mark's which tasted like chocolate candy. Thinking of Mark made me feel a little uneasy. But I couldn't stop now even if I wanted to, and I didn't want to. *Mark is my partner, my lover, always will be...This experiment with Peggy is just a dalliance...A one-time thing...It's just a way to clear the air...A ride on the Barge of Curiosity.*

"Let's go to the bedroom," Peggy uttered between kisses.

"Do you want to take showers?" I asked.

"No," she said. "Maybe after, but not before. I want to taste you, and I want you to taste me."

Peggy flopped onto the bed on her back. "Slide off my panties and enjoy my vagina," she said. "I am certainly going to enjoy you enjoying it."

She raised her ass, and I slid the panties down and off. *Holy shit!..She is awesome...I can't believe Sandy Roberts and Peggy Mayhew are going to have sex...We do have a special friendship...* "I can't believe how sexy you are." *I want to taste you...I want to smell you.*

"So you like what you see?"

"Yes," I said. The mystery was gone. The curiosity was satisfied. Light brown, almost tan, in color, beautiful to behold. I licked; I kissed; I sucked; I smelled. Her smell was different than my smell, experienced via Mark's mouth. I could see why Mark loved to eat my pussy. This was certainly exciting.

"Swing around so I can eat you too," Peggy said. I laid next to her on the bed and started to take off my panties.

"Let me do that," she said.

I let her. Then I swung around, got on top, and offered her my vagina while I resumed what I had been enjoying.

Girl-girl sixty-nine. We came together. Then I swung back around, and we kissed, and kissed, and kissed. "Oh my God, Peggy. Oh my God!" Then I blew a stream of air into her face.

"I guess you liked it," she said. "I did too. I have wanted to do this for a long time, Sandy Roberts." *Me too...But this is the only time...I really mean that...Just Mark from now on.*

We showered together. Then we sat in the living room to finish our Cokes. We had both put our panties back on.

"Well, are you satisfied?" Peggy asked.

"Yes, it's not hanging out there anymore," I said. "But I think this was a one-time shot for me."

"Wasn't I worth a repeat performance?"

"Most definitely," I said. "But it's not my thing. Mark is my thing. I just let my curiosity get the better of me. When I want to taste pussy in the future, I'll suck my taste and smell out of Mark's mouth after he eats me. You have given me a great memory, however."

" 'Suck your smell and taste out of Mark's mouth' – I like that. You've given me a great memory too. I still have Gina and Betsy, and Fred. Fred! Nice as he is, I don't think it's going anywhere. Mark on the other hand, if you ever want to discard him, send him my way."

"Never going to happen," I said.

"Yeah, I know. You and me, we were just scratching an itch, but if you ever feel itchy again, I'm here."

"Thanks. Our secret?"

"Absolutely."

Peggy and I became deeper friends after that afternoon. Our "event" removed the sexual tension that had been building. When we are together, we still touch each other, touches with a little sexual undertone, holding hands while we talk, a hand on the other's arm, an arm around the other's shoulder or waist when we're standing side by side, legs touching. Every so often I do think of that afternoon. It was memorable. There sure was nothing hanging in the air after we scratched that itch. I decided to limit my lovemaking to Mark. He does satisfy me. But that physical attraction for Peggy, and only Peggy among the world's women, never dissipated. As you will see.

I returned to Dunkin' Donuts and purchased two coffees from the take-out window. When I picked up Mark, I handed him a hot coffee. I wanted him right then, right there. But that would have caused quite a stir in the CHS parking lot.

"Thanks," he said. He then smiled at me. "Sandy, I am so horny." *He always comes through for me, doesn't he?..Could he smell my desire?*

"Me too," I said. "Let's go home." I never referred to it as "Mark's house"; it was "home" or "our house" now.

"Chinese after?" he asked.

"Of course."

"Let's call Peggy and ask her and Fred to join us?"

"Let's," I said.

They did, and we went to the Chow Fun. Where else?

That afternoon with Peggy Mayhew was my one flirtation with lesbianism, or rather with girl on girl sex. I didn't tell Mark about it until after we were married. He didn't get mad at me. He never gets mad at me. I think it excited him. We made love again after I told him.

Chapter Twelve
Senior Moments

I have had some memorable years in my life, both before and after my senior year in high school.

When I was eight years old, a 35-year-old pervert tried to grab me and force me into his car. Mark Tuttle, also eight, beat the pervert senseless with a baseball bat. If Mark had not been there that day, there would not be any Sandy and Mark history to relate.

The year I was twenty-two, Mark saved my life again, saved me and Maddie, inside my womb at the time. I'll tell you about that later. Mark has been, is, and always will be there for me. And for Maddie.

Another memorable year was the year I was twenty-three. That was the year Maddie was born. Maddie, my *primogenita.* Also twenty-four (Bobby), twenty-six, (Jimmy) and twenty-seven (Annie), my precious little Annie. But you seem to remember your first birth in a special way.

When I was twenty-nine I published my first of many *Alexandra the Mouse* books, children's books inspired by Maddie that have made me personally famous.

But if I had to pick one year of my life to call the most memorable, it will have to be my senior year in high school. It produced so many "senior moments."

The Deaths:

It was September of that year, just after classes at CHS had begun, that Mark was called out of our Advanced Placement Calculus class. I had no idea why. Later I found out that his parents, whom I always thought would be my in-laws, had been killed in a nightmarish automobile accident. I went over to his house after school, and stayed at his side all week, including during the wake and at the funeral. Strange as it may sound, we got engaged that tragic week, on the day of the wake. He gave me his mother's pearl necklace and diamond ring, with his sister Patty's blessing. We set the following June for the wedding.

Mark and Patty had each inherited close to $650,000, plus half the value of the house, mostly from life insurance. His father's agent was a big believer in term life insurance. Mark explained all this to me a few days after the funeral. He promised me that, the Monday after our wedding, his share would become legally our joint property. It did. Mark and I always share things. We had to wait until after the wedding for tax reasons.

We made love before the Tuttles died, but infrequently. Mark never wanted to have sex with me in any place or at any time that could cause me embarrassment if we were discovered. Sex in the back seat of a car was never an option. Patty was no longer living at home when the Tuttles passed away; she had an apartment in North Providence near where she taught. Now with Mark living alone, we had a place to have sex whenever we wanted. We took advantage of that. Almost daily. At first we used condoms; then I asked my doctor for a prescription for birth control pills. We had made the assumed commitment actual with our engagement. I never spent the night at Mark's, but I did keep clothes and toiletries there. It was wonderful, but I could not wait until we lived together, slept together. I hated it when he dropped me off at my house at night after we had made love. I wanted to bury myself in his arms and legs for sleep. He hated it too. We counted down the days until June. I had to sleep in my bed all alone. At least Mark had my smell, from the lovemaking, in his bed when he went to sleep.

The "Event":

This is a condensed retelling of the incident I revealed in *Scratching an Itch*. At first I was going to leave it out of this chapter, but I find even the retelling so arousing that I left it in. It only happened once, but it has happened innumerable times in my imagination.

Mark, Peggy Mayhew, and I were always together, classmates since first grade. I discovered in first grade that I loved both of them. I loved them in the same way, but I did love Mark more. Peggy and I were teammates on CHS's basketball and softball state championship teams. On and off during grade school, and deeply during our sophomore year, Peggy had a crush on Mark. But Peggy was, and is, my good friend, and never made any attempts to woo Mark away from me. *Thanks, Peggy.* Peggy is gorgeous, but I don't think she would have made any headway. Mark fell in love with me when he was six, and he has never, not for a minute, fallen out of love with me. The same is true for me, even when I was scratching that itch.

What itch? Five of us girls including Peggy were talking about pubic hair one day, the big question being "Have you shaved off your public hair?" It turned out that, of the five, only Peggy and I still had our bushes. The stalls and changing areas in the girls' locker room at CHS are private. I realized that I had never seen Peggy nude, and also realized that I wanted to. It became an obsession. Not sexual, or at least I pretended the obsession was not sexual; just curiosity. One day, after basketball practice, Peggy and I were the last two in the locker room. She was in one of the shower stalls. I, wearing a towel, knocked on her door and asked to borrow some soap. She opened the door and invited me in. *God, she was awesome in her natural state, a Venus.* I was awestruck, but thankfully, not aroused. She told me to take off my towel – she wanted to see me too. I did. She told me I had to kiss her to get the soap. I was reluctant -- how reluctant? -- but **allowed** her to kiss me. She slid her tongue into my mouth and I enjoyed it. I ran out of the stall, and avoided her for a while.

I knew there was no comparison between my feelings for Peggy and my feelings for Mark. I loved sex with Mark, but that was just a part of our whole. Mark was my whole life. But I had enjoyed that kiss. I couldn't deny that. Could I have sex with Peggy and Mark? That wouldn't work. I was smart enough to know that. And if I had to make a choice, there was no choice. It was Mark. Hands down. But---

I realized I had not seen all of Peggy. I had not seen her vagina, her sexual essence so to speak. The obsession came back. I really wanted to see Peggy Mayhew's vagina. Not only see it, but smell it and taste it. Using Mark's car (**Mark's car!),** I drove her to Dunkin' Donuts for a chat. We had discussed the matter briefly, and she was aware that I was struggling with an attraction for her. I also knew by then that she was having the same problem. *I knew we were in love with each other.*

She told me she was more than willing to allow me to explore her vagina. She wanted to explore mine as well. She invited me over to her house that very day. She told me that, unless we scratched that itch, it would continue to bother us, creating tension, putting obstacles in the path of our friendship. And, in truth, we both valued that friendship.

I reluctantly said "No." I did not want to do anything to interfere with my relationship with Mark. There was nothing more important to me than that relationship. She tried to convince me that we had to do it. Otherwise it would just fester. I drove her home and returned to Dunkin' Donuts. I had an hour and a half to kill. I ordered a coffee, stared at it, said "Fuck," and then drove to Peggy's house. She was waiting for me on the Barge of Curiosity.

We didn't know how to start. We were not beginning a relationship, just on a sexual excursion. She suggested wrestling (**wrestling?**). We stripped down to our panties and wrestled. Almost immediately we were excited. We kissed passionately, and then went to the bedroom where we satisfied our curiosities, quite well.

I loved it, but once the itch was scratched, I had no need to explore Peggy's vagina again. Or any woman's. I think Peggy would have liked one, or more, repeat engagements, but I no longer had the itch. I realized that it was very different than my sex with Mark. I want sex with Mark every day. It is not just an itch to be scratched. In fact I was thinking about sex with Mark while Peggy and I straightened up in the living room. When I picked him up at six, we went straight to his house.

But, and this is very hard to explain, my feelings for Peggy were never the same after our "event." They were amplified. I didn't want to have sex with her anymore – only God knows if that is true -- but I wanted to be with her. The attraction was still there. She felt the same toward me. Well, to be honest, I think she might still want to have sex with me, play with my vagina, but she knows that's not going to happen. She's okay with that. We became, and still are, best *girl*friends. Mark is my best friend. Peggy and

I do talk about sex all the time; girlfriends do that. We touch all the time. We hold hands when we talk; when we stand side by side, she'll have her arm around my shoulder, or I'll have my arm around her waist. We double date a lot, and, as she predicted, the "event" took away the sexual and relational tension that was beginning. I have never regretted scratching that itch. I told Mark about the event after we were married. To my relief, he had no problem with it.

Relationships:

Peggy and I were together all the time. I convinced her that she was too good for Billy Walsh, the Neanderthal football player she was dating. When I told her how sensitive a lover Mark was, she realized what a dud she had. She had called him, "***A good fuck without the trimmings***."

"Another great bumper sticker," I said. Peggy just laughed.

I convinced her to find a "good fuck with the trimmings." She came close. She started dating an honors student named Fred Williams. Billy told Fred he was going to "beat the shit out of him" after class when he discovered he had been replaced. I related this information to Mark, and he went with Fred to the pre-arranged spot. Peggy and I went too. Mark told Billy that he, Mark, was standing proxy for Fred. He had to explain what that meant, but, once Billy grasped the idea, the fight never materialized. Peggy dated Fred the rest of our senior year.

I mentioned in the chapter, *Scratching an Itch,* that Peggy occasionally called Gina or Betsy, or both, two lesbian lovers in our class, to get some vagina action. Hearing about that, from Peggy, especially the "both," was a contributing cause to my own "Peggy's vagina obsession." She still called them throughout our senior year. I guess Fred was not quite sufficient, and I, the preferred vagina, was not available. After Gina and Betsy broke up – Peggy was somehow involved in that, but I don't know the details – Peggy called Gina. She told me she liked the wildness of the Italian. There was biting involved. That disturbed me, frightened me a little. I had visions of Gina's gnashing teeth coming after my vagina. No, thank you. And Peggy told me Gina did in fact have a wild black bush, as I had imagined. Betsy found a new lover, a junior at CHS. Gina didn't go to URI, so I had no idea what Peggy was going to do for vaginas in Kingston.

Kisses and Fingers:

Our undefeated girls' basketball team travelled by bus to South Kingstown to take on the Lady Rebels. Mark and Fred Williams, Peggy's new boyfriend, drove to the game in Mark's car.

The Lady Rebels were not very good that year, and we got out to a 39 – 7 lead with two minutes to go in the first half. I fed Peggy with a great pass, and as she was going in for the lay-up, one of the South Kingstown girls deliberately drove her to the court. It was a very flagrant foul. Peggy has a fiery temper and jumped up screaming at the opponent. The other girl got right in Peggy's face and said, "Fucking cunt. Want to do something about it?" That was all Peggy needed to hear. She starting swinging. Another Lady Rebel jumped on Peggy, and I tackled her. The four of us were fighting as the other girls milled around, pushing and bad-mouthing each other. The referees and the coaches put an end to the fight quickly. Luckily no fans, including Mark, had left the stands.

The floor was cleared, and we stood in front of our bench as the referees and both coaches discussed what to do. Our coach, Linda Thompson, was irate. She believed that the South Kingstown coach had put in two subs to start the fight with the hope that we, Peggy and I, would take the bait, and be ejected from the game, along with the South Kingstown subs.

If that was the plan, it was successful. Peggy and I and our two opponents were ejected. Coach Thompson was furious, not at us, but at the South Kingstown coach.

Coach Thompson turned to us and said, "Go directly to the locker room and stay in there." She sent one of her assistants with us to make sure we did not leave the locker room. She did not want to hear about a resumption of the fight under the stands.

At halftime, she pulled the two of us aside and said, "You can't retaliate. Teams will use that as a weapon against us. There's no other way they can beat us. I know you were set up. We lost our two best players, and they lost nothing."

"It's my fault, Coach, Sandy was just defending me. The bitch called me a 'fucking cunt,' and I lost it."

"She called you what?" said Coach Thompson.

"A fucking cunt, Coach, a fucking cunt."

"Okay, as far as I'm concerned, it's over. Both of you, write out a note for Mr. Wells (the CHS Principal) explaining what happened. Bring them to me when they're done. Peggy, be sure to put in what she called you. Sandy, just say that a second girl jumped on Peggy, and you were just trying to get her off. I just hope we can hold onto this lead in the second half. You two have to stay in the locker room."

CHS held on to win 45 – 41.

Three South Kingstown police officers escorted our team to the bus. There must have been forty to fifty girls and boys in the vicinity of the bus. I saw Mark in the back of the crowd. Just making sure I was all right. A few adults, probably teachers, were helping with crowd control. We heard some pretty mean comments from the crowd:

"Cunts…"

"Just keep walking," I said to Peggy. I could feel her tensing up.

"Lezzies…

"You're lucky the police are here….

"Bitches…..

"Assholes….

Peggy and I took seats on the bench seat at the back of the bus. We looked out and saw nothing but angry, screaming girls. Peggy said to me, "Give me a kiss, and then do what I do."

She gave me a good kiss and then took her middle finger, sucked on it, and presented it to the crowd. I did the same. That was the last view of us they had as the bus pulled away. Something hit the rear window of the bus. It was a tomato, not a rock.

"At least we won," I said.

She put her arm around my shoulder and said, "The kiss was nice. We should do it more often."

"Maybe," I said. "Maybe." And I smiled at her. I do have feelings for Peggy. Not Mark-feelings, but feelings. She is a great kisser.

Mark and Fred met the bus, and the four of us went to Chow Fun for dinner. We then dropped Fred and Peggy off at her place, and Mark and I went home.

"Good fight," he said.

"Yes. It has me all worked up. Want to help me unwind?"

"Of course."

We won the return game, on our court, 77 – 21.

College Announcements:

In October, I received the academic scholarship offer from Harvard that I was expecting: full room, board, and tuition. I called Admissions and explained that I was getting married in June, and that my husband was going to be attending MIT. The Admissions Clerk told me I would have my tuition, fees, and books fully covered, and, since I would be married and living off campus, I would be given a meals and rental allowance of one thousand dollars a month for ten months, September through June.

Mark received his offer from MIT two days after I received mine from Harvard. He called Admissions and received basically the same information. MIT was a little more generous on the meals and rental allowance, twelve hundred dollars per month, for the same ten months.

That would give us non-taxable income of two thousand, two hundred dollars per month. In addition, we would have close to $700,000 in our joint investment, checking, and savings accounts. We would be financially fine. Even in July and August. The Tuttles' house sold for a net $200,000 after we were in Cambridge. We sent our share, $100,000, to Denny McIntyre to add to our investment account.

I received and rejected athletic scholarship offers from, among other schools, UConn, Tennessee, URI and Providence.

Mark received and rejected athletic scholarship offers from, among others, Duke, Kansas, Kentucky, Stanford, UCLA, North Carolina, URI, Providence, and Boston College.

Peggy Mayhew was accepted to URI, and offered a full room, board, and tuition Centennial Scholarship. She planned to major in Education and Physical Education, hoping to get a coaching job in a high school upon graduation. Fred Williams was accepted to RPI, which was his first choice. I saw that as a death knell for their relationship. It was.

The Taco Bell Fight:

I borrowed Mark's car after school one day in May, and Peggy and I headed over to the K-Mart Superstore in Cranston. Mark would say I used our car, not borrowed his. He considers everything we have, including the investment accounts, ours. Not legally yet, but the only reason for that is the tax code.

We stopped at a Taco Bell for a snack on the way. There were two black girls on the order line in front of us and, purely by accident, Peggy bumped into one of them. Peggy had turned around to look at me, and wasn't watching where she was going.

"Watch out, bitch," said the black girl Peggy had bumped.

"Sorry," said Peggy.

"What you mean, 'Sorry'? You think you can just bump people and say, 'Sorry.' That makes it all right?"

"What do you want me to say?"

I could see Peggy getting angry. "Let's get out of here, Peggy," I said, tugging her sleeve. I wasn't frightened. I just did not want the trouble, the hassle.

"You looking for a fight or something?" asked the black girl. People started moving away from us. "If you is, that's okay by me."

"I'm not looking for a fight. I just want tacos. But I'm not running away from a fight either."

"Peggy, come on. Let's leave," I said.

"You wanna fight, bitch? I think you wanna fight." The black girl was getting loud.

"Take it outside," yelled the manager.

"I'm leaving," said Peggy to the manager. And to the black girl, "If you want to follow me, fine. If you want a fight, fine. It's up to you. I'll be waiting outside."

"We gonna fight, bitch. One on one, me and you. Let's go."

Peggy turned to me. "You got my back?"

"Of course."

Peggy walked out into the parking lot. I was right at her side. The two black girls **did** follow us out.

"One on one," said the other black girl. She pointed to Pegy, "Just you and Maybelle. No jumping. No two on one shit."

Maybelle turned to her friend. "Hold my purse, Shaneen. Watch that other white bitch."

"I'm watching, Maybelle," she said. "I got my eye on dat bitch."

Maybelle turned to Peggy, "Okay, let's fight, bitch. Street fight. No rules."

"One on one," said Shaneen. "You hear me, bitch," she said to me. "No jumping."

Maybelle and Peggy squared off like boxers. Then they started exchanging punches.

"Kill her, Maybelle. Beat that white pussy."

"Kill her, Peggy," I said. I wanted her to know I was right there. "I got your back."

"You shut up, white girl," Shaneen said to me.

"You gonna make me?" I said, surprising myself. *Here we go…I can take her…She's my size…With all Mark taught me…Bring it on, bitch…I want to fight…Ruin my trip to Taco Bell, will you…Let's go…I can beat the shit outta her.*

Peggy landed a great right sending Maybelle to the ground. *Maybe this shit is over,* I thought. *Maybe I won't have to fight Shaneen…I want to fight Shaneen.*

Maybelle got back up and charged Peggy yelling, "You motherfukka." Peggy hit her again. Hard. Maybelle staggered.

Shaneen was in my face, "You want me to make you? Dat what you want?"

I pushed her away. "Fuck you, Shaneen."

She rushed back and stuck her face right in mine. Eye to eye. Nose to nose. Mouth to mouth. I could smell her breath. Feel her spittle. She had garlic for lunch. There was an unpleasant undersmell. *I definitely don't want to put my tongue in your mouth.* "What you say? You wanna fight? I gonna whoop your white ass. Come on let's fight, bitch. Me and you," she said. "Let's go."

"Fuck you, bitch. Get out of my face," I said, pushing her away again.

"Fuck you, cunt," she said, and rushed at me. I side stepped, grabbed her arm, and tossed her to the ground. *Thank you, Mark.* He taught me that move. I dived on top of her, and we rolled around throwing punches. I ended up on top. She struggled but was unable to get up. I was kneeling on her arms. We had rolled onto the dirt next to the parking lot. "Let me up, bitch," she cried.

"Now, why would I do that? You think I'm stupid?"

I glanced around. Peggy had Maybelle in a headlock and was pounded her head with punches.

"I'm gonna kill you, motherfukka," Shaneen said. She spat toward my face. None of the spit hit me. Most of it clung to her dry lips.

It still pissed me off. I grabbed both sides of her head and pounded the back of her head into the dirt. "You like that, bitch," I cried. "Don't you ever spit at me."

"Let go my hair, bitch," she cried. "I'm going kill you. Let me up."

I could hear sirens in the distance. The manager must have called the police. *Nice trip to K-Mart.*

I grabbed her hair with my left hand and started punching her face with my right fist. Her nose started bleeding, and she was losing some of her fight. The curses were still pouring out of her mouth, however. The sirens were getting closer.

Just then someone grabbed me from behind. *Shit, they've got friends.* But it was Peggy. Maybelle was curled up on the ground, moaning, her face bloody. "Let's get out of here, Sandy. Now. Before the cops come."

I jumped up and, holding hands, we ran to the car. I drove out of the parking lot without looking back. We could hear the police, but we didn't see any police cars.

"Still want to go to K-Mart, Peggy?" I said.

"No, let's go to my place. Thanks for sticking with me."

"You're welcome. What are friends for? It looks like you took care of Maybelle," I said.

"Yeah, and you took care of Shaneen. Did you enjoy the tacos?"

"Yeah, they were great."

I was driving in silence when Peggy, squeezing my right arm, said, "What are you thinking?"

"Just that I sure don't want to smell Shaneen's vagina."

We laughed all the way back to Peggy's house.

I collapsed on Peggy's couch. She got us two Cokes. She sat down and put her arm around me. She looked at me and raised an eyebrow. *She wants to have sex with me again...Fight must have turned her on...Turned on too...But I can't have sex with her...Only Mark...Maybe we can just kiss...That would be nice...Exciting too.*

"No, Peggy, I can't," I said, shaking my head.

"A kiss?"

"Okay, but I will only make love with Mark. Ever."

"I understand. But you're my best girlfriend, maybe my best friend period. I really appreciate you standing with me today. I want to kiss you so bad."

"I'll always stand with you. You know that. And I already said we can kiss."

"You said you'd kiss me?"

"Yes."

I put down my Coke. She put hers down. We hugged. We touched lips, then opened them and exchanged tongues. She tasted great.

"You taste great, Sandy," she said.

"You too," I said.

"Don't stop," Peggy said.

"I won't."

We spent the next half hour in a passionate embrace, letting our tongues play with each other, swapping saliva, licking each other's face, occasionally blowing breath into each other's mouth.

"Thank you," she said when we finished kissing. We were still hugging each other, breathing hard. "That was nice." She blew into my face. It smelled and felt exciting.

"That **was** nice. You can do that anytime," I said, and I meant it.

"Anytime?"

"Anytime," I answered. I looked right into her eyes as I said it. I blew into her face.

"Now?"

"Now."

We started kissing again. It was as sweet as before.

When we pulled apart, she said, "I could do that forever, with you."

"Yeah, I liked that too. A lot. Kissing friends. Maybe that's enough." We both smiled.

"Kissing friends, I like that," Peggy said. "Like kissing cousins."

"Nothing like 'kissing cousins,' " I said. We both laughed.

We sat silently and held hands. I took another sip from my Coke. It was a little warm.

"That was a good fight today," Peggy said. "We're unbeatable as a team."

"And a good post-fight too." I burped from the warm Coke.

"You did like kissing me?" she asked.

"Yes."

"We can continue to kiss at times?"

"Yes," I said. "But I would like us to have three rules."

"What rules?" asked Peggy. "Anal Sandy Roberts always has rules." She laughed.

"We only kiss in private, we do nothing more than kiss, and we keep it as our secret," I said.

"Deal," she said and held out her pinky. We joined pinkies.

"Time to pick up the boys," said Peggy. "Chinese?"

"Sure. Those two guys are going to get lucky tonight."

"Another kiss?" asked Peggy. "We have time."

I didn't even answer. Just attacked her lips with mine. I burped into her mouth. She laughed and bit my tongue, playfully. *I really like you, Peggy Mayhew…My kissing friend.*

That was the beginning of my and Peggy's Phase II, our kissing phase. We consider our friendship very special. Mark is my sole lover, and my best friend. That will never change. But Peggy is my closest girlfriend. And, when we get the chance, we kiss the hell out of each other. As I said elsewhere, we have developed a special bond. And I have Mark's blessing to kiss Peggy Mayhew. I don't know if he realizes what he has unleashed.

226

The Wedding:

Just two weeks after graduation, Mark and I got married. Mom wanted a large wedding; I didn't. We compromised and limited invitations to immediate family and friends. I wore a white dress and my pearl necklace. Peggy Mayhew was my maid of honor. Margie Baylor and Mark's cousin, Annie, were the bridesmaids. Annie was thrilled that I remembered my promise to her, given at the wake. *A promise made is a debt unpaid.* And we did invite Uncle Andy and Aunt Millie, and they flew in for the wedding of Uncle Andy's godson. Uncle Andy told one and all that he was the first to know we were getting married. "I knew it before they told me; I could tell." Actually he was the fourth to know; we had told Annie, Luisa, and Peggy earlier that day. But we did not correct him.

Billy Smith, who is now a good friend, told me that I made his day, and probably secured him a wife, when I chose him for the "Bride's Special" dance at the reception.

Coaches Wilson and Thompson attended. So did Bill Reynolds.

When I put a piece of wedding cake in Mark's mouth, Dad came up to me and told me the story of his vision at the Tuttles' dining room table that night oh-so-many years ago, the day Mark saved my life. "It was exactly as it happened tonight," he said. "Then I blinked and you were two little kids sharing ice cream. I told Mom that night, but never told anyone else."

The night of our wedding, we went to *our* house, and I did the thing I had wanted to do since I was a little girl: I slept in Mark Tuttle's arms. I did not have to go to my parents' house after we made love. I felt so loved and so safe curled up in our bed with him. We woke up still entwined with our faces three inches apart. We kissed. We made love. We showered together. We had coffee in **our** kitchen. What a great way to start the day and our new life.

227

Denny McIntyre, our financial advisor and money manager, was at the wedding. The wedding was on the second Saturday in June. On the following Monday, Mark and I went to Denny's office where Mark signed the paperwork to change *his* investment account into *our* investment account. That afternoon we went to Citizens Bank to do the same. We share everything.

On Tuesday afternoon we flew out of JFK to Fiumicino Aeroporto in Rome for our two week honeymoon. Peggy insisted on driving us down to New York for the flight. We hugged and kissed when she dropped us off at the international terminal.

"I'll meet you at Logan," she said. Our return flight was direct: Milano to Boston.

"You're a good friend, Peggy," I said.

"I'm more than that," she said.

"I know that. We both do."

"Send me some postcards," she said. Then she hugged and kissed Mark. Then she hugged and kissed me again. We looked into each other's eyes. "You're much more than a good friend, Peggy," I said. "I love you."

"I love you too. I'm going to miss you."

"I'll miss you too."

"Even on your honeymoon?"

"Even on my honeymoon."

We hugged and kissed a third time.

After eight years of Italian, Mark and I were both fluent. We were prepared to speak *la lingua Italiana alla Citta' Eterna.*

On Wednesday morning, we stood in St. Peter's Square, and I remembered, and I cried. I cannot tell you how much I loved Mark Tuttle that day.

Chapter Thirteen
La Luna di Miele – Part I
Nella Piazza San Pietro

ROMA:

La luna di miele nella Piazza San Pietro – Honeymoon in St. Peter's Square. Actually we were spending two weeks throughout Italy, not two weeks in St. Peter's Square, but the honeymoon started there, and, despite the many wonders we saw on the trip, I consider the *Piazza* the highlight of our honeymoon. Especially for the memory it generated.

We had considered a tour, but decided against it. We agreed a tour would be too constricting. We wanted to be free to spend as much or as little time in any one place as we wished. We inquired about a rental car, but discovered we were seven years too young. We purchased a one-month, first class rail pass.

We packed what we needed into two medium-sized backpacks, suitable for carryon. It's amazing what you can stuff into a backpack – we made one heavier than the other; Mark would carry the heavier one. We didn't take much. I brought two pair of light cotton slacks, two tan shorts, one pair of sandals, a week's worth of panties (quick drying -- I wondered if Mark would like to find panties hanging in his bathroom -- I figured he would love them if they were my panties), colored T-shirts, a Red Sox hat, a few blouses, toiletries, a lightweight, yellow, hooded rain jacket, and two books, *To Kill a Mockingbird* and *Catch-22.* Mark packed similar items: two pair of tan khaki pants, two tan shorts, one pair of sandals, a week's worth of boxer shorts (washable, quick drying), colored T-shirts, a Red Sox hat, a few short-sleeve oxford dress shirts, toiletries, a lightweight, blue, hooded rain jacket, and two books: *To Kill a Mockingbird* and *Catch-22.* We still team read. Peggy had the same two books for her reading while we were away.

We packed together in our bedroom Monday after we got home from Citizens Bank. Every time I looked at him I thought, *Mark Tuttle is my husband…Oh my God, Mark Tuttle is my husband…How great is that!* Then I would kiss him and say, "I am so happy."

"Me too," he answered. And I knew he was.

Then we rolled together onto the bed. It took us three hours to pack, but they were enjoyable, action-packed, play-while-you-pack hours.

The only limiting factor on the trip would be the hotel reservations which we made in advance. We booked four nights in Rome, one in Assisi, three in Florence, three in Venice, three in Stresa on Lago Maggiore, near the Swiss border, and one in Milan. We would fly home from Milan to the waiting Peggy Mayhew and Margie Baylor in Boston.

On Tuesday morning Mom and Dad came over to our house – I loved saying "our house" -- to give us a send-off. (Mark's sister Patty still owned half the house, but we lived in it.) Patty was in attendance for the *bon voyage.* And, of course, Peggy and Margie Baylor. Peggy insisted on driving us to JFK, and Margie was coming along to keep

Peggy company on the return drive to Rhode Island. Mark told Peggy she could use the car while we were away. Mom and Dad brought us a surprise gift, a 35mm Pentax camera and twelve rolls of thirty-six exposure slide film. We packed the camera and film, our tickets, our passports, our prepaid rail passes, our hotel reservations, our Fodor's *Italy*, and the two copies of *To Kill a Mockingbird* into a little bag that Mark carried. I let Mark plan the whole trip – trusting huh? – but isn't he the Captain of the Barge of Curiosity? He had been studying Fodor's *Italy* for weeks before we left.

After our plane landed at Fiumicino, we took a taxi to our first hotel, *La Pensione delle Suore di Misericordia,* on the *Via della Conciliazione*, the wide street running from the *Castello Sant'Angelo* on the Tiber to St. Peter's. It was late Wednesday morning when we arrived at our *pensione.* We had lost a night on the plane – there is a six-hour time difference between Coventry and Rome – but decided to make do with the naps we took over the Atlantic. We ate a meal an hour after take-off, then we huddled together, covered ourselves with blankets, and slept as best we could. I actually slept better than Mark. As my protector, he began his lifelong habit of sleeping with one eye open when we sleep in public. We planned to retire early that first night in Rome.

Our room wasn't available when we arrived, but the young postulant at the front desk let us store our backpacks in a secured room off the lobby. We knew our backpacks would be safe with the good sisters! The postulant was amazed that we spoke Italian so well. We exited the *pensione* onto the *Via della Conciliazione* and just stood frozen, holding hands, dazzled by the mid-day sun. *I am in Rome, Italy, with Mark Tuttle, and Mark Tuttle is my husband...I am going to sleep wrapped in his arms again tonight, and every night for the rest of my life…How good is that?..And, by the way, he adores me…And I adore him.*

"Well here we are in Rome," I said, giving him my best smile. "Where to first, my husband?" I loved to say that, "my husband."

"Where else?" he said. "*La Piazza San Pietro.*"

It was a five minute walk from our *pensione* to the *Piazza*. A five minute walk! We held hands and walked toward the most famous basilica in the world. We stopped at the edge of the square, standing near the horses and carriages for hire, bewitched by the sight in front of us. We knew St. Peter's Square was large, but we were not prepared for how grand it actually was. We were speechless before the hugeness of the *Piazza*, enclosed by Bernini's columns, and we were awed by the majesty of St. Peter's itself with the twelve apostles staring down at us from the top of the façade, the first pope, Peter, in the middle, of course, holding the keys to the kingdom. If you are a Catholic, there is nothing in the world more impressive than the initial view of this first church of Christianity.

In the center of the square was the four thousand year old obelisk that Caligula had moved to Rome from Egypt. We walked over and stood next to the obelisk still looking at the basilica. We couldn't take our eyes off the basilica.

I suddenly had a flashback. We were in Mark's pool. We were thirteen. I was sitting on Mark's shoulders looking down at him. His face, looking up, was upside-down.

"I'd rather see you topless than Peggy," he said.

"Really?" I asked.

"Really."

I kissed him. "You don't want to see Peggy topless?"

"I didn't say that. I said I would rather see you topless than see Peggy topless."

"So you would like to see her topless."

"So would you, I bet," he said.

I laughed. "Yeah, I guess I would."

"Sandy, let me tell you something that is absolutely true. If I die without ever seeing Peggy Mayhew topless, I will feel aesthetically deprived, but otherwise I will be fine. If I die without ever seeing Sandy Roberts topless, I will not die happy."

Then we were in the pool shed. It was later that same day. I had let him take off my top. That was a major step for us. He was gazing at and kissing my bumps for the first time.

I told him, "There's nothing to see or feel."

"Oh yes there is," he said. "What do you think is getting me so excited?" he asked.

"My awesome bumps?" I was laughing.

"Yes," he said. "Your fantastic little bumps. And you standing here displaying them to me and to no one else. Now I can die happy. I have seen Sandy Roberts topless."

"You're not going to die any time soon, Mark Tuttle," I said. *"I need you."* God, is that ever true!

"No, I'm not going to die. There is too much of Sandy Roberts I still have to see, and too many things I want to do with Sandy Roberts before I die."

"What things?"

*"Make love with you, of course, when we're older, but so much more: travel the world, hike in the Grand Canyon, walk on the Great Wall, look at the ceiling of the Sistine Chapel, admire Michelangelo's David in Florence, **stand in St. Peter's Square**, own our own house, share everything we have with each other, have children, maybe four, take them to Disney, go to Fenway, vacation on the Florida Atlantic coast, eat Chinese food whenever we want, go to sleep every night*

233

with you in my arms, wake up every morning looking at your glorious, smiling face, kiss that face, fondle your breasts and your ass, bring you a cup of coffee in bed," Mark said.

Stand in St. Peter's Square. **Stand in St. Peter's Square**!

And we were there, together, holding hands, married! I started to cry and squeezed his hand as tight as I could. "You promised me we would stand here. I was only thirteen years old, and I believed you. You're not going to die on me now, are you?"

"There are still too many things on that list, one of which we will be able to cross off tomorrow."

"What?"

"Standing together in the Sistine Chapel. Looking at God the Father stretch out his hand to Adam."

"Life with you is going to be wonderful," I said.

"My goal is to make your life wonderful," Mark said. "That's been my goal since I was six. And if I ever fall short, let me know."

"I will." We kissed. It had only been five days, but I loved our life together already. "And my goal is to make your life wonderful too, Mark Tuttle."

"I know that, Sandy," he said. And he smiled at me. I love that smile. Love it!

"Now that we're married, I have added things to the list of things I want to do with you," he said. "Further postponing the date of death."

"What?"

"Well, for starters, make love to you ten thousand times."

"Ten thousand times?"

"At just once a day, we will be close to eleven thousand times in thirty years. And we'll only be in our forties."

"My lover, the math whiz. And what makes you think we will only make love once a day?"

"I was just being conservative. There were multiple variables to consider: your period, times of childbirth, the occasional sickness, or excessive tiredness, of either of us. I didn't want to be too optimistic. It was a fairly complicated formula. Heavy algebra."

I just shook my head. "Let's go inside St. Peter's," I said. The reason I brought two pair of cotton slacks was for the church visits – shorts or short skirts are prohibited for women inside the Italian churches. Men can wear shorts; I don't know if they can wear mini-skirts. Or short kilts if they are from Scotland. I was wearing a salmon-colored T-shirt. I thought it went quite well with the tan cotton slacks. Mark thought so too; he told me I was the most beautiful woman in Rome. He always tells me ridiculous things like that, but he believes them. He constantly tells me that I have the most beautiful face in the world. And that, now that we are married, waking up to that face every morning is the highlight of his day.

St. Peter's inside was as awe-inspiring as St. Peter's outside. We planned to start each day in Rome with Mass at one of the side altars. Mass was being said almost continuously during the morning hours, in all languages. We would search out Mass in Italian, easy to find in Rome. Well that was our plan until something fantastic changed it.

Before heading back to *La Pensione delle Suore di Misericordia*, we decided to have dinner at one of the outdoor *trattoria* near St. Peter's. It was a little after four, and the restaurants and shops were re-opening after siesta. We found a small trattoria on a side street, and occupied a table outside under an awning advertising *Birra Peroni*. Mark sat across from me, smiling.

"What?" I asked.

"You are absolutely the most beautiful woman I have ever seen. You look so good in that salmon shirt, good enough to eat."

"You can do that later. For now, you will have to settle for spaghetti."

The waiter came over interrupting our little love banter. We ordered two bowls of *minestrone*, served with warm bread and a dish of olive oil for dipping, and then spaghetti and meatballs family style. And the house red wine, a half-liter. We sat across from each other, enjoying the meal – we had not eaten a meal since an hour after take-off -- watching the Italians and tourists go by, sipping our wine, speaking Italian with our waiter. I looked at Mark and, in my mind, heard him say again, *"Ever since I was six, I have wanted to make your life wonderful."*

"You have," I said.

"Have what?" he asked puzzled.

"Made my life wonderful."

"What brought that on?" he asked laughing.

"Sitting here with you, feeling so comfortable, so safe, so in love, knowing that this is just the beginning, that's what brought it on, my love." I held up my glass of wine; he clinked it with his; and we drank.

"*Sempre!*" he said.

"Yes, always," I answered.

After dinner, we walked back to the *Piazza*. We washed our faces in the cool water in the central fountain. We dried off using Mark's handkerchief. Mark led me to a little circle off-center in the square. He instructed me to stand on the circle and look at Bernini's columns. There are four rows of columns, but standing on the circle created the illusion of a single row.

"How did Bernini manage that?" I asked.

"Because he was Bernini," Mark said.

"How did you know about these circles?"

"I read about them in Fodor's."

We saw a young priest approaching us. We could tell he was American even in his black cassock. I don't know how, but you can always tell an American when you're abroad. He obviously recognized us as Americans too for he opened the conversation with, "Hi, where are you two from?"

"Rhode Island, here on our honeymoon," I said. "Sandy and Mark Tuttle."

"Father John Michael. Excuse me for asking, but how old, or rather, how young are you two?"

"We're both eighteen," I said. "But we have been in love since we were six."

"Six?" he said.

"This is hard to believe, Father," I said, "but when we were eight, he saved my life, really, and I took both his hands in mine, and, looking directly into his eyes, I said, 'I am going to marry you someday, Mark Tuttle.'

" 'Nothing will make me happier, Sandy Roberts,' he said. 'We are going to get married.'

" 'Promise?' I said.

" 'Promise,' he answered.

" 'I'm going to hold you to that promise, Mark Tuttle.' I said, and, Father, I have. Haven't I, Mark?"

"Yes, you have," he said.

The young priest laughed. "I'm a Salvatorian Father working on my doctorate in Philosophy at the Gregorian University. I live at our motherhouse right here on the *Via della Conciliazione,* number fifty-one."

"We're staying with the Sisters of Mercy just up the street from you."

"I know the place well. They will take good care of you."

"We're both students too, Father. I'm starting at Harvard in September, and Mark is starting at MIT. We don't plan on having children until after we graduate, then we want four." I did not mention what method of birth control we were going to use, and he didn't ask.

"Are you Catholics?" he asked.

"Yes," I said.

"When are you leaving *Roma?*"

"Sunday morning. We're taking the train up to Assisi."

"I am saying Mass, in English, tomorrow and Friday morning in the Chapel of the *Pieta'* in Saint Peter's, at eight o'clock. Why don't you join me?"

"Michelangelo's *Pieta'?*" I asked.

"The one and only," he answered. "Be my servers. There's nothing to it; just hand me the water and wine, wash my fingers, and answer the prayers – you'll have cards -- and you will be within five feet of one of the world's great works of art."

"Thank you, Father," I said. "What time do you want us there?"

"Meet me outside the motherhouse at seven thirty, and we can walk over together."

"We will be there. Thank you so much," I said. "Before you leave, Father, can you take our picture with St. Peter's in the background?"

"I'll do better than that. I'll take your picture and give you my blessing, for the success of your marriage."

After taking the picture, which I still treasure, and handing me back the Pentax, he put his hands on our bowed heads and said, "May your Christian marriage last as long as the basilica behind you. Actually longer, for all things physical must end, but things spiritual are eternal. Amen."

He then headed off toward the basilica. Mark and I just looked at each other. "Did that just happen?" I asked. "Are

238

we going to serve Mass in St. Peter's? In the chapel of the *Pieta'*?"

"I believe it did," Mark said. "We'll know tomorrow morning. Did he say Peggy was going to be there?"

"Peggy?" I said, giving him a funny look.

"Father said we would be near one of the world's great works of art."

I punched him on the shoulder right there in *La Piazza di San Pietro.*

We got back to the room at seven-thirty. The same postulant – what are her hours? – showed us to our room on the second floor. We showered together and then dressed for bed. I put the salmon-colored T-shirt back on and slipped into a pair of matching, salmon-colored panties. Mark just wore a pair of boxers. We should not have bothered. We were both exhausted from the trip, the lost hours, and the visit to St. Peter's, but that tiredness left us when we got in bed. We started kissing, and I took off my T-shirt. I wanted my "bumps" against his chest without cotton between us. I love the feel of my skin on his skin. We were both getting very excited. Then Mark slid off my panties and went down between my legs.

"Are we allowed to do this in a hotel run by nuns?" I asked.

"I won't tell if you don't, but I am not stopping," Mark said.

"Who wants you to stop?"

After he had me fully aroused and ready to receive him, he sat up in bed and put me on his lap, facing him. He entered me while we kissed, and we made love for an eternity in the Eternal City. I love kissing Mark, exploring his mouth with my tongue, receiving his tongue into my mouth, smelling his breath, letting him smell mine, sucking on his lip, letting him suck on my lip, while we make love.

After we came, at the same time, I collapsed in his arms. "How do I smell?" I asked. He is a connoisseur of my smells.

"I love your post-coital smell," he said. "The 'I have taken care of you; now protect me' smell. I love your pre-coital 'I'm ready' smell too."

"I meant my breath," I said, laughing.

"You did not!" he objected.

I just laughed.

"Your mouth smells great too."

Next morning, on the way to the Salvatorian Motherhouse, I handed him a note. He opened it and laughed.

It said: "9,999 to go."

Father John Michael was waiting for us.

"Can we take you out for breakfast after Mass, Father?"

"Yes, thank you, but just coffee and a roll. I have to be at The Greg by ten-thirty."

Father John Michael led us into the basilica through a side door patrolled by Swiss guards in their working blue uniforms. One saluted Father John Michael. I whispered to Mark, "Is this really happening to us?"

Mass in the Chapel of the *Pieta'* was an experience Mark and I will never forget. The three of us, Mark and I side-by-side in front, marched from the sacristy down the center aisle of St. Peter's to the Chapel. Again I whispered to Mark, "Is this really happening to us?" Father John Michael, fully vested, carried the chalice; Mark carried the cruets of wine and water on a crystal dish; I carried a small gold container filled with the unconsecrated hosts. There were about seventy-five people standing in front of the altar, outside the altar rail. Mark and I, and Father John Michael, were standing behind the altar next to Michelangelo's masterpiece, one of them anyway. We

240

would see more of his sublime creations on our honeymoon, but we would never be this close to one again. That's not true; we were next to the *Pieta'* the following morning as well.

Father John Michael led us to a small café where we had *café lattes*, rolls, and sweet Italian butter.

"Where are you two off to today?" he asked.

"The Vatican Museum," Mark said. "I promised Sandy when we were thirteen that we would stand together looking at the Sistine Chapel ceiling. And today we will."

"You two are amazing. I have to run. Thanks for breakfast, and I'll see you tomorrow at seven-thirty."

"No, thank **you**," I said. "And we will definitely see you at seven-thirty."

The Vatican Museum – the most compelling reason not to be part of a tour group. You can spend a month exploring the Vatican Museum, or you can rush through it, seeing a lot fleetingly, or you can, as Mark planned for us, pick out a few treasures that you really want to see and enjoy them.

Our treasures: the Laocoön sculpture, the *Stanze* of Raphael, and the Sistine Chapel. We saw many other works of art, amazing works of art, and we lingered anywhere either one of us wanted to linger, but we spent hours with the favored three, watching tour groups, following their guides with the flag-topped poles, rush by us.

I found it amazing that I was walking through the Vatican Museum with Mark Tuttle, and that Mark Tuttle was my husband. I still have a hard time grasping that. *Mark Tuttle, the little boy I fell in love with and never fell out of love with, who has always been my best friend, who has saved my life and always protected me, who will always protect me, the Captain of the Barge of Curiosity,* *the smartest, the nicest, the most athletic man I even met…**That** Mark Tuttle is my husband and loves me, adores me, and would die for me…And we are walking through the Vatican Museum, holding hands, heading eventually to the Sistine Chapel where he will keep another made-at-thirteen promise to me.*

We were in the hall of the map-tapestries when I pulled him into an alcove. I held his hands and said, "I just wanted to tell you that I love you and always will. I hope you will always love me. I don't want to be too demonstrative here, but I need to kiss you. I really need to kiss you."

"You can kiss me anytime," he said, and we kissed. "And you never have to worry about me. I am a one-woman man – it's my nature -- and Sandy Roberts is my woman. I think you knew that the first day of school at St. Michael's. I certainly did."

"I did," I said. "I just love to hear you say it."

We only spent a half hour at the first of our three special attractions, the Laocoön Group. Mr. Carlson, our junior year Honors Art Appreciation teacher, had showed the class a slide of this remarkable sculpture. An ancient sculpture, artist unknown, showing a father wrestling with a serpent, with one son already despairing, and the other still looking with hope at his father. How much better in reality than on the projection screen! Peggy and I had loved it, but it had captivated Mark. That was all he talked about that day after school. And now we were looking at the original.

"How could any man carve that out of marble?" Mark asked me. "Any man other than Michelangelo, that is."

We stood, holding hands of course, and staring at the statue. Every once in a while, Mark would shake his head and say, "Unbelievable." I had to agree.

"This morning, the *Pieta'*, and now this," I said.

I looked at Mark engrossed in the sculpture, and said to myself, *I can't believe this is happening to me.* But it is!

I bought Mark a marble reproduction, about eight inches high, in the gift shop on the way out. Mark still has it on his desk. It is heavy so it went in his backpack.

We also bought a postcard of the Laocoön Group and mailed it to Mr. Carlson in care of the high school. "We stood and admired this magnificent work of art today. Thank you for introducing us to it. Sandy and Mark Tuttle." *Sandy Tuttle…I wonder if he knows we got married.*

On to the *Stanze,* the Rooms, of Raphael. We spent time in each room, but lingered – I liked that word – in front of *The School of Athens* fresco. Plato, pointing up, and Aristotle, pointing down, in discussion, surrounded by the great philosophers of ancient Greece.

Then Mark said to me, "Time to keep a promise."

And off we went to the Sistine Chapel, where Michelangelo painted, and popes are elected.

"Wouldn't it be terrible to be here during a Papal Conclave," Mark said. "When the Sistine Chapel is closed to everyone but the College of Cardinals?"

"I would make you bring me back," I said. "A promise made is a debt unpaid."

He leaned over and kissed the top of my head. The Sistine Chapel was crowded. Tour groups were constantly flowing through like a river through a gorge, tourists getting time to view the ceiling or the Last Judgment, but not both. Mark put his arms around me and guided me to a spot near the center of the floor. "Let me keep my arms around you, honey. No one will move us from this spot until we are ready to move on."

We looked up at God the Father touching the tip of Adam's finger with the tip of His finger. The creation of man as the mind of Michelangelo saw it. A few gawkers bumped into us, but Mark protected me, and we held our spot.

There are too many things I want to do with Sandy Roberts before I die -- look at the ceiling of the Sistine Chapel. I started crying. "I am so happy, Mark. I can't tell you how happy I am."

He squeezed me tighter.

"This is unbelievable. Being here, seeing this, with you," Mark said. My Mark. My husband.

He kissed the top of my head again. And held me tight. I glanced at his face; he was crying too.

"Our life **is** going to be wonderful, isn't it?" I said.

"Don't ever doubt it," Mark said.

He then led me, still encircled by his arms, to Michelangelo's Last Judgment, the ceiling to floor fresco covering one entire wall of the Chapel.

"How can one man paint this, carve the *Pieta'*, and engineer the dome of St. Peter's?" Mark asked.

"I am so glad we did not take a tour," I said.

"Me too. That would have been awful."

When we left the museum, it was already five-thirty. We stopped at an outdoor bar and ordered two *birra Peroni.*

"Do you want to have dinner early?" Mark asked.

I leaned across the table so that only he could hear me and whispered, "No. Let's go back to the room and make love. Right now. I think I want to do that much more than eat dinner. Then we can have a great dinner and walk around the *Piazza.*"

We finished the beers and then headed to the hostel of the Sisters of Mercy. I don't think I ever enjoyed making love with Mark more than I did that day. But I say that every time, don't I?

We had a great dinner at a little out-of-the-way *ristorante* on a side street near the *Piazza.* Mark and I were the only non-Italians there. We had the soup of the day, a variety of *minestrone,* but creamy, and *fettucine carbonara.*

"If they make this right," Mark said, "there will be no thick cream sauce, just egg, peas, cheese, and bacon. Back home, they always make it with a cream sauce."

"That's *alfredo,*" I said.

The fettucine came out in an egg, cheese, peas, and bacon mixture that was divine. The helpings were enormous, but, after sex, we were famished.

We ran into Father John Michael in the *Piazza.* He was with three other priests. He told us that none of the three spoke English.

I surprised him by saying, "*Noi parliamo Italiano.*"

"Wonders never cease with you two," he said.

In Italian, we told them about our day, excepting the sex.

When we got back to the room, I said, "I want you again. Are you up to it?"

Mark picked me up and carried me to the bed. We didn't shower, before or after. I did not want to separate myself from him and his smell. When we finished, Mark got up to pee. When he returned, I lifted the sheet and invited him to join me again.

I curled up in his arms and asked, "Do you like sleeping with me?"

"Yes, especially when you're naked," he said.

"Do you think my body is better than Peggy's?" Loaded question.

"I have never seen Peggy's body – *good answer* -- but there is only one female body in the world that turns me on, and it belongs to Sandy Roberts."

"Really?"

"Yes. Let me prove it to you."

Oh God, did he ever.

We served Mass with Father John Michael and Michelangelo again the next morning. Then we went back to the same café for coffee and rolls.

"What are you planning today?" Father asked.

"Secular Rome, Imperial Rome," I answered. "The Spanish Steps, the Forum, the Colosseum, the Pantheon, the Piazza Venezia, the Piazza Navona with the Fountain of the Four Rivers, the Trevi Fountain---"

"Just up the street from the Trevi Fountain, on the little street to the left when you're facing the fountain, is the Greg," said Father John Michael.

"We'll take a look," I said. "Mark has a map and we plan to walk most of the day. Maybe grab a bus or taxi back to St. Peter's if we get tired. First thing we are going to do, however, is go back to the *pensione* so I can take off these long pants."

"You might want to stay in slacks today, Sandy," he said. "There is a sight on the *Via Veneto*, near the *Piazza Barberini*, that I recommend you two see. There is nothing like it anywhere else in the world."

"What, Father?"

"The Capuchin Crypt in the basement of the church of *Santa Maria della Concezione.* I won't tell you what's there. I don't want to spoil the surprise. But visit the crypt if you can."

"We will," said Mark. "I want to show Sandy the *Via Veneto* anyway. It's the Park Avenue of Rome, Sandy."

"I have really enjoyed meeting you two. Please come to the motherhouse tomorrow morning for Mass. I'm celebrating it at eight. Then we can have a little breakfast. The porter at the front door will be expecting you."

"Thank you," I said. "We would love that."

"And Mark, don't read about the crypt in your guide book before you go."

"Okay, Father," he said. "I won't." And he didn't – *a promise made is a debt unpaid.*

We walked all day ending up back in St. Peter's Square at seven-thirty. I won't tell you about all we did and saw, but we had a great second day in Rome.

One experience that might interest you was the photo taking outside the Colosseum. As we approached that ancient amphitheater, we noticed legionnaires from Julius Caesar's army standing about.

"I wonder if they'll let you take a picture of me with them," I said to Mark. *What a dumb question that was!*

One of the soldiers saw our camera and approached us. "Picture with me?" he asked.

"Yes, thank you," I replied. I went to his side, and he put his arm around my shoulder. Oh my God, the smell. *He hasn't taken a shower since the Gallic Wars,* I thought. *Or washed his uniform.*

"Quick, Mark," I said.

Mark snapped the shot, and, after saying, "Thank you," I began to walk away. The legionnaire grabbed my arm and said, "Money," in English.

I said, in Italian, "Don't touch me; he will kill you."

Mark concurrently gave him a look that screamed, "**Get your fucking hands off her!**" and took a step in his direction. The soldier immediately let go of my arm; he understood the seriousness of the look. But he protested, "This is my job. You have to pay me. This is how I feed my wife, my *bambini*." *The sympathy play.*

"It's okay, honey," I said. Then I turned to the soldier and said, "We didn't understand. How much?"

"Ten thousand lire or ten dollars U.S."

I could see Mark, seething internally, wanted to argue. I said, "Pay him, honey. We should have asked."

As you know, Mark always does what I ask. Or what Maddie asks. Or what Annie asks. Mark gave him the ten dollar bill. At the exchange rate of six hundred lire to the dollar, that was the only choice for my mathematically minded husband. He winked at me. The internal seething was becalmed.

As we headed toward a Colosseum entrance, I said, "Well, lesson learned. I'm glad you didn't hit him. We could have ended up in an Italian jail."

"Or fighting one hundred legionnaires," he said, laughing.

"We always take care of each other, don't we?" I said.

When we stood at the Trevi Fountain, I asked Mark for a coin. He took out two ten-lire coins and handed one to me.

"Do we make a wish or does this just guarantee that we'll come back to Rome someday?" I asked.

"I don't know, but I have a solution," he said.

"What?"

"Make a wish that you'll come back to Rome someday," he said.

"My brilliant husband," I said. "What is ten lire worth?"

"A penny and two-thirds," he said.

"Can you possibly get your wish for less than two cents?"

"It's not the amount but the act itself that creates wish fulfillment."

"You **are** brilliant."

We had to visit the Greg since *a promise made is a debt unpaid*. It was about fifty yards from the Trevi fountain. Known as "the Harvard of the Catholic Church," it was nothing like my Harvard. The Pontifical Gregorian University is an indoor atrium surrounded by four floors of lecture halls. That's it.

"We can tell Father John Michael that we have seen it," I said.

In the Pantheon Mark told me that the dome was the largest dome in the world for thirteen hundred years, until Brunelleschi constructed the dome on the cathedral, the *Duomo*, in Florence.

"We will see that, won't we?" I asked.

"Brunelleschi's red dome is the most visible thing in Florence. We will see it," he answered.

We had lunch in the *Piazza Navona* at an outdoor *trattoria* adjacent to *La Fontana dei Quattro Fiumi*, the Fountain of the Four Rivers. Each corner of the fountain features a river god, the gods of the Nile, the Danube, the Ganges, and the Rio de la Plata in South America. In the center, there is another Egyptian obelisk.

We sat at a table ten feet from the fountain. We had two grilled ham and cheese *panini* and two bottles of *acqua con gas*.

"Do you know who designed this fountain?" Mark asked.

"No," I said. "Let me guess, Michelangelo?"

"No, Bernini," he said.

"The same Bernini who designed our columns?"

"**Our** columns?" Mark asked.

"You know what I mean," I said.

"Yes, the same Bernini. And if you stand on a circle to the left of the fountain, you only see one river god, not four, due to the alignment."

"Really," I said amazed.

"No, my gullible little wife," he said.

I couldn't reach him across the table so I waited until we were walking again before I punched him on the shoulder.

Another never-to-be-forgotten part of the honeymoon in Rome was the Capuchin Crypt in the basement of the church of *Santa Maria della Concezione*. Father John Michael was right: wearing the long pants was worth it. Three rooms filled with the bones of dead Capuchin monks, arranged by bone type, in macabre designs.

"Why did they do this?" I asked Mark.

He pointed to a sign in English and Italian:

What you are now, we used to be;
What we are now, you will become.

"It's like the ashes on Ash Wednesday, a reminder of our mortality."

"I'll stick with the ashes," I said.

Since I had on long pants, Mark suggested a quick stop at the church of San Peter in Chains, a small, out-of-the-way church containing one of the world's great sculptures, Michelangelo's Moses.

"Why does he have horns?" I asked.

"I read up on it, but no one really knows. Some experts say they are not horns."

"They're horns," I said.

"Maybe Michelangelo thought he was horny," Mark said.

I punched him on the shoulder.

"You can't hit me in church," Mark protested.

"Yes, I can. I just did, didn't I?" Faultless logic.

As I said earlier, we arrived back at the *Piazza San Pietro* at seven-thirty. We washed our hands and faces in the central fountain and, refreshed, headed back to the same *ristorante* where we had eaten the night before. The *carbonara* had been delicious. That augured well for other items on the menu.

"Do you want to try the *vitello Milanese*?" Mark asked.

"I know that means veal Milan style, but what is Milan style?"

"Wiener Schnitzel," he said.

"Yes!" I said. I love veal cutlets.

Mark ordered two bowls of kale soup, two orders of *vitello Milanese* with French fries, a mixed greens salad for two, and two bottles of *birra Peroni.* The waiter brought a basket of hot bread and olive oil for dipping.

The *Weiner Schnitzel* was *delizioso.* And the *birra Peroni* went down so smoothly we ordered two more bottles. And they were half-liter bottles.

When we finished eating, but while we were still drinking our beers, I looked at Mark and said, "Do you want me for dessert?"

He nodded his head vigorously.

"Then what are we doing sitting here? Pay the bill and take me home, husband."

Another wonderful night amongst the Sisters of Mercy. If they only knew.

We rang the bell of *Via della Conciliazione 51* at seven forty-five Saturday morning. The porter, Brother Vincenzo, greeted us, "*Buon giorno, Signore e Signora Tuttle. Padre*

251

Giovanni Michele vi aspetta." He then led us up a wide marble staircase to the chapel on the second floor. At the top of the stairs, a lifesize marble statue of Father Francis Jordan, Founder of the Salvatorians, greeted us. At eight, Father John Michael exited the sacristy and began Mass, in Italian! We finally attended Mass in Italian.

After Mass Father John Michael led us up to the roof to take in the spectacular view: the top of the façade, the giant statues of the twelve apostles, the dome of St. Peter's, the Jesuit Motherhouse with the large statue of *Gesu': "Io sono la tua salvezza"* ("They are the Society of Jesus after all," said Father John Michael), the *Castello Sant' Angelo* at the other end of the *Via della Conciliazione,* and the Tiber.

"Do you come up here often?" I asked.

"Every day," he said.

Father John Michael then pointed out a window near the top of one of the buildings next to the *Piazza.* "That's the window from which the Pope addresses the crowds in the square every Sunday when he's in Rome. He's at his summer residence now, *Castel Gandolfo.*"

He then led us to the refectory for a light meal. We were the only ones in the dining hall.

"The Community has Mass at six-thirty with breakfast at seven. I asked Sister Veronica, our cook, to prepare something for us." He rang a little bell that was on the table, and two nuns came out of the kitchen. One had a pitcher of *café latte* and three cups; the other nun had rolls, jelly, butter, and three soft boiled eggs.

"Grazie, Suor Veronica," said Father.

She smiled, said, "Prego," and both nuns returned to the kitchen.

"So this is good-bye for us. I have enjoyed meeting you two. You are a special couple. I could tell the moment I met you."

"Thank you, Father. You have given us the opportunity to do and see things we never anticipated," I said.

"Did you get to the Capuchin Crypt?"

"Yes," I said. "What you are now, we used to be; what we are now, you will become."

"It's not on the standard tours, but I wanted you two to see it. A reminder of our mortality. At your age, you probably never think about that.

"Talking about death, Sandy, you told me that first day in the *Piazza* that Mark saved your life when you were eight. How?"

I told him the story of the attempted abduction. As I related the incident, he kept looking at Mark and shaking his head.

"How did you have the courage to do that, Mark?" he asked.

"Courage wasn't involved, Father. I knew from the day I met Sandy that somehow it was my job to protect her. Always. I really believe that. If Sandy is in trouble, I just act. I don't ever consider the odds."

"That's true, Father," I said. "On the day of our first date, my father asked Mark what he considered his main responsibility to be concerning me. What did you say, Mark?"

"To always treat you with respect and to defend you with my life."

"And he has, Father. The day he beat up the pervert, when Mr. Ross told him it was over, the first question Mark asked was, 'Is Sandy all right?' And he told Mr. Ross that I was his best friend, and he would never let anyone hurt me. And he won't, Father. He won't."

"I told you you're a special couple. May God always keep you together. What are your plans for today?"

"We're going to visit the four main basilicas of Christianity, our own private mini-tour," said Mark. "We have already visited St. Peter's, of course, but we will spend some time there. We want to say good-bye to the *Pieta'*. Then St. Mary Major, St. John Lateran, and we'll take a subway to St. Paul's outside the Walls."

"Oh, and Father," I said, "We did visit the Greg."

"You do know the official Latin name of the school?" he asked.

"No," I said.

"*Universitas Pontificia Gregoriana.* The **Pontifical** Gregorian University. The Pope is the Honorary Rector. Every September, all the students gather on the main floor in the atrium, and the Pope, standing on the balcony on the second floor, addresses them. Doesn't happen at Harvard and MIT, does it?" He laughed. "Have a great day today, and a great life. God bless you. If I'm ever in Rhode Island, I'll look you two up."

Before we started our minor pilgrimage, I bought four postcards, filled them out, and mailed them: one to Mom and Dad, one to Patty, one to Margie Baylor, and one to Peggy. On Peggy's I wrote:

"A priest asked us to serve Mass next to one of the world's great works of art. Mark asked, 'Peggy?' The priest was referring to Michelangelo's *Pieta'*. We miss you. We love you. Riding the Barge. Wish you were here. Really. Love, Mark and Sandy."

We had a wonderful final day in Rome. I love St. Peter's. I'll never forgot walking into the *Piazza* our first day and looking at that majestic basilica, but the *Basilica Papale di San Paolo fuori le Mura* (The Papal Basilica of St. Paul outside the Walls) is a close second – I had not seen the *Duomo* in Florence yet. We took the subway out to St. Paul's, and when we walked into the enclosed garden in front of the main entrance, the sight took my breath away. The bright yellow facade, the columns, the large statue of St. Paul holding a sword in the middle of the garden – I thought it was one of the most beautiful churches I had ever seen. Inside there are paintings of every Pope, starting with Peter, in circles near the ceiling. I loved that church! I never would have thought of coming here. Thank God Mark is the Captain of the Barge of Curiosity, and I ride on it with him. My only regret was that Peggy was not there with us. On our honeymoon? Yes, on our honeymoon!

We ate lunch at a small *trattoria* near St. Paul's, also outside the old city walls. It was one of those restaurants that tourists never see. The food was homemade, the prices low, the language was Italian, and the waiter was flirtatous, with me, not Mark. He went down on one knee and serenaded me. Mark loved it as much as I did. We shared a half-liter of the house red, walked back to the basilica for a second visit – St. Paul, the Apostle to the Gentiles; that's us -- then took the subway back to St. Peter's.

It was too early for dinner so we went back to the *pensione* where we made love and then took a nap. I woke up before Mark and washed my panties and his boxers and hung them on the shower rod.

We went back to the same *ristorante* – why give up on a good thing? We had soup, of course – Mark loves soup – a chicken escarole, then shared a family style helping of *spaghetti bolognese*. With warm bread, olive oil, and a half liter of their house red.

We walked throughout the *Piazza* after eating, to work off the dinner, and to say a farewell to one of the wonders of the world. I stood again on Bernini's magic circle. Then we went home and went to bed. We were both very tired – it had been a long day – and I planned to just snuggle and sleep. Mark, sensing how tired I was, wrapped me up in his arms and said, "Good night, honey," and kissed my forehead.

But I discovered again that it is almost impossible for me to snuggle with Mark Tuttle without getting horny, like Moses. We were so closely entwined that you could not slide a single piece of paper between our bodies. I looked at his face, eyes closed, so peaceful, so handsome, so mine! I slid my hand between his legs – he was horny too. I started blowing air into his face, streams of "my honey breath" as he calls it. When he opened his eyes, I said, "Want me for dessert?" He slid off my panties and went down between my legs. God, I love it when he does that.

"You smell and taste so good," he said. "And I love your little inverted triangle."

"It's there to guide you home, my love," I said. *And it works so well!*

After feasting he pulled me on top of him and attacked my mouth as he entered me. I sucked my smell right out of his mouth. He massaged my ass; I had both of my hands around his head. As was becoming the wonderful norm for us, we came together.

We were now too worked up to sleep. We lay there talking, about St. Paul's, Father John Michael, the *carbonara* without cream sauce, getting our two cents worth at the Trevi Fountain, serving Mass at the Chapel of the *Pieta',* Assisi, our next stop, how wonderful our life together is going to be, Peggy Mayhew – yeah, we talk about Peggy; she is a crewmember after all – kissing, sniffing, sucking, licking, blowing air at each other, playfully nipping each other, hands all over each other, just being in love in Rome, guests of the Sisters of Mercy.

When we calmed down a bit, Mark got up.

"Where are you going, honey?" I asked.

"To pee," he answered.

"Hurry back. I need you next to me."

"I will."

Then I heard him cry out from the bathroom, "I can't see, I can't see. I've gone blind. Sandy, help!"

I jumped out of bed and rushed to him. He was standing at the edge of the shower with a pair of my panties over his head, covering his eyes.

I pulled them off. "You jerk," I said. Yes, I did punch him in the shoulder.

"A miracle! I can see," he cried out. "Did you use spittle?"

"Don't be sacrilegious. I'm going to tell everyone you were wearing my panties," I said.

"Well, I am kinky."

"I like kinky," I replied and pulled him into bed.

Yes, we did make love again. We are putting a dent in that ten thousand!

Chapter Fourteen
La Luna di Miele – Part II
Assisi, Firenze, Venezia and Stresa

<u>ASSISI:</u>

On Sunday morning, we took a cab from St. Peter's Square to Roma Termini, the main train station. We arrived at the station at eight thirty for a nine o'clock train to Assisi. Assisi is on the Roma-Firenze line, so we would be getting back on the same train the following afternoon after our one-night stay in the City of Saint Francis. We entered the first class car and were pleasantly surprised. We took two seats facing each other with a table between us. The windows were spotless. I was wearing my tan shorts. I knew I would need the long pants to visit the basilicas, St. Francis and St. Clare, but decided to travel in comfort and change in our hotel room. We had a room in the Hotel San Francesco, the closest hotel to the Basilica of St. Francis. We had paid extra for a room with a balcony overlooking the basilica.

The train left at nine, right on time. A matron with a tray of goodies came down the aisle soon after departure, and we bought some fruit, almond cookies, and two bottles of *acqua con gas.* The conductor just checked the dates on our rail passes and gave them back to us with a smile. I kicked off my sandals and put my feet on Mark's lap. We shared our breakfast looking out at the Italian countryside, once we had left the Roman suburbs behind.

I have said this before, but I still cannot believe that I am traveling in Europe with Mark Tuttle, and that he is my husband. I always knew he would be my husband, but the reality is still incomprehensible to me. I wouldn't trade the reality for the world, but it is still beyond my comprehension. For the rest of my life, he will be at my side. I thought of the evening of the Day of the Pervert when we shared a chair and a dish of ice cream in Mark's house. I knew then. I really did! I remember his sister, Patty, saying, "He never shares his Breyer's vanilla ice cream with **me**." *But he does with me... And he always will.*

I turned my eyes from the countryside and looked at him. He was eating an orange and making a mess all over his right hand. I said, "Give me your right hand." He did, and I licked it clean. Mom wasn't there to disapprove. It tasted delicious, both the orange and his hand, my husband's hand.

"You can expect little favors like that now that you married me. I told you you would never regret it."

He smiled, leaned across the table, and kissed me. "I will never regret it, not for a moment."

The ride, with stops, took two hours. We sat mainly in silence, watching the activity in the fields and villages -- women washing clothes, men with their oxen, children playing -- looking at each other, smiling, loving each other, loving our life, sharing almond cookies, occasionally playing footsie under the table.

Assisi is on a hill; the train stops in the plain. There is a bus running up to town center from the train station, but we decided to splurge and took a taxi. Our room indeed had a balcony, small but sufficient with two plastic chairs and a plastic table, overlooking the square and the *Basilica di San Francesco*. I changed to the obligatory long pants, and we headed over to see the basilica and the Giotto frescoes. Mr. Carlson had shown us slides of those too; he called Giotto the "father of modern art."

We went into the upper church first. It was crowded. The noise increased little by little until it became a roar. Then a portly Franciscan monk appeared and cried out, "*Silenzio*," and the noise fell precipitously to a low level hum. Then the noise cycle would repeat, steadily increasing to roar levels, causing the reappearance of the monk: "*Silenzio*."

"I could do that job," Mark said.

"Is your Italian good enough?" I asked.

"With practice, I could get there," he said.

I have told you a few times that I couldn't believe Mark and I were actually a couple. But there was something else, something palpable, something spiritual, happening. We were no longer Mark and Sandy. We had become MarkandSandy. *And the two shall become one flesh, and one mind.* As much as I had always loved Mark, and he had loved me, we were now more comfortable with each other than I would have thought possible. And this was only the eighth day of our married life. There was absolutely nothing I wouldn't be comfortable talking to him about. I had absolutely no inhibitions with him, and I know he had absolutely no inhibitions with me. How absolutely wonderful! And I wanted to make love with him all the time. I know there's a time and place, but I had that exciting feeling all the time now. My body ached for him.

"Let's go see the life of St. Francis as depicted by Giotto," I said.

The frescoes were around the outer wall of the upper church. As we were heading toward the first one, the cuckoo clock Franciscan Monk popped out and intoned, "Silenzio." The roar subsided to a hum.

"I **could** handle that job," Mark said.

I just squeezed his waist. *God, I love you, Mark Tuttle.*

Giotto's frescoes were exactly what Mr. Carlson had led us to expect: lifelike in a semi-primitive way. I could see Mr. Carlson lecturing as he presented the slides to us, "Giotto painted lifelike figures, a break from the byzantine style of the time."

"You know, honey," I said, "Mr. Carlson was a great teacher. He made us love great art."

"Let's send him another postcard," Mark said. We bought one depicting Giotto's *The Death of St. Francis*. I wrote, "You were a great teacher, Mr. Carlson. *Tante Grazie*. Mark and Sandy Tuttle. P.S. Yes, we got married. We're on our honeymoon."

Since I was church-dressed, in long pants, we walked down to the *Basilica di Santa Chiara,* the Basilica of Saint Clare, and viewed the church dedicated to the other major saint of Assisi. We had to give equal time to Assisi's female patroness.

I changed to shorts after that. We ate dinner, family style, in the hotel dining room. Dinner was served at six. Hotel guests sat anywhere and shared space with other guests at eight-person tables. Dinner was delicious: minestrone soup, hot bread, spaghetti and sausage, spicy or sweet. A bottle of house red, of course, and a liter bottle of *acqua con gas* on each table. We sat with a family of six from Padua. They were pleasantly surprised to discover we spoke Italian. The younger of the two sons, age six, fell in love with me. He kept moving his chair closer and closer to mine. We actually shared my chair for dessert, fruit and dates.

"I think he is in love with me," I said to Mark in English.

"He's not the first six-year-old boy to fall in love with you."

"Really?" I said. "Who was the other one?" I smiled at the other boy who fell in love with me when he was six. "You never fell out of love with me, did you?"

"No," Mark said. "And I never will." *I love my Mark...And he is **my** Mark.*

"*Come ti chiami?*' I asked the little Paduan boy. ("What's your name?")

"Marco," he answered.

I looked at Mark. "Can you believe that?"

"*Anch' io mi chiamo Marco,*" Mark said to the boy. They high-fived each other. "*Ed io anche la amo,*" Mark said. ("And I love her too.") Little Marco blushed. I kissed him on the forehead. He broke out in a big smile.

One other memorable thing happened in Assisi: we went for a walk after dinner and stopped at a little outdoor cafe' in the *Piazza del Comune* (City Council Square). While we were having two Coca Colas, a group of twenty or so teen-aged boys and girls, in school uniforms, marched into the square, led by a young priest in a cassock. They formed a circle, boy-girl, boy-girl, and, led by the priest, danced and began singing a hymn to Mary. Many of the adults in the *piazza* started clapping and singing along.

I love dancing. Mark and I often go line dancing with Peggy back home. I stood up, pulled Mark up with me, and joined the circle. The youngsters, not really much younger than Mark and I, joyfully welcomed us to their dance. The words of the hymn were repititious, and, within a minute, Mark and I were singing as well as dancing. I then noticed the family from Padua sitting at a table at another cafe'. Marco was watching me dance. I motioned him to join us.

262

He looked imploringly at his mother, who nodded. His eyes radiated joy, and he ran out and entered the dancing circle between me and Mark. He smiled up at me. I kissed his forehead.

"You're giving him a moment to remember," Mark said.

The teen-agers sang and danced to three hymns before heading out of the square. Mark, Marco, and I participated in the entire performance. The priest came over to us before he departed and said, *"Lode a Dio!"* ("Praise to God!")

"Si, Padre, lode a Dio, e grazie a Dio ed a lei." ("Yes, Father, praise to God and thanks to God and to you.") He made the sign of the cross on my forehead with his thumb, and smiling, joined his retreating flock. *"Dio sia con te,"* he called back to me. ("God be with you.")

Mark reclaimed our table while I walked Marco back to his family. We walked back holding hands. Marco asked me, *"E' Marco il suo marito?"* ("Is Mark your husband?")

"Si'. Anche il mio guardia del corpo." ("Yes. Also my bodyguard.")

He nodded his little head up and down. *"Si'. Si'. Lo capisco."* ("Yes. Yes. I understand.")

When we arrived at the Paduans' table, Marco turned to me and said, "Tante grazie, Signora. Lei e' molto simpatica." ("Thank you, Signora, you are very kind.")

"No, grazie a te, Marco. Sei tu chi sei molto simpatico." ("No, thank you, Marco. It is you who are very kind.") I then kissed him on the forehead.

"Signora, come si chiama?"

"Sandy," I answered.

"Un nome bello per una donna bella," he said blushing. ("A beautiful name for a beautiful lady.")

"Grazie, Marco."

"*Sandy*," he said. "*Il suo Marco e' molto fortunato.*" ("Your Mark is very lucky.")

Walking away, I turned back for a final glance at my young admirer. He was still watching me. He smiled and waved his little right hand at me. I smiled and waved back.

When I got back to Mark, he said, "He does love you."

"Doesn't everybody? You're lucky it's you **I've** chosen. Little Marco said you are a very lucky man."

"I agree with him. I'm honored to be the chosen one."

"The chosen one better save room for dessert."

"The chosen one always saves room for dessert. What is it tonight, pecan sandies?"

"No pecans." God, I was getting horny.

We went back to the room. Mark had dessert, we made love, and then we sat on our little plastic chairs looking at the lighted basilica.

"I was thinking today, honey," I said, "we have only been married for eight days, but our relationship has changed, grown. I am no longer Sandy. I'm part of Sandy and Mark. Later we'll be Sandy, Mark, and the kids. Wow! I cannot imagine not being with you. I will never go to sleep again unless I am wrapped up in your arms. Give me your pinky."

Mark did.

"Let's make a promise with St. Francis as our witness.

"We are a couple, best friends, forever. Promise?"

"Promise."

"Wanna make love again?"

"Yes. Little Marco was right. I am a very lucky man."

We mailed out five postcards the next morning. On Mom and Dad's, I wrote, "Mark and I are getting closer and closer every day. We love Italy and we love mariage. Love, SandyandMark."

On Peggy's I wrote: "A young Italian fell in love with me. He's six and his name is Marco. *Deja vu.* Love, Sandy and Mark."

FIRENZE

I was riding facing backwards as the train approached Florence, looking at Mark sitting across from me. Suddenly Mark exclaimed, "There it is!" looking out the window.

"What?" I asked, turning my head.

"Brunelleschi's Dome on the *Duomo.* Come around to this side."

Mark stepped into the aisle and let me slide in next to the window on his side of the table. He then scooted in next to me and put his arms around my waist. Enfolded in his arms, leaning against him, I looked at the distant, but approaching, *Duomo.*

"Magnificent," I said.

"It does dominate the landscape of Florence."

"Magnificent," I repeated. "When did Brunelleschi build that?"

"Fourteen thirty-six, fifty-six years before Columbus discovered America."

I just shook my head. What could I say?

"I love sitting like this with you," I said. "I love being married to you. Can't tell you how much."

"Me too, both the sitting with and the married to parts. God, you smell good."

"You're looking at one of the wonders of the world," I said laughing, "and that's what you're thinking."

"I'm using my eyes to appreciate Brunelleschi's masterpiece, and my nose and my arms to appreciate you. My brain can't decide which wonder is greater, but I think you're winning. There is no olfactory or tactile input from the dome."

"Good vocabulary," I said. I kissed him on the cheek. "I'm getting horny too."

"Too? How do you know I'm getting horny?"

"I can tell. It's a good bet in any case, isn't it? I always make you horny."

I discreetly slid my left hand between his legs under the table. "See. I was right."

We took a cab from the train station to our *pensione*, an inn run by an elderly woman and her daughter. The daughter, in her thirties we guessed, led us up to our room on the second floor, or, at least, we thought our room was on the second floor. When she opened the door, we entered a hallway with another stairway at its far end. We followed her up that stairway which opened into a suite that filled the entire third floor.

"*Piace a loro?*" ("Do you like it?")

"*Si'* ", I said. "*E' magnifico.*"

The suite had a kitchen/dining area, a sitting area with comfortable furniture, a raised sleeping platform with a king-sized canopy bed, a bathroom with a giant round bathtub, a separate shower, and two sinks, and a large balcony with two chairs and a table, wooden, not plastic. We were only eight blocks from the *Duomo*, but the balcony faced the opposite direction.

"When Mamma told me that you were on your honeymoon, I said you had to have the suite. It was vacant, so it is yours. No extra charge. Congratulations. May God bless your marriage."

"Thank you," I said.

When she departed, Mark and I went out on the balcony. What a view! We were looking over the red-tile-roofed dwellings of Florence, the winding streets, the Arno in the distance. Two little boys were playing marbles below our window. There was a cool breeze blowing through the doorway. "That breeze will be nice for sleeping," Mark said.

"Yes, it will. What time is it, honey?" I asked.

"Three," he answered.

"Still *siesta* time. I'll be right back," I said. "Wait here."

"Where am I going to go?" he asked.

When I came back, I said, "Here is my plan. I'm running warm water in the tub. We can take a bath together, then try out the king-sized bed – you're still horny, aren't you?"

"What do you think?"

"Me too. Then we can walk down to the *Duomo*, explore, get some dinner. Sound good?"

"Sounds great," Mark said.

"Let's go bathe."

We helped each other disrobe then submerged our bodies in the warm water. It felt wonderful. We sat facing each other, smiling, playing footsie. "This is our first bath as husband and wife," I said.

"Husband and wife," Mark said. "Mark and Sandy, husband and wife. I have wanted to say that since I was six years old. And now I can say it everyday for the rest of my life."

"Did you ever think we would be sitting together, naked, in an enormous, round tub in Florence? Playing footsie?"

"Never," Mark said. He reached to a shelf behind the tub and grabbed two bars of soap. He unwrapped them and tossed one to me. "Come over here and I'll soap you up," he said.

I went over and sat on his lap – he was still horny – and we kissed and soaped each other. "Do you want to make love here or in the bed?" I asked.

"In the bed. I want to eat you before we make love," Mark said.

"Dessert before dinner?"

"Yep."

"Let's rinse in the shower and then dry each other," I said.

We started kissing in the shower. Eventually, when we were dry, Mark carried me to the bed. He wrapped me in his arms and we kissed, more passionately than we had ever kissed. We knew better things were coming, but we didn't want to stop. My whole body tingled as it touched his body. I was about to explode.

"I love kssing you," I said. "Love it!"

Mark took his tongue out of my mouth, took a deep breath, and blew a stream of air into my face. "Can I eat you now?" he asked.

"Yes. But kiss me again first," I said, opening my mouth wide joining his. *God, I love kissing you: the taste, playing with your tongue...the wetness...the smell...the rushes of air... nibbling, sucking, licking, exchanging exhales and inhales...rubbing our bodies together as we kiss...My whole body aches for you, Mark Tuttle...Aches for you.*

"Now," I said, pushing his head down between my legs.

I came three or four times then pulled him up so we could renew our kissing. He entered me. We kept kissing. We didn't come together; we exploded together. We kept kissing. I held him as tightly as I ever had. "I love you!" I cried out. "My husband."

"I love you too," he said. "My wife. Did I ever tell you I love the way you smell?"

"No. You like it?"

"Yes."

We started kissing again.

"I love being married to you, Sandy."

"I love being married to you, Mark. It's all I've ever wanted."

"Me too. Since I was six."

We walked down to the *Duomo*. It only took eight minutes. "Another good choice of *pensione*," I said. It was already six o'clock. Our lovemaking and related activities had taken almost three hours, three delightful hours.

"We'll have plenty of time to see the *Duomo*, honey," said Mark. "You hungry?"

"Starving," I said.

We found a little *ristorante* a few blocks from the *Duomo*. We took an outside table.

Mark again did the ordering. We started with *pasta e fagioli* soup, the pasta and bean soup we call "pasta fazool" back in Rhode Island. We then had a chicken and vegetable dish with a light chicken gravy and angel hair pasta. Warm bread, of course, and a half liter of white wine. We had worked hard and we were hungry. The meal was delicious. *Mark Tuttle, my **husband**, and I are having dinner in Florence.* I looked at him and smiled.

"What?" he asked.

"I love you, that's all," I said. "And I am happy."

We walked around central Florence after dinner, for an hour or so, and then stopped at a small market before heading back to the *pensione*. Mark had noticed that there was a coffee maker and coffee in the suite. We stopped to get milk and a six pack of *birra Peroni*. The beer was warm, but we had a small refrigerator back in the room.

I sat on the balcony when we got back. The marble game was over; the boys were now playing some variation of tag. Mark came out with two glasses of *birra Peroni* on ice. I had never had beer on ice before, but it was very satisfying.

We sat holding hands and looking out over the city.

"I never told you this, Sandy, but I had a recurring fantasy when I was little. It started when I was six, after I met you. When I went to bed at night, I used to imagine that you and I shared a bedroom. I hated the fact that we were together all day and apart all night. We had two single beds about one foot apart. In my fantasy we were always wearing pajamas, cotton in summer, flannel in winter, and--
-"

"Did you see me change into the pajamas?" I asked.

"No. There was nothing sexual about the fantasy. We were just in pajamas. We would talk, laugh, tell jokes, tell stories. Often we were lying on our stomachs, holding hands over the space between the two beds, looking at each other. Even then I thought you had the most beautiful face. And when you smiled, oh my God! Turned me to butter. Still does.

"Then an adult would come to the door, mostly my mother, sometimes your mother, and say, 'Okay, you two, get to sleep.' Like we were supposed to share a bedroom. Then one of us, sometimes me, sometimes you, would get out of bed and get into the other bed, and we would hug and go to sleep together. Every night. Even in my fantasy, you smelled great. Then I would wake up in the morning hugging my pillow.

"I couldn't wait to get to school to see you. After third grade I couldn't wait to get to your house to pick you up. Then we stopped at Peggy's, and the three of us walked to school together. I can't tell you how proud I was walking to school with you two, the two prettiest girls in St. Michael's. I was proud walking with Peggy, but I was proud and happy walking with you.

"Our sex is wonderful, Sandy, and I love making love with you. Love it! But nothing makes me happier than going to sleep with you in my arms. We have done that for nine days now, and are going to do it again tonight, and tomorrow night, and every night from now on. That, I think, is one of the great rewards of marriage, sharing a bed with you."

"This is unbelievable, but I had that same fantasy. In mine, we had bunk beds. You were on top. You would hang over the top looking down at me, and I would look up at you. We would talk and laugh and touch hands. My adult was usually my father. He would come and say, 'You two, cut the noise.' I then lifted up my covers, and you climbed down into my bed. We kissed and then we hugged and went to sleep. Didn't we ever kiss in your fantasy?"

"When I got a little older. Every night after that spin-the-bottle kiss in fourth grade. That's when I discovered the delights of a Sandy Roberts kiss. I would kiss my pillow."

"Me too. I couldn't wait until I saw you in the morning. Remember the day the pervert tried to kidnap me? When I said 'I'm going to marry you someday, Mark Tuttle?' Do you know what I thought married meant?"

"No."

"I thought it meant sleeping together. Not sex, but just sleeping together. Kissing. Cuddling. We wouldn't need that bunk bed anymore. And having a family and children, but I had no idea how you acquired children. I just knew when you got married, they came along. I agree with you, we have great sex now, and have had for the last year, but this, being married, is so much better."

"Give me your pinky," Mark said.

I did, and we locked them together.

"Sandy, I promise you that we will sleep together every night for the rest of our lives. For me and you, marriage is forever. We're not just lovers anymore."

271

"We never were **just** lovers, Mark," I said, and squeezed his pinky. "But I know what you mean. Nine days ago we crossed the Rubicon. Our lives have changed, irrevocably. I committed to you, before God, our family, and our friends. And you committed to me, before God, our family, and our friends. And knowing us, we keep our committments."

We both said, "A promise made is a debt unpaid," and laughed.

We held our pinkies joined together, looked into each other's eyes, then smiled. "You are my wife forever, Mrs. Tuttle," Mark said.

"I know. There's nothing else I want."

"Another beer?" he asked.

"Yes, and more ice," I said.

I watched my husband walk into the kitchen. Yes, I did have a tear in my eye.

When I woke up, at eight o'clock, I was alone in bed. For just a moment, I felt a chill. *Where am I?..Where's Mark?* Then Mark jumped on top of me and pinned me to the mattress.

"Where were you?" I asked.

"Making you *caffe latte* and breakfast. Put on your shorts and go sit on the balcony. I will bring it out to you."

"I gotta pee," I said. "I'll be right out. Give me a kiss."

He leaned down and gave me a good morning kiss. "You have the most beautiful face in the world."

"Better than the Mona Lisa?"

"No comparison."

"Kiss me again."

After I peed I put on my tan shorts and went out to the balcony. Mark had placed a pot with *cafe latte* on the wooden table. There were also two mugs, two plates, two knives, two spoons, a jar of strawberry jam (*marmellata di fragole*), and four pieces of warm toast on the table."

"Where did you get the jam and bread?"

"At the market last night."

He poured my coffee and then put strawberry jam on two pieces of toast and handed one to me.

"Thank you," I said. "Why the special treatment?"

"I just want you to know how happy I am that you are my wife."

"I know that, Mark. And you know how happy I am, right?"

"Yes. Knowing that you love me fills me with joy."

"How poetic."

"But true."

I leaned over and kissed him.

"I was thinking about what you said yesterday about sex," I said. " I don't think any two people ever had better sex than we had yesterday. As good, maybe, but better, no way. And since we love each other, are so athletic, make each other horny, and know how to take care of each other's horniness, we are going to have many sessions like that. There will be days when we don't have sex, however, for whatever reason; but there will never be a night that we don't sleep together, kissing and hugging each other. Because you're my husband, and I'm your wife, and we have committed to each other for life."

"That rhymes," he said, holding up his mug. I clinked it with mine. "Sandy, you have made my childhood fantasy come true. I will never do anything to jeopardize that."

"Me neither. And there's another reason why I will never leave you."

"What?"

"You make great *latte*."

We had arrived in Florence on Monday afternoon, and were leaving for Venice on Thursday morning, so we had two full days to tour Florence. Mark had studied his Fodor's, and made a list of "can't miss" attractions: Michelangelo's David, of course; the Laurentian Library (Mark told me he had a surprise for me there); the *Piazza della Signoria*; the *Ponte Vecchio*; and the *Duomo*, the *Campanile* ("another surprise"), and the Baptistry in the daytime. We had seen them briefly Monday evening before dinner. I was so happy to have the Captain of the Barge of Curosity as my tour guide. Again, I wished Peggy were with us – during the daytime anyway.

As we finished our *cafe lattes* and delicious strawberry jam toast on the balcony, Mark said, "Well, what do you want to see this morning?"

"Your choice, Captain." I said.

"Let's put the best first, Michelangelo's David," he said. "Fodor's says there might be a wait of up to two hours to get into the Academy of Fine Arts."

"Two hours. That's like the Magic Kingdom during school vacations," I said. "But I guess it's worth it."

There was a sign at the front entrance of the Academy: *ATTESA – DUE ORE.* (Two hour wait) We walked around the block and added two bodies to the already long line. It was nine fifty. I mentioned earlier in this narrative that you can somehow recognize another American overseas. We had just joined the line, when a young girl came up to us. "You're Americans?" she asked, expecting the answer to be "Yes."

"Yes," I said, meeting her expectations.

"Our group is going in at ten, and we have two extra tickets. Two of the girls got sick. Mr. Rohm, our tour leader, asked me to see if I could find two Americans near the back of the line to sell the tickets to. We're not trying to make a profit; we just don't want to lose money."

"We would love to buy them," I said.

"Ten dollars," she said. "They're five dollars each."

Mark took out a ten dollar bill and handed it to the girl.

"Not to me. To Mr. Rohm. Let's go; we gotta hurry."

We followed her to the front entrance and to Mr. Rohm. Mark handed him the ten dollars, and he gave us two tickets to go in with their group. A win-win. At ten o'clock, the Girls Choir of St. Vincent's Church, Chicago, with two substitute Rhode Island choristers, entered the *Accademia di Belle Arti* to view Michelangelo's David.

"I never realized it was so big," I said.

"And no fig leaf," Mark said.

I punched him in the shoulder. As I hope you have realized by now, that is a gesture of love.

"And no horns. I wonder why Moses got horns and he didn't," I said.

"Seriously, it is hard to believe Michelangelo carved that out of marble, isn't it?"

"Yes."

It was crowded, but we were able to work ourselves quite close, and then Mark, holding me in front of him, held our place until we could fully appreciate this, our third, Michelangelo sculpture. With Michelangelo's David in front of me, and Mark behind me, I felt like the luckiest young woman in the world. In retrospect, I probably was.

"Let's get lunch and then go to the Laurentian Library," Mark said.

"What's so special about the Laurentian Library?" I asked.

"You don't remember it from Mr. Carlson's class?"

I stopped and looked at him. I was nibbling on my lower lip. "Something's coming back. One of his slides. I got it! The staircase flowing like lava from the second floor to the first."

"Designed by?"

This was just like back in the dining room with Peggy. Mark teaching; Peggy and I learning. I loved those dining room days. "Michaelangelo!" I said.

"Bingo," he said.

"God I love being with you."

"Let's get lunch."

We exited the Academy arm in arm.

"I love being with you too," he said.

"We are going to have a great life, aren't we?"

"Yes, we are, my beloved Sandy Roberts. Yes, we are."

I just squeezed his waist. And smiled at him. My husband! "I know." *There is no doubt in my mind, Mark Tuttle, my beloved Mark Tuttle.*

It did flow like lava from the second floor to the first.

"How can one man be so talented?" I asked.

"This was the library of the Medicis. Michaelangelo did a lot of work for Pope Clement VII, who was the Medici Pope. I guess when the Pope asks you to do some carpentry work around the family library, you can't say, 'No.' " Mark was massaging my shoulder as he told me this.

"We have to send another postcard to Mr. Carlson," I said. "Is there a gift shop here?"

"Yes," Mark said. "We have to go through it to get out."

We bought a postcard depicting the staircase. I wrote on the back: "Mr. Carlson, Yes, it does flow like lava from the second floor to the first. Sandy and Mark in the library of the Medicis. Thank you." I figured he would know Sandy and Mark without the Tuttle by now.

"Can we call Mr. Carlson when we get back and go see him?" I asked.

"Of course. I would like that."

We walked to the shore of the Arno about a tenth of a mile from the *Ponte Vecchio*, the most unusual, and beautiful, bridge I have ever seen.

"I wanted you to see this from a distance before we walked on it," Mark said.

"Are those apartments on the bridge?" I asked. There were buildings on the bridge from shore to shore.

"There might be some apartments, but they are mostly shops, a lot of jewelry shops."

"This is another unbelievable sight. Thank you, my Captain."

"You're welcome. Too bad Peggy's not here."

"On our honeymoon?" I said laughing.

"You know what I mean."

Yes, I did.

We then walked to the Old Bridge where Mark, as he so often does, surprised me. He led me to a jewelry shop specializing in bracelets. I love to wear bracelets. But my bracelets are costume jewelry, in the three to five dollar range. The only real jewelry I have are my pearl necklace, which I left at home at my mom's house, my diamond ring, and my wedding band, which two rings I never take off. This shop offered eighteen karat gold, handcrafted bracelets.

"How did you know about this shop?" I asked.

"I did my homework," he answered.

I chose three bracelets. They were beautiful. Mark would not let me know the prices until after I had made my choice. Nine hundred dollars each! He put the expense on his American Express card.

"Mark, this is too much," I said.

"It's my wedding gift to you."

"But I didn't give you anything," I protested.

"Yes you did, Sandy. You gave me the one thing that I have always wanted."

I hugged him right there on the *Ponte Vecchio.* Yes, I was crying.

"Wear them," he said.

"I will never take them off." I love my *Ponte Vecchio* bracelets, my wedding gift from Mark Tuttle. I guess he didn't consider making me joint owner of assets worth three quarters of a million dollars a wedding gift. As soon as we were married, everything he had was ours. There was never any discussion about that. And yet Mark always insists that I gave him more than he gave me. I gave him his Sandy and later four beautiful children whom he adores. There is nothing anyone could have given Mark Tuttle that he would appreciate more than that. And it is a biological impossibility that any other female in human history could have given him Maddie, his beloved, irreplaceable Maddie. Only Sandy Tuttle could give him that girl.

That night I was lying next to the sleeping Mark. The breeze was delightful. I was on my side with my right arm under his shoulders, my left leg over his legs, and my left hand flat on his chest, rubbing it. My new bracelets were dangling on my left wrist. He had his left arm around me. I could feel his heart beating – strong, steady – under my hand. I was wearing a T-shirt, one of his, and panties. He was wearing his boxers. No T-shirt.

My protector...my lover...sleeping, so happy, so peaceful, yet he would be in fighting mode at the slightest hint of danger or threat to me...He told my father, "I will always treat her with respect and I will defend her with my life" – not an empty promise...God, my father loves him – ever since third grade...I'll never forget that day at Joey's..."Get your fucking hands off her or I will kill you"...He meant it as those fuckers found out...my *bodyguard...mio guardia del corpo – why did I tell little Marco that?...How many girls have two six-year-old Marks fall in love with them?..I can feel his heart beating...Let me listen to it...*I put my right ear against his chest – strong, steady. *He really is happy and I'm the reason for that...He loves me, always has, I hope always will...I'll make sure he does...I'm just as happy, and he's the reason...I love the looks he gives me...Margie Baylor said she would die happy if a man ever looked at her like that...He tells me I'm a twelve on a scale of one to ten...He never saw anything in this world as pretty as my face...Even my little girl face...How could he beat up a thirty-five year old man when he was only eight?..Don't mess with Sandy Roberts...That breeze is so nice...There is a smell in it, human, but not bad...What is it?..God, he is handsome, and he's mine...He's that rare breed – truly a one-woman man, and I am that woman...If you ask anyone in Coventry, "Who is Mark Tuttle's woman?", they will tell you, "Sandy Roberts"...What is that smell, cooking? Sex? No, I don't think it's sex...I know what sex smells like...It's a pleasant smell...God, how he loves to smell me, my hair, my breath, my pussy, even my feet, my armpits...Sounds kinky, but I could do kinky with him...Haven't yet, probably never will, but I could...Might be fun...No hurting...Mark Tuttle would never hurt Sandy Roberts...And he is not only a one-woman man in the real world, he is a one-woman man in his fantasy world...He tells me, and I believe him, that I am the only woman he ever fantasizes about...Hard to believe since he spends so much time with Peggy Mayhew, but I believe him...Yes, I still fantasize about Peggy, mostly just kissing fantasies, but sometimes more...Mark knows I love her and he's okay with that...I think he loves her too, in his own way...He got a black eye defending her...Maybe he fantasizes about me and Peggy...No, I don't think so...But* *my Peggy fantasies are only fantasies...Mark is my only real world lover...That one time with Peggy was nice, but we were just kids...Well, I wasn't married yet anyway...And Mark told me I can kiss Peggy...Peggy's kisses are delicious...Does he know how passionate our kisses are?..Probably not...I have never kissed Peggy the way Mark and I kissed yesterday...God that was good...I didn't want to stop...Starting in the tub then moving to the shower...I'm getting horny...I think we will take showers together a lot...Even when we were fucking, we were kissing...Something's changing in our relationship...for the better if that's possible...What is that noise?.. A man and woman are arguing – he took money from her kitchen jar to buy wine... There's a door slamming...Out for more wine?..I hope Mark and I never fight like that...We won't...Mark won't fight with me...I was punching him, challenging him to a fight the second day at St. Michael's...He could have killed me..."I don't want to fight with you, Sandy. I want to be your friend"...God I'm horny...That's good, getting horny with your husband...He always makes me horny...I haven't masturbated since junior year...I don't have to; he always takes care of me...I wonder if he masturbates...I've never seen him...Why would he? – I always take care of him...That's my duty and responsibility – I'm his woman...His wife...I am Mark Tuttle's wife, and he's my husband...Believe me, taking care of him is not an onerous duty...Oh God no...It's his duty and responsibility to take care of me too...I know that's not an onerous duty for him...I don't know who loves it more when he goes down on me...He loved my little bumps...I thought he was kidding at first, but he wasn't...He was so excited that day in the pool shed when I let him take off my top...looking at my little bumps, then touching and kissing them...One happy little boy...I always make him* *happy...He had his hand inside my bottoms squeezing my ass...I told him he could...We were hugging, flesh against flesh...He still loves my ass...And my bumps...Actually his left hand is caressing my ass now...Feels good...I've read about anal sex, but that's something we will never do...It would hurt me, and Mark will never hurt me, wouldn't even consider it...I wonder if he's horny...Let me see...He's getting hard...Maybe if I stroke him...Oh yes...I always make him horny...God, it's great to be horny together...Husband and wife, horny together – what could be better than that?..He's big too, like David...Not that big but perfect for me...Should I wake him up?..Will he get mad?..Will he get mad if I don't?..Mark never gets mad at me...Never...Yeah, I'll wake him...I'll blow my honey breath in his face...(*My sweet air is flowing over his face*)...He's stirring...Wake up, Mark. I've got something for you... He's waking up... He's looking at me...He's smiling, of course he's smiling...My face makes him smile...He loves my face...He says it's the most beautiful face in the world...He believes that...He's squeezing my ass...We're going to fuck...Mark Tuttle and I are going to fuck...and kiss... God I love being married to him... He's reaching up and touching my face...Oh my God!!!!*

"Your breath smells so good, and you have the most beautiful face in the world," Mark said. "Your ass is not bad either."

"This girl with the beautiful face and nice ass is horny."

"Well then, why don't we fuck?"

"I was hoping you would suggest that. I love you, Mark Tuttle."

"I love you too, Sandy Tuttle."

'Sandy Tuttle' – I am getting used to that.

"Know what I want to do right now, even more than fuck you?' I said.

"What?"

"Kiss you. Play with your tongue. Thinking of it is getting me so excited."

"Me too. God, your breath smells exciting, and so sweet."

Oh God!..Oh God!..Oh God!..I love you, Mark Tuttle.

"You'll have to wear your long pants this morning, Sandy. We'll visit the *Duomo,* the *Campanile* (the bell tower), and the Baptistry." We were sitting on the balcony drinking *cafe latte* that Mark made and having the toast with *marmellata di fragole* again. "You can change to your shorts at lunchtime." A whole gang of boys and girls were playing in the street beneath our balcony. *I wonder how the fighting couple are handling the new day...We will never fight like that...I won't let that happen...And what **was** that smell? ..I still can't place it.*

"Your *cafe latte* is as good as any I've had in Italy," I said.

"Grazie."

"*Prego.* Where are we going this afternoon?" I asked.

"*La Piazza della Signoria.* The site of the rise and fall of Savonarola."

"The evil monk, the dark monk."

"He would burn all your colored T-shirts and panties. Even the word 'panties' would be anathema. And he would confiscate those decadent bracelets."

"Nasty man. Can we climb to the top of Brunelleschi's Dome this morning? We need the workout."

"Yes. As soon as we get there, I'll get us tickets. Why don't you get ready, and I'll clean up here?"

"I want to take a shower, but I'll be fast. Wanna shower with me?"

"That could end up being a long shower. Maybe at lunch time."

No 'Maybe,' Mr. Tuttle. "Give me a kiss anyway."

There was no wait for the dome climb. It is steep with four hundred and sixty-three steps, but we are young, athletic, and healthy. Mark climbed up behind me. He didn't say why, but I knew. No, not to watch my ass make the ascent. I'm sure he enjoyed that, but he trailed me to protect me. If I slipped, he would be there to catch me. Always my protector, even in the mundane daily activities of living. He does it without thinking. It's his job. He always puts himself between me and potential danger. He does the same for Peggy and Margie, but if there is ever a choice between me and one of them, my safety comes first. I'm going to be the mother of his children. But I digress. The highlight was the cupola's outdoor balcony which gave us a three hundred and sixty degree view of Florence and the Tuscan Hills. I loved looking at the Arno and the *Ponte Vecchio* from on high. I turned to Mark and said, "My husband bought me these bracelets in a shop on the *Ponte Vecchio*. He must love me."

"Maybe he just wanted to get into your pants."

Yes, I punched him on the shoulder. "My husband doesn't need to buy me jewelry to get into my pants. He can live in there if he wants to."

"I was just kidding," Mark said.

"I know that. The day we stop kidding is the day I will start worrying." I had turned and was facing him. He had his hands around me holding the railing. I kissed him.

"God, you have a beautiful face," he said.

"You've never told me that before."

At the *Campanile*, the bell tower almost as tall as the dome, Mark assumed his Captain of the Barge of Curiosity role.

"Who do you think designed this?" he asked.

"Is class starting? Let me get Peggy," I said, laughing. "Let me guess, Bernini?"

"No."

"Michelangelo?"

"No. Our friend from Assisi."

"Little Marco?"

"Good guess, but no. Giotto."

"God, they were all polymaths."

"Good word. Yes they were."

It was lunch time. "I have an idea," I said. "We are going back to the *pensione* so I can change. Why don't we get some bread and cheese, butter, maybe some pepperoni, and eat on the balcony. We have cold beer. Maybe take that shower before we visit Savonarola."

We enjoyed our lunch on the balcony, looking over the red rooftops. The street was quiet – *siesta* time had begun. Mark had dessert in the shower, a delightful first for us. Savonarola would not have approved. We were clean and refreshed when we headed back out. I was in shorts.

In the *Piazza della Signoria*, we stopped first to view the sculpure *The Rape of the Sabine Women*.

"You wouldn't let any men rape me, would you?" I asked.

"I was ready to fight one hundred Roman legionnaires for you, wasn't I?"

He was. That's what's amazing. He was.

"This is Giambologna's masterpiece," Mark said.

"John Baloney?" I said. "I don't know him. Did Mr. Carlson cover him?"

"No. But just look at that. Carved out of one piece of marble. Rape didn't mean rape back then."

"What did it mean?" I asked.

"It's from the Latin, *raptio,* which means abduction. The first Romans needed wives so they adbucted them, raped them, from the locals, the Sabines."

"How do you know all this?" I asked. Peggy and I were always asking him that question.

"That's why I'm Captain, and you two are measly crewmembers."

I punched him on the shoulder.

"Come over here. I want to show you something," he said. I followed him to a white circle in the *piazza.*

"You know about the Bonfire of the Vanities?"

"Yes," I said. "That was when Savonarola ordered the burning of all luxury items, things that supposedly took your mind away from the important ideas, things like my colored T-shirts and fancy bracelets. What would he have thought of my skimpy colored panties?"

"He would have burned them with you still wearing them," Mark said.

"You wouldn't let him burn me at the stake, would you?" I asked.

"No," Mark said.

"Just, 'No?' "

"What more do you mant me to say?" he asked.

"I don't know, but more than just, 'No.' "

"No, I would not let him burn you at the stake."

"That's better."

"And how did Savonarola end up?" Mark, back in captain mode, asked.

"Burned at the stake," I said.

"Right here," he said, pointing to the white circle. "Feel it. It's still hot."

Always gullible with Mark, I reached down and felt the white circle. It was very warm. "That's amazing. How does it stay warm?" I asked.

"White stone, summertime, hot sun, Italy," he said.

Yes, I punched him again.

We sent out more postcards from Florence.

On Mom's and Dad's, I wrote, "I am glad we got married when we did. It would have been a crime to postpone the bliss for four or five years. Love SandyandMark."

On Peggy's: "Mark said he wished you were with us. Really. Me too. Love Sandy and Mark. P.S. I love you. xoxo."

VENEZIA

We rode side by side on the trip to Venice. Mark let me have the window, and I leaned against him the whole way. Napped a bit with my head on his shoulder. Something happened in Florence. I don't know exactly what, but I liked it. I wanted to touch him all the time, kiss him. I wanted everyone to know that I am his woman. I wanted my actions to cry out, "Women, he's mine. Mess with him and you'll be fighting a tigress." I was falling more in love with Mark every day.

Our train pulled into the Santa Lucia train station at noon on Thursday. We walked to our hotel, the Hotel Carlton, on the Grand Canal. It makes it easy traveling when you only have backpacks. Mark had booked an upper floor room with a canal view. I couldn't believe it – I was in Venice, with my husband Mark Tuttle, madly in love, and staying in a room on the Grand Canal. A month prior I had been sitting in Honors English class at Coventry High School.

The room was small, but the view compensated. All we needed in the room were a bathroom and a bed. We definitely needed a bed! The room had both. We stood on the balcony looking at the Grand Canal: gondolas, the water taxis, the *vaporetti* (water buses), which we would be using, private boats, little cross-canal ferries, water bus stops all along the Grand Canal.

"Put on your church pants, honey," said Mark, "we're taking a water bus to my church."

"Your church?"

"Yes, the Basilica of St. Mark in the *Piazza San Marco.* I don't think there is a *Piazza* Sandy here."

"Can we take a gondola ride while we're here? Just me and you?"

"Of course. I'll check at the front desk as soon as we go down."

"Make sure we get a singing gondolier. Another thing I'd like to do while we're here is spend one day at *Lido di Venezia,* the beach on the Adriatic. I read it is a spectacular, white-sand beach. We might even see some movie stars."

"Sure. Why don't we sightsee today and tomorrow and spend all day Saturday at *Lido. "*

"I'll change, and we can go catch us a water bus." I took off my short pants and was extracting my long pants from the backpack.

"God, you are sexy," Mark said. "Standing there in your panties. No inhibitions. I love that. I love living with you."

"Come here," I said. "We'll fuck later, believe me, we'll fuck tonight, but kiss me now. I am getting addicted to your kisses. Can't get enough of them. I want to kiss you all the time."

"You can kiss me anytime you want."

We kissed passionately for five minutes. He had both his hands on my butt the whole time we kissed. I think he is getting kiss-addicted too. And ass-addicted. My kisses; my ass. "Let me get dressed, or we'll never see Venice."

At the front desk, Mark booked us a private gondola ride for eight that evening. We had two choices, four or eight. I thought it would be more romantic in the dark with lights. The desk clerk promised us that our gondolier, Antonio, would enthrall us with Italian love songs.

We boarded the *vaporetto* going down the Grand Canal to the *Piazza San Marco* and the Doge's Palace, the giant L-shaped *piazza* that was the gateway to the Orient when Venice controlled the world's maritime traffic.

"Marco Polo left from here to go to China. He brought back the noodle." Mark said.

"One noodle?" I said, laughing. "Speaking of noodles, are you hungry?"

"Yes," he said. "These restaurants here all look expensive and touristy. Do you want to eat here or find a more secluded restaurant?"

"Why don't we find a local restaurant, and have Cokes here later to people watch?"

We headed off down a side canal and found a *ristorante* that did not seem to have any tourist customers. We sat at one of the three outdoor tables. Of course we ordered noodles: *fettucine bolognese*, served family style, with a half-liter bottle of *acqua con gas*. Mark had a bowl of vegetable soup; I passed on the soup. I took a couple of spoonfuls from his bowl, however. Mark did not mind. I even used his spoon. That made it more tasty for both of us.

"We can eat dinner after we get off the gondola," Mark said. "There are three or four restaurants near the Carlton."

"I noticed," I said. "One of them is Chinese."

"Really?"

"Yes. *Re di Cina*." (China King)

"Chinese it is," he said.

He sat there, looking at me, smiling.

"What?"

"I love you. I absolutely love you. I want to kiss you all the time too."

"Good, because I absolutely love you too. And you better kiss me a lot, or I'll die of kiss deprivation."

"Did I ever tell you you have a beautiful face?"

"Just a thousand times."

We walked back to the *Piazza San Marco,* visited the Doge's Palace, walked along the lagoon, sat and looked out to sea, stopped at Harry's Bar for a beer -- Mark had read that Hemingway hung out there when he was in Venice – and went into St. Mark's to see the famous relic of St. Mark, brought to Venice by pirates. There were street musicians and jugglers performing in front of the Doge's Palace. We stopped and watched them for a while; I put six hundred lire in their pot. There were mimes there too. Mark and I find mimes creepy. I didn't put any lire in their pot.

"Let's go sit at one of the tables in the *piazza* and have a Coke," he suggested.

We got a table at the edge of the *piazza,* perfect for people watching.

"A Chinese restaurant in Venice!" he said. "China King. There's a China King in Warwick."

"Maybe it's a chain. I read once that, no matter where you are on earth, there is a Chinese restaurant within one mile of you."

"That's hyperbole, but not far from the truth," he said.

"They have *gelato* here," I said.

I ordered a dish of *fragola* (strawberry), and Mark ordered *pesca* (peach). You have to be very careful when you order peach. *Pesca* is peach; *pesce* is fish. Fish ice cream would be unpleasant. We shared. We have been sharing everything since we sat at his table sharing

289

Breyer's vanilla bean ice cream the night of the aborted abduction. I started crying.

"What's wrong, honey?" he asked.

"Nothing. I am so happy. I was thinking about the time we were eight, sharing a chair and ice cream in your dining room. We always share everything. You just shared three quarters of a million dollars with me."

"There's no mine and yours anymore, Sandy. All there is is ours."

I reached across and squeezed his hand. "I love being married to you. What time is it?"

"A little after five thirty."

"Let's take the *vaporetto* back to the hotel and get ready for the gondola."

The *vaporetto* was packed. We had to stand, but Mark enfolded me in his arms, and we stood near the front looking at the houses along the Grand Canal.

"They're so colorful, honey," I said.

"Like your panties," he said.

I started laughing and couldn't stop. People were looking at me.

"*Scusi, scusi*," I said to those nearby. "*Il mio marito e' molto sciocco.*" (Excuse me...my husband's very silly) "That means 'jerk,' " I said to Mark. He kissed the top of my head.

When we got back to the room, at six fifteen, I suggested we take a nap. "Set the alarm clock for seven-fifteen, just in case," I said.

I stripped down to my colorful, tangerine, panties and joined him in the bed. We didn't make love – we were saving that for later, after the romantic gondola ride and the Chinese dinner – but we didn't nap either. First we talked. About us. About marriage. About our marriage. About how something had changed for me in Florence -- how something unbelievably good had become better. About tomorrow. I said I would like to take one of the half-day boat tours of Venice, going down many side canals, and then take a public *vaporetto* out to some of the islands in the lagoon. Of course, since I suggested it, it became our plan. Mark always does what I want.

Then we hugged and kissed. That was becoming one of my favorite pastimes. When the alarm went off, I reluctantly separated myself from my husband and went into the shower. We would have taken a shower together, but the stall was too small. A one-person shower, a very thin person. When Mark finished, he cried out, "Help, I'm stuck."

"*Sciocco!*" I said.

Antonio and his colorfully lighted gondola were waiting for us at eight. The gondola dock was fifty feet from the front door of the Carlton. Antonio helped me in, and Mark and I sat together, close together, in the back of the gondola. We were both wearing short pants. Antonio handed me a blanket. "You may need this. Just in case." It wasn't cold, but I put the blanket over us for romantic purposes.

"You can't come to Venice without doing this, honey," I said to Mark. I snuggled even tighter. Antonio moved us away from the dock out into the Grand Canal. He took the first left into a side canal where he began to serenade us. Beuatiful love songs, one after another. He had a marvelous voice.

Non dimenticar....
Ciao,ciao, Bambina....
Come prima....
Al di la....
Volare....

If possible, I snuggled even tighter. "Kiss me, *mi amore*," I said. *Kissing Mark Tuttle in a romantic gondola in Venice with Antonio singing Italian love songs for us -- how is this happening to me?* Mark kissed me. I laughed. Mark looked at me, not expecting that reaction.

"A month ago," I said, "we were in Honors English. Now we are on a canal in Venice, in a gondola, curled up together, kissing, being serenaded. How did this happen?"

O sole mio....

Anima e core....

Domani....

Santa Lucia....

Amore scusami....

The ride was over too soon. "I love you, honey," I said to Mark, kissing him.

Mark gave Antonio a ten dollar tip, in US dollars, which was appreciated.

"*Tante grazie, Signore*," said Antonio. "*La faccia di sua sposa e' bellissima.*" (Thank you, sir. Your wife has the most beautiful face.)

"*Io lo so*," said Mark. (I know.) And to me, "See!" I kissed him again. I love Mark Tuttle.

And the young lovers went to China King in Venice. I enjoyed writing that sentence; I don't know why. It was almost ten o'clock, but *Re di Cina* was packed. We had won ton soup, egg rolls, and mu shi chicken. We could have been in Rhode Island. At China King. Or Chun Fun.

Then we went to our room and made love. We kissed before, during, and after. Then I slept wrapped up in his arms. When I woke up, he was looking at me and smiling. "I love to wake up with your face in front of mine," he said. "It is the most beautiful face in the world." He says that a lot, but I never tire of hearing it. I blew a stream of honey breath into his face and then we kissed.

292

It was eight when we arrived at the front desk. Mark signed us up for a canal tour, four hours, beginning at nine. There would be eight people on the tour, not too many. We had *cafe latte* and rolls in the hotel restaurant before boarding the boat.

The most intriguing part of the tour was the passage under the Bridge of Sighs, *il Ponte dei Sospiri,* which bridge connects the New Prison with the Interrogation rooms in the Doge's Palace. You did not want to be led across that bridge, and if you were, you sighed. Your last sigh. *Il suo ultimo sospiro!*

We took a *vaporetto* down to the *Piazza San Marco* and took public transportation, another *vaporetto,* out to Murano, an island in the lagoon famous for glassblowing. The desk clerk at the hotel tried to sign us up for a free tour of Murano, but Fodor's had instructed Mark to avoid the free tours. "You won't get off Murano without buying something unwanted," warned the guide book. So we went out on our own. We did not buy anything.

We rose early on Saturday, at seven, and I packed Mark's bathing suit, my black bikini, a pair of my panties, a pair of his boxers, two T-shirts, and two towels into one of the backpacks. We left the camera and my gold bracelets in the room safe. We were definitely going to swim, and didn't want to risk losing them. We were wearing shorts and our Red Sox hats. Mark put some lire, our passports, and a credit card in a plastic bag that he placed in his zippered bathing suit pocket. He did not take his wallet.

We took one *vaporetto* down to the lagoon and another *vaporetto* over to *Lido di Venezia.* The *vaporetto* stop on *Lido* was at one end of the *Gran Viale Santa Maria Elisabetta,* and the beach was at the other end of that majestic street. It was a twenty minute walk. I loved walking down that street arm-in-arm with Mark. Mark and

Sandy walking together on the *Gran Viale Santa Maria Elisabetta*. Wow! There were cabanas for rent at the beach – locks for rent also. We rented a cabana and a lock, used the cabana to change, and locked our clean clothes and backpack inside. I love being married to Mark. We have no inhibitions. We changed in front of each other as if it were normal. It is normal for us. Halfway through changing, I pulled him to me and kissed him. I love being married to Mark. Didn't I just say that? He loves being married to me; I can tell. We also rented two bamboo mats and an umbrella. We were all set for a day at *Lido di Venezia.*

We went for a swim after we staked a claim to a spot on the beach by laying out our mats and putting up the umbrella. I laid out the mats; Mark put up the umbrella. The beach was not crowded. The Adriatic was clean and azure blue. The bottom sandy. We swam, kissed, and then ran back to our claimed spot, dried off, and stretched out on the mats under the umbrella. We held hands and talked. Even when we weren't talking, we were looking at each other. *Life is wonderful,* I thought. *Mark Tuttle and Sandy Roberts on the Lido di Venezia...So much more romantic than Narragansett Beach in Rhode Island...To be fair, Narragansett Beach is nice, but Lido di Venezia...I wonder what Peggy is doing now...Maybe she's at Narragansett Beach. In a bikini – what a body on that girl...I know Mark thinks I look sexy in my bikini, but Peggy is a goddess...Mark is funny – he thinks I'm prettier and sexier than Peggy...He says I'm the only woman who turns him on...And I turn him on all the time...I love you, Mark Tuttle..You turn me on too...I'm horny right now.*

"Peggy is going to be way ahead of us on *Catch-22*. We haven't opened the books since we've been here," I said.

"We can catch up on the flight home. I bet she hasn't opened it either."

It was a lazy, beautiful day. We swam, playing together in the water like kids, kissing of course, coming back to the mats to dry off, relax, nap, and talk. Most of the time we lay on our sides facing each other. We touched each other a lot, chaste touches, but wonderful touches. Mark likes to massage my shoulders when he talks to me. His hands are strong, but gentle with me. We found a vendor at noon and had panini – ham and cheese -- with Cokes.

"I'm going to run down to the water and wash the sand off my hands," I said. "Be right back."

As I ran back to the mats, Mark was sitting up staring at me, shaking his head.

I stood in front of him with a questioning look on my face.

"Sandy," he said, "you are the most beautiful woman in the world. I can't even begin to express how good you look in that bikini. I can't believe that you are with **me.**"

I stood there speechless.

"I will do everything I can to make your life wonderful and happy. I don't ever want to lose you. I want to prove myself worthy, as Aunt Marion would say. You are not only beautiful, but you are the most amazing person I have ever met, so smart, so nice, so athletic, amazing in every way...

"And that face of yours – the first time you smiled at me I thought I was being visited by an angel or by Helen of Troy, the face that launched a thousand ships. For twelve years I dreamed about that face every night. Now I wake up and find it in my bed...

"Don't misunderstand me. I know we are together, and I know we are together for life. The choices have been made, and you chose me. I thank God that you did. I just find it hard to believe that Sandy Roberts, who really is the goddess, not Peggy, chose me. Thank you. I love you."

What do you say to that?

I knelt down in front of him. I pulled him up on his knees. I was crying. Of course I was crying. I always cry when I'm happy. We were kneeling face to face, six inches apart. I held both his hands in mine. Some people nearby were watching, but I didn't care.

"Mark, I want you to look at this sexy young lady in her black bikini, look at this beautiful face, this angelic face that you love, and listen to me. You're putting me on a pedestal. This is the second time you've done that. Let me tell you something, Mark Tuttle – no matter how high a pedestal you put me on, I will always be looking up to you. I have put you on a higher pedestal. I am your woman. You are my man. There is no **fucking** way you are ever going to lose me. And no way I am ever going to lose you...

"All the way through school, you amazed me. Mark Tuttle, the handsomest, smartest, nicest, most athletic boy in school, the boy every girl wanted to date, chose **me.** Me, you, and Peggy were always together. Every person in Coventry except one – you! -- said Peggy was the prettiest girl in Coventry, maybe in Rhode Island, maybe in the whole world. I loved that you were the dissenter. So I never had to worry about Peggy. You chose **me**. Peggy told me many times she had a crush on you. She never did anything about it because we were best friends, but she also said that making a move on you would be a waste of her time, because you chose **me**, you loved **me**...

"In high school, I was worried for a couple of years. As you know. You never asked me for a date, and the girls sniffed around you like lionesses in heat. You never gave them the time of day. You were always with me and Peggy. But if you had shown any interest in any of those bitches, there would have been some vicious fights at CHS...

"I asked Peggy for advice in high school, and she told me to start fucking you. That's Peggy. But I decided to bring it to a head at that EG basketball game. That's when you told me I was on a pedestal, that I was the P-GOAT, the 'Prettiest Girl Of All Time', untouchable and intimidating. Me, untouchable and intimidating to Mark Tuttle. I thought I broke that pedestal back then...

"I lay in bed the other night in Florence. You were asleep. The first things that came into my head looking at you were 'my protector' and 'my lover.' And you are both of those things. I started getting horny, and, with my help, you started to get horny too, and do you know what I thought?"

"No," he said.

"I thought, 'Husband and wife, horny together, what could be better than that?' So no more pedestals. I'm worthy of you, and you're worthy of me. We're a couple, a team, partners, equals, best friends. Nothing will ever pull us apart. Okay? I love you. There is no **fucking** way you are ever going to lose me. You're stuck with me, Tuttle. And I'm stuck with you."

He pulled me to him, and we hugged and kissed. He was crying too. I wanted to fuck him right there on the beach at *Lido di Venezia*, but I didn't want us to get arrested. I could tell he wanted to fuck me too -- our genitals were touching, minimally separated by the thin material of two bathing suits.

"Let's go in the water," I said, "to cool down." And we ran to the Adriatic hand in hand. Me and Mark Tuttle, my husband.

We showered at the outdoor showers in the cabana area, changed into dry clothes in our rented cabana, which procedure took longer than it should have due to hugging and kissing interruptions. The thought of fucking there crossed my mind, but I was afraid we would tip over the cabana. "Tonight," I whispered into his ear. We walked back up the *Gran Viale Santa Maria Elisabetta* and stopped at an outdoor *ristorante* in *Santa Maria Elisabetta Piazza* for dinner.

"They specialize in fish," I said. "How about Mediterranean sea bass served over a bed of linguini? The soup of the day is Venetian Chowder."

"Sounds delicious."

I ordered the sea bass and two small bowls of chowder, and asked the waiter to bring us a bottle of the house white, a half-liter.

The waiter poured two glasses and then left the bottle. I held my glass up in front of me, extended toward Mark. He raised his glass to meet mine.

"To us," I said. "Partners and lovers forever."

"Amen!" said Mark.

We took the *vaporetto* back to *Piazza San Marco* and, after walking around the walkway bordering the lagoon, we stopped at the same *trattoria* for *gelato.* This time I had the *pesca* (not *pesce!*) and Mark had the *fragola.* We shared. We then boarded the Grand Canal *vaporetto* back to the Carlton.

We were kissing before Mark locked the door. Our final night in *Venezia* was memorable. We did not have a giant bathtub, but we compensated. Did we ever!

When we had finished, and I was lying in his arms, I popped him in the nose with my right index finger and said, "No more pedestal shit, okay?"

"What's a pedestal?" he asked. We started kissing again, and soon we added to the memories and took another chunk out of that ten thousand figure.

Stresa:

On the train ride to Stresa, I sat on Mark's side of the table again. The seat facing him was just too far away from him. It was a four-hour ride from Venice, our longest leg. We would arrive at Stresa at four in the afternoon on Sunday, the second Sunday of our trip. The first had been spent in Assisi. We would head to Milan Wednesday and fly home on Thursday. Peggy and Margie Baylor would be waiting. I miss Peggy, Margie too, but not the way I miss Peggy. We were passing beautiful countryside: mountains, vineyards, farms, lakes, forests. Sparcely populated. I was wrapped up in Mark's arms looking out the window between naps. The only time we weren't wrapped up together was when either of us went to pee. I would have brought him in to pee with me, but that was frowned upon. We were headed to one of the most beautiful lakes in Italy, *Lago Maggiore,* the Greater Lake. *Greater than what?..Other lakes, I guess.* Geographically the lake is half in Italy and half in Switzerland, but we were staying on the Italian side of the lake. We don't speak German.

"Can we get closer together?" I asked.

"How?"

"I don't know, but let's try."

He held me tighter.

I looked at him and smiled. "No more fucking pedestals, okay? Or if we need a pedestal, let's sit on it together."

He smelled my hair – he loves to do that – and said, "No more pedestals, fucking or otherwise."

"Our honeymoon is almost over," I said.

"But our marriage is just beginning," Mark said.

I looked at him and smiled. "How wonderful! I..love..you..so..much. Always will."

"I love you too. Fell in love with you when I was six. That love never waned. The honeymoon has been wonderful, but it just set the tone for the rest of our lives."

" 'Just set the tone for the rest of our lives.' I love you more every minute, Mark Tuttle. Hug me tighter."

"Impossible."

"Just shut up and do it." I kissed him.

The train pulled into Stresa Station fifteen minutes late, at four-fifteen, not bad. We took a cab to the Belvedere. Our room was ready.

Mark had booked a room with a balcony overlooking the lake at the Hotel Belvedere. Another fabulous choice. I told him if his career as a novel writer – that's what he wants to do; very few people know that, since he's going to MIT – didn't pan out, he could work as a travel agent.

"Or noise controller in Assisi," he said. "Don't forget that."

"What are we going to do in Stresa?" I asked.

"This is the relaxing, scenery-enjoying part of our honeymoon," he said. "There is an on-and-off, all-day ferry that goes to the islands and to Verbania across the lake. That will take a whole day. We can do that either tomorrow or Tuesday. The hotel has an outdoor pool, and there is a little beach on *Isola dei Pescatori*, the Isle of the Fishermen. That will give me a few opportunities to gaze upon my bikini-clad wife. After we get settled in our room, maybe go for a swim in the pool, then we can walk along the lakeshore and find a nice outdoor *ristorante*."

"You would make a great travel agent. However, when you give that spiel, leave out the part about gazing at your bikini-clad wife."

The balcony was the largest of our honeymoon. You could have placed five or six of the Carlton balconies on the Belvedere balcony. We stood looking at the lake, feeling the heavenly breeze. *Isola Bella*, the Beautiful Island, was right in front of our window.

"There is a surprise in store for you on *Isola Bella*," Mark said.

"What?"

"Can't tell you. Then it wouldn't be a surprise."

I kissed him. I was getting horny. *Husband and wife, horny together...What could be better than that?..Bet he's horny too; I always make him horny...I want to fuck him right now.*

"What do you want to do now?" Mark asked. *Accommodating question, eh?*

"Make love, go swimming, go for a walk along the shore, sit together on a bench looking at the lake, find an outdoor *ristorante*, walk some more, find some *gelato*, come back here, you can have a second, more enjoyable dessert, kiss passionately, make love, and then cuddle and sleep. How does that sound?"

"A second dessert more enjoyable than *gelato?* "

"Infinitely," I said. I popped him in the nose.

"Sounds like a woman who knows what she wants. It sounds great, especially the second dessert."

I led Mark into the room and pushed him onto the bed. What a nice way to start the relaxing, scenery-enjoying part of our honeymoon. We took off each other's clothes. *I know he still loves to take off my panties and my bra...*I wear soft, colored bras that match my panties. Pastel colors. Sometimes white with white or black with black, but mostly pastels. The color coordination turns him on. *Every time he takes off my bra, he's back in the pool shed...He still loves to look at me, my inverted bush, my little bumps, not so little anymore, my pussy...Just at me...No other woman...I satisfy him in every way...Good...He can look at* *me anytime he wants...Always has an exciting ending...He is so hard...I love to play with his penis... I have never given him a blow job -- I've never given **anyone** a blow job...I wonder if he'd like it...I never thought I would, but now I think I want to do that with Mark...I think I **would** like it...I know he would...But not now...Now I just want to kiss him and fuck him...Maybe we'll talk about it later...There is nothing we can't talk about...I love that....I'm shy, but not with him...He probably thinks I'm a sexual extrovert...That's good...Oh God he is giving me such pleasure...He's loving it too...We share everything...We're going to spend the rest of our lives together...You're stuck with me, Mark Tuttle...That's not such a bad thing, is it?...I gotta kiss him...Play with that magic tongue...Fuck him while we kiss.*

I pulled him up. "I need to kiss you," I said. "I want to taste me and you. I want to suck my smell and taste out of your mouth." *Stop laughing, Peggy Mayhew.*

"Put me inside you while we kiss," he said.

I didn't say anything. I just put him inside me. *I love to kiss him while we fuck, or fuck him while we kiss...A chicken and the egg thing, I guess...Oh my God!..Oh my God!..He's coming too...Husband and wife, horny together -- What could be better than that?..**Nothing!!!!!**..It's not so bad being stuck with me, is it, Mark Tuttle?..You are never getting rid of Sandy Roberts.*

We lay there, hugging, his penis still inside me, blowing air into each other's faces, smelling each other, heavenly smells, our private smells, enjoying the breeze off *Lago Maggiore.*

"Hungry?" I asked.

"Starving," he said. "Sandy, I always thought being married to you would be wonderful, but the reality is infinitely better than anything I could have imagined. And not just the sex, which has become beyond great, but the living with you, the sharing our lives, doing anything with you is better than doing it with anyone else."

I was crying, of course, and I hugged him tighter. "And, trust me, Mark Tuttle, it is only going to get better."

"I know. Hard to believe, but I know that. God, you have a beautiful face."

"Thank you."

I pulled him up, "Let's shower, go for a swim, and then search out a *ristorante*."

We showered together – this room had a large shower, unlike the Carlton – without any hanky-panky. We were hanky-pankied out, at least until after dinner. But we did enjoy it. "Our marriage **is** wonderful," I said. "And I agree with you – doing anything with you is better than doing it with anyone else."

We did kiss – we're both kiss-addicted now – but it was a husband and wife "I love you" kiss, and not a passionate lovers' "We're gonna fuck" kiss. I love both. I just love kissing Mark.

We were the only guests in the pool; perhaps because it was dinner time. We raced, ten laps. I won, but I think he let me win. Every time I looked at him, he was smiling at me. Probably thinking I have a beautiful face. Even when it's wet. Even when I stick my tongue out at him.

I hung up our suits in the shower to dry, and we went out for a walk along the lakeside. My hair was wet so I didn't tie it up in my usual ponytail. I just let it hang free. Mark loves both styles. Mark loves me. That is such a nice feeling.

Stresa is small, pristine, and delightful, so different from Rome, Florence, and Venice. Even from Assisi, which is a small city on a hill. Stresa is a vacation spot on a beautiful, serene lake. We passed a few restaurants, but decided to walk along the lakeside for a while. It was so refreshing. I was beginning to notice that objects in the distance were not as clear as they used to be. *Maybe I should see an optometrist when we get home...Will Mark still think my face is beautiful if I am wearing glasses?...Silly question...Of course, he will.*

"I think I should see an optometrist when we get home. My distance vision is a little fuzzy."

"I'll go with you. I think I should get my eyes checked too."

"We're getting old," I laughed. "An old married couple."

We picked a *ristorante* right at lakeside. They had a full menu, the familiar pasta dishes, chicken, veal, but the special that day was "Fresh-water perch caught today in *Lago Maggiore*, poached, served with roasted, herbed, baby potatoes, and fresh asparagus; 12.000 *lire*."

"How does the perch sound?" I asked. It was funny, but throuhgout the trip, we ate the same dinners or lunches. We both had the veal, or the *carbonara,* or the *lasagna*; we never ate different things. We do share everything.

"With a half-liter of the house white," Mark answered.

That was another thing – we are eighteen. We never drink at home -- well the occasional beer – but here we were having wine with our meals, and beers at the *cafes.* And enyoying it, especially the wine. "We're going to have to gct my father, or Patty, to buy us wine and beer at home."

The perch was delicious, melt-in-your-mouth delicious. And the little potatoes! There was something different about the asparagus. Softer. Less stringy. I asked the waiter. "We peel the asparagus, *Signora.*"

Peel the asparagus...How ingenious...I will have to do that...And I think I can duplicate these potatoes.

"Penny for your thoughts," Mark said.

"I was just thinking that I am going to make some delicious meals for us at home. We can invite my parents, my brother, Patty, Margie, Billy and Maureen, and, of course, Peggy, over for dinner. Peggy will probably be living at our house this summer, with the pool."

"Peggy's always welcome. And Margie, Billy Smith and Maureen. I have made arrangements for the pool guys to come next Friday to open the pool. I will have it ready by Sunday or Monday, with your help. We're still the pool team, you know. The only difference – it's now our pool."

"Friday?" ***Our*** *pool...**our** pool shed, too...Mark is my husband...I'm his wife...We don't have to sneak around in the pool shed anymore...God, those days were exciting...How he loved my little bumps!..I think he just loved me...Still does...Look at him sitting there drinking a glass of white wine...You can't drink wine – you're only eighteen...My little boy husband.*

"Yeah, we leave Milan Thursday morning at ten-thirty and arrive at Logan at one thirty that afternoon," Mark said. "We pick up six hours on the flight. Peggy knows the arrival time. We'll be home by mid-afternoon Thursday."

"Wow. The honeymoon is almost over."

"Remember what I told you: our married life is just beginning."

"I know. Something happened to us on this honeymoon. I feel closer and closer to you every day. We have grown so together. You know what I mean."

"Yes. Our relationship has changed – hard to believe, but it's better, much better."

"Let's go find some *gelato* and then go home and ravish each other."

"Sounds good to me, the *gelato,* but especially the ravishing. *The Rape of the Coventry Woman,* by John Baloney."

Another sunny day on Monday. I suggested we take the ferry around the lake that day in the unlikely event that Tuesday would not be sunny. And another nice surprise: the Belvedere had a full breakfast buffet included in the room price. We had scrambled eggs, soft and wet the way Mark and I love them, crisp bacon, fried potatoes, and little rolls. We made little bacon and egg sandwiches. *Cafe latte,* of course. I packed a backpack with a change of underwear, our bathing suits, two towels, and two T-shirts, and we headed down to the ferry dock. It is so wonderful speaking the language. We helped an American couple who were having trouble buying their tickets. They were from New Hampshire, and loved our Red Sox hats. We talked on the ferry ride to *Isola Bella.*

They were amazed at our ages – on our honeymoon at eighteen. They were more amazed that we were going to Harvard and MIT on full scholarships in September.

"We promised my mother that we would not have children until after we graduate," I said. "Then we plan to have four."

"How long did you know each other before you got married?" the woman asked.

"Twelve years," Mark said. "I fell in love with Sandy when I was six. And I have never not been in love with her."

"He saved my life when he was eight," I said. I told them the pervert story, short version. They were amazed.

"My father loves Mark," I said.

"I can see why," said the man.

We separated when the ferry docked at *Isola Bella.*

"Do you know of St. Charles Borromeo?" Mark asked.

"Yes, I think there's a school named after him in Providence," I said.

"His family owns this island, and the other islands in the lake. They're called the Borromean Islands. Let's go around to the gardens and I'll show you your surprise."

"Did I ever tell you I love being with you? Peggy should be here."

I was looking at him as we walked around the building. He pointed into the gardens and said, "Look."

"What? Oh my God," I cried out. "White peacocks. I didn't know there **were** white peacocks. There must be twenty."

"Beautiful, aren't they?"

"Breathtaking. Absolutely breathtaking."

"That's why you can never prove a universal negative," Mark said.

"What's a universal negative, Captain?" I asked.

"There are no white peacocks. There are no black swans."

"I see. There is always the possibility of finding one."

We boarded another ferry to the *Isola dei Pescatori*, the Isle of the Fishermen.

"We can go for a swim at the little beach and then have lunch. Fodor's says there are three or four *trattorie* near the landing. There's a place to change near the beach."

"I have to pee," I said. We were walking toward the changing place. "There's a public restroom," I said.

I came out laughing, doubled over laughing.

"What's so funny?"

"The toilet is a hole in the ground bracketed by two cement feet. The feet face away from the hole, so I knew it was the ladies' room---"

"Or the men's shitting room," Mark said.

"Didn't think of that. Anyway, good thing I'm athletic. I was successful."

"Wish I would have seen that," Mark said.

"I bet you would," I replied. "Maybe after swimming if you're lucky."

We changed together in an old, unlighted shed. It may sound silly, but I would have been nervous changing in that dark, dank shed alone. But I was with Mark. I never worry when I'm with him.

"God, you are sexy," Mark said, looking at me in my black bikini.

"You're not bad yourself, Mr. Tuttle," I said.

When we got to the beach, I froze. It was a topless beach. I stood there biting my lower lip. There were twenty to twenty-five women on the beach, the young and perky, the middle-aged and voluptuous, the old and droopy. All topless. No one has ever seen me topless except Mark, and Peggy a few times. *Did Mark know this was a topless beach?...I hope not.*

"What are you going to do?" asked Mark. "You can keep your top on if you don't feel comfortable going topless in public."

"Did you know this?" For the first time in my life, I **almost** got annoyed at Mark.

"No, I swear to God. Fodor's didn't say anything about the beach being topless. I would have told you, honey."

I kissed him. "Sorry for snapping at you. I should have known better. Mad at me?"

"I don't get mad at you, Sandy. Never." I hugged him and we kissed again. "This is crazy. I'm the one who stands out and it's because I'm wearing both parts of my bikini."

"That's not why you stand out," Mark said. We sat on our towels.

"Thank you." I squeezed his hand. "Stop looking around."

"I'm not."

"I know. I'm just kidding. I'm very nervous."

"Why?"

"I'm very shy, Mark. You don't realize how shy I am because I'm not shy with you. I don't know if I should go topless or not. I don't know if I **can**. It makes me nervous. I feel vulnerable. There's only one thing I'm glad about."

"What?"

"That you're with me. I only feel comfortable showing my breasts to you. If Peggy were here, she'd be in her glory, parading around, everyone looking at her."

"Not everyone."

"Thank you. Okay I'll go topless. When in Rome...You stay with me, okay. Do you want to take my top off?"

"I heard that before, on one of the most exciting days of my life."

"Remember that?"

"Never forgot it. You were on my shoulders in the pool. You said I was right, that you had nothing on top but little bumps. I asked if I could see them. That took courage on my part. You hesitated, and then you said, 'Yes.' I couldn't wait until we got in the pool shed. When you let me take off your top, I thought I was going to wet myself. My hands were shaking. Do you remember that? How I loved those little bumps. You let me touch them and kiss them. I dreamed about them. I was so afraid my mother would say something when she did the wash."

"Did you ever dream about Peggy's breasts?"

"No, just yours. You're my goddess. All my sex fantasies, even now, are about you."

"I believe you. I want to talk to you about your fantasies later. Take it off. I'm ready."

Mark unhooked my top and put it in our backpack.

"How do I look?"

"I've seen you topless, in fact every night. I love you topless. I think you look great."

"How do I compare with the women on this beach?"

"Do you want me to look around?"

"I guess not. Just look at me." I kissed him on the cheek.

"You don't have to leave it off," Mark said.

"No, it feels good. I'm adjusting. These little puppies are beginning to like the freedom. I think they want to take a swim in *Lago Maggiore.* Come on." I started running toward the water. He followed me. No one seemed to notice; perhaps I was being foolish. But I couldn't help it. I did feel vulnerable. We lay on the towels when we came back to the beach, I mostly on my stomach.

We had lunch at one of the *trattorie* near the boat landing. We sailed, after lunch, to the third major Borromean Island, *Isola Madre,* and visited the gardens. No white peacocks. Instead of sailing on to Verbania, we took a ferry back to Stresa. It was late afternoon. I cuddled up with Mark at the front of the ferry. *Tonight I have a surprise for you, my husband...I don't know why I was so inhibited today...My nature, I guess...I have great boobs...Not Peggy boobs, but perfectly proportioned...Mark tells me that all the time...He already loved them when they were only little bumps...God, did he ever...Unbelievable...I am so glad I have no inhibitions with him... None... Funny, isn't it?... When he's at the bathroom sink, I have no problem going in there to pee...I never thought I could pee in front of someone...One day after school at his house, **our** house, he looked at me and said, "Can I watch?"..I just smiled...He can watch...Of course, he can watch...He's my* *man...I'm his woman...No inhibitions with Mark...Love that...I thought he was only kidding, but he wasn't...He didn't know if my pee came out in a stream or a spray...He is so innocent at times...Love him...I told him a stream, "just like yours"..."How?" he asked..."Watch," I said..."I have a hose like you, only mine doesn't have the external extension"...I thought he would pee himself; he was laughing so hard...He did watch...We both got excited...Made love on the bathroom throw rug...I was on top...Never thought we would do that, but I wouldn't mind doing it again...Not here...In our bathroom at home...This is nice on the boat...Wrapped up in his arms...Nice breeze...God, he smells good.*

"I love you, honey," I said. "Hug me tighter."

He did, and he smelled my hair. Did I ever tell you he loves to do that? He loves all my smells. *All* my smells.

"Here we are," he said. "Stresa."

We stopped for dinner at the same lakeside restaurant. The special was fresh-water bass with angel hair pasta. I ordered it for both of us.

"What did you think of me today?" I asked. We were each drinking a *birra Peroni,* waiting for the bass and pasta. Mark was eating a piece of the warm bread, dripping olive oil.

"What do you mean?"

"I acted so inhibited at the beach. I don't think you realize how shy I am. I'll do and say anything with you, but not with others. Peggy and I talk about everything, but I only talk about those things with you and Peggy, no one else. Thanks for putting up with my foolishness. I will never see any of those women again. Why should I care what they think about my bumps? None of them were looking at me anyway."

"I love your bumps. I was looking at you."

311

"When we get back to the room, I want to discuss something with you."

"What?"

"Your fantasies."

"My fantasies? They're all about you."

"I believe you. I'd have to beat you up if they weren't. I think you'll be surprised."

We lay together in bed. I had stripped down to my peach-colored panties. We started kissing. Then I pulled back and said, "Let me ask you something."

"Okay."

"What do you fantasize about?"

"Kissing you, eating you, fucking you, playing with your bumps, seeing you in your panties. Not all sex though. Sometimes I just think about us doing something together, a Red Sox game, a movie, a PC basketball game, line dancing, watching you pitch, even shopping. But it's always doing things with you. Wrestling in the gym, but I guess that's about sex, isn't it?" He laughed.

"You only fantasize about me?"

"Yes." I liked hearing that, especially since I believed him.

"Do you ever come during the fantasies?"

"Before we started having sex, yes, but not after that. You take care of me---"

"You take care of me too," I said. "You always satisfy me."

"Good. I want you to be satisfied too. This is about us, not about me---"

"That's beautiful." I kissed him. "I believe that too. It **is** about us."

"I started masturbating that summer after seventh grade, thinking about your little bumps. I would get excited and start playing with myself. I don't think you ever

312

understood how much those little bumps excited me. I couldn't wait each day to take off your top in the pool shed. I was embarrassed, but I am glad, in retrospect, that your mother stopped us. We could have gotten in trouble."

"My little bumps excited you that much?"

"Yes, your little bumps drove me crazy."

"We can talk about anything, right?"

"Yes, you know that," Mark said.

"Do you ever fantasize about me going down on you?"

Mark hesitated. "Yes. Sometimes I think about us going down on each other."

"Is it an exciting fantasy?"

"Yes."

"Why didn't you ever ask me to give you a blow job?"

"I figured since you never did it, you didn't want to do it. And I am very happy with what we do."

"Did you ever have a blow job?"

"Sandy, you are the only girl or woman I have ever had sex with. The only woman I want to have sex with. So you know the answer to that."

"Good." I popped him on the nose. "Would you like one? Tonight? I'm ready. I've been thinking about it, and I want to do it. I want to taste you. We can add it to our repertoire."

"Only if you want to do it. I am happy with our current repertoire."

"I want to do it."

"Okay," Mark said.

"Well?" I asked.

"Whew. It was good. I liked it. Of course, I liked it, but do you want to know what I really think?"

"Yes," I said. "Do tell." I blew a stream of my breath at his face.

"I think, now that we have ridden the Barge of Curiosity, we should shelve blow jobs for occasional use only."

"Wasn't I good?"

"You were great. How could you not be great? But when I come, I want to come inside you, together with you, while kissing you. I want my tongue in your mouth when I come."

"Your tongue?"

"Yes," he said.

"Yeah, that's what I like too, fucking and kissing, kissing and fucking." *And the two shall be as one.*

"And while you were taking care of me, I wasn't taking care of you. Do you want me to satisfy you now?" Mark asked. "It's about us. Sequential orgasms are okay, I guess, but what I want are simultaneous orgasms."

"Let's kiss for a while and see what develops. Take off my panties just in case."

The breeze off the lake was invigorating.

The next morning during breakfast, at the hotel buffet, while enjoying our bacon and egg sandwiches, I surprised Mark again.

"Do you know what I want to do today, honey?"

"No," he said.

"Go back to the *Isola dei Pescatori*. I want these puppies to play in the fresh air one more time. It might be their last chance. This time I am going to lay on my back to give them some sun. I'll let you take off my top again. I know how much that turns you on."

"Why so brave?"

"Because you're with me. What do I have to worry about if you're with me." I leaned across the table and kissed him.

314

"God, you have a beautiful face," he said.

"Thank you, my husband."

As the ferry pulled into the first stop, at *Isola Bella*, I asked Mark if we could get off to see the white peacocks again.

Then we headed out to *Isola dei Pescatori* to let the world see Sandy Roberts's little bumps.

Milano:

We left Stresa for *Milano* (Milan) at eleven on Wednesday morning. We had a big breakfast before checking out of the Belvedere. It would have been foolish not to – we paid for it. The trip to Milan was the shortest leg on our journey, one and a half hours. We had to be at the airport at eight-thirty Thursday morning for our ten-thirty international flight, so we only had one afternoon in Milan. I again sat side-by-side with Mark on the train, at the window.

Why do I always get the preferred window seat? If there is ever a choice between good and better, Mark always gives me the better. He can't not do that. If there was ever a conflict over the use of our car, I got the car. Mark's insistence. In addition, automatically and unconsciously, always and at all times, as we say at Mass, he assumes his role as Sandy's protector. Thus he takes the aisle seat, between me and any possible danger or threat.

Cuddled in his arms, I looked up and asked, "What are we going to do in Milan today, Captain?"

"There are only two things I want us to see, the *Duomo* and DaVinci's Last Supper---"

"That's in Milan?"

"Yes. We'll go there first in case there's a wait. It's in the church of *Santa Maria delle Grazie.*"

We stayed in the Hotel *Spadari al Duomo*. The room was only slightly bigger than our room in Venice. The shower, however, was a two-person shower. "We'll have to take advantage of that later," I said. I put on my church pants, and we headed out to see DaVinci's masterpiece.

"John **does** look effeminate," I said. "I thought that in Mr. Carlson's class."

"And all twelve are still at table," Mark said. "So this is before Jesus told Judas, 'What you must do, do quickly.' I always wondered about Judas – did he really have a choice?"

"Dante has him in the very pit of Hell, which is ice, not fire, in the *Inferno*. Satan is stuck in the ice from the waist down, and he is chewing on Judas for all Eternity," I said. You don't ride the Barge of Curiosity with Mark Tuttle, and not know the *Inferno.*

"I know," Mark said, "but I still wonder. We might be surprised when we get to Heaven, Sandy."

"Deep subject, Captain," I said.

"Another postcard to Mr. Carlson?" Mark asked.

"Yes. We **are** going to see him when we get home?"

"Yes."

On the postcard, depicting The Last Supper, I wrote, "Final day of our honeymoon, and we thought of you! HaHa. We thought of you often on the trip. Thank you for our art education. Sandy and Mark."

The *Duomo di Milano* is huge and Gothic. So different from St. Peter's, St. Paul's, or the *Duomo* in *Firenze*.

"This is the fifth largest church in the world, and the second largest in Italy," Mark said.

"St. Peter's, I presume," I said.

"Yes," he said.

"What are the three other bigger churches?"

"I don't know," said Mark.

"You don't know. Should you be teaching this course?"

We had *Vitello Milanese* with French fries and *birra Peroni* for dinner. What else would we have in Milan?

We showered together; Mark had dessert, his favorite, me; then we made love in the Hotel *Spadari al Duomo.*

We were wrapped up in each other's arms when we finished, our favorite post-coital position. Our faces were inches apart.

"So our honeymoon is over," I said. "Thank you for two wonderful weeks."

"No need to thank me," he said. "They **were** wonderful, weren't they?"

"And our life together is going to be wonderful too, isn't it?" I asked.

"Never doubt it," Mark said. He always says that. He believes it. **I** believe it.

"You love making love with me, don't you?' I asked.

"There's nothing in the world I enjoy more. Joining our bodies together, coming inside you, my tongue inside your mouth, in a few years creating children together."

"Nice answer. And you love eating me, don't you?"

"There is neither taste nor smell more pleasing to me. And it is so moist---"

"Be serious," I said.

"I am."

I stuck my tongue out at him. Then I licked the tip of his nose. I don't know why. I just started laughing. Couldn't stop.

"Be serious," he said.

It made me laugh more. I was tempted to let him ravish me, but I was trying to get somewhere with these questions. "Just one more question," I said.

"Go ahead," Mark said.

"You love kissing me passionately, don't you?"

He just started kissing me, passionately. I couldn't resist and opened my mouth wide. *How great his mouth, his breath, smells,* I thought. *I love his tongue inside my mouth, playing with my tongue.* "God, you smell so good," I said.

"Did that answer your question?" he asked.

"Yes. Give me your pinky."

He did. I wrapped mine around his.

"Mark Tuttle, anytime you want to fuck a woman, you will fuck me, and only me. Anytime you want to eat a woman, you will eat me, and only me. And anytime you want to kiss a woman passionately, you will kiss me, and only me. Promise?"

"I promise. I made that promise to you two weeks ago in church – not in exactly those words, but the same meaning. (We both started laughing.) I will make it again now, and anytime you want, and I make it voluntarily, with sound mind, and in perpetuity."

"Perpetuity?"

"Forever."

"And I promise you that you will never regret it. I will always take care of you, whenever you want, always satisfy you, always love you. I promise that with all my mind and all my heart."

"Me too," Mark said. "There will be nothing more important to me than taking care of you and our children, the four of them."

"Our children! I love that. Yes the four of them."

We squeezed pinkies. Then kissed. Then lay entwined. You could not have slid a piece of paper between our bodies, between my bumps and his chest.

"Want to join our bodies?" he asked.

"Oh God, yes," I said. "In perpetuity."

The alarm went off at six. We had arranged for a seven-thirty taxi to the airport. We had only been sleeping together for two weeks, but I couldn't imagine not sleeping with Mark, not waking up in his arms. Our faces were still inches apart. I blew a stream of breath into his face; he did the same to me. *God, his breath smells so sweet in the morning...He tells me mine is like honey.* He smiled and said, "Good morning, Sandy. I love you and I always will. And I thank God everyday that you are my wife." I smiled back and said, "Me too. All of the above." That has become our morning mantra. We say it every morning. We **mean** it every morning. Our honeymoon has set the tone for the rest of our lives. Only then did Mark reach back and turn off the alarm. Then he rolled right back around me.

"Do you want to have a final honeymoon fuck?" I asked. I could feel that he did.

He just started kissing me. I knew that meant "Yes."

Peggy Mayhew and Margie Baylor met us at Logan. I gave Peggy a big kiss. I missed her. On the drive to Rhode Island, Peggy, riding in the back, said to me, "There's something different about you two."

I squeezed Mark's shoulder – he was driving – and said, "Yes, there is."

"I can tell. It doesn't seem possible, but you two are closer, more together, more a couple. I love it."

I called Mom as soon as we got home.

"Where are you?" she asked.

"Home," I said.

She was silent, then started laughing.

"What, Mom?"

"I forgot you don't live here anymore. How are you and Mark?"

"Mom, let me tell you what Mark said to me the other day. He said, 'Sandy, I always thought being married to you would be wonderful. But the reality is infinitely better than anything I ever imagined.' And I feel the same way. Does that answer your question?"

"Yes it does. Makes me very happy. And how was Italy?"

"We had a fantastic time, Mom. I'm taking our slide rolls to Photomat tomorrow. We'll have you two over for a slide show, and dinner, as soon as we get them back."

"Why don't you two, and Peggy, come over for dinner tomorow?" *I love you, Mom. She doesn't exclude Peggy, even now.*

"That will be great. Mark has the pool guys coming in the morning to open the pool, and we'll be back to our pool duties in the afternoon. Peggy will be here helping. We hope to have it ready by Sunday. Then you and Dad will have a pool for the rest of the summer. We'll be over at five."

"Honey, I can't wait to see you, and Mark."

We went to bed at ten; our bodies thought it was four Friday morning. We just cuddled and slept. *Mark's right...Sleeping together is the great benefit of marriage.* Peggy stayed in the guest room; she was our alarm clock – to get us up at eight. The pool crew was due at nine. We entered the kitchen to the smell of hot coffee. The table was set for three. Peggy placed a platter of scrambled eggs and a platter of crisp bacon in the middle of the table along with a plate of buttered rye toast. Peggy had filled the larder while we were in Italy. I had given her a key to the house. I had no plans to ask for it back.

"Thank you, Peggy," Mark said.

"You're welcome, my Captain. Welcome home."

The Barge of Curiosity was sailing again. It was great having the three of us together.

Chapter Fifteen
College Years

We did go see Mr. Carlson, the week after we got home. It's funny, but you never visualize your teachers in their private lives; you never imagine that they even **have** private lives. When I called, Mrs. Carlson answered the phone. She was so excited to hear my voice, even though she had never met me.

"He loved those postcards. You two are the first students who ever contacted him after taking his class. His was so excited. Thank you. That was so considerate."

"Mark and I want to come over for a visit, to thank him. His classes made the trip so much more enjoyable. We were inside the world he taught us about."

"Can you come tomorrow for dinner?" she asked, surprising me.

"Yes," I answered without hesitation. "We would love that."

The next evening we discovered that there are four Carlsons. The twins, Charles and Antonia, had just finished their freshman year at Coventry High. Their heroes? Mark Tuttle and Sandy Roberts. I noticed a basket over the garage entrance and asked if they would like to play a little basketball before dinner. You would have thought I asked if they wanted to go to Heaven! We played boys against girls, and, as usual, my team won.

Charles and Antonia were thrilled that their heroes had come to pay homage to their father. I could tell they loved him, but now they raised him onto a pedestal. (It's okay to put your father on a pedestal.) Mr. Carlson spread the the postcards around on the table. "I loved this comment," he said, holding up the picture of the Laurentian Library staircase. " 'It does flow like lava from the second floor to the first.' I was so gratified that you remembered that."

"We loved your class, Mr. Carlson. Peggy, Peggy Mayhew, Mark, and I discussed your lectures a lot when we were taking the course. Mark talked for two days about the Laocoön Group, and then, two weeks ago, we were standing in front of it. You should have seen the look on Mark's face. We met a Salvatorian priest in Rome and served Mass for him two times in the chapel of the Pieta'; we were five feet from that masterpiece of Michelangelo's."

"What are you plans now? Going to college, I hope," he asked.

"Yes, I have a full scholarship to Harvard, and Mark has a full scholarship to MIT. We're moving up to Cambridge in September."

"That's impressive, but, I guess, to be expected for you two. Peggy?"

"URI, on a Centennial Scholarship," I said. "But we will keep in touch. Mark's father called us 'The Three Musketeers.' A little distance will not be a deterrent."

"Mark, I was so sorry about your parents," said Mr. Carlson.

"I saw you at the wake, Mr. Carlson. I appreciated that."

Our final summer in Coventry flew by.

Mark, Peggy, and I took care of the pool. There was always a gang using it: Margie Baylor, Billy Smith, Maureen Sullivan, Patty, her boyfriend, Bill, my parents, my brother Bobby and his girlfriend, Leslie. I loved Leslie and prayed that she and Bobby would connect permanently. My prayers were answered, and Leslie and I are now sisters.

Peggy's boyfriend, Fred Williams, came over often in June and July, but then headed off to RPI, and out of Peggy's life, in August. *What a fool,* I thought.

As our separation grew nearer, Peggy spent most nights in one of our guest rooms. I tried to reassure her that we would remain close, but she feared that the Barge of Curiosity was about to go into dry dock. It wasn't, but she couldn't know that. I would never abandon Peggy Mayhew. She should have known that. We did kiss a lot that summer, Peggy and I, at times quite passionately, but nothing more. There would be nothing more now that I was married to Mark Tuttle. But I did enjoy those kisses. I have said this before, but it bears repeating: Peggy Mayhew has the most delicious mouth. And I love her. She loves me too.

We ate a lot of Chinese food that summer, both Chun Fun and China King. At China King, we had won ton soup, egg rolls, and mu shi chicken, to remind us of Venice.

I made a special dinner for Mark and Peggy one evening: poached, fresh-water perch, small, herbed, roasted potatoes, and peeled asparagus. I was able to find the perch at Stop and Shop. Dad bought me a bottle of white wine.

"How does it compare?" I asked Mark.

"I am back on *Lago Maggiore*," he said. "I think this is actually better."

Love you, Mark Tuttle.

"This **is** delicious," said Peggy.

Love you too, Peggy Mayhew.

I did need glasses, for distance. Mark's vision was still okay. I wear my glasses all the time, except for reading or close work. I had no need to worry. The day I picked them up, Mark looked at me and said, "You still have the most beautiful face in the world."

The honeymoon was, in fact, a preparation for the rest of our lives. Our sex life kept getting better. "How is this possible?" I asked Mark.

"It's because we love each other more each day," he said.

Love that Mark Tuttle...But he's right...We do...He just walks into a room, and my whole body starts to ache...To yearn for him...The way he looks at me...His body aches too...He yearns for me...Working together at the pool...Slipping into the pool shed for old time's sake...He still loves my bumps...Shopping together...Fighting over who's going to push the cart...Drinking soda out of the same can...Knowing his lips just touched the lid...Silly little things...I love being married to Mark Tuttle more each day...It's the same for him...Sometimes I just stop what I'm doing and look at him...If we're alone, at home, I whisper, "Want me?"..He has never said "No" to that...Never...God, fucking him is so unbelievably exciting and satisfying...For both of us...Sometimes we just look at each other...He nods his head...Off to the bedroom...Love it.

"Yes, we do," I said. "But you were right on our honeymoon," I said.

"What did I say?"

"You said the best part of being married to me, the greatest benefit was sleeping with me each night, sharing my bed. For me, the best part of marriage is sleeping with you each night. I would rather sleep in your arms on the floor than sleep alone in a big comfortable bed. Really."

The two-bedroom apartment we rented in Cambridge was unfurnished. Patty told us to take any furniture we wanted from the Coventry house. We took two beds, one queen-size, for me and Mark, and one double for the guest room, two dressers, two end tables, the kitchen table set (which seats eight when extended), cooking and eating utensils, some living room furniture, and Mark's desk. I took my old desk and my dresser from my Mom's house. Peggy, Margie, Billy Smith, Maureen Sullivan, Dad, Bobby, Leslie, Patty, and Bill helped us load everything into a U-Haul truck, and to unload it in Cambridge. The unloading was more problematic since our apartment was on the second floor.

Peggy and I set up the guest room.

"This is my room, right?" she asked.

"Yes," I said, and we both knew I meant that. "The Barge is still sailing, Peggy."

She kissed me. She does have a delicious mouth.

Patty had an estate sale the last week-end in August. Mark, Peggy, and I worked the sale with Patty and Bill. Every item went, some at rediculously low prices on Sunday afternoon. We and Patty each pocketed seventeen hundred dollars from the sale. We took Peggy to dinner Saturday evening, at Chun Fun, and to breakfast and dinner on Sunday – Chelo's for reubens, steak fries, curly fries, onion rings, much sharing. Mark also gave her two hundred dollars. Peggy did not want to take it, but we insisted.

Patty then listed the house. It sold in less than one month, adding $100,000 to the net worth of Mark and Sandy Tuttle. We would not have financial troubles during our college years.

The first day at MIT, registration day, Mark came home with a stranger, a fellow MIT freshman, a young man from

Croatia, Kristijian Kovasevic. The first thing Kristijian said to me was, "Sandy, I love your husband."

"I do too," I said, laughing.

"When I went into the gym to sign up for classes," Mark said, "I saw this young man sitting in the corner, head in his hands. I never saw any man more dejected. So I went over and asked him what was wrong."

"When he came over," said Kristijian, "I thought he was an angel. I had no idea what to do, and my English is only okay. It was all too difficult for me. But he helped me, Sandy, like I was an old friend. He got me signed up for my classes and took me to the housing lady. They have room for me, but not until two days. Your husband said I can sleep here two nights." He looked at me sheepishly.

"Of course you can," I said. "You can sleep on the couch. It opens up into a bed."

"Thank you," he said. "You are as good as your husband, and beautiful. You have a beautiful face, Sandy, and a very kind one."

"I always tell her that," said Mark.

"As you should," said Kristijian. "It is one of the world's great faces."

I just shook my head.

"No, really, it is," said Kristijian. "If you were not married to Mark, I would woo you."

Woo me?..Does anyone woo anymore?..You know, Mark would kill anyone who wooed me..."Don't you dare woo Sandy"...Woe to you, wooer. I laughed.

Kristijian became a good friend. Still is. We have visited him and his family two times in Croatia. Kristijian lives in Zagreb, and his family has two homes, a winter one in Split, and a summer one in Boska Voda, a little piece of paradise on the Adriatic. He never slept in our apartment after he moved into the dorm, but he was there all the time.

326

He became one of a group that survived on my mac and cheese. He told me something one day that made me cry. He said, "Sandy, the day I met Mark I thought he was the most wonderful person I had ever met. Now I think he is only the second most wonderful person in the world. You are number one."

It must be nice to have two friends who are one and two on the most wonderful persons list. Lucky Kristijian.

I majored in English and American Literature. Mark in Computer Science. My first class was at nine; Mark's at nine thirty. I finished up at four thirty; Mark at five. We left the house together each morning at eight fifteen, stopped at Dunkin' Donuts for a coffee and a breakfast sandwich or a bagel, then Mark walked with me to Harvard. At four thirty I went to the Harvard Library where I waited for Mark. The times varied, but never that routine, all four years. I never walked through the city to class alone. I loved that. Both because I felt so safe, but more because I loved being with Mark. That has never changed. When I had the occasional evening class, Mark walked me to Harvard, then did some work in the library while he waited for me. Then we stopped for Chinese or pizza.

I first met Bill Skwor when Mark brought him over for dinner – mac and cheese, of course. Bill became another aficionado of my mac and cheese. At times our kitchen could barely handle the crowd for dinner: me and Mark, Bill Skwor, Kristijian, Peggy, later Peggy and Warren, Billy Smith and Maureen, Bill Reynolds, my brother Bobby and Leslie, and Philip Andrews, who was involved with AODS, when he was in town. Even Margie Baylor a few times.

Bill Skwor was intense. All he talked about was the company he wanted to found: Alpha-Omega Data Systems.

He recognized a brilliance in Mark that he did not have – the ability to solve **any** problem logically, and then to put that solution into computer language. All of that is beyond my comprehension. Bill convinced Mark to be his partner in the new venture. Bill offered a 50/50 split, but Mark insisted on 55/45, with the fifty-five percent for Bill. "There would be no Alpha-Omega if it weren't for you," Mark said. I think that statement made Bill appreciate even more the treasure he had found in Mark.

When they hired a lawyer to draft the agreement, Mark insisted that the forty five percent ownership was: "Mark Tuttle and Sandy Roberts Tuttle, JTWROS." I did not ask for that, but I did expect it. Mark would have it no other way. There is no Mark; there is no Sandy; there is only MarkandSandy. In everything.

During our junior year, Bill introduced us to Philip Andrews, a venture capitalist from Seattle, Bill's home town. They renogiated the deal. Mark and Bill each gave fifteen percent to Philip in exchange for the capital to go big time. Within six months, the company went public in one of the largest IPOs in history. Overnight the thirty percent owners, Mark Tuttle and Sandy Roberts Tuttle, JTWROS, were worth over six hundred million dollars! *Holy shit,* I thought. *I guess I married the right guy...Only kidding...I would love Mark Tuttle no matter what...I don't even know what AODS does...It seems every computer manufacturer uses AODS...God, Mark is so smart...And I know the wealth will not change us...Mark told me the other night that he still wants to be a novelist...Now he will be able to do it without financial worries...Bill Skwor is going to leave MIT and return to Seattle...Give full-time to the company...Mark is going to finish at MIT...He told Bill he would be happy to be a consultant, but not a full-time employee...He told me that he will fly out to Seattle for meetings only if I go with him...“I am never sleeping without you”...Love that Mark...I am never sleeping without you either...Never...Was Dad ever surprised when we told him about the IPO...“Six hundred million dollars!” he said...“And how is the stock owned?” he asked...“Jointly, Dad,” I said. “We share everything. Always have; always will.”...If he loved Mark before...Saved his daughter's life when she was eight...Now this.*

Bill Skwor loved Mark. How could he not? Without Mark, his idea would have gone nowhere. But there was a side of Mark he did not know. The three of us were walking in Cambridge one evening during our junior year, returning to Mark's and my apartment, before the IPO, coming home from a Chinese restaurant if I remember correctly. Mark stepped into a convenience store to get some half and half. Bill and I were waiting outside the store.

Three young punks came up to us and demanded money. That's why Mark always walks me to and from school – why he walks with me everywhere in Boston or Cambridge -- to protect me at times like that. Bill was terrified. He is smart, but he is not a fighter, not athletic in any way. He started to take out his wallet, but I said to the obvious leader, “Get the fuck outta here.” I saw that Mark was exiting the store. Bill looked at me, stunned, disbelieving, shocked, both by my language – he had never heard words like that coming out of my sweet mouth – and by my courage. The punk leader said, “What did you say, bitch?”

“I said, ‘Get the fuck outta here’ before you get hurt.” Mark's approach had emboldened me. He was now standing at my side. The punk in the middle pulled out a knife. Mark, with lightning speed, smashed the punk's wrist causing the knife to fall on the pavement. I kicked it into an open drainage hole. We are a good team. The leader's wrist was broken. He was grasping it in pain, screaming. The other two disappeared, quickly. They wanted no part of Mark. I couldn't blame them.

"Let's get out of here," Mark said. He picked up the half gallon of half and half that he had placed on the sidewalk and led me and Bill away from the scene toward home. Bill was trembling. I don't think he fully comprehended what had happened.

When we got to the apartment, Bill sat on the couch, still shaking. I gave him a Miller Lite and asked if he was okay.

"I was scared shitless," he said. "How were you so brave, so calm, Sandy?"

"Bill, I knew two things that you did not know."

"What things?"

"One, I knew that Mark would never let anyone hurt me, and two, I know how dangerous and competent Mark is when he is fighting for me."

Bill just shook his head.

"He told me that he would never let anyone hurt me, Bill, and he won't."

We offered to let Bill sleep on the couch, but he wanted to go home. We walked him home. He appreciated that.

Mark's value ratcheted up in his eyes that night. So did my worth in his eyes.

When we got home, I re-enacted John Baloney's Rape of the Sabine Women with Mark. I was the raptor; he was the raptee. I know there is no such word, but I don't know any words to describe how good our sex was that night. Danger enhances arousal. I was glad it was a Friday night. We did not have classes on Saturday so there was no impediment to a long night of marital bliss. *Husband and wife, horny together. What could be better than that?* I stopped to catch my breath. I was on top, leaning forward, my pendant bumps inches from his chest. Mark was caressing them. *God, he still loves my bumps.* I inhaled deeply, then blew a stream of my honey breath into his face. Then again, I inhaled deeply and followed it with another stream of honey breath into his face. *God, he's enjoying this...He loves the smell of my breath...Loves me...*I did it a third time. My whole body was tingling, aching for him, wanting to fuck him again.

I grabbed the side of his face and yelled (How loud was it?), "**I love you Mark Tuttle**. I have wanted you since I was six years old. Now I have you, and I am never going to let you get away. Never."

"I'm not going anywhere," he said. "To whom should I go?"

What St. Peter said to Jesus...Nowhere, Mark Tuttle...There is nowhere you can go...There is nowhere you want to go...We belong together...We committed to that... Joyfully...Willingly...In perpetuity...Your word, Mark Tuttle...God, he's hard again...Let me put it in...We're going to fuck again...How many times is this tonight?..Not enough!

I kissed him. *I love kissing you, Mark Tuttle...My whole body tingles when we kiss...So does yours...I can feel it...Husband and wife, horny together...What can be better than that?*

Saturday morning. We woke up simultaneously at nine, smiled at each other, and then, you guessed it, made love. Twice. We might have made it three times, but we were starving. Before we got out of bed, Mark said to me. "Sandy, you have the most beautiful face in the world." What a surprise. I think, if we weren't so hungry, food hungry, we might have spent the whole day in bed, alternately fucking and arousing each other for another fuck.

We called Bill and Kristijian, and they joined us for a late breakfast. They were shocked at how much we ate. A sex marathon builds up your appetite.

I was not the only accomplished cook in our house. Mark made an unbelievable lasagna. When I asked where he got the recipe, he told me it was an old Tuttle family secret.

"The Tuttles aren't Italian," I protested.

"But we do have our culinary secrets," he said.

I finally got it out of him. There's nothing I can't get out of him. The secret Tuttle family recipe for lasagna is on the back of the Ronzoni lasagna noodle box. "But I mix in two eggs with the ricotta cheese," he said.

I had to admit he made a great lasagna, even if it was the Ronzoni family recipe, and not a Tuttle family secret.

Mark and I don't keep secrets from each other. As you know, it is one of our rules: *No lies; no secrets.* But there was one secret I had been keeping from him since junior year in high school. You probably can guess what I am talking about. *Why don't I tell Mark?..I really don't know…Fear?..Me afraid of Mark – Never…Embarrassment?..No…I'm not embarrassed by my feelings and relationship with Peggy…Do I think he will attempt to drive Peggy out of my life?..Give me an ultimatum?..No…We don't do that to each other…He loves Peggy too…Not like he loves me…But she is a part of our life, a crewmember on the Barge…He told me I could kiss her…That's all we do now…Pretty heated kisses, but just kisses…Mark knows Peggy and I love each other…Not with the intensity that I love him, but real love…He told me he*

332

thinks that is great...He has no worries about Peggy...No need to...Mark is the only person I will have sex with...Want to have sex with...Really...Yeah, I do daydream about Peggy once in a while....Just a fantasy...Nice fantasy, but just a fantasy...Mark takes care of me...Does he ever...I'll tell him tonight...Stop this foolishness...It's been four years now...That long?..Yes, we were juniors then; we're juniors now...It might even excite you, Mark Tuttle...Add a little spice to the sex tonight, as if we needed any!

"Mark, can I talk to you?" I asked. We had just finished dinner. It was one of those rare occasions when we had dinner alone in the apartment. We heated up some leftover lasagna – Tuttle family secret recipe lasagna. We both think it tastes better the second day. The juices soak into the noodles and the cheese. I was a little nervous. *Nervous with Mark?..There's no need for that, Sandy Roberts.*

"Of course. What's up?" he asked.

"Let me get right to the bottom line," I said. "When we were juniors at CHS, Peggy and I had sex one time, just one time, at her place. I don't know why I never told you. Maybe I thought you might get upset."

"What do you mean, you had sex?"

"You remember the day we were talking about shaving our bushes?"

"Yes," he said. "You, Peggy, Margie, and two other girls."

"I started thinking about her bush. I wanted to see it. Just curiosity. To compare it with mine. Then I did see her naked in the locker room. But I wasn't satisfied. I wanted to see her vagina. Maybe more than just see it. Play with it like you play with mine. Taste it; smell it. She told me I could. At first I said 'No' but then curiosity got the better of me. I went to her place one afternoon – you had a meeting at school – and I said, 'Let's get this out of the way.' We didn't know how to start, so we stripped down to panties and wrestled. That was wild, wasn't it? Anyway we got aroused, of course we got aroused, started kissing, then went to the bedroom where I played with her vagina, and she played with mine. When we finished, I told her, 'Never again. I scratched that itch.' And we haven't done it again. Yes, we do kiss, but nothing more than that. My only sex is with you."

Mark was smiling.

"What?"

"I always figured you two had sex. I know you love her. That doesn't bother me. I know you love me more. Some other guy – that would bother me. I would have to beat the crap out of him---"

"Would you beat the crap out of me too?" I interrupted.

He gave me a look, an "it's not in my nature" look, a "that's impossible" look.

"Or if you and Peggy were still having sex – that would bother me," he continued. "But you two playing around in high school. That's not a problem for me. You two kissing now – that's not a problem for me."

I kissed him. "I swear that it was a one-time thing."

"I believe you."

"You're not mad?"

"No. I don't think I **can** get mad at you. Actually I'm a little excited. (*What I was hoping!*) Maybe you should give Peggy a call," he said. "Suggest a wild *ménage a trois* the next time she's up." I think his mental image of the panty wrestling match was more of a turn-on than the mental picture of our sixty-nine. Men love to watch women fighting. And kissing. *You are excited, not mad, Mark Tuttle…I think we're going to fuck, not fight…We never fight.*

I **knew** he was kidding about the *ménage a trois*. At least I **hoped** he was kidding. I punched him on the shoulder anyway. "There's no way I'm letting that goddess in my bed with you in it. Do you think I'm crazy?"

"I thought you and Peggy were best friends," he said.

"We are, but if she ever tries to get in my bed with you, we're going to fight."

"Another fight in panties?" he asked, laughing.

I punched him on the shoulder again. His shoulder must hurt, but he never complains.

"Want to wrestle?" he asked. I knew that image turned him on. He is a man, after all.

"Why don't we wrestle and then fuck?" I answered. I was getting hot too.

He picked me up and carried me into our bedroom. I let him remove my shirt, pants, and bra, but not my lemon-colored panties. We rolled around on the bed; I ended up on top. Mark let me win the wrestling match. Of course, he did. Mark Tuttle will never beat up Sandy Roberts, even in a play fight. I knew that since the second day of first grade. *"I don't want to fight with you, Sandy…I want to be your friend."*

Even though I won the fight, the fuck was a draw. Equally satisfying. Equally satisfied. Nothing like a good fuck to clear the air.

Now I can honestly say that Mark Tuttle and Sandy Roberts have no secrets from each other. But I **do** wonder now what Mark thinks when he sees Peggy. She **is** a goddess.

- *Ménage a trois?*
- *Me and Peggy wrestling in our panties?*
- *Me and Peggy eating each other?*

- *Mark and Peggy having sex? No, not that...I would bet my life on that...And I would have to kill them, both of them...I can see the headlines in the Herald: Husband and Wife's Best Friend Killed by Jealous Wife...Wife Says She Had No Idea...Details and Lurid Pictures on Page 3.*

- *None of the above. I'll go with that.*

Mark picked up four box seats at Fenway for a Friday night game with the Tigers. Same junior year, but after the IPO. Box seats at Fenway had become very affordable for the Tuttles. My brother, Bobby, and his girlfriend, Leslie, both Holy Cross graduates, were living in Worcester. Bobby teaches; Leslie is a marketing rep. We had invited them to join us for dinner and the game. Mark grilled four steaks; I baked potatoes and made a tossed salad.

During dinner, Leslie said, "I want to tell you guys something."

We stopped eating and looked at her.

"Bobby and I are getting married."

I leaped out of my chair and almost tackled Leslie. We hugged, cried, laughed, kissed, even bounced like little kangaroos. I think I was as happy as Leslie. Mark and Bobby were more subdued. They exchanged manly handshakes.

"We want you two to be part of the wedding party. My sister, Beth, is the maid of honor, but Sandy, please be one of my bridesmaids."

"Of course," I said.

"And Mark, will you be one of the ushers?"

He echoed my response.

"When?" I asked.

"This August, third Saturday," Leslie answered.

The game was great, as all games at Fenway are. We had hot dogs -- even after the steaks -- beers, and peanuts. Seats were great; right behind the Sox dugout. The Tigers tied the game 8 – 8 with a five run rally in the top of the ninth, but the Sox won with a run in the bottom of the ninth, a Yaz walk-off homer! Leslie and I bounced like kangaroos again.

When we got back to the apartment, Bobby said one of those things that you never forget.

"What can be better than to go to Fenway with your best friend, who knows baseball as well as you do, who loves the Sox as much as you do, have hot dogs, a few beers, maybe some peanuts, see Yaz hit a walk-off homer, then go home and make love, because your best friend is your wife."

"Thank you," I said.

"Why are you thanking me?" he asked. "I was talking about me and Leslie."

"She's not your wife, not yet anyway," I said. "You said, 'Because your best friend is your wife.' So it only applies to me and Mark in this foursome."

We all laughed. Leslie sat on his lap; I sat on Mark's. They were staying in our guest room, in Peggy's room, that night.

"Everyone ready for bed?" Mark said.

We all were.

I'm going to love having another sister. I will now have three, Peggy, Patty, and Leslie. Oh, yes, Peggy is my sister, ever since first grade. Kissing friends, kissing sisters.

I told Mark one night in bed, after we had made our two bodies one, that there were only three people in the whole world who had ever made me come.

"Who's the third?" he asked.

"Me," I said, laughing. "Before we started sleeping together, before senior year, I would think of you at night and play with myself. I never did after we started fucking. There was no need to. Did you masturbate thinking about me? Do you ever masturbate now?"

"I told you. Beginning that summer after seventh grade, I thought about your bumps and your ass every night. Played with myself every night. My mother never said anything when she washed my underpants or pajamas. She had to know. I guess she thought it was normal for a young boy. I didn't stop until we started fucking every day. Since then I have never masturbated. As you said: Why would I? You take care of me."

"And my number two, Peggy, was just that one time. But you and me – we're every day. I still want to fuck you every day. I hope that never stops. I don't think it will. We're lucky that way. We get horny all the time. I don't think I ever said this to you, but I think it all the time."

"What?"

"Husband and wife, horny together. What could be better than that?"

"Nothing," he said. "Let's fuck again."

Love that Mark.

I asked my gynecologist, way back in freshman year, if we could have intercourse (I never say "fuck" to my doctor. I told you that, other than with Mark and Peggy, I am very shy.) when I am having my period. I had heard ("Street medicine?") that it was bad for both partners, but I had read that it was fine, but messy.

She told me that there was no medical reason not to have intercourse. "Put an old towel on the bed or just fuck in the shower," she said. *Fuck in the*

338

*shower?'...'**Fuck?'**...And I thought I had to say 'intercourse' with her...She's smiling...*

"I know you two love to have sex, Sandy. There's no reason not to, just because you're menstruating. It can be dangerous for the male, however."

"How?"

"If he doesn't satisfy his mate, she might just devour him."

We both starting laughing. I appreciated my gynecologist a lot more after that day.

We didn't always have sex in the shower during my periods. Sometimes we satisfied each other in different ways. Not blow jobs. I told you we put that on the shelf after that night on our honeymoon. Honestly, we have never taken it off the shelf. It is still there, collecting dust. Mark wants to come with his tongue in my mouth, only his tongue. We would put a towel on the bed and then play with each other while we kissed passionately. We both came. Always. Sometimes we did that when I was not having my period. Without the towel.

The more we lived together, the more we loved living together. The favorite part of the day for both of us was late in the evening, when one of us would say, "Ready for bed?"

Usually Mark asked me.

I always said, "Oh, yes." I knew three great things were about to happen:

- Mark was going to eat me.
- Mark was going to fuck me.
- I was then going to sleep wrapped up in his arms, safe and loved.

I asked Mark to stop at the neighborhood Dunkin' Donuts one month before graduation. We always go to Dunkin' Donuts to discuss important matters. I had decided is was time to take a very important, life-changing step. I was not looking for Mark's permission; we do not operate like that. I am his partner, not his subordinate. Likewise he is my partner, not my subordinate. I was looking for agreement. If we didn't agree on any important matter, we didn't do it. Honestly though, I can not think of one important matter that we disagreed on. The main reason being: Mark Tuttle always agrees with Sandy Roberts. I think he still has me on that pedestal. That's okay; I have him on one too. We're just not allowed to say that word about each other..

After we sat down with our two coffees, cream no sugar, I threw a little plastic holder on the table.

"Do you know what that is?" I asked.

"Yes, your contraceptive pills," he said.

"I want to throw them away. Right now. Right here."

"Let me do it," he said.

"So you agree. It's time to start our family?"

"We made this decision four years ago, didn't we?" he said.

"Yes, we did. You still want four?" I asked.

"Yes, but only if you do too."

"I do. Ideally two boys and two girls."

"Can we afford to have children?" he asked. "I hear they are very expensive."

I punched him on the shoulder.

"Have you thought about a name for the first one?" Mark asked.

"Yes," I said. "Maddie if it's a girl, and Bobby if it's a boy."

"I hope it's Maddie, but a boy will be fine too," he said.

"Let's go home and get our family started."

"How do we do that?" he asked.

I punched him in the shoulder again.

I told you my major was literature. I took a great course the first semester of my senior year, *An In-depth Look at James Joyce's Ulysses*. As always, Mark and I read it together. We discussed it. We both loved it. We got Peggy to read it too. Riding the Barge of Curiosity together.

We graduated the last week in May, Mark on a Friday, me on a Saturday. Both 4.0. Both *Summa cum Laude*.

After graduation, Mark handed me an envelope.

"What's this?" I asked.

"Open it."

Two tickets, round trip, Boston to Dublin on *Aer Lingus*. Leaving Boston June 13, arriving Dublin June 14. Returning from Dublin June 18.

I lunged at him. I can be scary when I am happy. Ask Leslie. At least Mark and I didn't bounce like kangaroos. That would have been a sight in my cap and gown.

"We're going to be in Dublin for Bloomsday!" I shouted.

"What's Bloomsday?" asked my father.

"James Joyce's *Ulysses* is one day in the life of Leopold Bloom, Poldy. The day is June 16. It is celebrated every year in Dublin."

"Oh," said Dad, not too impressed. "And?"

"And this year, my wonderful husband and I are going to be part of that celebration."

Chapter Sixteen
Stately Plump Buck Mulligan

SANDY AND MARK ON THE SANDYCOVE MARTELLO TOWER OVERLOOKING DUBLIN BAY

"*Stately, plump Buck Mulligan came from the stairhead,*" I read as Mark re-enacted the opening scene from *Ulysses*, "*bearing a bowl of lather on which a mirror and a razor lay crossed. A yellow dressinggown, ungirdled, was sustained gently behind him by the mild morning air. He held the bowl aloft and intoned---*" I stopped reading and looked at Mark, my personal Buck Mulligan.

Mark intoned, "*Introibo ad altare Dei."*

"I will go unto the altar of God," we said together.

"I always loved," I said, "that the Mass and *Ulysses* begin with that."

"Joyce was Catholic and Jesuit trained," said Mark.

"But in many ways irreligious," I added. "Buck Mulligan was mocking the Mass. By the way, you look great in yellow, ungirdled, your robe gently sustained by the air."

Mark twirled causing the flowing yellow robe to spread out around him. We had rented the dressinggown, the bowl, the mirror, and the razor. We purchased a small can of shaving lather. Prop rental had not been considered – we did not even know it was a possibility -- but we spotted the items in a small shop near the Tower. Good locational marketing. The up-front price to rent the items was the same as the price to buy them. However seventy-five percent of the price was returned to the renter when the items were returned. That removed the temptation not to return the rented items.

Mark and I were standing on top of the Sandycove Martello Tower overlooking Dublin Bay, the location of Chapter One of *Ulysses.* The Martello Tower was the first stop on our personal, graduation-gift, from Mark to me, Bloomsday tour. "Leopold 'Poldy' Bloom doesn't enter the novel until Chapter Four," I said. "The first three chapters are about Stephen Dedalus. His day starts at eight o'clock. The book jumps back to eight o'clock to begin Leopold Bloom's day in Chapter Four."

"Stephen Dedalus, the hero of *Portrait of an Artist as a Young Man,* was a little pissed at Buck Mulligan, wasn't he? Why?"

"Now I'm the Captain of the Barge, eh?"

"Aye, aye, sir," said Mark.

"Two reasons. He and Buck were sharing the Tower, and Buck introduced an Englishman – Heaven forbid! – into the mix.   And Buck made light of the death of Stephen's mother, or at least Stephen thought so. Probably a case of irreverent Buck being Buck." I opened my copy of *Ulysses* – we each had one -- "*When Stephen arrived, Buck said, 'Oh, it's only Dedalus, whose mother is beastly dead.'* I would be pissed too. Shows a lack of respect. What would you think if someone said, 'Oh, it's only Tuttle, whose parents are beastly dead'?"

"I'd be pissed too."

"Nice view of the sea from here," I said. "It looks rough today."

"The *snotgreen sea,* the *scrotumtightening sea,* Joyce's image-provoking phrases, although the second image makes me want to cross my legs."

"What did Homer call the sea in the Odyssey, the original voyage of Ulysses?"

"The *wine-dark sea,*" Mark said.

"Which do you prefer, *wine-dark* or *snotgreen*?" I asked.

"Definitely w*ine-dark.* My own suggestion, *peasoupgreen sea,* would be so much more appetizing than *snotgreen,* and anything is preferable to *scrotumtightening sea.*"

"You men, so penis protecting."

"I only protect it for you, honey."

"Thank you. But I'll go with Joyce on this one; the sea does look *snotgreen.* I don't think I would like to go swimming here today."

"Because of the roughness or the *snotgreeniness?"*

"*Snotgreeniness?"*

"If Joyce could make up words and phrases, so can I," said Mark.

"Go ahead, give me a Joycean phrase," I challenged.

"Okay. How about *the pussypink pig.*"

"Gross. And that doesn't work for all pussies. All are not pink."

"How would I know that?"

"Love you, Mark Tuttle. Peggy's is tan."

"Really?"

"Really. I can know that. You can't."

"But now I **do** know that," Mark said.

"Vicariously. And that's the only way you'll ever know it."

"How about the *pussytan sand* or the *pussytan lion*?"

I punched him in the shoulder.

344

SANDY AND MARK EAT IN POLDY FASHION

"Leopold Bloom ate with relish the inner organs of beasts and fowls," I said.

"I eat hot dogs with relish," said Mark.

"He ate them with **gusto**, you *sciocco,*" I said. "Not with pickle relish."

"Oh. Nevermind."

"When we first meet Poldy, in Chapter Four, he is going out to buy some kidneys for breakast."

"For breakfast? What's wrong with bacon and eggs?"

"Nothing, but Poldy likes kidneys. '*Mutton kidneys which gave to his palate a fine tang of faintly scented urine.*' "

"Sounds delicious."

"Do you remember what happens at the butcher's? All men are the same."

"He is attracted by the lady who bought two hams."

"She didn't buy two hams. She bought sausages. When she left the shop, he hurried behind to watch her moving hams. '*Pleasant to see first thing in the morning.*' It's like you looking at my hams during volleyball or running to the ocean in my bikini or climbing the stairs to the top of the *Duomo* in Florence. All men are the same."

"I was behind you in the *Duomo* for your protection."

"That too. I'll admit that. But didn't you like my hams?"

"Don't you like me looking at your hams?"

"Of course I do, but only **my** hams. Not some lady you waited behind at the butcher's."

"That wasn't me. It was Poldy," Mark said.

"Tuttle, party of two," cried out the hostess.

"I'll only look at your hams," Mark said. "I won't taste any others either."

I punched him on the shoulder.

"We're Tuttle," I said to the hostess. *God, I loved saying that sentence.*

"And when poor Poldy came back from the butcher's," I said to Mark. "He found a letter to Molly from her lover, Blazes Boylan. She was still in bed, and he brought it up to her. He had to walk around Dublin all day worrying about that.

"You're lucky I don't have a boyfriend making you walk around Cambridge all day worrying."

"I'd beat the shit out of him."

"You really are a Philistine."

We were at Davy Byrnes Pub where Poldy had lunch on June 16, 1904. Fictionally of course.

"What did he eat?" I asked. Captain Roberts quizzing her pupil.

"A cheese sandwich."

"What kind of cheese?" I asked. "Be more specific."

"You're as tough as Alex Trebec on Jeopardy."

"Yes, I am. What kind of cheese?"

"What is gorgonzola?" Mark asked/answered, Jeopardy correctly.

"Very good. And what did he drink?" I, Captain Roberts, asked.

"What is a glass of burgundy?" he asked/answered.

"Very good."

When the waiter came over, he said, "Two gorgonzola sandwiches and two glasses of burgundy?"

I just smiled and said, "You must sell a lot of gorgonzola."

"Only on June sixteenth," the waiter said.

The sandwiches were on the table within minutes. Along with two glasses of burgundy. I had never had a gorgonzola sandwich before. Probably never will again. But, on Bloomsday, in Dublin, in Davy Bryne's Pub, with my husband Mark Tuttle, I ate a gorgonzola sandwich. And I loved it. I loved being there with Mark as well. There is nothing I don't love doing with Mark.

"You better brush your teeth before you kiss me," Mark said. "Gorgonzola breath."

"And you better brush **your** teeth before you kiss me, Mr. Tuttle. And that's gorgonzola-honey breath, still delightful."

After we left the pub, Mark pulled me into the doorway of an adjoining building, and, you guessed it, kissed me. Passionately. Let me tell you this – it will take a lot more than a little gorgonzola to stop me from enjoying a Mark Tuttle kiss. I know he enjoyed it too. He told me so, and Mark Tuttle does not lie. Especially not to Sandy Roberts. But he did say he would draw the line at *"the fine tang of faintly scented urine."*

"Really?" I said, raising an eyebrow.

"Well, maybe not the fine tang of **your** faintly scented urine, my love."

SANDY AND MARK SET OFF IN BLOOM'S FOOTSTEPS AROUND DUBLIN

We went to Sweeney's Pharmacy where Mark bought me a bar of Citron-lemon soap. Poldy paid fourpence. Mark paid a lot more. Did Bloom buy it for Molly? I don't know. Mark bought it for me – that I do know. But there is no Blazes Boylan in my life, never will be.

We walked down to Sandymount to see if Gerty MacDowell would be exposing herself for Bloom's sake. Gerty caught Bloom looking at her and exposed her legs and undergarment to excite him. There were a lot of young mothers near the water, with their children, but none were modern day Gertys to Mark's Bloom. If Mark masturbated with me next to him, I would have killed him. Even randy Bloom did not have Molly with him that day in 1904.

We visited 7 Eccles Street, where Poldy and Molly lived, where Bloom ate his urine scented mutton kidneys, where Molly awaited her assignation with Blazes Boylan, where Molly concluded *Ulysses* with her eight-sentence, no punctuation, forty-five page thought-monologue.

MARK'S AND SANDY'S VISIT RELATED AS A SERIES OF NEWSPAPER STORIES

ERIN, GREEN GEM OF THE EMERALD SEA

Mark and Sandy Tuttle, AODS millionaires, visited Erin for Bloomsday this year. Sandy, a *Ulysses* aficionado, received the trip as a Harvard graduation gift from her loving husband.

They were sighted at eight o'clock yesterday morning viewing the Emerald Sea from Sandycove's Martello Tower. "I prefer *wine-dark* to *snotgreen*," said Mr. Tuttle, choosing Homer over Joyce.

They were seen eating gargonzola sandwiches at Davy Byrnes Pub, and kissing afterwood *sans* a tooth-brushing interlude. A brave American couple.

One of our reporters asked Mr. Tuttle how he liked the sandwich. His reply, "Better than urine tainted mutton kidneys."

IN THE HEART OF HIBERNIAN METROPOLIS

The Tuttles were spotted at Sandycove Martello Tower. Mr. Tuttle, emulating stately, plump Buck Mulligan, was seen in a flowing yellow dressinggown offering prayers in Latin to his Creator.

They were also spotted at Sandymount Strand where the couple sat and watched the mothers and their children frolic. Gerty MacDowell did not make an appearance.

They paid a visit to the long deceased Mina Purefoy at the maternity hospital. She was unable to see them. Neither was the baby available for visitation. Rumor has it that the beautiful Mrs. Tuttle is with child. Perhaps that was the *real* reason for the visit.

Mr. Tuttle inquired at the Westland Row post office if there were mail for him. He identified himself as "Henry Flower." There was a letter, perfume scented, contents unknown. He discreetly placed it in an inner pocket, with the lemon soap, while a bemused Mrs. Tuttle looked on. What did she think of the surreptitious pocketing of the letter? And of the pseudonym?

SHORT BUT TO THE POINT

Mr. Tuttle won fifty pounds betting on Throwaway at the local betting shop.

Mr. Tuttle denied that he encountered Mr. Macintosh in the cemetery. He claimed that he did not know any Macintoshes, here or in Boston.

MEMORABLE BATTLES RECALLED

---"She's my best friend, and I will never let anyone hurt her," said the eight-year-old boy.

---"Make fun of me all you want, but make fun of Sandy, and we fight."

---"That little sophomore who can't make up his mind which one he wants." "He wants me."

---"I thought Peggy and I were going to have to fight Mac, but then Mark was beside me."

---"I kicked the knife down the drainage hole. Mark had broken the punk's wrist."

---"I came in here for tacos, but if you want to fight, that's okay with me."

---"She gave me the finger. Didn't even look back. I should have broken it off."

---"What you going to do about it, cunt?" We both got thrown out of that game.

---"Your girlfriend has a shit mouth." "I think she has a beautiful mouth."

THE GRANDEUR THAT WAS ROME

Mr. and Mrs. Tuttle chanted together the opening line of the Tridentine Catholic Mass: *Introibo ad altare Dei.* I will go unto the altar of God. Other visitors to the Martello Tower actually knelt during the intonation. Mr. Tuttle was vested in a flowing yellow robe.

"What does the IHS stand for on the priest's chasuble?" Mrs. Tuttle asked her husband during Mass the day following Bloomsday. "I'm not sure," he answered, "but Molly said it means either *I have sinned* or *I have suffered.*" "Molly who?" "Bloom, of course."

SPOT THE WINNER

Mr. Tuttle came out of the betting shop with a smile on his face. With his Throwaway winnings and the beautiful Mrs. Tuttle on his arm, it is easy to spot the winner.

EXIT MRS. TUTTLE

Mrs. Tuttle was seen exiting an adult products establishment in the area formally called Nighttown. She was carrying a semi-large brown paper bag filled with items useful for fulfilling sexual fetishes, fantasies, and transgressions. What else could she have purchased there? Why else would she have a plain, brown bag? She covered her face, a beautiful face to be sure, with her free hand and rushed to a waiting cab.

WHAT?----AND LIKEWISE---WHERE?

No doubt as to what. The plain, brown paper bag tells us that. But where? Their hotel room? God only knows. The Dublin House is a respectable lodging establishment, not a bawdy house. Will the *nouveau riche* Americans sully that great hostel? God forbid.

350

RHYMES AND REASONS

Sandy..randy..handy..

Mark..hark..bark..

Mouth..south..

What is going on? What is coming off?

Shuck..suck..fuck!

Q&A ABOUT SANDY AND MARK (STAND-INS FOR POLDY AND STEPHEN)
(Items in bold print quoted from Ulysses.)

How did the young couple get to Erin, Green Gem of the Emerald Sea?

On Aer Lingus.

What type of plane was it?

A big one.

Did the youngsters fly coach?

No, first class. They decided to always avoid the dismayingly unpleasantly crowded condition of coach class now that Mark's brainpower had enriched them.

Was the meal satisfying on the plane?

Yes, but it was not the corned beef and cabbage that Mark expected on Aer Lingus.

Did they have the Irish soda bread that Sandy desired?

No.

Was there any Irish treat during or after dinner?

The young couple each had a glass of Bailey's Irish Cream.

Who drank more quickly?

Mark. He was ready for his second glass concomitant with Sandy's finishing half of her first one.

What did the female member of the duo say to the male member at that time?

"Sip it. Savor the taste."

Did the stewardess ask them for ID before serving them the Bailey's Irish Cream?

No. It was not necessary over international waters.

Would it have been a problem if she had?

No. Mark and Sandy were both twenty-two at the time of the flight.

Were any of the three stewardesses in first class from Northern Ireland?

No. All three lasses were from the Irish Republic, good Catholic girls, nun-trained.

Of what did the duumvirate deliberate during their itinerary?

Of Ulysses, of Peggy, of Margie Baylor, of the possibility that Sandy was impregnated, and if so, whether the growing baby was male or female, of new sister Leslie, and old sister Patty.

Did the sex of the baby matter to Mark?
No. Only the health.

Did he have a preference?
Yes. He wanted a Maddie.

Were their views on some points divergent?
Yes, but not on this. Sandy also wanted a Maddie.

On what points were their views divergent?
On the desirability of kissing Peggy Mayhew, on the speed of imbibing Bailey's Irish Cream, on the adequacy of Sandy's bumps, on watching each other pee.

Didn't Sandy like to watch Mark pee?
Yes, but not as much as Mark liked to watch Sandy pee.

Did they have other bathroom differences?
Yes, Mark **liked to read at stool.**

And Sandy didn't?
Not as much as Mark.

Did Mark like to watch Sandy at stool?
We will never know. That was not permitted by Sandy.

Why not?
She did not want to introduce a possibly disagreeable smell into her multiple, oral and vaginal, Mark-appreciated smells.

Was she sure he would not like to smell her at stool?
No. She knew it excited dogs.

Are men like dogs?
In some ways, perhaps in that way.

What action did (Mark) make on their arrival at their destination?
He looked in his pocket for the room key.

Was it there?

No. He had left it on the counter at the hotel's check-in desk.

Why was he doubly irritated?
Because he had forgotten and because he remembered that he had reminded himself twice not to forget.

What were then the alternatives before the inadvertently keyless couple?

For Mark to return to the desk, for Sandy to return to the desk, for both of them to return to the desk, or for the couple to stand in the hall hoping the key would miraculously appear.

What did they do?
Mark returned to the desk.

What did Sandy do?
She waited patiently, expectantly, lovingly, longingly, passively, willingly, non-irately, happily, slightly worriedly for her beloved husband's return.

Did she miss him?
Yes.

Was she lonely?
Yes.
Alone what did (Sandy) feel?
The cold of interstellar space.

What did she do when he returned?
Kissed him.

What did he do?

He opened the door.

What qualifying considerations allayed his perturbations?

Sandy led him to the bedroom where they enjoyed each other in a sensual way.

What satisfied him?

Sandy.

What satisfied her?

Mark.

What is Sandy's favorite phrase from Ulysses?

"The ineluctable modality of the visible."

Does she know exactly what that means?

No.

Does Mark.

Also no.

What is Mark's favorite phrase from Ulysses?

"Snotgreen sea."

What did Sandy do to him when he told her that?

She punched him on the shoulder.

What is Mark's most frightening phrase from *Ulysses?*

Scrotumtightening sea.

Did they plan to celebrate Bloomsday in any special way in their hotel room?

Yes. Sandy planned to re-create Nighttown in their hotel room the evening of June 16.

Did Mark know that?
No. Sandy wanted to surprise him.

Had they done kinky before?
No.

Did she think Mark would like kinky?
Yes. Mark likes anything to do with sex and Sandy.

Would he hurt her?
Never.
Would she hurt him?
Never.

Will they have fun?
Yes.

SANDY AND MARK SPEND AN EXCITING EVENING IN NIGHTTOWN

"What's in the paper bag?" Mark asked me.

"Take a look," I said.

He began removing items from the bag: a blindfold, a pair of handcuffs, a whip…

"A whip?" he said.

"It's foam, soft," I said. "For play."

"Foreplay?" Mark asked.

"No. For…..play," I answered.

"What games do you have in mind?"

"You'll see."

He continued removing items from the bag: strawberry-flavored gel, a little electric fan, two pair of plastic gloves, a pair of my black panties, which I had added to the bag upon arriving at the hotel, one of my matching black bras, also added after arrival, a dog collar, and a whistle.

"What are we going to do?" Mark asked.

"It will be our secret. No one will ever know, not even the readers."

SANDY'S SOLILOQUY (A MUCH SHORTER VERSION OF MOLLY BLOOM'S SOLILOQUY)

The first day I saw him at St. Michael's...so handsome...so nice...I wanted to kiss him...really that first day...Then he scribbled all over my Marble Composition book with purple crayons...Actually he didn't but that bitch Missy O'Donnell lied to me...I should have beaten her up...Mark told me to forget it...He liked me not her...I bought him a Coke that day at the candy store...I really wanted to kiss him...we just held hands walking home...Then he did kiss me, just a peck, a wonderful peck...it was nice...I knew then that he was going to be my boyfriend...I really did...Right from the start he liked me more than he liked Peggy...If he chose me over Peggy, I had nothing to worry about from any other girl...When did we kiss the first time?..A real kiss?..At Molly Davidson's birthday party...In the closet...We didn't want to come out...I never imagined how exciting it would be to just touch tongues...I still love touching his tongue with mine...sucking on it...tasting it...blowing streams of my honey breath...that's what he calls it...my honey breath...into his face...He loves it...really loves it...He says even today that he wants to come with his tongue in my mouth...I would not be here if it wasn't for Mark Tuttle...How can an eight-year-old boy beat up a man, even with a bat?..She's my best friend and I will never let anyone hurt her...God is that ever true...That was the first time I told him I was going to marry him...Nothing will make me happier, Sandy Roberts...We will get married... Promise?..Promise...That little boy has kept that promise...Peggy says when I hugged Mark that day I never let go...She's right...I will never let go of Mark Tuttle...Those big kids were making fun of us that day we were playing behind the school...Ignore them...They'll go away...Then they started making fun of me...You can make fun of me all you want, but if you make fun of Sandy, we're going to fight...Bully walked away fast...Mac too...I thought me and Peggy were going to have to fight Mac...But then Mark was there...He's always there for me, isn't he?..He takes care of me...In every way...I was on his shoulders, my little vagina touching his neck...Can I see your little bumps?..My answer was Yes right away, but I made him wait...He was pleading with me with his eyes...Yes, you can see my bumps...Touch them?..Kiss them?.. Yes...Later I let him take off my top...How he loved that...Thought he was going to come right there in the pool shed...He didn't see my vagina until junior year in high school...But he saw my bumps when he was still a little boy...Still loves my bumps...Loves my vagina too...Loves me...Tells me all the time I have the most beautiful face in all the world...Not true, but he believes it...So for Mark it is true...We love each other...That day in the pool, his heart was going like mad...Will you let me see your bumps?...Yes I said yes I will Yes.

Chapter Seventeen
Riptide

The Friday after we returned from Dublin, I asked Mark to walk with me to the local Dunkin' Donuts. He knew something was up. We sat at a back table with our medium coffees, cream no sugar. I held up my cup, and he tapped his against mine.

"Well?" he asked.

"I missed my period."

He almost spilled his coffee. He stood up, came over to me, hugged me, and kissed me. I cried as is my wont when happy.

My doctor, Barbara Majewski, the "just fuck in the shower" Dr. Majewski, confirmed my pregnancy the following Friday. Not that it was a girl -- she couldn't confirm that so early in my term -- but I already **knew** the sex of the baby. Maddie was on the way!

I turned to Mark as we walked out of Dr. Majewski's office. "How wonderful it this," I exclaimed. I was crying. "We've made a baby. Little Sandy and little Mark have made a baby."

He kissed me and said, "I can't wait to meet Maddie."

"You'll see her in nine months, but you will play with her and feel her long before then."

"And love her," he said.

I love Mark Tuttle. "Yes, and love her. I love her already."

"So do I," he said, and kissed me.

I mentioned earlier that the lifelong love affair between Mark and Maddie began the day he held her in the maternity ward. That's not correct; it began that day walking out of Dr. Majewski's office. We stopped at Dunkin' Donuts (where else?) and, after Mark placed my coffee on the table, he patted my stomach and said, "Hello, Maddie. I love you." I cried again.

The following morning, Peggy and Warren drove up from Rhode Island for the week-end. They had both graduated from URI in May, and had already obtained teaching positions for the fall, Peggy at Coventry High School as a physical education teacher and junior varsity basketball coach, Warren as an English teacher at Bishop Hendricken High School. Peggy found a job at the Coventry YWCA for the summer; Warren was teaching summer school at Hendricken. Their wedding date was the third Saturday of the following April. I would be the maid of honor, and Mark would be Warren's best man. They had an apartment in Coventry and were sharing expenses and other things.

We, Mark and I, had rented a second parking spot, another patch of dirt, close to our original parking spot. Also two hundred dollars per month. We rented the second spot primarily for Peggy and Warren. They spent most week-ends in Cambridge. Peggy needed her Sandy fixes. We maintained our close relationship throughout our college years and thereafter.

When Peggy entered the apartment, I kissed her and said, "Big news!"

"You're pregnant," she cried out.

"How did you know?"

"Can Sandy Roberts keep secrets from me? Your glowing face told me. I'm going to be an aunt," she cried out. "A real aunt, not a biological one."

"You're the first to know. Don't tell my Mom or Patty, okay? I want to tell them in person."

"They shall not hear the news from me."

"Peggy, there is no way I can know this yet, but I am positive it is a girl. Maddie is growing inside me."

We hugged as only two best friends can hug. There is no one I would rather share this news with than Peggy. She has been my best girlfriend, my sister, since I was six years old. I knew she was as happy with this news as I was. Peggy Mayhew and Sandy Roberts will always love each other and rejoice in each other's good news.

Working backward later, Dr. Majewski, Mark (my mathematician), and I concluded that Maddie was conceived during the first week of June. She came with us to Dublin, but, at the time, she was very tiny and sheltered inside my warm, loving, nurturing, nourishing womb. I don't think she'll remember any part of our Bloomsday adventure. I hope she doesn't remember her father and I re-enacting Poldy's escapades in Nighttown in our hotel room. You can be assured she will not learn of that from me or Mark. Notice I say "Maddie." I really had no doubt.

Mark and I had promised Mom that I would not get pregnant until after I graduated from college. I had graduated from Harvard in late May. Mark graduated from MIT at the same time. Therefore we had met our commitment to Mom. We were going down to Rhode Island the following week-end for a party at Margie Baylor's house. We decided to kill two birds with one stone, and make the announcement to Mom, Dad, and Patty at that time.

Peggy was with me when I called Mom, that Saturday afternoon.

"Hi, Mom."

"Hey, honey, what's up?" she asked.

"We're coming down to Rhode Island next weekend. Can you put us up?"

"Of course, no need to ask," she answered. "What's the reason for the trip home?"

Mom always considered Coventry, Rhode Island, our "home," not Cambridge. She expected us to move back to Coventry when we had children. "Who would raise children in Cambridge?" she asked. We probably will move back "home," but we had not committed to do that.

"Just a get together at Margie Baylor's house next Saturday," I answered. "She's having a summer swim party." That was true. We **were** going to the party at Margie's house, but the main reason for the visit had changed to my personal *Annunciation* to Mom and Dad.

"And we would like to take you two out for dinner Friday evening," I continued. "Where would you like to go? We'll meet you at the restaurant."

"The Seven Suns," she suggested. I knew she would. The Seven Suns is a Chinese restaurant in North Kingstown where the four of us often dine when we're in Rhode Island. The Seven Suns has delicious food, reasonable prices, and a relatively elegant ambiance. Mark calls it "Chinese Renaissance" décor, whatever that might be.

"Seven o'clock okay?" I asked.

"Seven at the Seven Suns. That sounds very lucky. That will be fine," Mom said. "I'll call and reserve a table for four."

"Make it for six, Mom," I said. "Peggy and Warren are going to join us."

After hanging up I said to Peggy, "Won't she be surprised?"

"I can't wait to see her reaction."

That evening Peggy and I discussed Maddie's godparents. I told her Mark and I had decided to ask his sister, Patty, and Bill to be godparents to Maddie and our future children. "I want the children to stay with family if something happens to us. You're not offended, are you?" I asked.

"No, of course not. I thought you would ask Patty and Bobby."

"If this were just an honorary title, maybe we would have gone that way. But it's not. We want them to stay together if....I can't even say it."

"Warren and I have talked about this too. Since neither of us has siblings, we want you and Mark to be the godparents of our children. I agree it's not just an honorary title. If something happens to us, will you take care of our kids?"

"Yes. How's that for a quick answer. I promise you we will raise them, and love them, as our own."

"I know you will."

We sat and hugged each other. Then we kissed. Peggy Mayhew and I love to kiss each other. Of course I will love her children, and take care of them, if I have to. Like my own!

Bobby and Leslie met us outside Fenway on Sunday. We had great box seats, again behind the Sox dugout. The girls sat in front, the boys in the row behind us. I was sitting between Peggy and Leslie. I turned to Leslie and said, "Leslie, I'm pregnant."

She started laughing.

"What?" I asked.

"Me too. Just found out."

We hugged and cried.

"We're going to tell Mom and Dad next Friday," I said. "We're going to dinner with them at the Seven Suns."

"Mind if we join you? We'll make it a double announcement."

"God, will she be happy. That will be great."

The Red Sox made our celebration complete, beating the hated Yankees 4 - 1. After the game, Bobby and Leslie headed back to Worcester, and my Peggy and her Warren drove back to Coventry. How delightful spending the day with two of my three sisters, and with Maddie. Maddie is always with me now. I still can't believe that! And don't forget Mark. He is always with me too – and nothing is better than that.

I called Mom back that evening. "Make that reservation for eight. Leslie and Bobby will be joining us and staying overnight. We're going to fill up your house."

"Is something up?" Mom asked.

"No," I lied.

"Okay," she said, but I could sense her mind working, trying to figure out what was going on. "And I love my home filled with family."

"I know," I said. *And there will be six family members staying there Friday night, not just four.*

Mark is ecstatic about Maddie. He loves to lay in bed with me and place his lips or his ears on my stomach. I'm not showing yet, but we both know she's in there. Mark is absolutely convinced it is a girl too. He kisses my tummy and speaks to Maddie. "I love you, little Maddie, and I can't wait to start feeling you move around in there. I know you're going to like me because I love you."

When we made love on the the night Dr. Majewski confirmed Maddie was living inside my womb, Mark was initially a little tentative. He was afraid that he might hurt little Maddie with his thrusts into the wet, dark interior.

I held his head between my two hands and said, "Honey, Dr. Majewski told us there is no way you can hurt the baby. As she gets older and bigger, she will know something is going on. She will hear me moaning and crying out and feel me moving around, after all. But our lovemaking will be like a little tickling sensation to Maddie and **cannot** harm her."

Now when he wants me, which, thank God, is daily, he says, "I would love to tickle Maddie. Okay with you?"

"Oh, yes," I answer. "I think both Maddie and I will enjoy that."

Mark loves to smell, lick, and kiss me in my wetness. Always has, right from the first day we made love. I love it too. He has asked me never to shave my pubic hair; he loves to twirl his fingers in my bush. He loves to blow streams of warm, moist air on me, both in my bush and then below it, which drives me crazy. He told me I was his first, and only, woman. I believe him, but I did ask him how he got to be so good without any prior experience.

"On-the-job training," he said, "with a great partner."

Love that Mark Tuttle.

Since my little visitor has taken up residence inside me, Mark has added a new twist. He whispers into my vagina, "I know you're in there, Maddie. Can you hear me? Can you feel the breeze?" The whispering and blowing not only tickle me; they arouse me beyond telling. Mark loves it when I show signs of arousal, and increases his blowing, sucking, kissing, and licking until I have one or more orgasms. He knows how to please me.

Did I ever tell you? I love Mark Tuttle.

After our delightful foreplay, I pull him up: "Now tickle Maddie while we kiss." We take care of each other during the tickling of Maddie. I seem to be getting the better part, two, three, or four orgasms to his one, but he is always satisfied. We have had a very exciting, inventive, and mutually satisfying sex life from the first day. After lovemaking, we lock arms and legs, and continue to smell,

365

kiss, lick, and caress each other. Mark loves that post-coital interaction as much as I do. Neither one of us ever rushes out of our bed. Often the contact leads to a repeat performance. *Husband and wife, horny together, what could be better than that?..Maybe husband and wife, horny together, with me carrying our child…It's not 'And the two shall become one'…It's 'And the two shall become three.'*

I walked into the lobby of the Seven Suns at exactly seven o'clock the following Friday. Mark and I have always been punctual, anally punctual. Mom and Dad were waiting for us in the lobby. Peggy and Warren were with them. So were Bobby and Leslie.

"Where's Mark?" asked Dad.

"Parking. He'll be right in," I said.

When I entered the Seven Suns's lobby, four young women rushed up to me.

"Sandy, how are you? Are you moving back to Rhode Island?"

"So good to see you. You look great."

"You going to Margie's party tomorrow?"

After I escaped my admirers, Peggy approached and hugged me. "I haven't said a word," she whispered.

Mom looked at me, and then at Peggy, and then back at me. Mom smiled, but did not say anything. *Does she suspect something?..How could she know?..How could she not?..She's my mother…You'll get the news very soon, Mom…Leslie's pregnant too, Mom…I bet you are going to be one very happy grandmother…Mom, a grandmother…Me, a mother…Leslie a mother…God, this is great.*

Peggy Mayhew is, and always has been, gorgeous: tall, well built, athletic, sexy, with an animal magnetism about her. Even when she was six! It's funny – I always considered Peggy beautiful, and she always considered me beautiful, but neither one of us considered ourselves beautiful. Well, I didn't. Peggy said she didn't, but that is hard to believe. The boys at CHS called her the "goddess."

The boys' basketball coach at East Greenwich High School told his wife, who later told me, that I was the most beautiful girl he had ever seen "not in a model sense, but in an athlete sense." I don't really know what that means. Mark thinks I am beautiful, so I guess that settles the issue. He says that waking up and seeing my beautiful face first thing in the morning is the best possible start to his day. He tells me that he never tires of looking at my face. Even when I'm wearing glasses.

Mom told the receptionist that the other couple, meaning Mark and me, had arrived, and the young Chinese hostess gathered eight menus and led us to a table in the rear next to the indoor fountain. I kept an eye on the front door, and waved to Mark when he entered. He had to stop at seven tables before he was able to join us. Mark gets more attention than I do even though I brought CHS four trophies to his measly two. I claim it's sexual bias.

Mark, Peggy, Warren, Leslie, Bobby, and I ordered beers. Mom ordered a white wine; Dad ordered a scotch and water, Dewars. When the drinks arrived, I asked for everyone's attention to make a toast.

"To the newest grandparents in Rhode Island, to Mr. and Mrs. Roberts who are just now finding out that they will have two little granddaughters in about eight months."

Dad said, "What? You're pregnant?" He looked from me to Leslie.

Mom, Leslie, and I stood up. Mom put her arms around us, hugged us, kissed us, and cried all over our beautiful faces. "Sandy, Leslie, I am so happy, so happy."

"Me too, Mom," we both said.

Peggy stood up and embraced the three of us, creating a quadrumvirate of joyous, crying, dancing women.

"You knew, didn't you?" Mom said to Peggy.

"Yes. I was up in Cambridge the day after Sandy found out, and with Leslie at Fenway the following day."

"I thought something was up when you called me back last Sunday, and I was positive when I saw you and Peggy whispering in the lobby. I had a feeling, a hope…This is so wonderful. Two granddaughters, coming at the same time… how do you two know they're girls? It's too early."

"Mom, I don't know how, but I am positive. Absolutely positive," I said.

"Me too," said Leslie. "Absolutely positive."

"We even have a name for her," I said.

"What?"

"Mom," I answered, "we are going to name her Madeline, after you, and call her Maddie. We call her Maddie already. Yes, we talk to her." I smiled at Mark.

Mom looked at Leslie.

"Melanie," she said. "After my mother's sister who died as a teen-ager."

Mom, who is as emotional as I am, who probably is the reason why I am so emotional, began to cry, hearing that one of her granddaughters was going to be named after her. She reached over and squeezed my hand."

"That's so wonderful." said Mom. "I can't wait to see my Maddie and my Melanie. To love them. To spoil them. Thank you." Then she turned to Mark and Bobby, "Let's not forget you two. Congratulations." She hugged them both.

"We're going to stop in to see Patty after dinner to tell her the news and ask her and Bill to be the godparents," I said. "We are sure she will raise Maddie, and any other children we have, with love if anything happens to us."

Mom looked at Peggy.

"We discussed this, Mrs. Roberts," said Peggy. "I would be a great guardian for the kids. Sandy knows that.

But I agree they should all stay together with family. I'll always be their aunt."

Patty is not only Mark's sister, she is my sister too, much more than a sister-in-law. It's the same with Leslie; she is my sister. We love each other. The day Mark's and Patty's parents died, Patty pulled me aside and asked me to stay at Mark's side all that terrible week. I had every intention of doing that. Nothing could have kept me apart from Mark that week. But hearing Patty ask me to do that was reassuring. Mark's Aunt Marion objected, but Patty put an end to that quickly. That cemented my and Patty's sisterhood.

Dad, always the less sentimental of my parents, then said, "Shall we call over the waitress and order dinner?"

"Good idea, Dad," I said. I was starving. I had not eaten since breakfast, saving my appetite for the Chinese feast. Mom and Dad always let me and Mark order. We had become Chinese food experts over the years in Cambridge.

We ordered a large bowl of hot and sour soup for the table to be followed by a medley of fried and steamed pork and shrimp dumplings. And an eggroll for Dad.

For the entrées, we ordered sweet and sour pork, which did **not** come with a red sauce, but with a light orange, almost translucent, sweet and sour coating, a Szechwan chicken and vegetables dish ("Not too spicy, please"), shrimp *mei fun*, a large bowl of white rice, and a platter of pork fried rice. Mom and Dad used plates and forks; the three younger couples ate Chinese style: rice bowls and chopsticks. There was more than enough food for eight. Peggy took the leftovers home.

Everything was *hen hao chi*, delicious. Mom asked if it was okay for me and Leslie to eat the hot Szechwan food. I told her Maddie loves spicy cuisine. "No, really, Mom, Doctor Majewski told me that spicy food is great for a growing baby. She told me the major items to avoid are

369

cigarettes, drugs, other than those she will prescribe, and alcohol. She knows that the first two are non-issues for me, and when I told her I only drink Miller Lite, and no more than two a day, she said that would be fine. Szechwan, Thai, and Mexican food are all okay for me, Maddie, Leslie, and Melanie.

We finished dinner around nine and, after telling Mom and Dad that we would be at their house around eleven, we headed over to Patty's and Bill's house. Peggy gave me a hug, and then she and Warren went home. We hadn't forewarned Patty and Bill of our visit, but they were home. Patty was as emotional as Mom. She and Bill said they would be thrilled to have the honor and responsibility of being Maddie's godparents. She and I had a hug and a cry over that. We truly are sisters.

Leslie, Mom, and I sat up to two in the morning talking in the kitchen. Mom loves Leslie as much as she loves me. Well, maybe not as much as she loves me. But very close. That makes me happy. Leslie is my sister.

Mark had gone to bed, but he was awake waiting for me. I was glad he was – Maddie wanted to be tickled. He held up the cover, and I slid into the bed and into his arms. *Husband and wife, horny together…What could be better than that?*

It was good seeing old friends at Margie's summer swim party. Margie will be a senior at the University of Rhode Island (URI) in the fall, and lives at home. She is in the nursing program. Billy Smith, also beginning his senior year at URI, is in the pharmacy program. He came with his fiancé, Maureen Sullivan, a senior at Rhode Island College (RIC) preparing to be a teacher. Billy had brought Maureen as his guest to our wedding. They have been dating ever since. She was impressed when I chose Billy for my special "Bride's Choice" dance, describing him to those at the wedding as, "with the exception of Mark, the most courageous man I know."

Peggy and Warren were also at the party. I spent most of my time lounging around the pool talking to Peggy, Margie, and Maureen. Margie assigned the grilling to Mark, Billy Smith, and Warren. *You are one lucky guy, Warren Jones...I hope you realize that.* The pool was delightful. Mark was in the water, and I dove in and grabbed his legs. He lifted me out of the water and put me on his shoulders. *How did you do that, Mark Tuttle?..You are so strong...God, Peggy, you look sexy in a bikini...I don't look bad...Actually I look pretty good...Mark can't take his eyes off me...I like that...With Peggy here, he can't take his eyes off me....Just like Kristijian's naked blonde with nice teeth...Love you Mark Tuttle...Want to see my bumps?..Remember that day?..I was on your shoulder that day too.*

Before we ate, Peggy called for attention. "I have an announcement to make. Can I have your attention?" Everyone stopped and looked at her. God, she is striking.

"Our friends from Massachusetts are a threesome." No one grasped what she meant.

"Duh," she said. "Sandy is pregnant."

That statement caused a rush in my direction. And many questions. My answers:

"Yes---"

"A little girl---"

"I just know---"

"Maddie---"

"In eight months---"

"We'll stay in Cambridge until she's born, then, we're not sure---"

"Maybe back to Coventry---"

Looking at Peggy I had to wonder what would have happened if she had made a play for Mark. She is gorgeous.

Well, she didn't, and he wouldn't….No, he wouldn't…He fought for her that time…Got a black eye for her…But I expect him to fight for her, or Margie, or Leslie…Let me ask him tonight in bed…Maybe at Dunkin' Donuts…See what he says…I know what he'll say…Yes, I do.

On the way back to Mom's, I asked Mark to stop at the Coventry Dunkin' Donuts. We have always had our important conversations at Dunkin' Donuts. I found a table for two, and Mark went to the counter for two medium coffees, cream no sugar, and a honey-dipped stick for us to share. I took the larger half. "Don't forget I have to feed Maddie too," I said.

"I'm not going to forget that," he said. "Ever. What do you want to talk about?"

"Did you know that Peggy Mayhew was in love with you during our sophomore year at CHS?"

"In high school? I thought so, but she never said anything."

"Yes. She never said or did anything about it because of me even though we were not 'formally' dating until our junior year. But she knew you belonged to me. Would she have swayed you if she had made her intentions known?"

"The gorgeous, statuesque, sexy Peggy Mayhew had a crush on me?"

"Yes."

"And you're asking what my reaction would have been?"

"Yes."

"Sandy, the world is full of beautiful women. Even little Cambridge is full of beautiful women. Has anyone ever turned my head?"

"No."

"What did Kristijian say about the naked, beautiful, blonde with nice teeth?"

I just laughed.

"Ever since I have been six years old, the only woman I have ever wanted to live with, to be with, to sleep with, to smell, to kiss, to taste, to make love with, is you. And that will never change."

"I know that. Just wanted to hear you say it again. Peggy is beautiful, though, isn't she?"

"I never noticed."

"Yeah, sure."

"Well, maybe I noticed, but I wasn't swayed."

"Good."

At the beginning of October, we went back to Dr. Majewski's office for a sonogram. The test confirmed what I already knew. Maddie was a girl, a healthy, normal, beautiful little girl.

We stopped at Dunkin' Donuts on the way home. "Let's scoot down to Flagler Beach for a week or ten days. Temperature should still be in the high eighties. We both love it there, and nothing is holding us here now. We can get a motel with a pool and enjoy both the pool and the ocean. You can work on your book down there as well as in Cambridge. Me too, on my stories."

"Sure," he said.

"That was easy," I said.

"I'm always easy, with you anyway."

"I'm glad you weren't easy with Peggy."

"I never knew about Peggy. Maybe---"

I punched him in the shoulder. "I'll still let you tickle Maddie tonight."

I made all the arrangements the next morning: round trip on Southwest, Providence, actually Warwick, to Orlando, leaving on a Tuesday in mid-October, returning eight days later; a rental car in Orlando; a room at the

Topaz Motel in Flagler Beach, just across A1A from the ocean. We love Flagler Beach: great restaurants, all informal, great beaches, fun nightlife, no high-rise hotels or high-rise condominiums. We found it by accident while still in college, and have returned numerous times, always staying at the Topaz. We drove to Mom's Monday evening. Mom's house is ten minutes from the airport in Warwick. Mom offered to drive us to the airport and pick us up on our return, but we elected to use one of the Park 'n Fly lots. Easier for everyone, and not expensive.

The Southwest non-stop flight landed in Orlando a little after noon on Tuesday afternoon, and, after stopping at the Topaz to change into our Florida uniforms, T-shirts, shorts, baseball caps (Red Sox or Patriots – we brought both), and sandals, we arrived at the Golden Lion, "The King of the Beach", at three for a late lunch. We chose a table on the upper deck overlooking the ocean and shared a large conch chowder and a pound of peel 'n eat shrimp. Temperature was eighty-seven; ocean breeze was heavenly. God, we love Flagler Beach! Maddie loved the shrimp, so I had to take a larger share than Mark. Oh, we had two ice cold Miller Lites to wash down the shrimp. The little fellas slide down so much easier with beer.

Michael Reyes, a local publisher and author whom we had met on previous trips, was having a beer at the next table. Michael runs a local author's event on the third Tuesday of each month at which local authors read from their work. He calls it "Writers Read." That day happened to be the third Tuesday of October, and Mike asked me, a published author, to read that evening. He still had a few slots open. I told him Mark was working on a novel, a very good novel, and he asked Mark to read as well. We agreed to be at the Beach House Beanery at seven.

We walked, at least a mile, beside the ocean after our late lunch before returning to the Topaz to change for the pool. Thinking of Maddie, I had a Coke. Mark had another Miller Lite poolside. I did take a few sips from his bottle, but that doesn't count. The pool temperature was in the low eighties. I could have stayed in the water forever, but, at six, we went back to our room to get ready for Writers Read. Since we were only five minutes from the Beach House Beanery, and since we were both horny, we tickled Maddie, and Mark spoke to her in his special way, before we gathered our reading material and headed out to perform. I told Mark that Maddie enjoyed the tickling so much, he would have to do it again later when we returned to the room. "Happy to oblige," he said. It gave me something to anticipate during the rest of the evening. God, he turns me on. And then takes care of me! I turn him on too, and, yes, I do take care of him. Always.

I read from my latest short story which was going to be published in the November issue of Alfred Hitchcock's Mystery Magazine. I finished half of the story and then left a copy with Michael. He said he would have a local writer finish reading it the following month. He introduced Mark as "the husband of a published author." I liked that. Mark read from the introductory section of the novel. It was well received, as was my reading. Mark kept his promise when we returned to the room. Then we opened the window to let in the ocean breeze, wrapped up in each other's arms, and went to sleep. His last words to me were, "God, you smell good." Nice last words.

The next day was almost the last day of my life.

After a run on the beach, we ate breakfast outside at Oceanside, another A1A restaurant. Then we decided to spend the day at the ocean. We brought beach towels and an umbrella from the motel, and staked out a spot not far from the mighty Atlantic. The surf looked friendly. We each brought a book, the same title actually. We have been team-reading ever since high school. I removed my T-shirt and stretched out on my towel to soak up the sun in my black bikini. Mark kissed my tummy and said, "Sandy, you are one sexy mother." He's a writer; he has a way with words.

After an hour of soaking up sun and reading, Mark suggested we go for a swim. I jumped up and raced toward the sea. He followed me. He loves to follow me when I run in a bikini. I wonder why.

"Looking at my hams, Poldy?"

The water was warm. Not as warm as the pool, but warm. I ran straight in and dived over an incoming wave. He followed me over the wave and caught me under the water. We came up kissing. There were no other swimmers in the area. Two lifeguards were on duty on their high wooden chair on the beach. Mark lifted me up and tossed me backwards over the next wave.

Then it happened.

All of a sudden, I was being sucked away from the shore. Fast. I tried to swim toward the beach to slow down the pull, but it was a losing struggle against the outwardly surging sea. *Is this the end?.. Is Maddie going to die inside me before she's even born?*

I could see the lifeguard stand receding rapidly. The shore was receding rapidly. Everything was receding rapidly. The lifeguards were running toward the ocean, blowing their whistles, but what could they do? I never felt so alone in my life. "Mark!" I yelled. And again, "Mark!" But I knew I had left him behind. *Mark, you must be frantic.* I think I gave up at that point. I cried out, "God, help me and Maddie. We don't want to die."

A hand grasped my shoulder. **A hand grasped my shoulder.** *Mark,* I thought. ***Mark!***

"Don't fight it, Sandy. Go with the flow. We'll be okay. I'm with you," he said.

Immediately relief washed over me. I had no fear, no anxiety. *Mark is here…Mark is always here when I need him…What is there to worry about?..Maddie, Daddy's here…We're okay.*

I yelled, "Mark, what do we do?"

I don't know if he could hear me, but his answer was appropriate. "Let the riptide take us out. Don't fight it. Swim toward the side. Do not let go of my hand. We can swim out of this. Do **not** let go of my hand," he screamed. He held my right hand in his left hand, and stroked with his right arm pulling us sideward as the ocean continued to pull us out. I stroked with my left arm. It will probably be hard for you, reader, to believe this, but I was completely, absolutely calm. Mark was with me.

Just as suddenly as the incident began, it was over. Mark and I were treading water, but in relatively calm ocean. "Let's take a few more strokes to the side," Mark said.

We did. We were far out from the shore, but, at least, we were not being pulled away from the beach any longer.

He said, "Are you all right, Sandy?"

I answered, "Of course I'm all right. I'm with you. I'm always all right when I'm with you." I kissed him passionately right there in the ocean. My tongue was all over his mouth. I think I would have fucked him right there if it were possible. "I love you," I said.

"I love you too, Sandy. Always have. Always will. Let's slowly make our way back toward the shore. Stay together."

"I'm not leaving your side," I said. We both smiled.

He then patted my tummy. I looked at him. "Reassuring Maddie," Mark said. *I love you, Mark Tuttle.*

"Don't let go of my hand," he said.

"Mark, Peggy always says I grabbed hold of you when I was eight, and never let go. I'm not letting go now."

377

He smiled, and we made our way back toward the beach, **together.**

We met the lifeguards about halfway to the beach. They swam with us until we reached the shallow water, then walked with us to the sand. Mark explained what had happened. When he realized I had been snatched by the riptide, he immediately dove into it following me out. Since he was fighting to move away from the shore, and I was fighting to stay close to the shore, he reached me rather quickly. You already know what happened when he caught up to me.

The younger of the two lifeguards, his name was Marty (his name was sewn on his trunks), smiled and said to Mark, "I guess you're going to get lucky tonight." He didn't think I heard him.

I said, "Marty, he gets lucky every night."

Marty blushed. I think he was envious. I do look good in a black bikini, even four months pregnant.

As we walked back to the towels, I asked Mark how he had known what to do. He said there was a sign at the entrance to the beach explaining riptides and giving instructions on how to proceed if caught in one. I had not even seen the sign. When Mark is with me, he is always in protector mode.

He asked me if I wanted to stay at the beach or head back to the Topaz.

"Topaz," I said. "Unless you want to make love here on the beach."

"Better head to the Topaz," he said. "And then how about lunch at The Lion."

"It's going to be a late lunch," I said. "You're not getting out of my bed for hours."

"I like late lunches," he said.

That night we had dinner at one of the outdoor tables of the Flagler Fish Company. Two ice cold *Dos Equis* beers, homemade potato chips, and a pound and a half of their colossal peel 'n eat shrimp. After the waiter brought the beers, I raised my bottle toward Mark, and, after he had raised his, we clinked bottles. "Thank you, my protector, my lover, my husband, my best friend, and the father of my baby. I will always love you." I was crying.

"You're welcome, my lover, my wife, my best friend, the mother of my Maddie. I will always love you too. Always."

I then said, "Maddie asked me earlier, 'Mommy, what happened today? I was scared.' I told her, 'We were playing in the ocean, honey, when we got caught in water rushing away from the shore. I thought we were in terrible trouble, but then Daddy was there. He saved us. He will always save us.' She said, 'He must love us, Mommy.' I said, 'Oh yes, Maddie, he loves us.' "

I looked at Mark. He had tears in his eyes, proof of the old adage that real men do cry. He looked so strong, so handsome, so fearless, and he is mine. I thought of a hymn we sing frequently in church, *Be Not Afraid*. I sang the second verse to him, very softly. I don't know if any of the other diners could hear me, but I didn't care.

"If you pass through raging waters, in the sea you shall not drown.

"If you walk amid the burning flames, you shall not be harmed.

"If you stand before the power of hell and death is at your side, know that I am with you through it all."

Then I sang the chorus, a little louder. All the other diners stopped eating to listen.

"Be not afraid.

"I go before you always.

"Come follow me, and

"I will give you rest."

I stood up, walked around to Mark's side of the table, and kissed him, and kissed him, and kissed him. I didn't care how many diners were watching us. A few began to clap. Then all joined in. The waiter asked if everything was all right. "Yes," I said, "Everything is more than all right. Can you bring us two more *Dos Equis?"*

The lady at the next table said, "That was beautiful."

I said, "He saved my life today, literally, and it's not the first time."

Then I added, "And I am carrying our first child."

She stood up and hugged me. She was crying too. Then she hugged Mark.

When I sat back down, I looked at Mark and said, "Did I embarrass you?"

He answered, "You never embarrass me. You thrill me."

How I love that man.

We walked along A1A back to the Topaz. I held Mark's hand tightly in mine all the way back. We couldn't see the ocean, but we could hear it off to our left.

"We're going back in the ocean tomorrow," Mark said. "Getting back on the horse and all that shit."

"Yes, we are," I said. "The ocean gave me its best shot today, but I have you, so its best shot was not good enough."

We sat on the porch of our room looking at the stars, listening to the ocean, enjoying the antics of the other guests. I wrapped myself in his arms, closed my eyes, and promptly fell asleep. He must have carried me into bed; I woke up the next morning in bed in his arms, wearing just a T-shirt and panties. We started the day the way I had planned to end the previous one.

The remainder of the vacation was uneventful. We arrived back in Rhode Island the following Wednesday, late in the afternoon. We had dinner with Mom and Dad and then drove home to Cambridge. During dinner, I told Dad, "He did it again."

"Who did what?" Dad asked.

"Mark saved my life. I was caught in an ocean riptide, and he saved me and Maddie."

Dad looked at Mark, a loving look, and said, "Thank you."

"I promised you, sir, that I would always take care of Sandy. I will."

Maddie was born five months later in Boston's Brigham and Women's Hospital.

Melanie was born a week after that in Worcester General.

Mark and I did give Mom and Dad their first granddaughter after all.

We bought a large house in Coventry a month after Maddie was born. Leslie was transferred to Providence by her firm, and she and Bobby relocated to Coventry as well.

Mom loved that. All her children and grandchildren were coming home.

Maddie and Melanie would grow up together.

Peggy and I would be together again.

Chapter Eighteen
Candi's Crisis

The month after Maddie was born, the same month Peggy and Warren got married, Mark and I found the perfect house in Coventry: a six-bedroom, three-storey colonial on an acre and a half of land. Of course it had an in-ground pool and a pool shed. The asking price was $425,000. We offered $400,000, cash, and closed in two weeks.

The Tuttle, Roberts, and Jones families immediately set about increasing the population of Coventry.

Maddie and Melanie were born in March of that year.

My Bobby, Peggy's Heather, and Leslie's Robby were born one year later. Peggy and I took a one-year break at that point. Leslie dropped out of the game completely.

Two years after Heather and Bobby entered our world, I had Jimmy, and Peggy had Larry. And the following year, I had my precious Annie, and Peggy had Candace, always to be known as Candi.

Peggy (Mayhew) Jones called me early, six o'clock, one Saturday morning when her youngest, Candi, was three. I had been sleeping, but as soon as I heard Peggy's voice, I was wide awake. Mark asked who it was.

382

"Peggy," I said to Mark. He sat up. *Why is she calling at six o'clock?*

"Sandy, something is wrong with Candi---"

"What's wrong?" I asked. Candi is like one of my own children. I love her.

"Something with her breathing, her chest, I don't know, I'm scared."

"What can I do?" I asked.

"Warren and I want to take her to the emergency room at Kent. Can you come over and get Heather and Larry?" Heather was six, Larry four.

"Mark's on the way." He didn't know it yet, but he was. "He should be there in five minutes. Don't worry about Heather and Larry. We'll take care of them as long as it takes."

"Thanks. Love you," Peggy said.

"Love you too. Take care of Candi."

I briefly explained to Mark, and he was out of the house in less than a minute. Mark is so good in a crisis.

Peggy:

At eleven thirty that morning, Candi was admitted to the cardiac care unit. The doctor-in-charge asked Warren and me to go with him to the Hospital Administrator's office. We followed, nervous, worried, wondering.....

"Mr. and Mrs. Jones," the Administrator began. "We have good news and less good news."

Less good? I thought. *What the hell does that mean?* I felt a shiver run through my entire body, from head to toe. *Oh God, let Candi be okay...Please, God, please.* "What do you mean good and less good, Doctor?" I asked.

"Your daughter, Candace, has a very rare heart valve disorder. Very rare. One in ten thousand---"

"And?" I interrupted, not one for statistical analysis at any time.

"It is curable, one hundred percent curable, with a new valve replacement procedure."

"What's the *less good* news?" I asked.

"The procedure is experimental, and it is not covered by insurance plans."

"What's the cost?" asked Warren.

"One hundred and seventy-five thousand," said the Administrator.

We, Warren and I, looked at each other. "We're teachers," said Warren. "We don't have that kind of money."

"Can you get a loan, a second mortgage?"

"Not for that much money," said Warren. "What are we going to do, Peggy?"

I don't know...God, help me... Then it hit me – Sandy...*I'll call Sandy...She always has my back...She loves Candi...She loves me.*

"Can I use your phone?" I asked the Administrator.

"Of course."

I dialed and waited, praying Sandy would answer.

"Hello."

"It's me," I said.

"How's Candi?" Sandy asked.

"We have a problem---"

Sandy:

My heart sank. *Oh no, God...Let Candi be all right...She's just a little girl, so innocent, so precious...What can the problem be?..Peggy must be dying...I'll do anything I can...Peggy knows that...I love you, Peggy Mayhew.*

"She has a rare heart valve disorder. It's one hundred percent curable, but the procedure is not covered by insurance. It's considered experimental," Peggy said.

"Then we don't have a problem," I said. "No matter the cost, we do **not** have a problem."

"It's a hundred and seventy-five thousand, Sandy."

"I'll have it wired to Kent today. Do you think I would let anything happen to Candi, or Heather, or Larry, if I could do something about it? I love them. I love **you**, Peggy."

"Don't you have to run it by Mark?" Peggy asked.

"No. Mark and I support each other one hundred percent in everything."

"We'll pay you back, I promise."

"No, you won't, Peggy. This is not a loan, not a gift, just good friends having each other's backs, like at Taco Bell. God, do you remember that day? I love you. I love Candi. Let me talk to someone with the hospital to make the arrangements for the wire."

Peggy was crying. "I love you too, Sandy. I don't know how to thank you."

"No need. Just take care of Candi. We'll never mention this again, okay? Let me talk to the hospital people. Heather and Larry are fine. Maddie has them all playing tag. Now I'm starting to cry. Love you, Peggy. Always have. I'll be by later. Mark will watch the kids. Get me that hospital person."

Peggy:

I was in tears when I handed the phone to the Hospital Administrator. He spoke to Sandy briefly and then transferred the call to the Billing Department.

"Are Sandy and Mark giving us a loan?" asked Warren.

"No, they're taking care of the expenses. 'Friend having a friend's back,' Sandy said."

"What?" Warren said. "I don't understand. It's wonderful, but why are they doing it?"

I looked at him. "They're good people, and Sandy and I love each other."

Warren looked at me. *You really don't know how much we love each other?..How could you?..That's our secret...Mark knows...The three musketeers...Sandy always has my back...Seems like she has mine more than I have hers, but I always have hers too.*

"Like sisters, honey, like sisters."

"Is it taxable to us?" Warren asked.

"Does that matter?" I asked. I shot a dagger at him with my eyes.

"No, I was just---"

The Administrator, overhearing, said, "It's not taxable. As long as the payment is made directly to the provider, which it will be in this case, it's a non-taxable medical transfer."

The doctor explained the medical procedure in detail while the Administrator's assistant started preparing the voluminous paperwork.

The phone on the Administrator's desk rang before twenty minutes had elapsed. The Administrator took the call, nodded, and then hung up. "Kent Hospital just received a wire transfer of one hundred and seventy-five thousand dollars for the account of Candace Jones. The memo simply stated, 'Advise if not sufficient.' I never saw such a fast response, especially on a Saturday."

I started crying. *God, I love you, Sandy Tuttle...You just saved my baby's life...You have always had my back...At Taco Bell...At South Kingstown...Mark fought for me too, because of you...I know that...But this is the best thing that anyone has ever done for me...I love you, Sandy Roberts...Always have...Always will.*

The procedure was scheduled for the next morning. Warren and I went to Candi's room to be with her.

"I'm staying overnight," I said to Warren. "I'm not leaving her side."

"Me too," said Warren. "Sandy and Mark will watch the kids?"

"Of course," I said. *Sandy will do anything for me. I'll do anything for her.*

Sandy:

When I arrived at Candi's private room, I found Warren sleeping in a chair in the corner. He had a book open on his lap. He looked drained. Peggy had moved another chair up to the head of Candi's bed. She was sitting on the front edge of the chair, leaning on the bed holding her sleeping daughter's hand. I walked up and stood behind her. I don't think she knew I was there. *I love you, Peggy Mayhew…Always have…Always will…Candi will be fine.*

Mark had once told me that the Chinese character for good, *hao,* is composed of two other characters, the character for woman and the character for child. God did the Chinese ever get that one right. Peggy and Candi. Woman and child. Good.

I gently placed my hands on her shoulder, kissed her on the top of her head, and whispered, very softly, "I love you, Peggy Mayhew."

Without taking her eyes off Candi, she whispered, "I love you too, Sandy Roberts."

She then stood and wrapped me in her arms. We embraced, crying, for what seemed an eternity, but could not have been more than thirty seconds.

"Thank you," she said.

"I've always had your back, Mayhew."

Peggy laughed. It made my heart feel good seeing her laugh.

"What did Mark say when you told him?"

"He just said that I was a good woman and a good friend, and that's why he loves me so much. He knows how much I love you. And he loves Candi too."

"He's a good man, Sandy."

"The best."

She hugged me tighter. "I love you, Sandy."

"I love you too."

A little voice piped up. "Hi, Aunt Sandy."

"Hi, honey. You're going to be fine."

"Mommy said I have to thank you."

"No you don't, honey. Just get better." I kissed her on the forehead. She smiled at me. That smile was worth one hundred and seventy-five thousand dollars. No, infinitely more.

"I'm glad you woke up. I brought you something," I said.

"What, Aunt Sandy?"

"Close your eyes."

When she did I reached into a bag I had left on the floor and pulled out an *Alexandra the Mouse* doll. "Open your eyes, honey."

She cried out and said, "Oh, thank you, Aunt Sandy.

"Can she stay with me in the hospital, Mommy?"

"Of course," answered Peggy. She had her arm around my shoulder, massaging it the way Mark does.

"And, Candi, this is a very special *Alexandra* doll," I said. "You cannot buy it in any store yet. My agent sent me five, and I have given them to the five little girls that I love most in the whole world."

"Me, Maddie, Annie….Heather?"

"Yes, Heather, and?"

"And…and…I don't know, Aunt Sandy."

"Who is at my house all the time?"

"Melanie," she screamed. My niece.

"Yes, Melanie."

Peggy kissed my cheek and whispered in my ear, "I can't tell you how much I love you."

An indescribably warm feeling coursed through my body. I turned to face Peggy, blew out a little exhale, and said, "You don't have to. I already know. Believe me, Peggy Mayhew, I know." We put our lips together and kissed, a sisterly kiss, but it was filled with more meaning, more feeling, more warmth, more love, than any of the many passionate kisses we had shared.

Our chatter woke up Warren. He came over and kissed me. "I can't thank you and Mark enough. I've never seen such generosity."

"Look, Daddy, a new *Alexandra* doll."

"Wow, you lucky little girl," said Warren.

"We love Candi like one of our own, Warren." I left it at that.

I stayed with Peggy, Warren, and Candi for a few hours. Warren found another chair for me and placed it next to Peggy's. Peggy and I held hands the entire time I was there, not talking, looking at the sleeping Candi. Every once In a while, Peggy looked at me and smiled. I smiled back. No words were needed. She squeezed my hand before turning back to Candi each time. We **do** love each other. To be sure, that love has changed since we were seventeen. It has matured and grown, become richer, deeper. It is not as strong as the love I have for Mark – nothing can compare with the love I have for Mark -- but it is true love.

Warren went down for dinner in the cafeteria at six promising to bring a sandwich back for Peggy. Peggy wouldn't leave Candi's bedside. When he returned, I told Peggy I had to get home to make dinner for the gang. Candi was asleep; I gave her another kiss on the forehead. *Please,*

God, take care of her. The look Peggy gave me as I left the room was priceless. I gave her an air kiss and mouthed, "I love you."

She mouthed back, "I love you too." Then she turned back to Candi.

I floated out to my car. *God, I love you Peggy Mayhew.*

I arrived home to find Mark preparing macaroni and cheese, my Cambridge recipe, for the kids. I hugged him and kissed him. *I am a very lucky woman.* I joined the nine of them -- Leslie had dropped off Melanie and Robby after school -- at the dining room table and had two helpings. It was *almost* as good as when I make it. I told everyone that Candi was going to be fine, and I told Heather and Larry that they would be sleeping at our house. We have two boys and two girls, so we have plenty of pajamas. Everyone cheered at the good news about Candi and at the announcement of the sleeping arrangements. Our kids get along great, which is extremely pleasing to me and Peggy. Melanie and Robby, of course, asked to join the sleepover. I told them it was up to their mother. Leslie, as expected, allowed it when she came back at nine.

Maddie whispered to me later that she had told Mark the mac and cheese was as good as mine. "I didn't want to hurt his feelings, Mom; he worked so hard on it. But it's not. Our secret, okay?"

"Okay."

She kissed me and went off to do her homework smiling. She and Melanie are in the same class at St. Michael's and do their homework together most nights. They are as close as sisters.

Leslie, Mark, and I were sitting in the den having a glass of wine when the doorbell rang. Mark answered it and then led Mrs. Mayhew, Peggy's mother, and Mr. and Mrs. Jones, Warren's parents, into the den.

When I stood up, Mrs. Mayhew, who loves me and Mark to begin with, just hugged me and said, "Thank you from the bottom of my heart." Nothing more was needed.

Mrs. Jones then hugged me as well. Mr. Jones shook Mark's hand, vigorously.

Later, while Mark was showing them out, Leslie asked what that was all about.

"Candi's surgery was experimental and not covered by insurance---"

"And you paid the cost," said Leslie.

"Yes. Gladly," I said.

"I have to ask. How much was it?"

"One hundred and seventy-five thousand," I said.

"I bet Peggy didn't even have to ask you. She just told you the problem.'

I said nothing.

Leslie then hugged me too. "You are one good friend." Then she held my face between her hands and kissed me. She was crying. "And you know what I know, and we'll never have to talk about it."

"What?" I said.

"You would do the same thing for me."

"Of course I would."

"You know, Sandy, you are a very special person. I know why Peggy loves you. I know why Mark loves you. And now I have fallen in love with you. You know what I mean."

"Yes, I do. I love you too."

We hugged, and then she kissed me again. "I am so glad you are part of my life," she said, "Part of Melanie's and Robby's life too."

"Me too," I said. Then I started crying too.

That night when we got in bed, Mark said to me, "Sandy, you are a very special person." He knows how much I love Peggy, but that just makes him love me more. He knows Peggy is not competition. Nobody is, or ever can be, competition for him with me.

"You're the second person today who told me I'm special."

"Peggy?"

"No. Peggy **does** think I'm special, but it was Leslie."

"You are."

"Thank you. You're pretty special too, Mr. Tuttle. Do you want to make love with me?" I asked. "I want to make love with you."

"When did I ever say, 'No' to that?"

"Never," I said, pulling down his shorts.

The operation the following morning was successful. Candi was home a week later, still recovering, but completely cured. For the following week, after Maddie and Bobby left for school, I took Jimmy and Annie over to Peggy's house where we spent the day. Peggy had taken a few weeks of leave. Annie and Candi stayed in Candi's room playing games. Jimmy and Larry played in the back yard or competed in video games in the den. Peggy and I sat, mostly in the kitchen, talking and drinking coffee. Sometimes we just sat and looked at each other and held hands. And smiled. We have become such good friends!

Leslie picked up Heather, Maddie, and Bobby when she picked up Melanie and Robby after school. She dropped them off at Peggy's and stayed for a few hours, talking with me and Peggy, before she and I headed to our homes. She never mentioned what I had done. It was during that week that Leslie, Peggy, and I entered a new stage in our relationship. We realized we would do anything for each other and our families. We all appreciated how great that is.

Chapter Nineteen
Alexandra the Mouse

Alexandra the Mouse has made me rich. Actually marrying Mark Tuttle has made me rich in more ways than one, but creating *Alexandra* would have been sufficient to make me rich had Mark not already done that with his brain and computer skills and his unending and totally unselfish love for Sandy Roberts.

And when I say that *Alexandra* has made me rich, I mean that in two ways. The books have been very successful financially. Every young girl in the country loves my little mouse, and many sleep with her or wear clothes expressing their love of the adorable *Alexandra*. I've seen her on little purses and lunch boxes; I've seen her on rain coats and fair weather jackets; I've seen her on pencils, bedsheets, kites, and even earrings.

But creating *Alexandra* really made me rich in a different and better way. *Alexandra* did not just pop out of my imagination. If there were no Maddie, there would be no *Alexandra*. I love all my children, but my firstborn child, my *primogenita,* my Maddie, has fascinated me in a very special way from the day she was born. No, from the day she was conceived. *I knew you, Maddie, when you were in your mother's womb...So did Mark...He saved your life when you were in there...He loves you in a special way*

393

too…He loves all his girls, you, me, Annie…And his boys, but…

I'll never forget Mark holding her for the first time and then turning to me and saying, "Sandy, I realized almost immediately that I love her as much as I love you, and I didn't think I could ever love anyone that much." And then to reassure me, a reassurance I did not need, he added, "And I did not take a part of my love for you and give it to her. Our love for each other just expanded to include Maddie." That it did, and still does.

I could say that *Alexandra the Mouse* is my daughter Maddie. Everything *Alexandra* has ever done has been inspired by something my precocious Maddie had done previously. I constantly look at Maddie and ask, "Now what have you done today that every little girl would love to read about or fantasize doing?" And when I find an answer to that question, another *Alexandra the Mouse* story is born. Maddie tells me the stories should be called *The Adventures of Maddie the Mouse*, and I agree, but only up to a point.

"Maddie," I tell her, "you're the inspiration for *Alexandra*, but you are not *Alexandra*, and *Alexandra* is not you. The stories are not about you; you just do something, and then I ask myself, 'What would *Alexandra* do if she were in your shoes but in her world?' And I love you much more than I could ever love a mouse!"

"Even *Alexandra*?"

"Even *Alexandra*."

"Okay," she says, "but can I tell my friends that *Alexandra* is really me?"

"Yes," I say. "You can do that."

"In the last story, Mom, *Alexandra* saved her little sister, *Annabella Mouse*, when she found some poison cheese. What did I do to inspire that? I have never even heard of poison cheese."

"At breakfast one day when Annie was a baby, she picked up a button that was on the table and put it in her mouth. You took it away from her and told her that buttons were not food. Now Annie could have choked on the button or it could have gotten stuck in her throat, and I would have had to take her to the emergency room. But after you took the button, which I didn't even know she had in her mouth, away from her, the danger was gone."

"But buttons aren't poisonous," objected Maddie.

"I know, but what you did gave me the idea. I thought: what if *Alexandra* and her little sister, *Annabella*, found some cheese that had been poisoned by that bad *Wilfred the Rat*. You know how much *Wilfred* hates *Alexandra* and her family because they're so good. Remember what he did to their school project to get them in trouble at the mouse school?"

"Yes, he filled it with catnip, and, boy, did that cause trouble," said Maddie.

"*Alexandra*, being as cautious and intelligent as you are, Maddie, smelled the cheese before she let her little mouse sister eat any of it. When she didn't like the smell, she stopped *Annabella* from eating it and brought it to her Mommy to show her the smelly cheese. The smelly cheese was the button. Remember what Mommy Mouse said?"

"Yes," said Maddie. "She said, '*Alexandra*, some cheese is smelly and not bad. But this cheese is cheddar, and if cheddar cheese is smelly, it is bad.' She then smelled it again, and told her daughters that she thought the cheese was poisonous. And Daddy Mouse agreed when he came home from work and took it out and buried it in the yard."

"So you just took a button out of Annie's mouth, and, voila', *Alexandra* saved *Annabella* from eating poison cheddar cheese."

"Now I understand," said Maddie. "I never stopped Annie from eating poison cheddar cheese, but when I took the button out of her mouth, it gave you the idea for the story."

"Exactly. And when you read any of the stories about *Alexandra*, if you think hard about it, you will think of something you did that made me think of that story," I said. "After dinner tonight, pick out one of the stories, and ask Daddy to read it with you. Then try to answer this question: 'What did I do that inspired Mommy to write that story?' Okay?"

"Yes, that sounds like fun," said Maddie.

Mark had been up in our studio working on his latest novel, *The Lost Years at Sunset Park*, and when he came down to help me set up for dinner, I told him that he had a special job after dinner.

"What?" he asked.

"You and Maddie are going to read one of the *Alexandra* stories, and then you two are going to try to figure out what real life episode of Maddie's inspired the story," I said.

"And what do I get if we figure it out?" he asked.

"I'll give you a passionate kiss and tell you I love you," I answered.

"We'll figure it out," said Mark. "I can't go to bed without a kiss from you."

"I'm sure you'll earn it. I know you and Maddie. You two will figure it out."

When we were going to college in Cambridge, me at Harvard, Mark at MIT, we rented an apartment near both schools. We married right after high school and went to Cambridge as a married couple. As readers of this book know, my mac and cheese carried us, and a few others, through the college years. The kids love it now, and I made it that night. My secret is four different cheeses, excluding smelly cheddar, of course, and stewed tomatoes. I do use cheddar, just not smelly, poisonous cheddar.

We had no guests that night, so the six of us, Mark, Maddie, Bobby, Jimmy, Annie, and I sat around our kitchen table for dinner. We usually eat in the kitchen unless we have company; then we eat in the dining room. I sat at one end of the table with the boys near me; Mark sat at the other end facing me with the girls on his left and right. As usual Maddie said Grace.

"Dear Lord, thank you for the food and for having all six of us together. I love it when we are all together because it makes me feel so good. And, God, help me and Daddy when we read the story after dinner. Amen."

"What story?" asked Annie, my baby.

"Mommy told me to pick any of the *Alexandra* stories to read with Daddy, and then Daddy and I will try to figure out what I did to give Mommy the idea for that story," answered Maddie.

"Can I listen when you read it?" asked Annie.

"Yes, and I'll pick a story that has *Annabella* in it. That's you, you know?" said Maddie.

"Yes, I know. And you know what *Annabella* means, don't you?" asked Annie.

"Yes," said Maddie. "Annie the Beautiful."

"I like that name, Mommy," said Annie. "Do you think I'm beautiful, Daddy?"

"Yes, Pumpkin, I think you are a real live *Annabella*," said Mark.

"Prettier than Maddie?"

"No, but she's not any prettier than you either."

"Prettier than Mommy?" She began to laugh as she sneaked a look at me.

"Annie, nobody on Earth is prettier than your mother," said Mark. I laughed too, but the crazy thing is, Mark really believes that. He tells me all the time that I have the most beautiful face in the whole world. He even tells me that I'm prettier than Peggy. In my opinion, no one is prettier than

Peggy Mayhew. *That's okay, Mark...You can go on believing that.*

That satisfied my little Annie the Beautiful. She sat there and smiled as she ate her mac and cheese.

Maddie turned to her father and said, "Daddy, I love it when you say that about Mommy. I really love it."

I do too! I thought.

"I mean it, Maddie," said Mark.

"I know you do, Daddy. That's why I love it so much."

After dinner, the boys volunteered to help me clean up, and Maddie went to her room and brought back one of her *Alexandra the Mouse* books. I, of course, have a full *Alexandra* set up in my and Mark's studio. Maddie has another full set, which she treasures, in her room. "Let's read this one, Daddy," she said handing him one of my little creations.

"Can I sit on your lap, Daddy?" asked Annie.

"You sure can, *Annabella*, and, Maddie, that looks like a good story. Do you want me to read it or do you want to read?"

"Why don't you read, Daddy? I'll snuggle up with you, like Annie is."

Mark, surrounded by two of his three favorite females, began:

Alexandra the Mouse and the Wicked Spider

One day, a fine sunny day in Sunnydale, Alexandra the Mouse woke up with a tickly, wickly, ickly feeling in her tummy. This made her very nervous, but she did not know why. She sat up in bed and looked out the window. She twitched her nose and wiggled her whiskers around to see what she could sense, but she did not sense any danger. The sun was shining, and everything looked and smelled normal. She didn't see or smell any cats. Oh, how she hated to see a cat first thing in the morning or, worse yet, to smell cat rain. It always gave her the wiggly-jigglies.

But, even though everything seemed fine, and she didn't sense any cats, she was afraid to get out of her bed. Her little sister, Annabella Mouse, was still asleep and looked calm and peaceful. ("That's me, Daddy," interrupted Annie. "Shush," said Maddie. Annie gave her a stare, but she did not say anything else.) *Annabella twitched her nose and rolled over on her back exposing her pink belly. She and Alexandra loved their pink bellies; they knew all the little boy mice at school loved them too. Alexandra reached over and tickled Annabella's tummy with a feather, waking up her little sister. "Hey," said Annabella, "what are you doing?"*

"Good morning, Little Sister," said Alexandra. "Did you sleep well?"

"I was still sleeping well until you woke me up," said Annabella.

"Well, it's time to get up. We have school today, you know."

"Yes, I know. I'm not stupid, Alexandra."

"Let's go down and have breakfast. I think I smell cheese pancakes, our favorite," said Alexandra. She really just wanted Annabella to go downstairs with her. She still had that tickly, wickly, ickly feeling in her tummy and did not want to go downstairs alone.

"Good morning, Alexandra. Good morning, Annabella," said Momma Mouse. "Did you sleep well?"

"Yes," they both said. Alexandra did not tell Momma Mouse that, although she slept well, she did not wake up well. And she did not tell her about the tickly, wickly, ickly feeling in her tummy.

"Where are Romulus and Remus and Daddy?" asked Alexandra.

"They went over to Farmer Gray's house to see if they could find some crumbs under the table. You know I love a little toast with my coffee," said Momma Mouse. "They should be back soon."

"Good morning, my princesses," said Daddy Mouse coming into the kitchen. Romulus and Remus were right behind him. Remus stuck his tongue out at Annabella. She did the same back to him. As often happens, the second person got caught, and Momma Mouse said to her baby daughter, "Annabella, is that nice? How do you expect to grow up to be respected like Alexandra if you do things like that?" ("Sometimes that happens to me too, Daddy," said Annie. "Shush!" said Maddie again. Another stare, but silence from Annie.)

"Did you find any crumbs under the table?" asked Momma Mouse.

"Romulus found almost a half a piece of rye toast, and Remus found a piece of a toasted bagel," said Daddy Mouse. ("Romulus and Remus are Bobby and Jimmy, right, Daddy?" asked Annie. "Yes," he said. "Shush," said Maddie a third time, with a little shake of her head. "Let Daddy read the story.")

Daddy Mouse then pulled Momma Mouse over to the stove and whispered in her ear, "I sensed something in the yard today. I don't know what. It gave me a tickly, wickly, ickly feeling in my stomach. I haven't felt that for a long time. That's why I stayed outside on guard when the boys went crumb hunting."

"What could it be?" wondered Momma Mouse aloud. "What could it be? Was it cat?"

"No, definitely not cat. But not something nice, I know that."

Momma and Daddy Mouse went back to the table, and Momma Mouse called all the mice children to breakfast. "I made cheddar pancakes this morning and I cut up some apples to eat with it," said Momma Mouse.

"Yum! Yum!" said Alexandra, Romulus, Remus, and Annabella in a little mouse chorus.

"I think I'll have a pancake too," said Daddy Mouse.

"I'm just going to have coffee and toast," said Momma Mouse. "Thank you, Romulus, for the rye toast, and thank you, Remus, for the toasted bagel. I think I'll have one of each."

"Should we say Grace before we eat?" asked Alexandra.

"Don't we always?" said Momma Mouse, looking sternly at Romulus who had a piece of cheddar pancake almost halfway to his mouth.

"I'll say it," said Alexandra. ("Just like in our house, Daddy," said Annie.) *"Dear Great Mouse in Heaven, thank You for the food on our table and for letting Romulus and Remus find toast for Mommy to have with her coffee. And please, please take away the tickly, wickly, ickly feeling I have in my tummy which I don't know why I have, but which I've had all morning. Amen."*

Momma Mouse looked at Daddy Mouse when she heard that.

"So you have a tickly, wickly, ickly feeling in your tummy this morning?" asked Daddy Mouse.

"Yes, Daddy, ever since I woke up," answered Alexandra.

"Does anyone else have it?" asked Daddy Mouse.

"No," said the boys and Annabella.

"Alexandra, I had the same feeling out in the yard," said Daddy Mouse.

"It wasn't cat, Daddy, was it?" asked his oldest child.

"No, it wasn't cat, but it made me feel tickly, wickly, ickly too."

"Well, it's time to go to school," said Momma Mouse. "I want the four of you to stay together on the way to school this morning, is that clear?"

"Yes, Momma," said the four children.

"And you two," added Daddy Mouse to Romulus and Remus, "carry a strong twig with you just to be safe." Daddy Mouse had taught Romulus and Remus how to fight

401

using the old strong twig method, but he had told them that they should never start a fight. He now addressed his two sons: "When is the only time I want you to fight?"

"If we are backed into a corner or to protect Alexandra and Annabella," they answered. "If Alexandra or Annabella is in trouble, we will twig and bite and scratch and keep doing it until they are out of trouble."

"Very good. Now off to school."

Momma Mouse gave them each a kiss and their little lunch bags as they left the house. "What's for lunch today, Momma?" asked Alexandra.

"Pieces of Swiss cheese and apple and orange slices," said Momma Mouse.

"Do you know what my favorite part of the Swiss cheese is, Daddy?" asked Annabella.

"No," answered Daddy Mouse, playing along with Annabella's favorite joke.

"The holes!" she cried out. ("That's funny, Daddy," said Annie.)

As they left the house, the tickly, wickly, ickly feeling came back to Alexandra's tummy. 'What is this?' she thought. "Romulus, do you sense anything?" she asked the older of her two brothers.

"No, do you?"

"Yes, but I don't know what. It's not cat, but I don't like it."

Romulus and Remus held their twigs in the classic twig-attack position as they went through the yard.

Then they left the yard and passed around the big hedge that Farmer Gray had put around his property.

Sssssssssssssssst, they heard.

"What's that?" asked Alexandra, feeling very, very tickly, wickly, ickly.

Sssssssssssssssst came again from inside the hedge.

Romulus and Remus, good brothers, placed themselves between the sound and their sisters. "Come out of there," cried out Romulus holding high his twig.

And slowly, very slowly out of the hedge came a big black spider, half as long as Romulus, who was big for a young mouse. The spider was hairy and kept snapping his fangs. "Sssssssssssst," he said. And pointing to Alexandra with three of his eight legs, he said, "You, girl mouse, you with the pretty pink belly, give me your lunch. (Annie said, "Annabella has a pretty pink belly too, Daddy.) I am hungry. If you don't give me your lunch, I will bite your cute pink belly and put poison inside your little mouse body."

"Go away," said the brave Romulus. "Or we will have to beat you with our twigs. There are two of us ready to fight you to defend our sisters. And stop snapping your fangs; it's an extremely annoying habit."

"Sssssssssssst," said the spider, deliberately snapping his fangs at Romulus. "You are only a mouse. I am not afraid of a mouse or of two mice! Nobody is afraid of mice!"

"Well, you should be," shouted Romulus who hit the spider over the head with his twig. Remus hit the spider in the middle of his back at the same time. The surprised spider backed up. Yellow and green blood was coming out of his head and out of his back. "Do you want to keep fighting?" asked Romulus. "We will not stop until the girls are safe."

"Sssssssssssssst," said the spider as he backed away. He had not expected any trouble from mice.

"And don't ever come back," said Remus.

The four mice children then went to school together. Alexandra and Annabella were so proud of their brothers. They never saw the wicked spider again. And the tickly, wickly, ickly feeling left Alexandra's tummy.

THE END

403

"I liked that story, Daddy," said Annie. "Can I have some ice cream?"

"Ask Mommy," said Mark.

I gave Annie some ice cream and then handed a dish of chocolate chip ice cream, her favorite, to Maddie. "Well? Where did I get the idea for that story?" I asked my husband and daughter.

"I know," said Maddie. "That was the time when I was in second grade, and the bully told me to give him my lunch cookies."

"And what happened?" I asked.

"I said 'No' and started crying. And he was going to take them, but Bobby came over and told him to leave me alone. At first he laughed at Bobby, but when he saw that Bobby was going to fight him to protect me, he walked away. I told you that story after school that day."

"Yes, and that very night after you went to bed, I wrote the story *Alexandra the Mouse and the Wicked Spider*."

"I understand now, Mommy," said Maddie. "And I see that *Alexandra*'s not me, but I just give you ideas and you make up *Alexandra* stories."

"Yes, that's right. And that night, Maddie, I was also thinking of a time when I was your age, and a very bad man tried to take me away in his car. There was no one there to help me but Daddy."

"Oh gosh, Mommy, what happened?" asked Maddie.

"Your daddy, who was only a little boy then, didn't let him hurt me; he saved me. He beat the man with a twig like Romulus beat the spider. Someday I'll tell you the whole story."

"Daddy beat the bad man with a **twig**?" asked Maddie.

"Well, actually, it was a baseball bat, but it became a twig in the story," I said. "Your daddy is very brave, honey, very brave. All the adults were very surprised that he could defeat the bad man. And do you know what daddy said when the fight was over, and the teachers finally arrived?"

"No, Mommy, what did he say?"

"He said, 'That man was going to hurt Sandy, and she's my best friend, and I will never let anyone hurt her.' And he never will, Maddie, and he'll never let anyone hurt you or Bobby or Jimmy or Annie. Never." I was beginning to cry. I always cry when I'm emotional.

"I know," said Maddie with a tear in her eye as well.

Maddie then went over to Mark and hugged him and kissed him and said, "Thank you, Daddy, for saving Mommy."

"You're welcome, Maddie."

"Daddy, *Alexandra the Mouse and the Wicked Spider* is now my favorite Alexandra story. Do you know why?" she asked her father.

"No, Maddie, why?"

"Because it's about me and you and Bobby, how Bobby saved me and how you saved Mommy from the wicked spider. It's funny, you know."

"What, honey?"

"That Mommy called a baseball bat a twig! Good night, Daddy, I love you."

"Good night, Maddie. I love you too." And Maddie went off to her room with a big smile on her face, carrying her new favorite *Alexandra the Mouse* book under her little arm.

After the children went to bed, I told Mark he had earned his passionate kiss. God, I love it when he wins prizes like that!

Chapter Twenty
Bunratty, County Clare

I almost called this chapter *Pub Crawling through the Emerald Isle,* but stuck with the above title for sentimental reasons. Mark always loved the photograph he took of me at the Folk Park in Bunratty Village in County Clare. He kept it framed in our den. I used it for the cover of this work in his honor. When my mother saw the framed photograph in our house, all she could say was, "Couldn't you wear jeans without holes, with all your money?" She just shook her head when I told her the style was trendy.

Leslie and I hosted a joint "Celebrate the First Decade" birthday party when Maddie and Melanie turned ten. We had it at our house on the Saturday between their respective birthdays.

That evening, my other sister-in-law, Patty, cornered me and Mark in the kitchen. "When was the last time you two were away together?" she asked.

"We go out to Seattle for a few days every year," Mark said.

"But that's business. I mean when did you two have a real vacation?"

"Bloomsday," I said, "right after graduation."

"That's eleven years ago," she said. "I want to make you an offer you can't refuse. Bill and I will stay here for ten days or two weeks. We will take care of the children. We will love taking care of our godchildren. Whenever you want. Just let me know."

I looked at Mark. "What do you think?"

"Let's do it," he said. "Where do you want to go?"

"It might sound crazy, but I want to go back to Ireland, to see the remainder of *Erin, the Gem of the Emerald Sea*, as Joyce called it."

"So that's all set," said Patty. "Book your trip."

"Thank you," we both said.

Mark suggested that this time, unlike on the Italy and Bloomsday trips, I should assume the duties of trip planner. I rose to the challenge. We went to Border's the following day and purchased Fodor's *Guide to Ireland*. Nine days later, on a Tuesday evening, we flew, first class, on Aer Lingus again, from Logan Airport to Dublin. Peggy rearranged her schedule and drove us to Boston.

"I expect postcards," she said, as she kissed me good-bye. "I'll be here to get you a week from Sunday."

We arrived in Dublin late Wednesday morning. Since it was late March, we packed accordingly. Mark brought jeans and khakis, oxford shirts, sweaters, a hoody, and his leather jacket. I brought two pair of jeans, with holes, a blue, fleece-lined jacket, a hoody, and a slew of blouses. I could always wear one of Mark's sweaters if I needed more warmth, or better, let him hug me.

We picked up our rental car, a small English Ford, at the airport. Mark opened the driver's side for me.

"You want me to drive?" I asked.

"Just get in," he said.

I did and found myself in the passenger's seat. *So it's the same here as in England -- the driver sits on the right side and drives on the left side of the road...The last time we were here, we didn't rent a car…We walked everywhere…How did I not notice anyway?..Oh well…I guess I just went wherever Mark led me…Trusting soul…No one better to trust…I bet Mark handles this like he's been doing it all his life…He is so adaptable…I think I wanna try it too.*

"Can you handle this?" I asked.

"Yes. And not only that, you're going to share the driving." *That should be an experience.*

"I read in Fodor's," said Mark, "that the real difficulty is driving in the roundabouts. You enter to the left and drive clockwise. The suggestion is to go around one full turn before trying to get out. To get your bearings."

We went around the first roundabout four times before Mark could get out at the correct egress. Horns were honking. Were they ever!

He looked at me. I was laughing.

"Don't you laugh at me, Sandy Roberts." *Wow! – that's what I said to him when I crinkled in McDonald's…Twenty-five years ago…I wasn't mad then…He's not mad now…He never gets mad at me, do you Mark Tuttle?..I can't think of one time he's been mad at me…or even annoyed at me…I've been mad at him twice, both times unjustified – when I thought he scribbled on my Marble composition book and when I thought he lured me onto a topless beach…Look at him…How handsome he is…MY Mark Tuttle.*

"I'm not laughing at you. I'm laughing at the situation," I said.

He squeezed my thigh. He was laughing too. *You never get mad at me, Mark Tuttle…That's one of the reasons – just one of many, many – why I love you so much.*

"Keep both hands on the wheel, driver," I said.

We arrived without mishap at our bed and breakfast.

"Why don't we leave the car parked here," he suggested, "and walk or take public transportation or a cab to get around. Just use the car for inter-city travel."

"Good idea. Can I drive the next leg to Cork?"

"You got it." *You have never said "No" to me, have you?..No, you haven't!*

We took a nap at our B&B, The Abberley House, and then took a taxi to Upper O'Connell Street for fish and chips at Beshoff's, highly recommended by the guidebook and by the owner of the B&B. I think the chips (fries) were the best I ever had. I reached across the table and whacked Mark in the nose with a chip. Why? Who knows? It seemed like a fun thing to do. He grabbed the chip out of my hand and ate it. We each had a Guinness draft with dinner. I still don't know if I like Guinness, but I vowed to learn to like it on the trip or die trying.

After dinner we stopped at a pub near Beshoff's and had a few more Guinness drafts while listening to a folk singer. Songs of the revolution and Irish love ballads – what else are there?

"Her eyes they shone like diamonds…
"I thought her the queen of the land…
"And her hair it hung over her shoulder…
"Tied up with a black velvet band."

Mark and I love this ballad and joined in, along with all the patrons, for the chorus. Then Mark, who always amazes me with his surprises, came around behind me and tied up my hair in a black velvet band. "I definitely consider you the queen of the land, this one and our own."

My eyes filled up with tears. "Where did you get a black velvet band?"

"I always come prepared," he said, and smiled.

You are truly amazing, Mark Tuttle…What other man would have thought of that?..Prepared for that?..Queen of the land…That I am for Mark…Getting horny.

The pub had a dart board that was not being used. I challenged Mark to a match and discovered, to my delight, that I could beat him. There is very little that I can beat Mark at. I could put the dart exactly where I was aiming, every time. Even after three or four Guinness drafts. I could do that with a softball too. Made me unhittable.

When we arrived back at the B&B, the combination of the lost night on the flight, the fish and chips, and the Guinness, primarily the Guinness, suppressed my earlier horniness.

"Mind if we just cuddle and sleep?" I asked.

Mark kissed me and wrapped me in his arms. "As long as I sleep with you, I'm happy."

Love that Mark Tuttle.

I woke up at four the next morning. Horny. I blew a stream of my breath into his face. Mark woke up smiling. "Guinness with an undertaste of honey," he said.

"Have a mouthful," I said. "In fact, have a few."

"I think I will." He put his lips against mine and began to enjoy the Guinness and the honey.

When he took a break to catch his breath, I said, "You still love to fuck me, don't you, even after all these years?"

"Yes," he said. "Every day."

"Me too," I said.

"And no one else," he said.

"I know." *I do know that…It's so wonderful to know that about your man…He is my man exclusively…Always will be…It's his nature…Like the scorpion and the frog…Scorpion asks frog for a ride across the river…Frog says, "You'll sting me"…Scorpion says "No. If I do that we both drown"…Frog gives him a ride…Half way across*

Scorpion stings Frog...“Why?” asks Frog...“It's my nature.”..Even if a playboy bunny, naked, blonde, nice teeth, were here, he would want me.

We celebrated our first full day in Ireland with an early morning coupling. Then slept for three more hours.

We discovered on this trip that "Eat breakfast like a king" was the B&B motto throughout the country.

The Abberley House had a breakfast buffet: rashers, which is Irish bacon, eggs, potatoes, fried tomatoes, sausages, baked beans, black and white pudding – both of which are made of pork meat, oats, spices, and, for the black variety, pork blood -- soda bread, brown bread, little tubs of soft, creamy butter, jam, and tea. No coffee. We sampled everything, even the black pudding. When in Rome...Or in Dublin, I guess...

We spent the morning at Trinity College. It is the only college at the University of Dublin, so Trinity Collge and the University of Dublin are synonymous. I didn't know that. I thought they were two different schools. What I wanted to see at Trinity College was the Book of Kells in the college library. Fodor's said it was a "can't miss" item.

"What the hell is a Kell?" asked Mark.

"I can tell you," I said. "It's a city in Ireland. There was an abbey there and the book was kept at the Abbey of Kells for four centuries. So the book is called the Book of Kells."

"Wow, I'm impressed. And what **is** the Book of Kells?"

"It's Ireland's national treasure, a magnificently illustrated book, actually four volumes, containing the four gospels of the New Testament, Matthew, Mark, Luke, and John, in the vulgate Latin of St. Jerome, created around the year 800 by Columban monks."

"You did your homework," Mark said.

"Of course I did. I'm Captain of the Barge for this trip."

"Acting Captain," Mark corrected. "Temporary Captain."

I stuck my tongue out at him.

The Book of Kells was indeed a treasure. I couldn't imagine how many hours the monks spent creating it, how much care and diligence was employed by those holy men of antiquity. "I'm glad we saw this," I said to Mark. He just squeezed my shoulder.

We skipped lunch – we were still full from breakfast – and headed to the Guinness Storehouse, the visitor attraction next to the Guinness St. James Gate Brewery. The glass atrium is shaped like a large, very large, seven-storey-tall glass of Guinness. On the seventh, and top floor, we entered the Gravity Bar for our first Guinness stout of the day, included in the price of admission. The bar afforded a great panoramic view of Dublin. We slowly sipped our stouts and enjoyed the view. Then we ordered another round not included in the price of admission.

Mark picked up his glass and held it toward me. I lifted mine and tapped his. "To the queen of the land," he said.

"Do my eyes shine like diamonds?" I asked.

"Oh yes," he said, "with your hair tied up in a black velvet band."

We just sat and stared at each other, smiling, surrounded by Dublin. "I love being married to you, Mark Tuttle."

"Being married to Sandy Roberts, one of life's greatest pleasures," he said, and tapped my glass again. "And no other man will ever experience that pleasure."

"You are right about that, Mark Tuttle," I said. "As little Marco said, 'Your Marco is a very lucky man.' "

We found a pub near the brewery which advertised, "Corned beef and cabbage."

"Want to eat dinner here?" I asked Mark.

"Yes," he said. Mark loves corned beef and cabbage.

It was delicious: the corned beef melted in your mouth, the cabbage was plentiful (what more can you say about cabbage?), the potatoes, onions, and carrots tasty. We had two more Guinness stouts. After dinner we went for a walk and then caught a cab back to the B&B.

Lying in bed that night, I told Mark I missed the kids.

"Me too," he said. "I've been thinking, now that Maddie is ten, and Annie six, we should take them to Disney."

"I've been thinking the same thing!" I said. "What I would like to do is take the whole clan. Our treat. Peggy and Warren, Leslie and Bobby, all the kids, even Mom and Dad if they want to go. Patty and Bill too. Get a few suites in one of the Disney Resort hotels. Okay?"

"Of course it's okay," Mark said.

I kissed him. I still love to kiss Mark Tuttle.

Suddenly I could feel rumblings in my stomach, my intestines. *What's going on down there?..I've had corned beef and cabbage before...Never felt like this...Could it be the Guinness?..Maybe the Guinness and the cabbage...Ooh, that was a big one...Silent, but...* "Oops. Sorry," I said.

"Whew," Mark exclaimed.

I moved to a kneeling position on top of him. I was naked. "What do you mean 'whew'? I'm not letting you out of bed."

"I just meant 'Whew,' " he said. "I don't want to get out of bed."

"What do you want?"

"I'd like you to move up a bit so I can eat you."

"And put yourself so close to ground zero?"

"The reward is worth the risk," he said.

413

I crept up to get in position. "Go ahead, but be aware, there are still rumblings."

"I like your smells."

I laughed. *Oh God, this feels good…He can turn me on…Oh no…*"Sorry."

"It smells delightful."

"You **are** like a dog," I said.

"Your dog, excited by your smells."

"You're kinky, but I love it."

"We do kinky well," he said.

The next morning, Friday, I drove to Cork. That was an experience, especially my first roundabout. We were staying in Cork, at the Metropole Hotel, but our primary objective was Blarney Castle, a little south of the city. After checking in, we drove to the castle to see and kiss the famous stone. I drove again; I was getting good at the roundabouts.

"What do you know about the Blarney Stone?" Mark asked me.

"According to legend, the lord Cormac McCarthy---"

"The author of *Blood Meridian* and *All the Pretty Horses*?' Mark asked.

I punched him on the shoulder. "His great-great-great-grandfather. Anyway Cormac was involved in a trial and he prayed to the goddess, Cliodhna, for guidance---"

"Cliodhna or Peggy?"

I punched him again. "Cliodhna. Let's call her Clio for simplicity. Clio told him to kiss the first stone he saw on the way to court the next morning, and he would acquire great eloquence, the ability to deceive without offending."

"Nice ability. I assume he did and, voila', the Blarney Stone was created," said Mark.

"Yes. Now let's go kiss it. I want the ability to deceive you without offending you."

"You already have that."

I punched him again.

To kiss the stone, you have to lean backwards from the top of the battlements. There are hand rails, but I made Mark promise not to let me fall. I did the same for him.

"Now I'll never know if you're telling me the truth," I said.

"You have to trust me."

"I do, Mark Tuttle, I do."

We had dinner, Irish stew, and Guinness at Gallagher's Gastro Pub in Cork. I beat Mark at darts again after dinner. Four games!

There were no rumblings that night during sex. "Must have been the cabbage-Guinness combination," I said.

"I didn't mind," he said.

*God, he really does like **all** my smells…They must enhance the full experience for him.*

On Saturday morning Mark drove us to Limerick.

"There was an old lady who had a duck---" Mark said as we approached the city.

"Sitting beside her in her yellow truck," I said.

We starting laughing. "What does the last line end with?" I asked.

"There are so many options," he answered, "Buck, luck, muck, suck, yuck…"

"You forgot one," I said.

"I know," he winked. "I'm saving that for tonight."

"You devil," I said.

We arrived at the Kilmurry Lodge at eleven.

"What's the schedule for today, Captain?" Mark asked.

"The Milk Market, King John's Castle, and then Guinness at a café on the River Shannon. Then a pub for dinner and some darts, if you're up to darts against me."

"I let you win."

"Bullshit," I said, punching him on the shoulder.

The Milk Market was a joy. Stall after stall of pastries, candies (mostly chocolates), cheeses, breads, and other gourmet treats. I enjoyed talking with the stallholders, most of whom grew or made their offerings. We sat and had cheese and bread, with tea, for lunch at a small table in the market. I wasn't wearing my black velvet band today – just letting my hair flow loosely – but I still felt like the queen of the land. How could I not – sitting with Mark Tuttle, the little six-year-old boy who became a man and never veered from his love of me along the way. *Why do you love me so much, Mark Tuttle?..Maybe you can never explain these things…They just are…But you do…That I know…And I love you too…Even before you saved my life when I was eight…*I leaned across the table and kissed him.

"What was that for?"

"Just because…Just because," I said. My eyes shone like diamonds, moistened diamonds.

"I love you too," he said, knowing what I was thinking.

Instead of visiting King John's Castle, we sat and admired it from a café along the Shannon. *This is perfect happiness…Sitting alongside the River Shannon with my Mark…Having a Guinness…Looking at the majestic castle…Watching the boats on the river…My eyes shining like diamonds…My heart full to overflowing…Beginning to enjoy the taste of Guinness…*"Know who would love it here?" I asked.

"Who?"

"Maddie," I said. "I miss her. I miss them all, but especially Maddie."

"Me too."

"When I talk to her, it's like talking to another adult."

We found Michael Flannery's pub, near the Milk Market, and ate corned beef sandwiches and drank Guinness for dinner. No cabbage. A local couple challenged us to a game of darts. We swamped them, winning us two drafts of Guinness. *Don't mess with the queen of the land!*

That night back in the Kilmurry Lodge, Mark completed the limerick. He is a man who keeps his promises. *A promise made is a debt unpaid.* We had an early day planned for Sunday, so we curled up together and went to sleep after completing our wonderful Irish ditty. I guess my cabbage-Guinness combination conclusion was correct. There was no foulness escaping from my hindquarters that evening. Mark said he missed it. I punched him in the shoulder before crawling into his arms for sleep. *So warm…so protected…so confident that he was loving my smells.*

We hit the road at eight the next morning, after a small breakfast, and drove east to Glenstal Abbey in the little town of Murroe, still in County Limerick. Glenstal is an active Bendictine abbey with forty monks, a school for boys, a farm, and a guesthouse. The main attraction for us was the chanted Latin Mass at ten. We would fulfill our Sunday obligation while listening to the monks sing Gregorian Chant.

We arrived a little after nine and toured the abbey before Mass. We entered the chapel at nine forty-five. The boys from the school were there as well as about one hundred local villagers and tourists. The monks filed in and filled pews to the left of the sanctuary.

The celebrant entered at ten and chanted, "*Introibo ad altare Dei.*"

Mark whispered to me, "Is that stately, plump Buck Mulligan?"

"Behave," I said. "You're at Mass."

The celebrant, at the conclusion of Mass, after intoning, "*Ite, missa est,*" (Go, the Mass is ended), invited the congregation to proceed to the refectory for a small meal. Mark and I accepted the invitation, and enjoyed a mid-day repast of warm bread, white and dark, honey, jams, creamy butter, milk, apple juice, and tea. There was no charge for the meal, but there was a donations box at the door. Mark and I each put a twenty-pound note in the box to support the sons of St. Benedict.

We arrived back in Limerick at three in the afternoon. We went back to the same café alongside the Shannon and enjoyed the river, the view of the castle, the Guinness, and each other's presence. The "each other's presence" most of all. Someone once told me, I don't remember who, maybe I read it, that a woman can always tell when a man has lost his desire for her. If that's right, and I believe it is, then Mark has never lost his desire for me.

We walked back to Michael Flannery's Pub for a repeat of the corned beef on rye and Guinness dinner.

We walked along the Shannon after dinner. When we got back to our room, I hugged Mark and said, "God, I want to make love with you." *He makes me so horny...Still...And I make him so horny too...Yes, I would know if he has lost his desire for me...He hasn't...Neither have I.* "Carry me to bed, my husband," I said. "And ravish me."

He always does what I ask him.

Love that Mark Tuttle.

I drove the next morning alongside the River Shannon to a village that has become legendary in Tuttle-Roberts lore, Bunratty Village, County Clare. As you probably guessed, it has become legendary because of the picture Mark took of me in Bunratty Folk Park. I had no idea at the time that Bunratty Village would become so memorable for us; Mark had not yet taken the photgraph, which he loved and which scandalized my mother -- the holes!

The famous Bunratty Castle stands on the shore of the Shannon, and we stayed at the Bunratty Castle Mews B&B. Our room had a view of both the castle and the river.

We found a pub riverside on the Shannon and had lunch with the castle as our backdrop. Not a sight one sees in Rhode Island. We had corned beef sandwiches and Guinness, no cabbage, and spent a few hours enjoying the scenery, absorbing the local atmosphere.

"I see you're wearing your black velvet band today," Mark said.

"Yes, someone I love gave it to me," I replied.

"He must think you're special, the queen of the land."

"He does. He told me my eyes shine like diamonds."

"He is romantic too."

"Oh, yes, he is."

I smiled at him. He loves my smile. I know because he has told me a thousand times. He can tell me a thousand times a thousand times. I never get tired of hearing it. Did I ever tell you he thinks I have a beautiful face too. Yes, I think I have told you that.

After lunch we toured the castle. The view from the top was spectacular. It was a challenge getting to the top – narrow, steep stairs -- but we are young and athletic. Of course Mark let me ascend in the front position. I almost fell once, but he placed both hands on my butt and kept me upright.

"Thank you," I said.

"The pleasure was all mine," he said. And it was. Cupping my hams. He's got one up on poor Poldy – he only got to watch the swaying hams of the lady exiting the butcher shop.

We then went to the B&B where I wrote out the postcards we had purchased. We sent one, depicting the goddess Cliodhna, to Peggy: "Peggy, Mark says she can't hold a candle to our goddess. See you Sunday. Love, Mark and Sandy."

To the kids, the Blarney Stone: "Maddie, Bobby, Jimmy, Annie. Miss you all. Dad and I are going to take you to Disney after we get home. Daddy held me while I kissed the stone so I wouldn't fall. Love, Mom and Dad."

To Mom and Dad, the Guinness Storehouse: "Mom & Dad, Getting to like Guinness. I found out I can beat Mark at darts. Drives him crazy! Love, Sandy and Mark."

To Patty and Bill, Bunratty Castle: "Patty & Bill, Thank you so much for watching the kids. Having a great time. Lotsa Guinness. Fun driving on left. Mark and Sandy."

To Leslie and Bobby, Glenstal Abbey: "Leslie & Bobby, We went to Mass here, in Latin. Gregorian Chant. Love to my dear Melanie and Robby. Love, Sandy and Mark"

We went to Bunratty's most famous pub, Durty Nellys, for dinner and post-dinner entertainment. We had a hearty Irish stew, with warm, dark bread, butter, and, of course, drafts of Guinness. We did play darts. I did win. Mark said he let me. I said, "Bullshit!" **again**. The entertainment was a female fiddle player accompanied by a female singer. Her sister, we discovered. What a lilting voice the singer had. We stayed in the pub until eleven enjoying the music, the

Guinness, and, of course, each other's company. We started out across from each other, but ended up side by side. I just wanted to be closer to Mark as the Guinness warmed me and mellowed my heart. I leaned against Mark and he held me against him. We sang along to the music, even the songs we weren't familiar with. You can do that after a few drafts. Heaven.

We had an upstairs room at the B&B. We opened the window to enjoy the breeze from the Shannon. I held Mark in my arms after we retired, and we started kissing. That led to pleasures beyond description, so I won't try to describe them.

He fell asleep before I did, but his arms never released me. I eventually fell asleep, so safe, so loved, so tightly-held. "I love you, Mark Tuttle," I whispered to my sleeping lover, my sleeping husband, my protector, my guardian, my everything. I said a little, "Thank you, God," and then drifted off to sleep.

After the usual "breakfast fit for a king" at the B&B (I was beginning to love rashers), we headed over to the Folk Park, not knowing what to expect. We both fell in love with the yellow cottages with thatched roofs, little houses from a gentler past.

"Take my picture," I said. It was a little chilly so I was wearing my blue jacket over a hoody. I leaned against one of the doorjambs, crossed my legs at the ankles, and bent my head a bit.

"These people must have been short," I said.

"Nae, you're a fookin' Yankee giant," Mark said.

After I stopped laughing, I asked, "Should I take off my glasses?"

"No, I love you wearing glasses," Mark said. *You love me no matter what I'm wearing... You even love me when*

I'm not wearing anything…Of course you do…That goes without saying. "And put the hood down," he added.

Mark took three pictures. "To make sure I get one good one," he said.

When we got home and developed the film, Mark absolutely fell in love with that picture. I don't know why, but he did. The three shots all came out. He had one blown up, 8 ½ x 11, and framed it in expensive wood. He placed it in our den, and it remains there to this day. No, he does not keep a lighted candle in front of it. As I told you, Mom just shook her head. "Why the holes?" She never understood that.

We sat at a pub on the Shannon for most of the afternoon, ate again at Durty Nellys, enjoyed the same two sisters fiddling and singing, then returned to the B&B where we enjoyed each other as only two loving married people can. *What can be better than this, husband and wife, horny together, loving each other, sleeping together, wrapped in each other's arms…So much more than sex…Incredibly more than just sex…Incredibly better than just sex… But I do miss the kids…Now why did I think of that?..I'll see them in five days…and Peggy…I'll see her in five days too…Mark is holding me so tight…No one will ever hurt me as long as I have Mark…Rather as long as Mark has me…I'm getting horny again…Isn't that wonderful?..That he always makes me horny…Let me pop him in the nose, blow my honey-Guinness-scented breath in his face…He's waking up…He's smiling…We're gonna fuck again…Thank you, Mark Tuttle.*

"Wanna fuck?" I said.

"Oh yes," he answered.

"Nice breeze off the Shannon," I said.

Next morning, I drove to Ennis on the River Fergus.

"Did you know," I asked Mark, "that Muhammad Ali's great-grandfather was from Ennis?"

"The boxer?"

"Yes."

"His great-grandfather was Irish?" Mark asked.

"Yes. His name was Abe Grady."

"Holy shit. I never would have thunk it. No wonder he was such a great fighter."

"Stick with me and you'll learn a lot."

The next day, Thursday, I drove to Galway, on the River Corrib, our last stop before the return to Dublin on Saturday. We drove directly to Flannery's Hotel where we had booked a room for two nights.

We did sightseeing on Thursday, starting at the Spanish Arch, an extension of the old city wall. The arch itself is an attraction, but I wanted to see the monument to Christopher Columbus in front of the arch. Columbus visited Galway in 1477, fifteen years before he discovered the New World.

"I had no idea Columbus was in Ireland," Mark said. "Did he know Muhammad Ali's grandfather?"

I punched him in the shoulder.

"*Sciocco*," I said. "Columbus was in Galway, not Ennis."

We visited the Roman Catholic Cathedral of Our Lady Assumed into Heaven and Saint Nicholas.

"That's a mouthful," said Mark.

"And how did Saint Nicholas get equal billing with Mary?" I asked.

"Well, he is Santa Claus, isn't he?"

The cathedral was at one end of the Eglinton Canal; Galway Bay at the other end. The length of the canal is about one kilometer, a little more than half a mile. We took a leisurely walk from one end to the other.

"So this is famous Galway Bay," said Mark.

"Let's find a pub and toast it," I said.

"Any excuse for a Guinness," he said.

We found a pub, ordered two drafts of Guinness and a rolled newspaper page filled with chips (fries). Delicious, but not quite as good as Beshoff's. I hit Mark in the nose again with a chip. A new Tuttle tradition. He ate the chip as he had done in Dublin.

We walked back up to Galway City, again along the Eglinton Canal, and made our way to Flannery's Hotel. We took a nap, showered and headed out for dinner and music. We had corned beef sandwiches and Guinness at the Cellar Bar and then went to the Crane Bar to listen to Irish music. Three Irish balladeers sang, what else, love songs and songs of the revolution.

"Oh we're off to Dublin in the green, in the green
"Where the helmets glisten in the sun."

If the Irish Republican Army had a recruiter in the pub, I would have enlisted.

We arrived back at the hotel at eleven. I was exhausted from all the walking, and the Guinness. We curled up in bed, started kissing, and then I fell asleep in Mark's arms. I didn't wake up until eight the next morning, still wrapped in his arms.

"I have a surprise for you this morning," he said, smiling.

"Another black velvet band?" I asked.

"No, better."

"What could be better than that?"

"You'll see."

After breakfast, we walked to Quay Street. We stopped in front of a large jewelry shop, Dillon's Claddagh Gold. Mark smiled at me.

"Are we going in here?" I asked, suspecting I would hear a "Yes."

"Yes," he said, not disappointing me. He never disappoints me.

"Welcome, Mr. and Mrs. Tuttle," said a salesman, greeting us at the door.

I looked at Mark.

"I called ahead," he said.

"But how did he know it was us?" I asked.

"Good guess," Mark said.

"He told me I would recognize you," the salesman said, "a young colleen with a beautiful face. You do have a beautiful face, Mrs. Tuttle."

Mark Tuttle, you are too much....But I appreciate that.

"Thank you," I said to Mark.

"Dillon's is the original maker of the Claddagh ring," Mark said. "The queen of the land has to have a Claddagh ring, doesn't she?"

God, I love you Mark Tuttle.

The salesperson brought over a tray of rings, various sizes, all 22k. Mark and I found two exactly alike that fit us perfectly. We put them on the ring fingers of our right hands, and there they remain to this day. I don't know the cost; Mark paid with his American Express card. (Actually with **our** American Express card – there is no Mark's or mine in our marriage.)

We spent the afternoon seaside at Galway Bay. I had left my gold bracelets from Florence back in Coventry, but I thought of them while sitting next to Mark at a pub overlooking the sea. He always surprises me with such wonderful gifts. And the value of the gift is not the cause of my satisfaction. I love my black velvet band as much as my gold bracelets and my Claddagh ring. I love Mark's thoughtfulness. We had corned beef sandwiches and Guinness in a pub back in center city and then went back to the hotel for an evening of lovemaking. As my brother once said, "How wonderful it is when your best friend is your wife." I am Mark's best friend, and he is mine. We wear our Claddagh rings to show that to the world.

Mark drove to Dublin on Saturday, and we flew home on Sunday.

I love surprises, and Peggy had a big one for me at Logan Airport. Standing next to her to welcome us home as we walked out from Customs was my beloved Maddie. When she saw us, she broke out in a big smile. So did I. So did Mark. Maddie came running and hugged both of us. "Welcome home, Mom, Dad. I missed you."

We both hugged her. "We missed you too, honey," I said. "More than I can ever tell you." I was beginning to cry.

"She asked to come with me," said Peggy. "When the others heard she was coming, they all wanted to come. I told them I only had room for one, and Maddie had asked me first. Bobby said, 'If any one of us goes, it should be Maddie.' You know, they all respect her, recognize that she is the leader of the Tuttle-Roberts-Jones clan."

"Yes she is," Mark said. Maddie gave him a warm smile. "Thanks, Dad."

"We had a great conversation on the way up. It was like talking to an adult," said Peggy.

"Nice ring, Mom," Maddie said. "Where did you get it?"

"Daddy bought matching Claddagh rings for me and him in Galway."

We walked through the terminal four abreast, Mark on my left, Maddie on my right, and Peggy on Maddie's right – the four most attractive people in Logan Airport!

Every man we pass turns his head to look at Peggy…Even the married ones with their wives sneak looks at her…Maybe they are looking at me too…Ha Ha…Maybe they are looking at Maddie...She is one beautiful little girl...No, they are looking at Peggy, our Cliodhna...Mark is in his protector mode...Protecting both me and Maddie, and Peggy...But mostly me and Maddie...I did catch him looking at me a few times, smiling, loving me...He's the only man in the terminal not sneaking looks at Peggy...Looking at his beloved Maddie too...Loving her...He has always loved Maddie...From the day he patted my tummy with her inside...No one inside for him to tickle, but he will still tickle me tonight...Always loved me...Great husband, great father...I read once that the most pleasing attribute of a man to a woman is his willingness to protect her children...They're Mark's children too, but that doesn't matter...Mark will protect my children with his life...And he'll protect me with his life...Can you imagine how wild he would be if someone threatened me or Maddie...Peggy too...He would fight for Peggy – already proved that...I would fight for Peggy too – I already proved that too...Would I fight for Mark and Maddie?..For all my children?..Like a tigress...Or, as they say in Ireland, like a fookin' tigress.

I don't think I have ever been happier in my life. Sandy Roberts Tuttle, the queen of the land, marching through Logan Airport with Mark, Maddie, and Peggy. I'm going to cry again.

Chapter Twenty-One
The Next Generation in Coventry

Mini-Precursor Incidents:

I called Chapter Eight *Precursor Incidents*, describing a few occurrences in Mark's and my childhood and young adulthood that were foreshadows of our future life together. In this section of Chapter Twenty-One, I want to tell you about a few incidents that occurred during our trip to Disney World that were indicators of our children's future.

It was six months before we made it to Disney World. We didn't want to go during summer school vacation – too crowded, too hot – and we had to arrange for eight suites! It is not easy getting eight suites in any one of the Disney Resort Hotels at one time.

We ended up with eight expensive (very expensive) suites in the Dolphin, one of Disney World's premier hotels, for the second week in September, the week after school started. Neither Peggy, Leslie, nor I had any qualms about taking the kids out of school for a week. Not our kids! Not one of them would have any trouble making up lost class time.

Why eight suites? One for me and Mark, one for Peggy and Warren, one for Leslie and Bobby, one for Patty and Bill, one for Mom and Dad, one for Mrs. Mayhew (Peggy and I talked her into accompanying us), one for the five girls (Maddie, Annie, Heather, Candi, and Melanie – 'my girls' -- the same five girls who received the advanced model of the *Alexandra the Mouse* doll when Candi was in the hospital), and one for the four boys (Bobby, Jimmy, Robby, and Larry).

Mark and I had invited all the adults to our house early in June, after our return from Ireland. We told them we wanted to pay for a trip to Disney World for the whole family, to include airfare, rooms, admissions, meals, snacks, souvenirs – everything. I had called Disney and tentatively blocked eight suites in the Dolphin. All of us, the kids and the adults, would have five-day park-hopper passes, good for unrestricted admission to all the parks, and individual charge cards to be used for meals, snacks, drinks, and souvenirs. No cash would be needed. The rooms would be pre-paid, by Mark and me, and all charges by any of the guests in the eight suites would flow to one account – mine.

Patty said, "You don't have to do this."

"I know, Patty," I said, "but we want to. We want the whole family to experience Disney World together, and this is the best way to do it. Believe me, this is our pleasure."

"I have tentatively booked 20 seats on Southwest, round-tip," said Mark.

"Consider it an early Christmas gift," I added.

Everyone sat there in stunned silence until Peggy said, "I'm in." She came over to me and hugged me. Leslie did the same. Since the three of us were the mothers of the nine kids, and the trip was for the kids, that settled it. Mom and Dad were ecstatic – going to Disney World with all their grandchildren. So was Mrs. Mayhew. She always loved me and Mark, ever since first grade when we befriended Peggy and invited her to sail with us on the Barge of Curiosity. And after what I did when Candi had her crisis, well you can imagine how high I went in her estimation after that.

Now she would be going to Disney World with Heather, Larry, and Candi, thanks again to Sandy Roberts Tuttle. She hugged me before going home and said, as I had so often heard from her daughter, "I love you, Sandy Roberts." Yes, I did cry. "I love you too, Mrs. Mayhew," I said. "And your daughter and your grandchildren. They are family to me." She was crying too as she left our house with Peggy and Warren.

There was one funny incident during check-in at the Dolphin. Peggy and Warren led our entourage to the check-in desk. The desk clerk asked their names and then, looking at my Bobby and Heather standing together, said, "You must be Larry and Heather." The children's names and ages were included in the pre-registration entry displayed on his computer screen.

"No. I'm Bobby Tuttle," Bobby said.

The desk clerk looked confused. I intervened. "He's mine. This is Larry." I pushed Larry forward. "We're all together, twenty of us in eight suites. My Bobby and Heather are inseparable. Let me tell you who is staying in which suite; that will be easier." When I said, "twenty of us in eight suites," the desk clerk looked overwhelmed. He called over a young woman to assist him.

We survived the sign-in process (it was much less complicated than the desk clerk had feared – with me taking charge, everything moved along smoothly. I am a Harvard graduate, after all.) Leslie, Peggy, and I then took the kids to their suites. The girls' suite had two double beds and a single. Annie and Candi chose one of the double beds, Maddie and Melanie the other, and Heather took the single. Her choice for a sleeping partner, if she had to make a choice, would have been Bobby, but that was not going to happen. Not on my watch. I remembered me and Mark, in the closet at Molly Davidson's birthday party. We were nine, their age. *God that was nice…It was the first time I tasted Mark's mouth, touched his tongue...Yes, that was very nice...I'm sure Heather and Bobby kiss...Well, I'm not sure, but I think they do...Probably...They are together all the time...Alone at times...But Peggy and I would be irresponsible parents if we let them sleep together...I don't know why I'm even thinking about this...It was never an option...Boys in one room – Girls in the other...Neither Heather nor Bobby mentioned sharing a bed...Why would they?..They're only nine!*

The boys' room had two double beds. My boys chose one, and Robby and Larry got the other one.

Mark had purchased four quality walkie-talkies before we left Rhode Island, and we divided into four groups the following morning, our first full day at the resort. Maddie and Melanie were Group One. Bobby and Heather were Group Two. Candi, Annie, and the adult women were Group Three. Larry, Jimmy, Robby, and the adult men were Group Four. Each group had to check in with Mark, overall Trip Commander, at least once every hour. We had no fears about the children's safety within Disney World, but with this plan, no one would ever be alone, and everyone would be in hourly contact with Mark. Mark and I are anal. The walkie-talkies had a twenty-five-mile range so the groups were never out of contact with each other during our stay. At times two of the groups ended up together, but Group Two, the young lovebirds, always remained separate from the other groups.

The person using the walkie-talkie could set the gadget's transmission switch to one, two, three, four, or all. Mark used the 'all' switch to let everyone know it was time to gather for dinner. The kids used the 'four' switch to report in to Mark.

Maddie made it a game: "Group One Captain to Trip Commander. Over."

431

"Trip Commander here. Over," replied Mark, with a smile.

"Group One happy and safe. In Epcot. The China Pavilion. Over."

"Enjoy the movie. Have an egg roll. Out."

"Will do. With duck sauce. Out," said Maddie.

Annie called in for Group Three. "Hi, Daddy, it's me. We're still on Main Street. Mommy said to tell you she loves you. Over."

"Tell her I love her too. Over."

"She knows that, Daddy. Everyone knows that. Out."

"Out, Pumpkin."

As I said, Heather and Bobby were inseparable. From the time they boarded one of the Disney busses in the morning until we all got together for dinner in the evening, they were off on their own. They did check in every hour, of course. Peggy and I asked them one evening what rides they liked.

"We like them all, Mom," Bobby said.

"But especially the ones," Heather said, "where we ride into the dark together."

"Oh?" I said, looking at Peggy.

"We don't do anything bad, Mom," said Bobby. *I hope not.*

"He just holds me so I don't get scared," said Heather. *Heather scared?..Heather, like her mother, has never been scared of anything in her life!*

"Sometimes we kiss," added Bobby blushing.

"We like to kiss," said Heather. "But we don't do anything else." *What else could she be talking about?..She's only nine!*

"Just kiss," said Bobby.

"And hug," I said. They had already admitted that.

"Yes. And hug," he agreed.

Later Peggy said to me, "They are a young Mark and Sandy."

"But they look like a young Mark and Peggy," I said.

"Don't worry," said Peggy. "Even though I might have wanted Mark and me to be a couple, it never happened. I love you too much for that to have happened."

"We wouldn't be such good friends if it did," I said, laughing.

"One of us would be dead," she said.

We returned each evening after our "family" dinner, as one group, to one of the parks for the fireworks. My favorite was the fire and light show at the lake in Epcot. Heather and Bobby, although they did go with us, remained slightly apart. They were like me and Mark twenty years ago. Bobby had his arm around her shoulder; Heather had her arm around his waist. I think they enjoyed each other's company as much as they enjoyed the displays. Probably more. Mark and Warren put Annie and Candi on their shoulders. Melanie and Maddie stood with me, Leslie, and Peggy. Larry, Robby, and Jimmy stood with Mom and Dad, Peggy's Mom, and Patty and Bill. They had not yet reached the age where adult relatives embarrassed them. Watching the whole family enjoying the fire and light show filled me with such warmth. I would have enjoyed it more if Mark were hugging me, but watching him lifting up Annie so she could see was a greater pleasure. He would be hugging me, and more, back in the suite after the show. *I should get a bumper sticker for my car...I fucked the Trip Commander at Disney World...That would raise some eyebrows...What can I say?..I did...Five times.*

Maddie told me something one evening after the fireworks that made me a little uneasy. It was probably nothing, but I did talk to Peggy about it.

When Maddie told me about the incident, she wasn't tattling, but revealing something that she thought was very cute.

"I woke up, Mom, and looked over at Candi's and Annie's bed. They didn't know that I was awake. They were whispering to each other and hugging each other. Then they kissed, and Annie said to Candi, 'I love you. You're my best friend.' Candi kissed her, and said, 'I love you too, Annie. We'll always be best friends.' How cute, eh, Mom? They are like little sisters."

"Yes, Maddie, they are."

They're only six, Sandy…Don't worry about it…Should six-year-old girls be kissing?..I don't know what kind of kiss it was…I couldn't ask Maddie that…Make her think I thought something might be wrong…Probably very innocent…I know they love each other…They're always together…Like Bobby and Heather…No, I hope not like Bobby and Heather…Like me and Peggy…We love each other…What would have happened if there had not been a Mark?..If there were no Mark, there would be no Annie, and I wouldn't be wondering about her now…I'll talk to Peggy later.

Peggy told me not to worry about it. "They're just little kids, Sandy. What were we like when we were their age?"

"Just good friends," I said.

"There," said Peggy. "Nothing to worry about."

"We didn't hug and kiss when we were six, Peggy."

"We would have if we had the chance. If our parents let us sleep together, we would have, don't you think? We would have talked, giggled, hugged, and kissed all night."

"Yes. That's why it worries me. Should we let them sleep together?"

"Of course. They're only six. I think it would only create a problem if we put ideas into their little heads. They're innocent. And we turned out fine, didn't we?"

434

"What if there were no Mark, Peggy? Then what would have happened between us?"

"I don't know. But whatever, we would be fine."

We just looked at each other. Then we smiled. "Yeah, we would be fine," I said. "No matter what." She leaned over and kissed me lightly on the lips.

"We would have been fine, Sandy. Different, but fine. Let's get Leslie and Patty and order some margaritas. The Tuttles are paying for them."

Gang War at Coventry High School:

Maddie and Melanie were in their junior year at Coventry High School when the following harrowing incident occurred. Robby, Bobby, and Heather were sophomores.

Peggy called me from school at two thirty. Peggy was the Phys. Ed. Teacher and girls' basketball coach at CHS.

"Can you get down here to school?" she asked.

"What's up?"

"The kids got in a fight, and the principal wants to see us."

"Which kids?"

"All of them."

"**All** of them?"

"Yes. Do you know where Leslie is? I tried to get her at her house, but no answer."

"She's here with me."

"Can you ask her to come along?"

"Leslie too?"

"I said **all** the kids."

"Oh shit. Are they okay?" I asked worried.

"They're fine."

"We'll be right there."

"Is Mark home?"

"Yes."

"Warren is picking up Larry and Candi. I'll have him drop off Jimmy and Annie at your house." The four younger ones were still at St. Michael's, in eighth and seventh grade.

"Thanks. We'll be right there."

I called Mark out from the den where he was working. "All the kids got into a fight at school. Peggy just called. The principal wants to see me, Peggy, and Leslie."

"What do you mean, 'All the kids'?" he asked.

"**All** the kids, Maddie, Bobby, Heather, Robby, and Melanie. All of them."

"Holy shit," said Mark.

"That's what I said. Warren will bring Jimmy and Annie home from St. Michael's. Peggy said all our kids are okay."

We arrived to find our five kids and Will Cox, Melanie's boyfriend, sitting outside the principal's office. Bobby had his right arm around Heather. *God, they look like me and Mark...More like Peggy and Mark...What a horrible thought...She is beautiful...Heather...Peggy too...Heather looks just like Peggy when she was fifteen...Lucky Heather...Lucky Bobby...You have good taste, Robert, my son...So does your father...*Melanie was in Will Cox's arms. Maddie and Robby were sitting side-by-side talking, cousins, but as close as brother and sister. When they saw us come in, they all lowered their eyes. They seemed a little embarrassed, having their mothers called to school.

"Will, is your mother coming?" asked Leslie. Will lived with his mother. There was no father in the picture.

"No, Mrs. Roberts. She's at work."

"Don't worry. We'll get you home."

"They got in a fight with six other kids after school," Peggy told me and Leslie. "The vice-principal has the other

436

six kids down in the Guidance area. I don't have all the details yet, but our kids did not start it. I know that."

Maddie looked like she was carrying the weight of the world on her shoulders, like she was wearing a lead-filled blanket. "Our kids didn't start it," was enough for me. *Maddie's the leader...She's taking responsibility for this...no matter how it started...She looks so miserable...No matter what happened I'm sure Maddie did the right thing...I know Maddie.*

I was about to head over to her, to hug her, tell her not to worry, when she looked at Peggy. Peggy smiled and winked at her. It was like someone lifted the lead-filled blanket off Maddie. She knew everything was all right. *I love you, Peggy Mayhew.* I looked at Peggy. She looked at me. I smiled and mouthed, "Thank you."

Then I walked over to Maddie. She stood up and said, "Mom, I'm sorry."

I hugged her. "You don't need to be sorry, honey. I'm not mad. I'm proud of you. I don't even know what happened yet, but I'm proud of you. I know my daughter."

"We didn't start it, Mom. Betsy Cerullo threw a punch at Heather for no reason, and it got out of control. It turned ugly, Mom. Fast."

"It's okay, Maddie," I said. "We'll get all the details later. I am on your side."

"Will Daddy get mad at me, for fighting?"

"Daddy never gets mad at you, or me, or Annie."

She smiled. "How about Bobby? Will he be mad at Bobby?"

"He never gets mad at Bobby or Jimmy either."

She smiled and hugged me tighter. "I love you, Mom."

"Love you too."

The vice-principal entered the outer office where we were standing and sitting and said to our six kids, "We want to make sure this is over, doesn't re-start tomorrow.

437

Can you six pick out someone to go to a meeting with me down in Guidance? The other kids will pick one representative too." He looked at Bobby.

"Maddie," said Bobby.

"Maddie," echoed the other four, including Will Cox.

"Do you want me to go with her?" I asked.

"No," he said. "We want to keep this low-key. Try to settle it without getting parents involved. The last thing we need is to have the parents fighting." *He must mean fighting verbally, yelling at each other, not fist fighting.*

When he said that, Peggy looked at me and winked. *She, on the other hand, is thinking fist fighting…She would love to have it out with the other parents…I don't think there are two female parents of CHS students who can take me and Peggy in a fight…Might be fun…Haven't had a fight since Taco Bell…With Peggy…All my fights have been alongside Peggy…I bet Leslie can handle herself too…Stop thinking like this…What the Hell…I would like to pound someone…Their kids messing with my kids.*

Maddie left with the vice-principal. She looked back at me and smiled. The smile said, "I'm okay, Mom."

I asked Bobby what happened.

"Betsy Cerullo got into an argument with Heather. Heather was beginning to walk away when Betsy punched her. Heather wasn't going to take that, and she punched back. *(Yes, she is Peggy Mayhew's daughter.)* I tried to break it up, but Betsy's boyfriend started a fight with me. Robin Reilly, a friend of Betsy's, jumped on Heather, and Maddie pulled her off. They started fighting. Then Ellen Cerullo, Betsy's cousin, punched Maddie from behind, a sucker punch. Melanie tackled her, and they started fighting. When I looked around, Robby and Will Cox were fighting with two other kids. It was like a gang fight, Mom. Seven or eight teachers broke it up. They brought us to the principal's office, and the other kids to Guidance."

"Okay, don't worry. Maddie will get it all sorted out."

"Will Dad be mad at us?" Bobby asked. *Why are they all concerned about Mark?..He has never been mad at them...Ever.*

"No, absolutely not," I said.

"You sure?"

"Yes. When has he ever been mad at any of you?"

"Never," Bobby said.

I tousled his hair.

"Bobby, listen to me. Dad and I consider all five girls 'our girls,' not just Maddie and Annie. We will never get mad at any of you boys for defending the girls, Maddie, Annie, Heather, Candi, or Melanie. We expect you guys to do that. We'd be disappointed if you didn't." Smiling at him I added, "And if you didn't fight for Heather, I would be shocked."

"I love you, Mom," he said.

The vice-principal came back with Maddie. Maddie was smiling.

"It's all over," said the vice-principal. "As far as the school is concerned, nothing happened. No one was hurt, and Maddie and Robin Reilly agreed that there would be no repercussions, no revenge seeking, no more fights. No suspensions, no detentions, nothing. It's over. Okay, you kids go home now. See you in school tomorrow."

When we got outside, Peggy said, "How about a stop at McDonald's?" *You can always count on Peggy to put everyone at ease.* We piled into our two vehicles and headed to Mickey D's. Maddie, Bobby, and Heather came with me. Leslie, Robby, Melanie, and Will Cox went in Peggy's van.

As we were entering McDonald's, Peggy pulled me aside. "Too bad we didn't fight the other mothers..."

"Do you mean that biologically or as part of a longer word?" I asked, laughing.

"Both ways," she said. "I would have liked a good fight. Do you know who Betsy Cerullo's mother is?"

"No," I said.

"Rosalie Torino."

"The girl you fought in seventh grade?"

"Yes, and I would love to fight her again. Her kid messing with Heather. Fuck that. I would beat the shit out of her."

"Mayhew, you'll never change."

"That's why you love me, Roberts."

Yeah, I guess that's right...I wouldn't love Peggy Mayhew if she wasn't Peggy Mayhew.

In McDonald's, Maddie asked if she could make a little speech. I said, "Yes."

"Mom, Aunt Leslie, Aunt Peggy, I know Dad's rule about fighting: 'Never start a fight and avoid fights at all costs.' We do. But he also says, 'There are times when you have to fight.' I know he has told Bobby, Jimmy, Larry, and Robby that they have to defend me, Heather, Melanie, Annie, and Candi. I assume that rule applies to us girls too. We have to stick together. Today was one of those times when we had to fight. Betsy started it, and there was nothing to do but fight after that. We had to defend each other. I think everyone learned something very important today."

"What?" I asked.

"If you fight with a Jones, you have to fight with a Tuttle and a Roberts too."

"And a Cox," said Will.

"Maddie," I said. "We had a similar motto when we were your age: 'If you fight with a Mayhew, you fight with a Roberts and a Tuttle.' But there were only three of us so we didn't engage in the mass warfare that you guys got involved in today. And we didn't have any Coxes to help us." I winked at Will.

I asked Maddie later if she thought there would be any renewal of the fighting. She laughed and said, "No, Mom. We were winning all six fights. All six! They won't mess with us again."

Love that Maddie.

"Did you and Aunt Peggy get in fights when you were our age?" Maddie asked me.

"Someday I'll tell you about the rumble at Taco Bell. When you're a little older, over a glass of wine, or two."

"I bet Aunt Peggy was tough," she said.

"So was I," I said.

She hugged me. "I love you, Mom."

"Love you too, honey, from the moment you were conceived."

"You loved me when I was still in the womb?"

"Yes. And Dad saved your life when you were still in there."

"What?"

I told her the story of the riptide.

When I finished, she went into the dining room where Mark was helping Annie and Jimmy with their homework. She stood behind her father and began to sing, "*If you pass through raging waters, in the sea you shall not drown---*" Tears were streaming out of her eyes, down her beautiful face. *God, she does have a beautiful face....I know what Mark means about me...She looks like me...Am I that beautiful?..Mark thinks so...That's all I care about...I love you, Maddie...I love you, Mark.*

"*If you stand before the power of Hell and death is at your side, know that I am with you through it all---*"

I stood in the doorway, watching my firstborn sing to her father, my husband, my lover, the verse I sang to him seventeen years earlier at the Flagler Fish Company. It might sound trite, but my soul was filled to bursting.

"Come follow me, and I will give you rest."

Then Maddie hugged her father and said, "Thank you, Daddy."

She hadn't called Mark 'Daddy' in a long time.

"You don't have to thank me, honey. It's my job to take care of Mom and the four of you. I will never let anyone or anything hurt any of you."

Annie and Jimmy were staring at their older sister and their father, mouths wide open, wondering what was going on.

Maddie told them.

Annie smiled and said, "Daddy, we are so safe with you. Even before we were born."

That's when Mark starting crying too.

A hand rested on my shoulder. "What's going on, Mom?" It was Bobby, attracted by the singing. "Why's everyone crying?"

"Tears of joy, Bobby," I answered him. "Tuttle family love."

Then I looked at him and said, "Bobby, did I ever tell you that I fell in love with your father when I was six years old, and still love him, and always will? Did I ever tell you that?"

"No, Mom."

"Well I did, and I do."

"He loves you too, Mom. We all know that. Everyone knows that."

Yes, everyone knows that…Thank you, Mark.

Only good things have happened since they got together….Love you, Maddie…Love you, Mark…Right now is one of those good things…All of us together.

A few weeks later, I saw Rosalie Torino Cerullo in Stop & Shop. She had gained weight, but still looked very tough. She was wearing blue jeans and a tank top. I bent over into the frozen vegetables bin so she wouldn't see me. It reminded me of an old joke – two teen-agers tell their parish priest that they can't stop fornicating. He tells them that he can't let them in church for Mass until they stop. They promise they will stop. But after ten days, the young woman bends over into the freezer, and the young man enters her from behind. Now they are not only banned from Mass; they're banned from Stop & Shop.

When I stopped chuckling, I looked around. Rosalie had vanished. *Yeah, she still looks tough, but Peggy* **would** *beat the shit out of her if they fought…Might be fun to watch…Maybe Rosalie would bring her friend Alex…Then we could finally have that fight…And I could break that fucking middle finger of hers.*

The Unexpected Visitation

It was a Saturday during Maddie's junior year, two weeks after the rumble. Mark had taken Bobby and Jimmy up to CHS to play some basketball in the gym. Maddie usually played with them, but she wanted to work on a project with Melanie. The four of us, Maddie, Melanie, Annie, and I, were in the kitchen having lunch when the doorbell rang.

"I'll get it," said Maddie.

She came back into the kitchen and said, "Mom, it's a priest. He said he knows you and Dad."

"Did you let him in?" I asked.

"No. I don't know him. I don't even know he's a priest. He's outside on the porch."

I went to the front door; the girls followed me.

"Oh my God," I said when I opened the door.

The priest smiled at me. "Remember me?" he asked.

"Of course, Father John Michael, the Salvatorian from Rome. Come in, come in."

"Maddie, Father John Michael took care of Dad and me when we were in Rome on our honeymoon. We served Mass for him in the chapel of Michelangelo's Pieta' in St. Peter's Basilica, and attended his Mass in the Salvatorian Motherhouse. How did you find us, Father?"

"I came to Providence College for a retreat and I said to myself, 'Why don't you look up that nice young couple from Coventry?' I found, 'Tuttle, Mark and Sandy' in the phone book. I knew that had to be you, and here I am. Are these three beautiful girls yours?"

"Maddie, the young lady who left you on the porch…."

"Mom!" she cried.

"is my oldest, our *primogenita,* and Annie, the little one, is my youngest, *mia bambina.* Melanie is my niece. Mark is up at the high school gym with the boys. He should be home soon."

"Boys? How many?"

"Two. We have four children altogether."

"That was your plan. And I bet you're still as happy as you were in Rome."

"They love each other, Father," said Maddie. "My Dad adores her. And she thinks he's a god."

"I'm not surprised. When I met them, I knew they were special."

"They still are," said Maddie. *I love you, Maddie.*

"How long can you stay, Father? Dinner?" I asked.

"Sure, I am finished for today. We only had a morning session."

Mark was shocked, pleasantly, to see Father John Michael sitting in the kitchen with the four of us when he got home.

"Sandy, your sons are as handsome as your daughters, and your niece, are beautiful. And, Mark, you look great. I've read all your novels. I loved them."

"Thank you, Father. Sandy's a writer too, children's books."

"I didn't know."

"Have you heard of *Alexandra the Mouse?*" asked Annie.

"Yes. My nieces have *Alexandra the Mouse* books and dolls," answered Father John Michael.

"*Alexandra* is Maddie. And *Annabella* is me. Mommy wrote all those books."

"Wow," said the priest. "Two authors in the family."

We relived our time in Rome with Father John Michael that evening. Maddie loved hearing the stories of Rome. She is our romantic. Father John Michael has become a family friend, and stops in to see us at least once a year. He has said an open-air Mass a few times for the entire Tuttle-Roberts-Jones clan in our backyard.

Mark and I made love the night of Father's first visit – we make love most nights – and then, after we kissed, Mark fell asleep. I looked at him sleeping peacefully beside me. His right arm around my chest, cupping one of my little bumps. He always loved them regardless of size. I don't think I could sleep without his right arm around me. *I love you, Mark Tuttle…You have never stopped loving me, have you?..When we were kids…In Rome…Now as adults…Father John Michael was right…We are very special…I don't know any other couples as happy as we are…Four kids and we still love to fuck each other…He still loves to eat me…"Required foreplay," he says…God, do I love that required foreplay…And we still love to do things together…What things?..Everything…You will always know if your man has lost interest in you…Mark has not…Believe me, Mark has not.*

A Day at the Health Club:

After Annie started at St. Michael's, Mark and I started going to the New England Health and Racquet Club to work out. We try to go all weekdays when the kids are in school. Occasionally we play racquetball – we are an even match, which makes it fun to play against each other. Even on the days we play racquetball, we do the Nautilus circuit then spend forty-five minutes on the stairmaster or the bikes. After the aerobic activity, we lay out mats in the stretch room, and Mark follows my lead through a series of stretching exercises. When we finished the other day, we were laying side by side on the mat facing each other.

I blew a stream of my breath into his face and asked, "Wanna wrestle?"

"Yes, but if we do, every man in this club will have a hard-on, and half of them will come in their shorts."

"Thank you," I said.

"For what?" he asked.

"For assuming that I am still exciting, that I can still arouse all these young men."

"Believe me, you can. You do. If I wasn't with you, you'd be propositioned every time you're in here. They all look at you. That's why I always come with you. To protect you from the wolves."

"Thanks." I leaned into him and kissed him. "Let's go to Dunkin' Donuts and then go home and wrestle."

"Is that a euphemism?"

"Fuck yes."

We both laughed.

Jolie Blon's Bounce:

I was coming out of the women's locker room at the health club one day; Mark was sitting waiting for me. He was reading a paperback: James Lee Burke's *Jolie Blon's Bounce.*

"Great title," I said.

When we got in the car, Mark said, "Let me read you something I just read."

"Okay, read away," I said.

"The moon was up and Bootsie's hair was the color of honey on the pillow. She was the only woman I had ever known who had a natural fragrance...

"I guess he never met you."

Mark has always loved the way I smell...Yes, he would say I have a natural fragrance...All of me...My hair, my mouth, my body, my armpits – yes, my armpits – my pussy...my ass...Every part of me has, to Mark, a natural fragrance...Wow, I am getting horny...Mark reading a line from a book to me, and I'm getting horny...Bootsie, whoever you are, you and I have something in common...Our man loves to smell us...Mark told me once that the greatest physical pleasure for him is hugging me while he smells me in bed..."The greatest?'" I asked..."Yes," he said...He means it too...Mark would rather hug me and smell me than fuck me...And he loves to fuck me!

"Wanna go home and fuck?" I said.

"Yes, after I enjoy your fragrance, every inch of your fragrant body."

God, if I was horny before....

Glory Days Return to Coventry High School:

Peggy once said, "Great players make a great coach." And she had great players. So did Coach Wilson who still coached the boys' basketball team at Coventry High School. Coventry had not come close to winning a state championship, in any sport, since Mark, Peggy, and I had graduated. But now that the Tuttle, Roberts, and Jones families had produced replacements, the glory days came back to CHS.

When Maddie and Melanie were juniors, and Heather a sophomore, the girls' basketball team rolled to the state championship with a 28 – 1 record. This was the first championship for CHS in any sport since our senior year. I said earlier that Melanie was not as good as Maddie, or as Heather for that matter, but maybe I was wrong. She had an uncanny knack of getting herself open, and whenever she did, Maddie hit her with a pass, and Melanie scored. And Heather, even at fifteen, was as tough on the boards as her mother had been. Many rival coaches that year thought Maddie and Melanie were sisters – they looked so alike – and were surprised to see they had different last names. They all knew Heather was Peggy's daughter. Just looking at them standing together at the bench removed any doubt. When Peggy looked at Heather, it was as if Peggy was looking into a way-back mirror. And fans of our generation seeing Maddie and Heather together thought immediately of me and Peggy.

Leslie and I sat together at all the games. Peggy, of course, was on the bench. The men, all three, sat behind us. Mark usually had one hand on my shoulder. Every time Maddie made a good play, he gave me a little squeeze. He gave me a lot of little squeezes that year. I didn't mind. Both for my sake – I like Mark touching me -- and for Maddie's – a squeeze indicated a good play on her part. The little ones, Annie, Candi, Jimmy, and Larry, sat in the row in front of us. They were so proud of their older sisters and were their sisters' biggest boosters. Bobby and Robby, sophomores, and on the boys' varsity, sat with their friends, but never missed their sisters' games either.

Maddie was a good softball pitcher, but her pitches did not have the zip my pitches had. Yet with her more than adequate pitching, and Melanie's, Heather's, and her hitting, they brought another crown to CHS in softball that spring. Peggy coached the girls' softball team as well as the girls' basketball team.

Bill Reynolds came to many of the games, basketball and softball, and mentioned the girls occasionally in his Saturday column. The *Journal* sent a reporter and photographer to most of their games as well. When Maddie's photo started appearing in the *Journal's* high school sports section regularly, I can't tell you how many people said to me, "My God, Sandy, she looks just like you." *I had to agree...She does have my face, and it is a beautiful face!..Didn't Mark tell us both that a thousand times!*

The girls repeated in both sports in Maddie's senior year. In the state final in basketball, Maddie scored 41 points against LaSalle Academy in a twenty point blowout. Melanie had twenty points, and Heather pulled down twenty-one rebounds in Maddie's and Melanie's final high school basketball game.

When Bobby and Robby were juniors, the boys' basketball team won their first state championship since the Mark Tuttle days. Jimmy, who was just a freshman, started and averaged fourteen points and seven rebounds a game that year. They repeated in Bobby's and Robby's senior year.

No one expected CHS to take the title the year after they graduated, but Jimmy, by then a 6'4" junior, had become the reincarnation of his father, the third coming of Jerry West! Larry, who took more after Warren than his mother, started, but it was Jimmy who propelled CHS to two more years of glory. In his senior year, they were 33 – 0, and clobbered Bishop Hendricken in the state final, 99 – 67. Jimmy had fifty-two points in the championship game at the Providence Civic Center.

I was watching Larry and Jimmy play one-on-one in our driveway one afternoon. All I could think of was the day Mark got 57 against Warren. *Mark's and my Alpha Point...Poor Warren...Poor Larry...Turned out, in retrospect, to be a great day for Warren.*

The kids, all of them, followed the lead of their parents, and did not play varsity sports in college. Mark and I had let Peggy, Warren, Leslie, and Bobby know that we were setting up a fund to manage all "family" tuition payments. Of course Peggy's and Warren's children were family. Maddie and Philip – you will meet Philip – managed this fund for the next generation of students.

Annie and Candi never played organized sports. They were athletic, but they used sports for fun, exercise, and as "something we can do together." They enjoyed bike riding, swimming, tennis, jogging, and later skiing. Swimming and tennis, of course, are competitive sports, but the two girls didn't compete for CHS. They competed against each other, and were satisfied with that. They were always together during their four years at CHS, and before, and after. They were like me and Peggy, without the Mark.

Chapter Twenty-Two
The Joining of the Families

The month after Bobby and Heather graduated from CHS, Warren walked Heather down the aisle and presented her hand to Bobby. I don't think anyone in the world could have been happier at that moment than Bobby Tuttle, except perhaps Heather Jones, soon to be Heather Jones Tuttle. Looking at the two of them together, so happy, so committed, was joy-producing for me, but it also filled me with an eeriness. *God, it looks like Peggy and Mark getting married...The image could only be scarier if it were Heather and Jimmy...Bobby looks a lot like Mark...No one would ever doubt he was Mark's son...But Jimmy looks **exactly** like Mark looked in high school...We had great times in high school...It still amazes me that Mark chose me over Peggy...He says there was never any competition...He loved me from the first moment he saw me at St. Michael's...Peggy was always his friend, one of the three musketeers, one of the crewmembers of the Barge of Curiosity, but Peggy was never Sandy...Not for Mark...There never was and never will be anyone for Mark Tuttle but Sandy Roberts...That thought gives me such pleasure...But still seeing Bobby marrying Heather is unnerving.*

I started crying. Those around me assumed I was crying because of the wedding ceremony. I was, a little, but I was crying because I was so happy. I leaned into Mark and kissed him on the cheek. I whispered in his ear, "I absolutely love you, Mark Tuttle." He smiled and said, "Me too, Sandy Roberts."

I had no concerns about Bobby and Heather getting married right after high school at eighteen. How could I object? Mark and I did it, and it worked out quite well for us. When Bobby and Heather told me they wanted to get married, I suggested the six of us – the kids and both sets of parents – get together to discuss it.

"Mom," Bobby said, "We're getting married whether you all approve or not. I know it will be a lot harder without your approval, but we'll manage." *Mark and I would have said the same thing to my parents…There was no need…Mom and Dad gave us their approval and their blessing…Dad loved Mark since third grade.*

"Mrs. Tuttle," said Heather, "We're not little kids infatuated with each other. We have talked about this for four years, longer really, since grade school. We understand what marriage is, and we are committed to each other for life. We realize there will be hard times, but it will be during those hard times that we'll really need each other. We want to go off to college up in Cambridge as husband and wife just like you and Mr. Tuttle did."

I smiled. "Bobby, Heather, I'm on your side. How could I not be? Mark will be too. Heather, I can't see your parents disapproving either."

Peggy and Warren, far from disapproving, gave their blessing to the young lovers.

"We're going to be reciprocal mothers-in-law," Peggy said to me.

"Riciprocal mothers-in-law?" I said. "Never heard that one."

"Well, we will be, won't we?" asked Peggy.

Heather and Bobby followed me and Maddie to Harvard. The newlyweds had partial scholarships, but the "Tuttle Education Fund" filled in all the gaps. Mark and I also gave them, as a wedding gift, a new car – so they could drive back to Coventry for visits -- and a $5000 per month stipend until they graduated. Peggy and I put them under the same restriction my mother had put me and Mark under – no children until after graduation. They agreed to that.

Four years later, after graduation, they settled in Rhode Island. Bobby is now a professor at Brown University, and Heather teaches and coaches basketball at West Warwick High School. They have given us four beautiful grandchildren, two boys and two girls.

When the first one, a little boy they named Warren, was born, I said to Peggy, "Now we're reciprocal grandmothers as well as reciprocal mothers-in-law."

Heather and Bobby are still together and, as far as I know, and I know a lot, they are still as happy and in love as they were as high-schoolers.

Eight years after Heather and Bobby were married, Mark walked Annie down the aisle and gave her hand to Candi. Yes to Candi. It was not in St. Michael's Church, of course. The ceremony was conducted in All Saints Episcopal Church in Coventry. Mother Frances Burney officiated at the wedding. Same-sex marriage had been approved by the state legislature in Providence, but not by the Catholic Church. That will never happen.

Peggy and I had anticipated this. From the time they were little girls, Annie and Candi were closer than sisters, always together, always laughing, always playing, always sharing, always touching each other. I actually had expected it ever since our family trip to Disney World when they were six. After graduating from CHS, they

453

enrolled at the University of Vermont (UVM) – four years as roommates, skiing partners, study partners, always together, always happy. They both majored in American Literature. Graduated with high honors. Were they lovers? I guess I assumed that they were. Did it bother me? Not as much as you might think. I would have been Peggy's lover by now if Mark Tuttle had never existed. I have no doubt of that. Mark and I gave them a car when they went off to UVM; we wanted them home for visits as much as we wanted Bobby and Heather home. Maddie had a car as well, but she usually rode home from Cambridge with her brother and sister-in-law.

Peggy and I had long discussions about our younger daughters before they told us their plans. We agreed it could very well have been us. And, the more we talked about it, the more comfortable we were with it. Peggy and I accepted the possibility – probability? -- long before it became an actuality.

"They will still make us grandmothers," Peggy said.

"They actually have two wombs," I said.

"Marriage with a spare womb. Not a bad concept," she said.

Mark did have a problem with their marriage when Annie first disclosed their plans, but he was able to keep his feelings hidden from his younger daughter. He never said anything to Annie, or did anything, to let her know he was having difficulty accepting the marriage to Candi. I think there were three things that brought him around.

First, as you know from reading this memoir of mine, Mark loves Annie. In a different way but as much as he loves Maddie. As much, too, as he loves me. He could not do anything, ever, that would cause a rift between him and his younger daughter. Note that I said "could not," not "would not." Mark **cannot** hurt Annie. Mark **cannot** do

454

anything to hurt Annie. Mark **cannot** do anything to alienate Annie from him. It is not in his nature; it is not Mark Tuttle.

Second, Mark loves Candi. He would never do anything to hurt her.

Third, Mark and Maddie, then twenty-six, had a long, serious discussion the day after Annie told us. Mark called Maddie, and they sat and talked in his study for three hours. I have no idea what they talked about, but that night, Mark told me, "I'm okay with it." That was all I needed to hear. I knew exactly what "it" was.

"Will you walk her down the aisle? Will you give her away?"

"Of course I will. I'm her father. I love Annie." I gave him a big hug, and, yes, I did cry.

And from that moment until today, Mark has accepted Annie's and Candi's marriage in the same way he accepts Maddie's and Philip's, Bobby's and Heather's, and Jimmy's and Sharon's. I'll introduce you to Sharon later. I love Sharon as much as I love Maddie, Annie, Heather, Candi, and Melanie. My six daughters. In truth, I love Maddie and Annie more than the others; of course I do. But I do love them all. Sharon is a wonderful addition to the family. She is beautiful, intelligent, and always has a smile on her face. And she is the mother of three of my granddaughters! Hannah, Sarah, and Samantha. Absolutely beautiful little girls. How could they not be – Jimmy and Sharon are their parents.

Annie and Candi have given us two grandchildren too: Maddie, named after her aunt and her great-grandmother, from Annie's womb, and Max, delightful, always impish Max, from Candi's womb. Same father – from a sperm bank.

"It's a different world," I said to Peggy.

Chapter Twenty-Three
Maddie's Soliloquy

I asked Mom if I could have a chapter in this book. After all she let Aunt Peggy have two chapters, and I only want one. Mom, of course, said "Yes." It is very rare when she or Dad say "No" to me.

Mom tells me that she and Dad have loved me since the day I first made my appearance in her womb. Dad patted her tummy and told me he loved me. He did that the moment he heard from Mom that I was in there. Mom told him if I was a boy, I would be a Bobby, and, if a girl, a Maddie. She asked him if he had a preference. He said he just wanted a healthy baby, but, if he had his choice, he would pick a Maddie. And he got one! He got a Bobby too, but he had to wait another year for that. He loves Bobby as much as he loves me. He loves Jimmy and Annie too, but I am, as he says, his primogenita, his first born, the amazing result of his initial participation in God's creative work. Mom said that every night I was in the womb, he kissed her tummy and told me, through her skin, that he loved me and couldn't wait to meet me. I have loved them from the moment I met them too. They have been caring, loving parents. Both of them.

Mom told me that Dad saved my life, and hers, when I was in her womb. He wouldn't let the Atlantic Ocean swallow us up. Jesus calmed the Sea of Galilee to save his apostles, but Dad conquered the mighty Atlantic Ocean to save me and Mom. I was sixteen when I found that out. It was the evening of the day of the rumble at CHS. Dad was in the dining room helping Annie and Jimmy with their homework. I walked up behind him and sang, "If you pass through raging waters, in the sea you shall not drown." Mom sang that to him the day he saved us, in a crowded restaurant in Flagler Beach. She asked if she was embarrassing him. He said, "You never embarrass me. You thrill me." I love it when he says things like that to her. And he says them all the time! He really loves her – I have no doubt of that. I was standing behind him in the dining room, crying, loving him so much it hurt, Annie and Jimmy looking at me like I was crazy. There are only two men I have ever loved. Dad and Philip, my husband. And they both love me. How wonderful is that? Oh, I do love Bobby and Jimmy, but that is different. That day in the dining room, I hugged Dad and thanked him. And do you know what he said? He said "You don't have to thank me, Maddie. It's my job to take care of Mom and you kids." My job! And you do your job so well and with love, Dad. I told Jimmy and Annie what he had done, and Annie, always so cute, always so loveable, said, "We are always so safe with you, Dad, even before we were born." Even before we were born! How theological is that.

The day I was born, Dad held me, kissed me, and said to Mom, "I didn't think I could ever love anyone the way I love you, but from the moment I laid my eyes on Maddie, I realized that I love her the same as I love you. And I don't love you any less." Mom said that was because God is Love and therefore Love is infinite. Mom told me that she understood the mystery of the Trinity that day in the hospital. The love of the Father for the Son creates the

457

Holy Spirit. The love of Dad for her created me. The Loving One, the Loved One, and Love itself. I have never forgotten that. Sometimes your parents really surprise you with their insights. When we first studied the Trinity at St. Michael's, in fifth grade, I told that story to my teacher, Sister Mary Rose. She actually cried and said, "Maddie, that is so beautiful." Thanks, Mom.

The day after I was born, Bill Reynolds, who is now a friend of mine, announced my birth to the world: WHAT A JUMPSHOT THAT GIRL IS GOING TO HAVE. He was right. I scored forty-one points in my last game at CHS, against mighty LaSalle, almost all on jump shots. I had Melanie and Heather to help me, my sisters. Melanie is my biological cousin, but my spiritual sister. And Heather. I love her as much as I love Aunt Peggy. Now she's my sister-in-law. More than in-law. In-heart. I love her and Melanie. I love Sharon too, Jimmy's wife. And their three adorable daughters, my nieces. Hannah, Sarah, and Samantha. Dad, who loves Woody Allen movies, calls them "Hannah and her sisters." There is no favoritism toward any of the grandchildren – Mom and Dad love them all equally, and fully.

There's a lot of love in our family. It all starts with Mom and Dad. I have never seen two people who love each other more than Mom and Dad love each other. Bill Skwor, "West Coast Uncle Bill," a classmate of Dad's at MIT, visits us often. He calls our house the Coventry House of Christian Love. And it is. I asked Mom recently -- maybe I should not have asked, but Mom and I talk about everything – if she and Dad still have sex. She smiled at me and said, "Honey, the day I stop having sex with your father is the day you will be burying me, or him." I hope Philip and I are like that. I think we will be. And I hope that Alexandra, my daughter, and I always have the open relationship that Mom and I have. We will. I will make sure of that.

It's funny I named my daughter after a mouse. I actually named her to honor Mom, to let Mom know how much I love her. Mom created Alexandra the Mouse to honor me. I created Alexandra the Person to honor Mom. I call her Alexandra, always. Others call her Alex. Mom told me she is the second Alex she knew. She didn't care much for the first one, but she adores the second one. I asked Mom why she didn't like the first Alex. She said, and I quote, "She is the only person who ever gave me the finger. I should have broken it off." Mom can surprise, can't she? I said, "I bet Aunt Peggy was involved." Mom just laughed.

Mom and Dad appointed me the family Grace sayer when I started school at St. Michael's. I usually said the traditional Catholic "Bless us, Oh Lord," Grace, but sometimes I improvised. I'll never forget one day at Chelo's. I was still little. We were all there, including Grandma and Grandpa Roberts. I said -- it was an inspiration -- "Thank you, God, for bringing Mommy and Daddy together. Only good things have happened since then." I looked up to see if that Grace was okay, and all the adults were crying. Mommy said, "Maddie, you, Bobby, Jimmy, and Annie are the things that have happened, and they are exceedingly good." I just said, "I know." And I did. And I still do.

Growing up in that house was a joy. I don't ever remember Mom and Dad fighting. I don't even remember them being mad at each other. Ever! I told Mom once that it was obvious that Dad loves her. He always treats her with respect. He always smiles when he sees her – his face lights up when she walks into a room. So does hers when he enters a room. I told her I hoped that someday a man would look at me the way Dad looks at her. She said the

459

right man would. And she was spot on. Philip looks at me that way. That special Mark and Sandy way! How marvelous is that!

During those growing up years, I remember the six of us going to Roger Williams Park Zoo. We went frequently after church on Sundays. When I was three and four, before Annie came along, I rode on Dad's shoulder in the zoo. Later Annie replaced me on Dad's shoulders, but I knew she didn't replace me in his heart.

Philip, Alexandra, and I went to the zoo with Mom and Dad last week. Sharon, Jimmy, and the girls joined us. Alexandra rode on Philip's shoulders; Samantha rode on Dad's while Dad walked hand-in-hand with Hannah and Sarah. After a while, Dad handed Samantha off to Jimmy, and he put Alexandra on his shoulders. "Hannah and Her Sisters." "My Little Mouse." How Grandpa loves his little girls. Mom tells me that he always had a soft spot for his girls: Mom, me, and Annie. When Alexandra was on his shoulders, Mom said to me, "Dad loves his granddaughters, but don't ever forget that he loves his daughters just as much. Still does." "I never forgot that, Mom," I said. And I haven't. How could I forget that Mark Tuttle loves me? The man who saved my life before I was born. He patted Mom's tummy that day to let me know everything was okay. During my entire life, I have never felt unsafe when he was around.

I still get along great with Bobby, Jimmy, and Annie. And with Melanie, Robby, Heather, Larry, and Candi. And now Sharon. We are one big family. I was the impetus for starting the Tuttle Family Dinner tradition. Most of us were in the habit of eating Sunday dinner at Mom's and Dad's. About five years ago, I suggested that we make it a plan – Sunday dinner at Mom's and Dad's. "Don't worry, Mom, we'll share the cooking and take care of the clean-up."

"I'm not worried, Maddie," she said. There is no requirement, real or implied, to attend. I understand that things come up, and we all have "the other side of the family." But you would be surprised, or maybe not, knowing us, how rare it is when we're not all there. In two cases, the "other side of the family" is Aunt Peggy and Uncle Warren, and they are usually there for Sunday dinner. Mom and Aunt Peggy are still the best of friends.

We are quite the clan now. Philip and I have our Alexandra; Bobby and Heather have two girls, Sandy and Peggy, and two boys, Warren and Mark; Jimmy and Sharon have Hannah and Her Sisters; and Annie and Candi have Maddie and Max. I try not to show favoritism to my niece and goddaughter, Maddie, but it is hard. Add to that number of attendees Mom and Dad, Aunt Peggy and Uncle Warren, and Larry, his wife, Mary, and their three children, two boys, Larry and Billy, and a girl, Maria, and we have a full house every Sunday. I accused Bobby and Heather of trying to curry favor with Mom and Dad by naming the children after their grandparents. Bobby just said, "We're not dumb." God, Heather is still so beautiful. So are her daughters. Another beautiful Sandy and Peggy. How can the world take such beauty? Alexandra is not a slouch either. Neither are Hannah and Her Sisters. And my precious godchild, Maddie – of course she is beautiful.

When we were little, Dad took care of the pool. When Bobby and Heather were in eighth grade, actually the summer between seventh and eighth grade, Dad turned over care of the pool to them. "That's when your mother and I started taking care of the pool at my parents' house. Don't spend too much time in the pool shed," he admonished. Bobby blushed.

I always wondered what Grandma and Grandpa Tuttle were like. Mom said they were wonderful. They died when *she and Dad were in their senior year at CHS. They didn't live to see their son marry his lifelong sweetheart, Sandy Roberts. They didn't live to see any of their grandchildren or great-grandchildren. How sad. Mom told me Dad proposed to her the day of the wake. She didn't leave his side that week. That was the day Aunt Patty gave her Grandma Tuttle's pearl necklace, the same necklace that I wore when I married Philip. Alexandra will wear that necklace when she walks down the aisle to her beloved. And I hope she has a daughter who will wear it at her wedding. I love traditions. As long as that tradition survives, the memory of the Tuttles will survive. I really wish I had known them. Dad once told me that his father would have loved me. He would have loved all four of us, but I would have been his first granddaughter, and being first, I would not have had to share his love with anyone else for a full year, until Bobby was born.*

I was sitting by the pool at Mom's and Dad's yesterday sharing a white wine with Mom. Alexandra was playing in the sandbox Dad had constructed for the grandchildren. It's funny how your mind works, but all of a sudden an image came into my head. Bobby blushing all those many years ago when Dad told him not to spend too much time in the pool shed with Heather. I told Mom what I was visualizing and asked her if she knew why Bobby would have been blushing. "Bobby and Heather were probably doing what your father and I used to do in the pool shed – making out." "You did?" I cried. "Yes, everyday until Grandma Roberts stopped us. Your father was so embarrassed that day. He had asked me to show him my little bumps, that's what I called them. How he loved my little bumps." "Mom!" I said, "Too much information." "Well, you asked, honey." Later I said to Dad, "Mom says you used to love her little bumps." "Still do," he said, and he kissed the top of my head. The things you don't know about your parents!

Mrs. Mayhew is dead now – that was so sad. I had never seen Aunt Peggy cry before. I cried too. As you know, I never knew my Grandma Tuttle. Aunt Peggy's Mom was my second grandmother growing up. I called her "Grandma Mayhew." We used to sit on the porch or around the pool in the summer and talk about everything. She told me so many stories about her Peggy and Mom and Dad. The first day of school, she told Aunt Peggy to pick out the toughest girl in school and beat her up. "That will keep the bullies off you," she said. Aunt Peggy never had to have that fight -- the toughest girl in school was Mom, and she and Aunt Peggy became best friends immediately. "My Peggy had a crush on your father, Maddie, for years, all the way to sophomore year in high school." "Really?" I said. "Yes, but she never did anything about it." "Why not?" "For two reasons, first she knew your father loved only one girl, and that's still true today, your mother. And my Peggy knew that, if she made a move on your father, she would lose her best friend. She never wanted that. I'll tell you something, Maddie, and this is God's truth: my Peggy's life has been wonderful because of her relationship with your parents. 'Riding the Barge of Curiosity together,' they called it. And she was smart enough to know that, if she wanted to stay on that barge, she couldn't make any moves toward your father." "The Barge of Curiosity, Grandma Mayhew. I like that."

The day of the rumble at CHS, the vice principal brought me to the Guidance Office to meet a representative of the other group. It turned out to be Robin Reilly, the girl I had been fighting with, and beating! Robin and I were actually friends; both of us were on the basketball and softball teams. When I entered the office, Robin stood up

463

and hugged me. That was a surprise. I hugged her back. The vice principal said, "Well, I guess this is over. Good." We both told him it was over. It was. That was the only fight I ever had. How did I get to be such a good fighter? I have two brothers and two almost brothers, Robby and Larry. They taught me, Heather, and Melanie how to fight, how "to take care of ourselves" if we ever had to. Heather also had her mother's fighting spirit; she had her share of fights. Always won, too. I can honestly say she never started a fight, but could she finish one when it got started! The day after the fight, Robin approached me before basketball practice. "I am very sorry about yesterday. I'm Betsy's cousin – my mother is Italian – and I thought you were getting in on Heather's side, so I grabbed you." "I was just tring to break it up," I said. "I realized that later. Sorry. How did you learn to fight so well?" Robin asked. "I have two brothers," I said. She just nodded her head. "Are we still friends?" she asked. "Of course," I said. And we remained friends while at CHS. Then our life routes diverged. I see her occasionally, shopping, at church, and she always gives me a big, "Hello." She has the distinction of being the only girl I ever beat up. Lucky Robin.

The night of the rumble, I said to Mom, "I bet Aunt Peggy was tough in high school." Mom said "I was too," and promised to tell me about the fight she and Aunt Peggy had at Taco Bell "some day when you're older over a couple of white wines." Sitting on her porch many years later, I reminded her of her promise. "We were going to K-Mart and stopped for some tacos at Taco Bell. There were two black girls in front of us on the line, and Aunt Peggy, not paying attention, accidently bumped into one of them. The girl got irate and asked Aunt Peggy if she wanted to fight. Wrong question. Aunt Peggy said, "I came in here for tacos, not a fight, but if you want to fight, let's go." "She's just like Heather," I said. "Yes, like mother, like daughter. Anyway, the manager told us to take it outside, and we did. Aunt Peggy said to me, 'You have my back?' Of course I said 'Yes.' We ended up fighting two on two in the parking lot. We were winning both fights when I heard sirens. Peggy and I rushed out of there."

"Did you two have a lot of fights?" I asked. "Only three that I remember, the Taco Bell one, one on a basketball court – we were playing South Kingstown and one of their players called Aunt Peggy 'a cunt.' " "What!" I said. "Yes, a cunt. Well all of a sudden four of us were going at it. We got kicked out of the game. Without us in there, we almost lost that game, but the team survived without us -- barely. And in seventh grade, again supporting Aunt Peggy, I had my run in with the other Alex. I thought we were going to fight, but she walked away giving me the finger as she left. I should have broken it off." I stared at Mom. Sometimes you don't know your parents.

"Do you want another glass of wine?" "Yes," I said. "Did you and Aunt Peggy ever fight against each other?" "Almost," she said. "What do you mean 'almost'?" I asked. "We were having a chicken fight in the Tuttles's pool. I was on Dad, of course, and Peggy on her boyfriend, not Uncle Warren – she met him at URI – and I won. Aunt Peggy said I only won because I was on your Dad. I said, 'I'm not on him now,' and we went at it. Thank God your father was there, and he put a stop to that immediately. Once we realized what almost happened, we vowed to never let that happen again, and it hasn't." "How old were you two?" "The summer after seventh grade, I think." "The same time Dad was exploring your little bumps?" Mom smiled at me, "One of many, many times he has explored my little bumps, honey."

One of my proudest moments growing up was going to Logan Airport with Aunt Peggy to greet Mom and Dad on their return from Ireland. I was a surprise. They expected Aunt Peggy to meet them, but not their Maddie. When Mom and Dad saw me, their eyes lit up. I ran to Mom and was engulfed by her arms, and by her love. Dad then engulfed both of us. "Engulf" – a word I don't often use, but it applied to Mom and Dad that day. We then walked through Logan Airport side by side by side by side. Mom said we were the four handsomest people in the airport. I had to agree. I think Mom is prettier than Aunt Peggy. I look like Mom so I am a bit biased. But every man in the airport turned to look at Aunt Peggy as we walked through the terminal. Every man except Dad. Dad only has eyes for Sandy Roberts.

I met Philip during my sophomore year at Harvard. We were in a few classes together, and I knew his name, but we hadn't talked to each other except to say, "Hello." I was in the cafeteria having lunch, by myself, reading a book, when he came over to the table and asked if he could join me. I invited him to sit with a gesture. He then said, "Did anyone ever tell you you have the most beautiful face in the world?" "You should see my mother's face," I said. We started dating that very day, and I never dated anyone else after that lunch. I was nervous the first week-end I brought Philip to Rhode Island. We drove down with Bobby and Heather. But I had no reason to be concerned. Dad loved him. So did Mom, but I was more worried about Dad. Mom told me years later that Dad said Philip was "Maddie worthy." No greater compliment can be given to a man than that from Dad. Philip was an accounting major, got his CPA designation a year after graduation, and worked for one of the big eight accounting firms until he and I became CFO and COO of The Tuttle Charitable Foundation.

Philip and I took a trip to Paris after graduation, and Philip proposed to me at an outdoor café on the Champs Elysees. I said "Yes." As you know, as a little girl, baking a chocolate cake in the kitchen with Mom, I asked her if she thought I would ever find a man to love me as much as Dad loved her. She said I would. And I did. Philip is the best husband I could want. Philip is my rock. He is also my best friend, my lover, my partner in all decision making, and my wonderful co-conversationalist. There is nothing we can't talk about. And to top it all off, Philip loves Alexandra as much as Dad loves me.

Philip and I were still living in Boston when Dad called, on a Thursday, and asked if Philip and I could come down to Coventry for the weekend. He said that he really needed to have a private talk with me. I asked if anything was wrong. He hesitated and then said, "No, I don't think so, but I need to talk to you about Annie." About Annie. About Annie and Candi, I thought. I still remember the time at Disney when I woke up and found them hugging and kissing in their bed. I thought it was so cute, and told Mom. Neither one had a boyfriend in high school, and then they went off to UVM together. I think we all knew they were lovers by then. Maybe Dad didn't. How could he not? Well we never spoke about it at home. Maybe he thought it was a phase they would outgrow. "What about Annie?" I asked. "She and Candi told me and Mom that they want to get married." I remained silent. "Believe me, Maddie, I did not say or do anything to let Annie know I had a problem with that. I don't really know if I do have a problem with it, but I need to talk to you. The world is changing." "We'll be down tomorrow at six," I said. "Join us for dinner, then we'll talk," Dad said.

467

*We went into the den after dinner Friday. I sat across from Dad and waited for him to start. "Maddie," he opened, "you know I love Annie as much as I love anyone in the world. Not more, but as much as I love Mom, you, Bobby, and Jimmy. I would never do anything to hurt her. I **could** never do anything to hurt her. When she told me she and Candi wanted to get married, I smiled. Like it was great news for me. I didn't let her see my disappointment." "Does she have any idea of your problem with the marriage?" "No, I don't think so." "Didn't you know they were lovers, Dad?" "How could I not, Maddie? But I always hoped it was a passing fancy. You know the acronym LUG?" "Yes," I said, "Lesbian Until Graduation." "Well, maybe that is what I was hoping for, that after college, they would each seek out a male partner for marriage." "Dad, I thought you knew. They have been in love with each other since they were little girls. Can you ever recall any time either one had a boyfriend?" "No," he said. "Dad, I think you have two choices, and only two." "What?" he asked. "One, let Annie know you disapprove. That will have consequences." "What consequences?" he asked. "First, she and Candi will get married anyway. Second, you may lose a daughter and, probably, any grandchildren that result from the marriage." "Grandchildren?' he asked. "They each have a womb, Dad, and each can get pregnant." "Have sex with a man?" he asked. "That's one way, but not the most popular one with lesbian couples." "How then?" he asked. "Some sort of artificial insemination, using a donated sperm. It's amazing what science can accomplish these days. And third, consider the possibility of you and Mom fighting about this. That would be awful." "More than awful," he said. "And what's the second choice?" he asked. "Accept it and continue to love Annie and Candi. Treat their marriage* *the same as you treat Bobby's, Jimmy's, or mine." "I will always love Annie and Candi, Maddie, even if I don't accept their marriage." "I'm sorry, Dad, I know that. I didn't put that too well." "Well, Maddie, thank you very much for coming down and talking to me. I will think it over, pray about it, and let you know what I'm going to do." "Talk to Mom, Dad," I said before leaving the den.*

The following morning before breakfast, Dad asked me to go with him out on the porch. "Choice two, Maddie. There really is no other choice, is there?" "No, Dad, there isn't. Not for you." "I told Mom last night. I think if I had chosen choice one, Mom and I might have had our first fight." "Did you tell Annie?" "There's no need, Maddie. Annie never knew there were any choices for me to make." "Will you walk her down the aisle?" "That's the same question your Mom asked. Of course I will. I'm her father. I love her." I cried and hugged him. Mark Tuttle will always do the right thing for his children. Especially me and Annie. Dad always loved his girls in a special way.

Dad was speaking the truth: he and Mom have never had a fight. It would have been awful if they fought over Annie. But they couldn't; they both love Annie. And they love each other too much to fight.

I will close this little soliloquy with a story Mom once told me. The last two words of this story truly amazed me, still amaze me. She and Dad were at Narragansett Beach during the summer after their junior year at CHS. She had gone down to the ocean to wash off her feet before she and Dad headed back to Coventry. As she ran back to their blanket, he was staring at her. She stood in front of him, the ocean at her back, and asked, non-verbally, with her eyes, "What?" He said, "Sandy Roberts, you are the most beautiful girl in the world. You have the most beautiful face I have ever seen. And your little bumps aren't bad either. I am going to spend the rest of my life with you, and I am going to love every minute of it, and I m going to do all in my power to make sure you enjoy every minute of it too." She looked him right in the eye and said, "You bet your ass you are, Tuttle. There is no way you're ever getting rid of me." Then she launched herself onto him, spun him around, and pinned him to the blanket. As she stared at him, a tear dropped from her eye and bounced off his cheek. "Together forever," he said. "I know," she said. **I know.** *Not "I hope," not "I think," not "I wish."* **I know.** *I always thought those were the two most amazing words I ever heard.*

Chapter Twenty-Four
Senior Moments II

Warren Jones died suddenly at sixty-six. An aneurysm in his brain. Peggy was devastated. My Bobby, her son-in-law, and Larry stayed at her side throughout the wake and the funeral. Mark and I, of course, did everything we could for her. I always have Peggy Mayhew's back.

Peggy and I became closer after Warren's death than we had been, if that is possible. She stopped in most mornings to have breakfast with me and Mark. We went shopping together, went to plays together, became "Friends of the Library" together, did things that best girlfriends do.

"We started as three, and we are ending as three," she said one day at breakfast.

"I think it was Robert Penn Warren who said, 'the friends of your youth are your friends forever,' or something like that," Mark said. "He was right."

We went out for dinner most nights, the three of us. Sometimes some of the kids would join us, Annie and Candi most frequently. Then the three of us would return to our house and talk, and laugh, and share a few glasses of wine while we relived our youth. Robert Penn Warren was definitely right.

Peggy ended up sleeping at our house many nights, more often than she slept at her house. Mark would never let her drive home after we had been drinking wine. Our main guest room became Peggy's room. That room had a private bath.

Four years after Warren died, on a cold November evening, Mark and I planned to go to a Providence College basketball game at the Dunkin' Donuts Center. I had a bad headache and suggested he go with Maddie. Worst suggestion I ever made. I still regret it. At eight oh three – I'll never forget that time – Maddie called, crying, gasping for breath.

"Dad collapsed in the lobby of the Dunk. The paramedics are here now. They're going to take him to Rhode Island Hospital---" *How can this be happening?..Mark is the healthiest man I know.* "I'll call Bobby, Jimmy, Annie, and Aunt Patty. Mom, get Aunt Peggy to drive you. You'll want her with you anyway. I'll drive Dad's car to the hospital."

"What happened, Maddie?" I said.

"The paramedics think he had a heart attack."

Oh God...Oh God...Don't leave me, Mark. "I'll meet you at the hospital, honey," I said.

Peggy had just come over. She was sitting at the kitchen table. "What is it, Sandy?" she asked.

"It's Mark. He had a heart attack," I said.

"Oh shit," she said. "He'll be all right, Sandy."

"I hope so."

"Who are you talking to, Mom?" asked Maddie.

"Aunt Peggy is here."

"Okay, Mom. Come with Aunt Peggy, all right? Let her drive."

"Yes," I said.

Peggy drove me to the hospital. She did observe stop lights, but not speed limits.

When we got there, we found Maddie, Annie, Candi, Mark's sister, Patty, and her husband, Bill, in the ER waiting room. They were crying. *Why aren't they in with Mark?* Maddie jumped up and embraced me. "He died in the ambulance, Mom. Massive heart attack."

I collapsed. Peggy and Maddie lifted me up and placed me in a chair. Soon Bobby and Heather, Larry and his wife, Mary, and Jimmy and his wife, Sharon, arrived. I made everyone kneel down, and we said a prayer. Sure I was sorrowful, but I was also thankful for the wonderful sixty-four years God had given me with Mark. Maddie's husband, Philip, arrived while we were praying. He understood immediately what had happened. Maddie went to him and buried her head in his chest. Maddie is so strong. All the kids – now adults -- have always looked up to her. They rely on her. She is the Tuttle-Roberts-Jones rock. But Philip is **her** rock.

When Mark walked Maddie down the aisle and gave her hand to Philip, he smiled. He then joined me in our pew, squeezed my shoulder, and whispered, "I am very happy." Of course, I cried.

I'll never forget the time Philip came to me and said, "Mom, you have the most beautiful face in the world, and you have given it to Maddie. Thank you."

I just smiled. *She does look like me, doesn't she? Annie takes more after Mark.*

Then he said, and I thought it was Mark speaking, "I tell Maddie every morning that she has the most beautiful face in the world. Maddie tells me that you always thought that Mrs. Jones was the most beautiful woman in the world. Mrs. Jones is beautiful, and I can understand why all the boys in high school called her 'the goddess,' but you and Maddie have something she doesn't have, that face, and it puts you two head and shoulders above her."

I just said, "Thank you, Philip."

At the wake, I remember kneeling with Peggy in front of the coffin. We were both crying. "Now we're only two," I said.

"No, we'll always be three," she said. "On the Barge of Curiosity."

I kissed her on the cheek. *Peggy's right; we will always be three...Kneeling there, looking at Mark Tuttle in the coffin, I found it hard to believe that this was really happening...I hoped he would sit up and say, "I'm just kidding. I'm not dead."...But of course that didn't happen...Thank God Maddie was with him at the end...He always loved Maddie with a special love...He loves Annie...He loves Bobby...He loves Jimmy...But Maddie is his firstborn..."Sandy, I love her as much as I love you, and I didn't think it was possible for me to ever love anyone the way I love you."...When Annie told him she was going to marry Candi, he called Maddie...I am so glad that worked out...You are a good man, Mark Tuttle...*

"Are you okay?" asked Peggy.

"As long as you're with me, I'll be okay," I said.

"I am with you, Sandy. Always," said Peggy. "We always have each other's back."

"Stay at my side," I asked.

Peggy just squeezed my shoulder. That is what Mark would have done. I knew it meant "Yes."

At the funeral, Bobby and Jimmy walked at my side. Everywhere I went, they were there. I love my children. There were hundreds at the funeral. Bill Reynolds was there. So was Coach Wilson, Coach Thompson, and Mr. Ross. Bill Skwor and Phillip Andrews flew in from Seattle. Kristijian Kovasevic came from Zagreb. Denny McIntyre, our financial advisor, attended. Mark's cousins, Annie and Luisa, drove in from Columbus. Margie Baylor and Billy and Maureen Smith led a large contingent of former CHS students.

Outside the church an elderly nun approached me. It was Mother Mary Agnes who had been principal of St. Michael's when Mark and I were in third grade.

She hugged me and said, "He was the bravest person I have ever known. You can be certain, my daughter, that he is with God."

I said Bobby and Jimmy supported me that day. And they did. But my girls never left my side either. Maddie, Annie, Heather, Candi, Sharon, and Melanie – always nearby. Leslie and Patty too. And, of course, Peggy. Peggy Mayhew always has my back.

Four months later, during breakfast, I said to Peggy, "Isn't it kind of foolish for us to maintain two houses? You're here more than you're at your house. Why pay two electric bills, two heating bills, two phone bills, two property tax bills? It doesn't make sense. We should consolidate."

"Is that a proposal?" Peggy asked.

"Yes," I said laughing. "It just makes sense. We're seventy. I know we are both very healthy, but we're not young women anymore. We should not be living alone."

"I agree," said Peggy.

"For security reasons," I said. "And if one of us gets sick or has an accident, the other will be there to take care of her."

"Again I agree," she said. "We have the kids, but they have their own lives."

"We have always had each other's back," I said. Then I added, "We have loved each other for sixty-four years.

There is no way this won't work. Who would take better care of me than you? Who would take better care of you than me?"

"No one. One question, my love," Peggy said.

"What?"

"What will be the sleeping arrangements?"

"Together, of course. That will be our wonderful secret. You think I'm going to live with you and not sleep with you? Not make love with you?"

Peggy got up, came over to my side of the table, and kissed me passionately. "I have always wanted to sleep with you," she said. "And make love with you."

"We will have to keep up appearances," I said. "The guest room will be your room, in which no one will ever sleep, and the master bedroom will be our room, in which we will always sleep."

Peggy moved in that day. The arrangement, as we **explained** it, made sense to all our children. They thought it was great that we would not be living alone, and that we would be there for each other in case of sickness or in an emergency. Peggy put her house on the market, and it sold in three months. I insisted she put that money aside; I, as you know, have more money than God.

We love our sleeping arrangement. My bed had felt so empty during the four months after Mark's death. When Peggy and I went to bed that first night, there were no inhibitions, no hesitation. Peggy and I rolled into each other's arms and hugged and kissed and slept with arms around each other and legs intertwined. Peggy also, like Mark and I, woke up with sweet breath, and we began each day with a kiss, a lingering, loving kiss. That became our routine. I loved the feel and taste of her tongue in my mouth. She loved starting each day with a taste of Breyer's vanilla bean ice cream.

476

Living together did not create any problems or clashes. How could Peggy Mayhew and Sandy Roberts not cherish living together? I told Peggy that Mark and I had a rule: never fight and never argue. We agreed to adopt that rule. It works. We shared the housework, the washing, the cooking, and the dishes. We did most of the shopping together.

We do love each other, physically as well as spiritually, and we are healthy seventy year old women. Consequently, there was no way I was going to live with Peggy Mayhew, sleep with Peggy Mayhew, and not make love with Peggy Mayhew. It is nearly impossible to lie in bed with a beautiful vagina and not want to play with it and explore its intricacies, especially if it belongs to a woman you love. We became lovers the second night together. I found her vagina as exciting as I had found it that one time at seventeen. It had aged well. So had mine. Peggy told me that. We both agreed that Warren and Mark would not be upset with our arrangement. They would be happy that we were taking care of each other and not involving strange men in our lives or our bedrooms.

Another custom of Mark's and mine that we adopted was the practice of having pre-sleep conversations. Being two women, we talked for hours. With the exception of the occasional doctor's visit, we had no reason to rise early, so talking into the wee hours of the morning was not a cause for concern.

Mostly we talked about the old days, when we were three.

"Do you remember how we used to sneak kisses on the lips during the Kiss of Peace at Mass?" Peggy asked one night.

"Yes, until Sister Mary Thomas stopped us," I said. "I wonder what she thought of two fourth graders kissing on the lips in church."

"She probably thought we were innocent little girls," Peggy said.

"Weren't we?"

"I was never an innocent little girl," said Peggy.

"Neither was I. I knew what you were doing. And I liked it."

"Me too."

"You better have liked it. You initiated the kisses," I said.

"You didn't push me away," Peggy said.

"I'm not pushing you away now either," I said, opening my mouth and surrounding her lips. I blew a stream of air into her mouth. That got us started. Sleep would wait that night.

"That fight I almost had with that Alex the day you fought Rosalie---"

"I remember. She said, 'Fuck you,' and walked away. Gave you the finger without turning back."

"I should have grabbed that finger and broken it. I really wanted to fight her, but when she walked away, I felt relieved. While we were staring at each other, I was excited. It was almost sexual. Strange, huh? When Mark walked me home that night, I pulled him into an alleyway and kissed him with my tongue. He loved it. I did too."

"You could have kissed me. At McDonald's that time, when Margie Baylor asked me if I really wanted to kiss you, and I threw it back at her, God did she ever turn red," Peggy said.

"Margie had a crush on me. I knew that. She was so good, and so innocent at that time."

"She still is." We both laughed.

"I still can picture Mark standing over that pervert with the bat, even though I wasn't there," said Peggy.

"There's a part of that story I never told you," I said.

"What?"

"When the pervert grabbed me, I got so scared I peed my pants. When I told Mark, I asked, 'Do I stink?' You know what he said?"

"Knowing Mark, I bet he said, 'No, Sandy, you smell wonderful.' "

"Exactly. Nurse Smith gave me a pair of plastic panties to wear home. When we got to McDonald's – my mother took us to McDonald's – I crinkled when I sat down. Mark laughed. I gave him my sternest look and said, 'Don't you dare laugh at me, Mark Tuttle,' and I punched him on the shoulder. But then I laughed too. That was the day I decided I was going to marry him."

"I know. You told me that the next day."

"Mark loved my smells, even that day when I peed myself: my mouth, my vagina, my body, my hair, even my ass. He said he could walk into a room blindfolded with fifty women in the room, and pick me out immediately just by my smell. The first time he ate me, he said he had died and gone to Heaven. He said he loved the smell more than the taste, and he loved the taste. He asked me never to wear perfume, and I never have. I got to love his smells too. I missed them for the last four months, but now I have your smells with me at night. You smell great too, Peggy."

"All of me?"

"Yes, **all** of you."

"Do you know that picture I have over my desk in the den?" I asked.

"The one Mark took of you in Ireland?" Peggy asked.

"Yes. I was in the doorway of a little farmhouse in Bunratty Village in County Clare. We had such a wonderful time on that vacation. We lucked out with good weather all week. Mark told me I looked beautiful standing in that doorway. He also said he loved my jeans, holes and all.

" 'I don't want anyone to know I'm a multi-millionaire,' I said.

" 'They won't,' he said.

"We went to a local pub for dinner – some kind of stew – hearty, and had a few Guinness stouts. Then we went to our room in an inn, window overlooking an undulating green meadow with the sea in the background, and made love all night."

"Undulating. Nice word. Were you an honors student?"

"Smartass."

"Do you remember that afternoon we made love, when we were seventeen?" Peggy asked.

"Never forgot it. That was a great ride on the Barge of Curiosity," I said.

"And do you remember how we got started that afternoon?"

"Yeah, we wrestled. That was silly."

"It worked, didn't it?"

"Yes, but we almost ended up having a real fight," I said.

"When I sensed you were getting serious, I stuck my tongue in your mouth. That stopped the fight."

"It sure did," I said. "I felt so guilty that day."

"Because we had sex?" Peggy asked.

"Yes, but more because I knew I loved you. I felt I was being disloyal to Mark. That's why we never made love again. I didn't want to lose Mark. As much as I loved you, I loved him more."

"I always knew that. But knowing you loved me, knowing you were my best girlfriend and always had my back, that was enough for me. I never wanted to be competition for Mark. I knew I couldn't be. I used to be so horny around you," Peggy said.

"I was too, but I would not allow myself to have sex with you. I was probably as horny as you were. I decided I wanted to kiss you, and convinced myself it was okay."

"What was the catalyst?" Peggy asked.

"I guess fighting gets me going," I answered. "It was that fight at Taco Bell. Both of us going at it with the two black girls. When we got back to your place, I really wanted you. I knew you wanted to have sex, but I told you I would kiss you. At first you didn't hear me. You were pleading for a kiss. You should have seen your face when I told you I had already agreed to that. God that was exciting. How long did we kiss?"

"A half hour. Then we kissed two more times. When you told me you would kiss me any time I wanted, I felt like I had won the lottery."

"I kept my word too, didn't I?"

"Yes, with two conditions: that nobody would know, and that we only would do it when we were alone," Peggy said.

"We met those conditions a lot, didn't we? We both saw to that."

"We are meeting them now," Peggy said.

"Yeah, we are, but they don't exist anymore. And you can do more than kiss me if you like."

"I like." Another deferred sleep night.

"The day Mark saved my life in Flagler Beach, pulled me and Maddie who was in my tummy out from the riptide, well that night at a local restaurant -- we were sitting at an

481

outside table, all the tables were occupied -- I looked across at him and began singing out loud, *"If you pass through raging waters, in the sea you shall not drown---"*

"From the hymn. How appropriate. What did Mark do while you were singing?"

"He just sat there smiling. Nothing I ever did embarrassed Mark. I sang the whole hymn, including the chorus, *Be not afraid, I go before you always. Come follow me, and I will give you rest."*

"What did the other diners do?"

"Nothing at first, then they clapped. One lady got up and hugged me. I told her that Mark had saved my life that day, literally, pulled me, pregnant me, out of a riptide. The lady who hugged me than went over and hugged Mark."

"I asked Mark if I had embarrassed him. He said, 'You never embarrass me, Sandy. You thrill me.' I did thrill him too. I always thrilled him. And he thrilled me. Always. So do you, Peggy."

"You thrill me too, Sandy."

"Life has been good to us, Peggy, hasn't it?"

"Yes, it has."

"Every time I look at Candi, I think of your generosity and your love. When the Hospital Administrator told us that we had to come up with one hundred and seventy-five thousand dollars, Warren and I were stunned," said Peggy. "I almost despaired. I didn't know what we were going to do. Then I figuratively smacked myself in the forehead and said, 'Sandy!' You immediately told me you had the cost covered before you even knew how much it was. Then you said, 'Now I'm starting to cry. Love you, Peggy. Always will. I'll be by later.' I started crying too. '*Love you, Peggy. Always will.*' What wonderful words.

"When you walked into Candi's room, I felt your presence before you put your hands on my shoulder and kissed the top of my head. I felt such love. Can't even describe it. When I stood up and said, 'Thank you,' and you said, 'I always had your back, Mayhew,' I knew that you loved me as much as I love you. Mark would always come first, but I would always be there in your heart. And now we live together. I never thought that would happen."

"Life has its pleasant surprises, Peggy. I didn't know what I would do without Mark, how I would survive without him. Then one morning I was sitting across the breakfast table from you, and I thought, *You still have Peggy. You love her; she loves you.* And my life is wonderful again."

"Let's take the Viking cruise on the Yang Tze," I said one morning after kissing my sweet Peggy. "With a post-cruise visit to Beijing and the Great Wall. That is the only place that Mark promised to take me when we were thirteen that we didn't get to, the Great Wall. So now I will go with you."

"Wow. That will be great. *Hen hao*," she said. (Very good.)

"I'll book it today. I'll get us an outside suite." It's nice to have money and time and a girlfriend whom you love.

That was Peggy's and my fourth cruise: Alaska land and sea, Viking river cruise from Amsterdam to Budapest, and a three-week Mediterranean cruise stopping at many of the Greek islands and Dubrovnik. Kristijian flew down from Zagreb to have dinner with us at Dubrovnik. Life is good. *What would Mark say if a playboy bunny, blonde, pretty, **with nice teeth**, stood in front of him?..He would say, 'Please move. I can't see Sandy.'...Kristijian is doing so well now, but that first day Mark brought him home – he was like a little lost puppy Mark had found...I was so* *happy and surprised that he came to the funeral... "I would never miss the funeral of Mark Tuttle," he said to me... "Mark Tuttle and you are two people I will never forget."*

On the Yang Tze river cruise, two elderly men tried to pick us up, two women traveling unaccompanied. They figured we were in our sixties. Peggy told them we were widows (true) and still mourning (untrue), and they left us alone.

I changed my will after Peggy and I began co-habitation. My net worth is astronomical, and two of Peggy's children are married to my children, so they will be taken care of. I put the house, checking account, savings account, and a substantial money market fund in joint name; they will go to Peggy automatically if I pre-decease her, and she has full access to them now. Our families don't know this, but Peggy and I married legally to avoid tax problems. Only our accountant, our money manager – we still use Denny McIntyre; we have made him rich, but he has always done well by us – and our attorney know of the marriage. (That is not quite true as I will tell you in a moment – one other person knows.) I also left fifty million to Peggy, and ten million to Larry, the only Jones who didn't marry a Tuttle. I promised Peggy that I will take care of Larry and his family should she pre-decease me. I will. Peggy agreed that the remainder of my estate, less bequests to Mclanie and Robby, should go to my children, which means in two cases to her children as well. We decided to leave large donations to charity, including The Tuttle Charitable Foundation and St. Michael's Parish. Father Newsome, the new pastor, will be shocked at the size of the bequest if he is still there when I pass away. My money grows faster than Peggy and I can spend it.

Peggy said to me one morning, after our begin-the-day kiss, that we should apprise Maddie of our arrangement. I agreed. So Maddie is the fourth person who knows of our legal marriage. She had to know; she is the executrix of my will.

Maddie later asked me, "You love Aunt Peggy, don't you?"

"Yes," I said. "I have loved her for over sixty years. Maddie, believe me, I always loved Dad more."

She smiled, hugged me, and said, "I am so glad you two have each other. I was afraid you would wither after Dad died." *Wither? Sandy Roberts wither? My wonderful Maddie.*

"Our marriage is a secret, honey," I said. "No one in the family knows of it. Please keep it that way; I don't want to shock anyone."

"It won't shock Annie and Candi," Maddie said smiling.

"No, that's for certain. And you can tell Philip. Refusing to keep secrets was one of the reasons Dad's and my marriage was so strong."

"What surprised me," I said to Peggy one night, "was Annie and Candi. Oh, I knew they were lovers, but somehow I did not expect a marriage. That would not have been possible when we were their age."

"It's a different world," she said kissing me.

"It sure is. Mark had a little trouble with it at first. He never let Annie know. And he loves Candi, so he came around. Maddie helped him. Annie never knew there was any coming around going on."

"And now they have given us two grandchildren, one from each womb," said Peggy. "Maddie and Max."

"I still find that amazing. Same father."

"Like me, the kids will never know their father. I guess that's okay."

"You turned out all right," I said.

"You know," said Peggy, "if it wasn't for Mark, we could have ended up like Annie and Candi."

"We did," I said. "Let's make love."

What a nice way to end the day. Back in seventh grade, I began to wonder what it would be like to make love to Peggy Mayhew. It is one of life's true delights.

My Jimmy married Sharon O'Rourke, a classmate of his at Providence College. He could have gone to Harvard, but chose Providence College. Sharon is a fourth-grade teacher in the Coventry School System. Jimmy always wanted to write and teach writing. He has accomplished both his goals. He published three novels, all moderately successful financially, and teaches at his alma mater, Providence College. He and Sharon have given me three granddaughters. Priceless little things who live in Coventry! "Hannah and her sisters," Mark called them. He always loved Woody Allen movies. Me too.

My *primogenita*, the little girl who gave me an insight into the Trinity, the little girl who survived the rush of the riptide inside my womb, the little girl about whom I asked, "Can you love all your children the same, and yet love one more than the others?", my living *Alexandra the Mouse*, the last family member to see my Mark alive, my beloved Maddie, Maddie who was afraid I would wither when Mark died, is now the Chief Operating Officer of The Tuttle Charitable Foundation. Mark and I put one hundred million dollars into the foundation twenty-five years ago. It is worth substantially more now. Her husband, Philip Rodgers, is a CPA, and the Chief Financial Officer of the foundation. All Maddie's brothers and sisters still look up to her. No, that's an understatement; they revere her. When I die, she will be the matriarch.

She, like me, went to Harvard where she met Philip. Mark and I love Philip. Let me correct that. I should say: I love Philip, and Mark loved Philip. The greatest praise I can give Philip is to relate what Mark once told me: "Philip is worthy of Maddie." You have to know the extent of the love Mark had for Maddie to fully appreciate that comment. I once told someone, I don't remember whom, that if you ever wanted something from Mark, have Maddie ask him. I added that either of the other two women in his life, me or Annie, would have worked as well as intercessors, but the Mark/Maddie father/daughter relationship was special from the day she was conceived until the day he died. If one family member had to be with Mark at the end, and it could not be me, then it had to be Maddie.

Maddie and Philip have one child, a young lady who is the splitting image of me. Maddie always tried to please me. Maddie always **did** please me. She named her daughter Alexandra. Whenever little Alexandra came to visit, I would pick her up and say, "Alexandra, you have the most beautiful face in the world." She would laugh and reply, "I look like you, Grandma." *Can you love all your grandchildren equally, and yet love one more than the others?*

Bill Reynolds was right when he said about Maddie, "Can you just imagine what a jump shot that little girl will have!" She, teaming up with her cousin, Melanie Roberts, and Heather Jones, who could rebound as well as her mother, Peggy Mayhew, and who would become Maddie's sister-in-law, led CHS to the state championship in basketball Maddie's junior and senior years. Maddie scored 41 points in the state championship game her senior year.

"You know, Peggy, I have only loved two people in my life. Not counting my children, of course. That's a different kind of love. Only Mark and you. And I lived with Mark, had my children with Mark, had sixty-four happy, loving years with Mark, and now I am growing old with you. I have had a great life."

"Me too. I did love Warren. Don't get me wrong. I had a wonderful life with him. He gave me three children whom I love. And I loved Mark, especially when we were young. But I never loved anyone the way I have always loved you. From that first day at St. Michael's. I have loved riding on the Barge of Curiosity alongside you with Mark as our tugboat."

"Me too."

"Sandy, I never got off that barge."

"Neither did I, Peggy. Neither did I."